MISS CHAMBERS TAKES CHARGE

Joy Reed

ZEBRA BOOKS
Kensington Publishing Corp.
http://www.zebrabooks.com

ZEBRA BOOKS are published by

Kensington Publishing Corp.
850 Third Avenue
New York, NY 10022

First Printing: April, 2000
10 9 8 7 6 5 4 3 2 1

Printed in the United States of America

*Dedicated with gratitude to
Anne Brooker Grogan,
beloved sister and chief donor to my
research library*

One

Miss Claudia Chambers looked first at the slip of paper in her hand, then at the house in front of her.

"Number Seventeen, Bridges Street, Mayfair." Yes, this was certainly the right address. Again Claudia looked at the house. She had been an hour and a half finding it, searching one genteel and bewilderingly similar street after another and in the process acquiring a painful blister on her heel. But now that her search was ended and she was standing in front of her destination, she wished nothing so much as to turn and go back home again.

Anxiously Claudia studied the house, hoping that its prim facade might reveal something of its owner's personality. But it was only an ordinary London town house: tall and narrow, with windows flanking its central doorway and an arched fanlight over the door.

"Still, it looks very tidy and well tended," Claudia told herself, striving to take what comfort she could from this meager evidence. "Lady Rexford evidently has servants enough to keep the place up properly. And it's a good-size house, too—much bigger than Edmund and Anthea's. Her ladyship obviously has money, and that to me must be the chief thing.

Claudia might have been pardoned for thinking money was the chief thing. She came of an old and respected family whose members were more distinguished for their breeding than their wealth. This fact had been a painful thorn in their collective sides for several generations.

Claudia's father had been a country gentleman whose ancestral property had come to him already saddled with a heavy mortgage. Urged by all his friends and relations to remedy this situation by the time-honored expedient of marrying an heiress, he had chosen instead to marry his childhood sweetheart, a lady as genteelly poor as he. He had then dedicated himself to settling his debts through the slower and less glamorous means of hard work and economical living.

If only Mr. Chambers had lived a little longer, these measures might have sufficed. Unfortunately he had died when Claudia was only nine and her brother Edmund twelve, long before the burden of debt on his property had been lifted. His widow, recognizing the difficulty of managing an encumbered estate on behalf of her minor son, had behaved with a prudence and resolution her background never would have suggested. She had found a tenant for the estate, a wealthy merchant who was desirous of establishing himself in county society and who was willing to pay dearly for the privilege of engraving the name of Ashdown Grange on his cards. Mrs. Chambers had then betaken herself and her children into lodgings; and there, by practicing the most stringent economies, she had succeeded not only in clearing a further portion of the debt on her son's estate, but in providing him with the public school and university education that his position demanded.

Claudia had recognized the necessity of these measures and had participated in them wholeheartedly. Even when the cost of Edmund's education had entailed a personal sacrifice on her part—the making over of an old dress instead of the buying of a new one, for instance, or having to take brown sugar instead of white in her tea—she had never found it in her heart to complain. Edmund was so obviously the Chambers family's only hope of ever reestablishing itself that she felt she had no choice but to support him.

Her support was made easier because Edmund himself was

so grateful for the sacrifices made on his behalf. He was a sober, studious, hardworking young man, keenly aware of his responsibilities and warmly attached to his mother and sister. He often spoke of the luxuries he would shower upon them when he had succeeded in establishing himself in his profession—for a profession he must have, both to occupy himself until the lease on his property ran out and to pay off the dwindling but still present mortgages. The profession he had chosen to that end was the law. And at the present date he had so far succeeded in his goals as to be spoken of as one of the rising young barristers in London.

Mrs. Chambers, sadly, had not lived to see her son's success. She had died a little more than three years ago, at a time when Edmund was only starting out in his new profession. But Claudia thought now that it was perhaps as well her mother had died when she did. For only a few months after Mrs. Chambers's death, Edmund had chosen to marry a young lady who was the sister of one of his fellow barristers—and from that time on, everything had become much more complicated.

It was not that Edmund slighted his sister in favor of his new wife. If anything, the reverse was true. He had insisted that Claudia make her home in the little house in Albany Street where he and his wife had set up housekeeping, and whenever his increasing income allowed an indulgence, he made sure Claudia had her share in it. But these measures, which he saw as simple justice for a sister's past sacrifices, were perceived by his wife in quite a different light.

Anthea was disposed to be jealous of Claudia anyway, for though she came of a respectable family, her pedigree was by no means so exalted as her sister-in-law's. There had been a painful occasion on which Claudia had received an invitation to a party at a certain Lady Worley's in Portman Square—an invitation in which Anthea was not included.

In vain had Claudia tried to soften the sting of this slight. "You know Lady Worley is my godmother, Anthea. She was one of Mama's oldest friends, and I am sure she had no intention of slighting you. Indeed, it may be that she is not even aware Edmund has a wife, for you know you and he were married very quietly on account of Mama's death—"

"I don't believe it," interrupted Anthea, her voice rising hysterically. "It's a deliberate snub—that's what it is. I'm not good enough for Lady Worley and your aristocratic friends, even though I *am* Edmund's wife. I daresay you think it's quite fair for you to go gallivanting off to *ton* parties, while I am left home caring for the children!"

"Oh, but this will not be a *ton* party, Anthea. Lady Worley lives very quietly, and her parties are always very sedate. I doubt we will do anything more exciting than talk and drink tea."

These reassurances did nothing to comfort Anthea. She had alternately sulked and stormed for days, until at last Claudia had offered to send Lady Worley her regrets and stay home with the children herself so Anthea and Edmund might have an evening out. Anthea had been pacified by this offer, but her ire was raised all over again when Edmund learned of his sister's sacrifice and insisted on praising her for it.

Claudia knew, of course, that Anthea was jealous of her. She could hardly help knowing it when Anthea voiced her resentment so freely, but what she did not realize was the extent of her sister-in-law's jealousy. Anthea was jealous not only of Claudia's birth, connections, and influence with Edmund, but of the attention that Claudia received wherever she went. For Claudia was a very pretty girl, though she would have been incredulous if anyone had told her so. The adjective she associated with her own looks was ordinary.

She was of medium height, with a figure neither voluptuously curved nor ethereally slender. "Merely ordinary," was how Claudia put it to herself, failing to see how very out of the ordinary were her elegant proportions and feminine grace. Her hair was neither dazzlingly fair nor fashionably dark, but only an undistinguished (though attractive) chestnut brown. Her eyes were brown, too, and Claudia was perfectly sure they could never slay anyone with a glance or beam forth with a scintillating light, as the blue- and violet-eyed heroines in novels were wont to do. And though her features were attractive enough, they had not that chiseled perfection that she supposed indispensable to anyone with pretensions to beauty.

But though Claudia might not be able to see her own attractions, she could see very well that her position in her brother's home was becoming increasingly untenable. Much as she loved her brother and the little niece and nephew who had been born in the three years that had elapsed since his marriage, there could be no hope of domestic peace and happiness while Anthea resented her presence so fiercely.

Edmund, of course, could not be made to see this. He loved both his sister and his wife unreservedly, and his profession kept him so busy that he was seldom around when Anthea staged her worst displays of jealousy. Claudia had not the heart to reveal to him the extent of his wife's resentment, but she was resolved to escape her uncomfortable situation by whatever means were available. So one evening, after a day in which Anthea had been particularly trying, she took him aside and told him that she meant to try to get a position.

"Get a position?" Edmund had repeated, regarding his sister with incredulity. "Whatever do you mean, Claudia?"

"Just what I say, Edmund. Why should you be the only one to make good in our family? I am sure lots of girls support themselves nowadays, and no one thinks the worse of them for it. I am tired of being dependent on your and Anthea's generosity."

Edmund had looked hurt by these words, but he had also looked slightly amused. "Ah, you have been reading Miss Wollstonecraft and Mrs. Macaulay," he said with a shake of his head. "I will not quarrel with you about the natural rights of women or the dignity of labor, for in truth I have always sympathized with those ideals myself. But all the same, I cannot like the idea of my sister hiring herself out to work. Cannot you be independent without that, Claudia? I am sure Anthea and I never meant to restrict your freedom in any way."

"You don't," said Claudia quickly. "Indeed, you don't, Edmund. It is only that I would like to do something toward my own support."

Edmund had looked at her keenly. "Of course, I know you have been forced to do without a good many things through the years, Claudia," he said. "No one knows better than I the sacrifices you have made. But I assure you that things *are* getting better. I am making quite a good income now, and if you need additional pin money—"

"Oh, no," said Claudia firmly. "You know I have a little income from the money Mama left me, Edmund. I don't need any more pin money than that."

Edmund regarded her with amusement. "To hear you speak, one would suppose Mama had left you millions rather than a mere three thousand pounds! I am sure the income from that is barely enough to keep you in dresses, Claudia."

Claudia smiled reluctantly. "What I mean is that I don't want any more money from *you*, Edmund," she said. "Indeed, I already feel as though I am taking more than I ought. If you have money to spare, it ought to go to Anthea and the children instead of me."

These words made Edmund look at her more keenly than ever. "It's not Anthea who suggested this, is it?" he said. "I know sometimes she seems to resent your presence here, Claudia, but I am sure nothing could be farther from the case. Indeed, she ought to be grateful to you, considering how much you help her with the children."

"No, Anthea did not suggest I seek a position," said Claudia, skirting the truth with what she congratulated herself was considerable diplomacy. "I thought of the idea all by myself. The fact is, I have a fancy to see if I can be independent, Edmund. I would like to try to support myself with no help from you or anyone else."

To her relief, Edmund seemed to accept this statement without further question. "I suppose that is a natural enough desire," he said slowly. "I am sure I remember feeling much the same way when I was fresh out of Oxford and panting to take my place at the bar. But—"

"But what?" said Claudia, relieved to find him so understanding. "I don't see why I shouldn't earn my living the same as you, Edmund."

"Yes, but—what would you do, Claudia? It's not as though you've been bred up to a profession, as I was."

Claudia laughed. "In a way I have. You know I have spent a great deal of time in your nursery, Edmund—and though I don't wish to boast, I think I have made myself very popular there! It seems to me I ought to be able to get a job looking after children without too much difficulty. Of course I have not education enough to be a proper governess or anything of that sort, but I could probably teach very young children."

Edmund shook his head over this and said he did not like to think of his sister hiring herself out as a glorified nursemaid. But after much coaxing and pleading, he gave a reluctant permission for her to seek a position such as she had described.

"Of course you don't know what you're getting into, but I can see you won't be satisfied until you try. Just remember there's always room for you here, Claudia, whenever you get tired of it." In a cheerful voice, he had added, "But there, I daresay you'll never find anyone to hire you in the first place. You're hardly out of your teens, and you haven't any real experience. And then, too, your appearance is against you."

"My appearance?" Claudia had repeated, surprised. "What is wrong with my appearance?"

Edmund had laughed. "Nothing, dear sister, except that you probably look more of a gentlewoman than most of your prospective employers! Don't be surprised if you find them less than enthusiastic at the idea of hiring you."

Although Claudia was disposed to think this speech mere brotherly teasing, a few weeks of job-hunting had obliged her to admit that Edmund was right. There were not many ladies looking for inexperienced governess nursemaids, and those who were all took one look at Claudia and declared her far too young. "You hardly look out of the nursery yourself," had said one matron, surveying Claudia's face with marked disfavor. "I am afraid I was looking for a more *mature* person."

It did not occur to Claudia that, when this woman said "more mature," she really meant "less attractive." But she could see easily enough that her appearance was against her when it came to finding a position taking care of children. She therefore determined to seek another kind of position, and when the following advertisement had appeared in the *Morning Post,* it had seemed an answer to her prayers:

WANTED: *a Gentlewoman of Good Family to serve as Companion to a Lady. Address Lady Rexford, Seventeen Bridges Street, Mayfair.*

Made leery by her previous failures, Claudia had resolved that her age should not be an issue on this occasion. She had therefore taken care to dress herself in a most mature style, even going so far as to beg the loan of a cap from Anthea to wear under her bonnet. Anthea, who had become much more amiable since Claudia had declared her intention of seeking employment outside her household, had not only willingly complied with this request, but had of her own volition lent Claudia a pair of lace mitts, her second-best cashmere shawl, and a raisin-colored pelisse, whose very lines seemed to breathe a matronly dignity. Feeling rather like a little girl playing dress up in her mother's clothes, Claudia had then set off for Bridges Street.

She had chosen to walk, though Anthea had pressed her to take the carriage. It was all very well to borrow clothes, Claudia considered, but a lady striving for independence ought not to be obliged to others for more than she could help. Besides, the day was a fine one, and the prospect of a walk enjoyable. But thanks to the elusive nature of Bridges Street, the walk had proved longer than she had anticipated, and she had begun to regret her attitude of independence more and more as her legs grew weary and the blister on her foot began to assert itself. Her hair, too, felt as though it were coming loose beneath Anthea's cap, and she felt altogether frowzy and disheveled.

Again Claudia looked at the address on the slip of paper, then at the house opposite. "It's probably no use even going in," she told herself with weary fatalism. "Lady Rexford will not hire me any more than those other ladies would. I am sure I am just as ill suited to be a companion as I am a governess."

Still, it seemed cowardly to go home without even inquiring about the position. It would also be foolish in the extreme. For she needed this position—needed it as badly as she had ever needed anything in her life. Unless she found some excuse for leaving her brother's house, she could expect to spend the rest of her life listening to Anthea's reproaches and feeling as though her sister-in-law begrudged every penny that was spent on her.

Galvanized by this thought, Claudia stepped forward to Number Seventeen. Drawing a deep breath, she grasped the knocker in both hands and rapped it firmly against the door.

For several minutes it seemed as though her knock had gone unheeded. Claudia had plenty of time to reflect on the futility of her errand and her own folly in supposing Lady Rexford would wish to hire her. Just as she had made up her mind that Lady Rexford must be away from home and that she ought to be going home herself, the door opened. A gray-haired woman in a cap and apron, as tall as a grenadier and almost as fierce looking, stood scowling down at her.

"Can I help you, miss?" she asked.

Unnerved by this reception, Claudia found herself stammering as she answered the woman's question. "I have come about the position—the position that was advertised in the *Morning Post*. Could I—is it possible that I might see Lady Rexford for a moment?"

The woman stared at her a moment, then nodded. "You'd best come inside, miss," she said and drew back from the door slightly so that Claudia might enter. Claudia, wondering if she had not better turn and flee while escape was still possible, stepped timidly into the house and tried not to flinch as the door was pulled shut behind her.

The hall in which she was standing was small, but very richly and fashionably furnished. Indeed, it struck Claudia as being almost overfurnished for such a diminutive room. But she had no time to take in the details, for the gray-haired woman was already stalking her way grimly amid statues, candelabra, and gilt console tables. She seemed to expect Claudia to follow, so Claudia did, moving cautiously and trying not to knock anything over. Despite her care, however, the skirt of her pelisse caught the edge of a vase of pink roses, and she was only just in time to keep it from falling over. With a guilty look toward her grim guide, Claudia righted the vase, then hurried on down the hall.

Having reached a door halfway down the hall, the gray-haired woman paused to allow Claudia to catch up with her. "Lady Rexford's in here, miss. If you'll give me your name, I'll tell her you're here to see her."

The words were spoken in a flat voice, but it seemed to Claudia that the woman's manner was slightly less hostile than before. "Thank you," said Claudia, trying to smile at her. "My name is Miss Chambers."

"It is, is it?" the woman said cryptically and vanished within the room. A moment later she emerged and nodded briskly. "She'll see you, miss. Right this way, and mind your step. The room's a bit crowded."

This, as Claudia immediately saw, was an understatement. Though the hall had been full, this room, which seemed to be a kind of parlor or sitting room, was so heavily furnished as to make movement almost impossible. There were statues and vases on pedestals, more gilt console and occasional tables, and a vast quantity of chairs and sofas upholstered in pale pink plush. Hectically colored landscapes covered the walls, interspersed with crayon portraits of a sentimental kind. Although it was broad daylight outside, the rose brocade draperies were tightly drawn. The resulting gloom was illumined by dozens of alabaster lamps, which emitted a low but pleasant glow and a nearly overpowering scent of ambergris.

Claudia, coughing slightly and with watering eyes, was at first unable to locate Lady Rexford amid the clutter. Presently, however, her eyes distinguished a small white-haired woman seated atop an upholstered chair. It was hardly surprising that Claudia should have overlooked her at first, for the woman's sarcenet gown was the same shade of pink as the chair she sat on, and her figure was almost as round and comfortably upholstered. "Lady Rexford?" said Claudia, coughing a little and dropping a curtsy.

"Yes, I am Lady Rexford," said the woman. She said it doubtfully, however, as though she herself were only half convinced of the truth of her words. Claudia saw her eyes flicker to the gray-haired maidservant, who had lingered in the doorway after admitting Claudia.

"This is Miss Chambers, my lady," said the woman in a minatory voice.

"Yes. Yes, of course. I'm very glad to meet you, my dear." Lady Rexford flashed Claudia a nervous smile. Her eyes were very round and blue, and they regarded Claudia with an expression of distinct apprehension.

"Why, she's even more nervous than I am!" Claudia marveled to herself. The idea had the effect of calming some of her own anxieties. She returned Lady Rexford's smile as she dropped another curtsy. "And I am very pleased to meet you, my lady. I have come to apply for the position of companion that was advertised in the newspaper. I take it the position is not filled as yet?"

These words seemed to cast Lady Rexford into an acute embarrassment. "No, oh, no. That is to say—no, not yet." She cast an agonized look at the gray-haired woman, who once more came to her aid.

"Lady Rexford has received a good many ladies wishful of being hired for the post, but none of them was quite what she had in mind," she told Claudia. "Why don't you tell her a bit about yourself, miss, and let her see if you might do better?"

"Yes, thank you, Hettie," said Lady Rexford, casting a grateful look at her mentor. "That's it exactly." To Claudia she added warmly, "Tell us all about yourself, Miss Chambers. And, Hettie, why don't you bring us some tea and a bite to eat, so that we may be more comfortable?"

Claudia, who was both thirsty and hungry after her long walk, happily accepted the tea and cakes that her hostess pressed upon her. As she ate and drank, she did her best to follow the maidservant's instructions. "My family is originally from Surrey. My brother has an estate there, although he lives in London right now." Not caring to dwell upon her family's financial embarrassments, she hurried on to give such additional details of her background and upbringing as she thought might interest Lady Rexford.

Lady Rexford did indeed seem interested in all she said. She listened closely to Claudia's words, putting in a question now and then when Claudia paused for breath. "That's good, my dear. That's very good," she said when at last Claudia had reached the end of her narration. "I've no doubt you're a gentlewoman through and through. Though to be sure, I might have known that from your pretty way of speaking. What's bred in the bone will come out in the flesh, as I've reason enough to know."

This idea seemed to plunge Lady Rexford into a momentary depression. But the next moment she was cheerful again, smiling and addressing Claudia in a friendly manner. "I don't mind saying I've taken a great fancy to you, my dear. In fact, I've a notion to tell you everything and let you see what you think of it all." She cast a glance at the elderly maidservant, who had lingered in the room after serving the tea and had listened in grim-faced silence to all Claudia had said. "What do you think, Hettie?"

The elderly woman surveyed Claudia narrowly, from the frill of the borrowed cap peeping demurely beneath her bonnet to the tips of her dusty boots. Her keen gray eyes seemed to penetrate past these outward trappings, all the way to Claudia's heart and soul (as it seemed to that young lady's nervous fancy). Finally the woman shrugged her shoulders and looked again at her mistress.

"What *I* think don't matter," she said in a brusque voice. "But it seems to me you might go farther and fare worse, as the saying is. If you've a mind to tell, my lady, then you'd best go ahead. It's easy to see you won't be happy until you do."

Claudia wondered what her hostess had to tell that could be of such moment. She waited in some trepidation, as Lady Rexford pushed away her teacup and leaned forward to address her in a solemn and confidential voice.

Two

"I think, my dear, that to begin with I had better explain how the late Lord Rexford and I came to be married."

Lady Rexford began her speech with these words, looking at Claudia as though expecting some response. Claudia, more mystified than ever, said cautiously, "I see."

Lady Rexford smiled and reached out to pat her hand. "No, you don't see, my dear, and it's not to be expected that you should. I'm making a fearful muddle of this business, I don't doubt. But I can put it to you so you'll understand everything in a trice. The truth is that Lord Rexford and I were not born to the same station in life, as you might say. In fact, not to wrap the matter up in clean linen, I used to be his house-keeper."

Lady Rexford brought forth these words with a defiant air, but her face was anxious as she surveyed Claudia. Claudia at once gave her a reassuring smile.

"I see, Lady Rexford," she said, and this time she really did see. Several points that had been puzzling her about her prospective employer were now made clear. Lady Rexford's initial nervousness in speaking to Claudia, her almost painful efforts to appear well bred; the ladylike gentility of her speech that nevertheless betrayed an occasional lapse into a more common dialect—all were perfectly understandable in a lady who had married into a social class in which she felt not quite at home.

Claudia's smile seemed to reassure Lady Rexford. She

smiled back warmly and patted Claudia's hand once more. "There, I knew you'd take it just that way, my dear," she said. Casting a look of triumph at the elderly maidservant, she added, "Hettie would have it I ought to keep it a secret about how I used to be in service, but as I told her, you can't expect to keep such a thing hidden in a chatty place like London. Besides, what's the use of pretending? I daresay you knew as soon as you walked into the room that I wasn't a lady born."

"Oh, no," protested Claudia, but Lady Rexford merely shook her head.

"There, there, my dear, you needn't spare my feelings. I never pretended to be anything other than what I am. Not when Lord Rexford married me, and not afterward either, though there were plenty no higher than I who would have put on airs fast enough if they'd ever had half as much excuse. But I don't hold with that kind of nonsense. What's bred in the bone will come out in the flesh, as I said before, and the fact is, I've got no breeding to speak of. Though I've always kept myself respectable, mind you. I wouldn't want you to get any wrong ideas about *that*."

"Oh, no," said Claudia hastily. Lady Rexford nodded, looking solemnly pleased.

"It's a fact that Lord Rexford was after me from the time I entered his service sixteen years ago," she confided to Claudia. "But I never would listen to a word of his lovemaking until he was willing to put a ring on my finger and make me his wife proper like—no matter what *some* people might say," she added, looking dark. "But that's all spite and foolishness, as Hettie can tell you. Respectable I have always been, and respectable I hope I am now, though I'm not a lady."

"I'm sure you are," said Claudia rather wildly. Lady Rexford threw another look of triumph at the maidservant.

"There you are, Hettie! There's the difference between your true Quality and your shabby genteels. I may not be a lady myself, but I can tell one when I see one—and I'm seeing a very pretty one right now, and no mistake." Again she smiled at Claudia.

Claudia, embarrassed by this fulsome tribute, gave a little laugh. "I don't know about that, ma'am," she said. "To be honest, I'm afraid I fall rather into the shabby genteel category. My family is not at all wealthy—although, like you, we have always prided ourselves on being respectable."

Lady Rexford shook her head decidedly. "Ah, but it's not money that makes a lady. I've a deal of money myself, but that don't make me a lady any more than my title does or my fine clothes." She plucked disparagingly at her pink dress. "But anyone can see you're a lady, my dear, even if you don't go about in silks and diamonds. And it's a lady I want for this job, not any of your shabby genteels. We've had our fill of them, haven't we, Hettie?"

Hettie vouchsafed an affirmative grunt. Lady Rexford smiled at her affectionately. "Hettie can't abide a shabby genteel any more than I can. We always did feel the same about that and about most other things, too. She and I were in service together with Lord Rexford, you know: me as housekeeper and her as undercook. But when Lord Rexford married me, I took her for my own servant, and we've been together ever since."

Hettie nodded, her face betraying a gloomy pleasure. "I told her ladyship she ought to have a grand ladies' maid in her position, rather than a great raw-boned creature like me," she told Claudia.

Lady Rexford laughed at this and said her dear Hettie talked a deal of nonsense. "What would I do with a grand ladies' maid if I had one?" she demanded rhetorically of Claudia. "I'm sure I'd never dare ask her to hand me my chocolate of a morning, let alone comb my hair or lace me into my stays. But I don't mind asking Hettie, because I know her and she knows me and we both know what I am without any nonsense about it. Besides, there's nobody whose judgment I respect more."

Hettie looked pleased by this tribute and unbent sufficiently to say, "Ah, get along with you, Lucy—Lady Rexford, I mean."

To Claudia, she added, "I've known her ladyship these twenty years, miss, and I can vouch for her character. You'll be getting a good mistress if she takes you into her service."

"But you know, Hettie, a lady like Miss Chambers might not be willing to work for someone like me," put in Lady Rexford, her expression solemn once more. "Being a lady herself, she mightn't want any truck with one who was only a gentleman's housekeeper before her marriage."

Both women looked at Claudia. Claudia looked back at them, her mind working rapidly. It might be true that Lady Rexford was not a real lady, but Claudia was not disposed to think the worse of her for that. Indeed, she was inclined to respect the widow for her openness in speaking of her past. And besides Lady Rexford's obvious qualities of candor and plain speaking, she appeared to be both kind and good-humored. Claudia had had dealings enough in the last few weeks with gentlewomen who were neither to value these qualities in their proper degree.

So she said quite readily, "Why, no, I should have no objection to working for you, Lady Rexford. Not if you think I might suit you."

"Ah, there's the rub, my dear. You're a gentlewoman right enough, and I don't deny I've taken a great fancy to you. But I must confess I was hoping to find an older lady for my companion." She surveyed Claudia's face dubiously. "You look very young."

Claudia said earnestly that she was not so young as she looked. "In fact, I am twenty-nine," she told Lady Rexford, recklessly adding seven years to her age. A lie it might be, but it seemed a harmless lie, and she could not bear to see the prospect of another position slipping away from her.

Lady Rexford looked surprised. "Are you indeed, my dear? You look very young for your years, and that's a fact. Though I can't say that cap makes you look any younger." She regarded Claudia's borrowed cap with disfavor. "There's nothing makes one look a dowdy quicker than a cap, is what I always say. I never could abide the things, though of course I was obliged to wear 'em when I was in service. But quick as I was married to Lord Rexford I threw them all away, and I haven't worn one since." She patted her fluffy white hair complacently.

Claudia smiled and nodded, but in truth she was eager to return to the subject of her own employment. Happily for her, Lady Rexford soon reverted to this topic of her own accord. "But even if you're twenty-nine, my dear—which let me say, I take leave to doubt—I'm afraid you're still a bit young for the job I have in mind."

"Am I?" said Claudia with disappointment. "I thought it was merely a companion you wanted. And surely my youth is no bar to my being that."

"Ah, but you see, there's a bit more to it than that, my dear." Fidgeting with the fringe on her shawl, Lady Rexford hesitated a moment, then went on, fixing Claudia with appealing blue eyes. "You see, Lord Rexford was a very well-off man. In addition to his City interests, he had a deal of property, including the family property, which was entailed on him along with his title. I've never been to Rexford Park myself, but I've heard it's a grand estate, for all that it is in an out-of-the-way place like Yorkshire."

"Yes?" prompted Claudia as Lady Rexford paused.

"Yes, and I never thought it would have aught to do with me," continued that lady disconsolately. "I always supposed that Lord Rexford meant to leave me this house and a nice little annuity and that the rest of his estate would go to his heir. That was his nephew John, you see, who was his younger brother's son."

"I see," said Claudia with a nod. "This John was Lord Rexford's heir presumptive."

"That's right. And to give you the word with no bark on it, I never cared for the man. To be sure, I never met him to speak to, but a woman always knows her enemy. Master John was my enemy and no mistake. None of the Rexfords were exactly delighted about Lord Rexford marrying me, mind you, but it was Master John who was most set against it."

"Because he was afraid of being cut out of the succession?" suggested Claudia.

Lady Rexford gave a snort of mingled amusement and vexation. "He must be a perfect nincompoop if he was afraid of that! I ask you, is it likely that a woman of my age would do any breeding? But to do him justice, I don't suppose that was Master John's objection at all. It was more the disgrace to the Rexford name he took exception to. Well, I don't hold that against him, for it's not to be expected a man like him would be pleased at the idea of having a woman like me marry into his family. But what I do hold against him is the way he insulted my character. Why, he had the gall to say that I was a scheming adventuress and that his uncle must be a dotard for falling prey to my wiles!"

Lady Rexford looked so indignant that Claudia could not help smiling. "Did he?" she said. "That was very bad of him, to be sure."

"Yes, it was," said Lady Rexford warmly. "As I said, I've always kept myself respectable, and that's something a deal of folks higher born than me couldn't say. But what hurt me even more than the insult to my name was the insult to Lord Rexford. Him a dotard, who was clever enough to buy and sell properties the way other men buy waistcoats! Why, he made a thousand on 'Change the very day he died!"

"He must have been a very astute man," said Claudia sympathetically.

"Aye, that he was, my dear," said Lady Rexford. She paused to apply a handkerchief to her eyes, then went on with as much heat as before. "And for his nephew to say he was failing in his mind was quite ridiculous. When Lord Rexford heard of it, he only laughed and shrugged his shoulders, but I think it must have displeased him all the same. For when he died, he left his estate tied up in such a way that I now have a life interest in Rexford Park as well as the bulk of his fortune."

"Indeed!" said Claudia. With a laugh, she added, "That must have put Master John's nose out of joint almost as much as if you *had* disinherited him!"

"Yes, I expect it did," said Lady Rexford with satisfaction. But the next moment her voice grew gloomy again. "Still and all, I'd almost as lief Lord Rexford hadn't gone and left me his estate as he did. It's been a deal of bother to me, what with one thing and another. There are times I think I'd almost rather turn it over to Master John and be done with it. If he hadn't been so rude about me and his uncle marrying, I'd do it in a trice, but it goes against the grain to do a favor for a man who's insulted one. I don't doubt you can understand, my dear, if you put yourself in my shoes."

"Oh, yes, I quite understand," Claudia assured her. "Naturally you would not want to benefit Master John after the way he behaved toward you. I am sure if I were in your place I would hang on to the estate as long as I possibly could, just to spite him."

Lady Rexford nodded vigorously. "Yes, that's it exactly, my dear. Only it turns out not to be as simple as that. If I could manage the estate from here and never set foot in Yorkshire, I'm sure I'd be happy to hang on to it, but it seems that's not possible. You see, though I have a life interest in the place, it really belongs to Master John now that Lord Rexford is dead. And that creates all kinds of problems."

"Oh, dear," said Claudia, whose upbringing had given her a fair acquaintance with the laws concerning entails. "Yes, I can see how that would create problems."

Lady Rexford heaved a sigh. "That it does, my dear, and no mistake. Mind you, I think Master John could make everything easy for me if he chose, but of course he don't choose, any more than I choose to turn the estate over to him. And so for the past year and a half we've been wrangling back and forth by letter, trying to determine what's to be done about the property. And it really looks as though I shall be obliged to travel up to Yorkshire and meet with him in person so we can decide what to do about drains and fences and cottages and a dozen other things I know nothing about."

Lady Rexford looked so gloomy at this prospect that Claudia was once more tempted to laugh. She quashed the temptation, however, and gave the widow a sympathetic smile. "Must you indeed go to Yorkshire? That is certainly too bad, when you prefer to remain in London. But I have heard the north country is very picturesque."

"Oh, I don't doubt it is," said Lady Rexford, looking more gloomy than ever. "Though I never cared much for picturesque places myself. But it's the idea of meeting Master John that's cast me into the megrims. That, and dealing with the servants at Rexford Park." She looked across the table at Claudia. "And that's where I hoped you would be able to help me, my dear. But seeing how young you are, I'm afraid it wouldn't do."

"You thought I would be able to help you?" said Claudia in puzzlement. "Help you do what?"

"Why, help me deal with Master John and with the servants at Rexford Park. Indeed, it's the servants I'm worried about as much as Master John." Lady Rexford's round blue eyes were very frank as she looked at Claudia. "You see, I've been in service myself, and I know how servants talk about guests who aren't—well, who aren't quite the thing, as you might say. And the servants at Rexford Park are mostly old family retainers, which makes it a hundred times worse. They'll be looking to take advantage of me every minute—and Master John will be, too, I have no doubt. So I talked it over with Hettie, and we agreed the only thing for it was to find a real lady who wouldn't let herself be imposed on and would see that I wasn't either."

"Ah," said Claudia with comprehension. "And that's the job you wanted me to do."

"Yes, if you *could* do it, my dear. But as I said before, I'm afraid you're too young. I had hoped to find an older lady, one who had some experience managing a household and who wouldn't be afraid to take charge where necessary."

Once more Claudia's mind was working. The duties Lady

Rexford had outlined did not sound especially attractive, nor did they sound particularly difficult. She was sure she had sufficient experience in managing her mother's and brother's households to take charge of matters at Rexford Park. Besides, what had she to lose? If she stayed in London with Edmund and Anthea, she would certainly be miserable, whereas she might find life in Yorkshire comparatively enjoyable. At the very least it would be a change for her, and after three years of feeling like an unwanted encumbrance in her sister-in-law's house, Claudia was ready to take any prospect of change that was offered.

Lifting her chin, she assumed what she trusted was an authoritative air. "I believe I am just the person you are look- ing for, Lady Rexford," she said. "I may be young, but I have had a great deal of experience managing servants and house- hold affairs. If you hire me, I assure you I will not let you be imposed on."

It was obvious that both her words and her manner had had an effect on her listeners. Lady Rexford looked impressed, but still a trifle dubious. "What do you think, Hettie?" she asked, appealing once more to her faithful friend and servant. "For all she is so young, she does have an air about her. Not like some of those poor creatures we've seen who didn't look as though they could say boo to a goose."

"I assure you that I am quite capable of saying boo to a goose," said Claudia, trying hard to maintain her authoritative manner despite a strong urge to laugh.

Hettie surveyed her a moment, then slowly nodded. "I think the same as you, my lady," she said. "She's young, but she's Quality. It seems to me that's the chief thing."

"And it seems the same way to me," said Lady Rexford with a satisfied nod. Smiling at Claudia, she said, "I'm blessed if I think I won't give you a try, my dear. You may consider yourself engaged."

"Wonderful!" said Claudia. "Indeed, you may depend on me

to do my best for you, Lady Rexford. I shall try not to disappoint you."

So elated was she by her victory that it never entered her head to ask what salary might be forthcoming in return for her services. Fortunately for her, Lady Rexford was more businesslike. "We have not settled the matter of your wages yet, Miss Chambers," she said. "I've never had any doings with companions before, so I don't know what salary they generally get, but it stands to reason you couldn't get by on ten pounds a year like a housemaid. Shall we say a hundred and twenty pounds, paid in quarterly installments?"

Claudia, who had existed for years on a smaller stipend, was staggered by this generosity, but she assented to it in a faint voice, and so the matter was settled. Lady Rexford then went on to discuss her upcoming journey to Yorkshire.

"I had thought to leave a week from today if that isn't too short notice for you, Miss Chambers. Of course your wages will be paid from today's date, for there might be matters on which I'll need your advice between now and then, and I'd like to feel myself free to call on you. In fact, I had thought it might be best to advance you your first quarter's salary today. There might be things you need for the trip—warm clothes, for instance. I've heard Yorkshire has a terribly harsh climate."

"Yes, but you know it's almost June, ma'am," said Claudia, smiling. "You are very generous, but I think I can manage with the things I already have."

Lady Rexford insisted on presenting her with her first quarter's salary, however, and urged her to provide herself with a warm pelisse and a couple of flannel petticoats. She likewise insisted on sending Claudia home in her own carriage, an offer that Claudia was glad to accept in view of her blistered foot.

"And do drop by tomorrow if you can, my dear," said Lady Rexford, warmly pressing her hand at parting. "I declare if just talking with you hasn't made me feel better about this business. There's no doubt in my mind I have made the right decision in hiring you."

"I'm glad if I helped, Lady Rexford," said Claudia. "Certainly I shall call on you tomorrow, and we will discuss your affairs in greater detail. Good afternoon to you. And a good afternoon to you, too, ma'am," she told Hettie. Hettie gave her a gruff good afternoon in return, and on this amicable note Claudia left Seventeen Bridges Street and started for home.

During the drive home, she divided her time between counting over the money Lady Rexford had advanced her and exulting over the delightful position she had won. "I haven't done a thing yet, and already I am thirty pounds richer," she told herself. "Why, if I were a dishonest person, I might simply take the money and vanish. Lady Rexford seems to put a great deal of trust in me and my gentility!"

It occurred to Claudia at this point that Lady Rexford was almost dangerously trusting. She was clearly a credulous, warmhearted, generous woman who acted largely on impulse. Of course Miss Claudia Chambers would never take advantage of those qualities, but others might not be so forbearing.

"I shall have to caution her against being so generous in the future," Claudia reflected. "It will do her no good with those Yorkshire people, I'm sure. They will only despise her for thinking she can buy her way into their good graces. It would be better if she were very close and demanding, for then at least they might know they could not impose on her. I shall have to give this whole matter a great deal of thought."

Claudia did give the matter a great deal of thought, for the rest of that day and long into the night. As she lay in her lumpy bed in Edmund and Anthea's second-best bedchamber, gazing up at the cracked plaster ceiling, she felt convinced that if Lady Rexford went into Yorkshire in her natural character, she was likely to be eaten alive. Yet could she sustain an assumed character for any length of time? Remembering Lady

Rexford's pretty, guileless face and chattering tongue, Claudia thought it doubtful.

"It's natural for her to talk and smile and be friendly with people and unnatural for her to hold herself aloof in any way," Claudia told herself. "But people do learn to do what's not natural to them, given the proper motivation. I suppose Lady Rexford might be able to damp down her natural impulses. All the same, it's likely to be uphill work. If only she were a woman like Great-Aunt Ermintrude! Then she would have no difficulty holding her own in Yorkshire."

The thought made Claudia smile, for aside from the similarity in their ages, no two women could have been more different than Lady Rexford and her own late Great-Aunt Ermintrude. Great-Aunt Ermintrude had been Claudia's mother's aunt, an elderly lady of unprepossessing looks and strictly limited means. Notwithstanding these disadvantages, she had managed to exert a degree of authority within her native village that would have done credit to a duchess. Ladies better born than she meekly gave her the precedence, and the local squire had ceded to her his own family pew at church, where she sat each Sunday listening to the service in grim and silent satisfaction. Servants and tradesmen went in terror of her. No butcher ever dared palm off an inferior cut of meat on Great-Aunt Ermintrude; no servant girl in her employ ever neglected to sweep under the rugs or to dust the unseen tops of doorways and picture frames.

"It's a pity Lady Rexford couldn't learn a trick or two from Great-Aunt Ermintrude," Claudia reflected with a sigh. Then suddenly she sat up in bed, possessed of a revolutionary idea. Why should not Lady Rexford study her great-aunt's techniques and do that very thing?

"Of course, she could never really be like Great-Aunt Ermintrude, but she might copy some of her mannerisms," Claudia told herself. "And her clothes—I am sure we would do well to copy her example there. Lady Rexford's frills and furbelows simply don't encourage one to take her seriously.

And first impressions are so important. If we can only make her seem formidable at the start, it wouldn't matter so much if she couldn't keep up the pretense later on. But—"

Again Claudia sat up in bed, as a second inspiration struck her. "But if we keep her contacts with outsiders to a minimum, she might keep it up almost indefinitely! Hettie and I between us could manage it, I think. We could give the orders to the servants and represent her as a very grand, strict, demanding person. She would only need to stand in the background and look as formidable as possible."

Claudia could see no flaw in this plan. With Hettie and herself to play the active roles, Lady Rexford might remain safely behind the screen of the public image they constructed for her. The only difficulty would be when it came time for Lady Rexford to meet with her nephew, Master John.

"I suppose he's really Lord Rexford now, but somehow I can't help thinking of him as Master John," mused Claudia as she composed herself to sleep. "Whatever he's called, he sounds a most disagreeable person. I am afraid he will not allow himself to be fobbed off with messages from me or Hettie like the servants. But forewarned is forearmed, and knowing your opponent is the first step to defeating him, as Edmund says. I must get Lady Rexford to tell me all about Master John tomorrow, and then I shall know better how to proceed."

Three

Claudia awoke the next morning impatient to discuss her plan with Lady Rexford. Knowing the ways of the fashionable world, however, she felt it would be a solecism to present herself in Bridges Street before early afternoon. The hours until then seemed to stretch endlessly into the distance; but fortunately Lady Rexford's ways proved not to be those of the fashionable world. Claudia was both pleased and surprised when, at ten o'clock, she received word that her employer's carriage was at the door.

"My Lady Rexford's compliments, and she hoped you might find it convenient to step around to her house for a few minutes," explained the footman who delivered the message. "If not convenient, I am to return at whatever hour suits you best."

"Oh, now will suit me best," said Claudia happily. Pausing only to put on her bonnet and pelisse—and the borrowed cap from Anthea, which she hoped would lend her an extra measure of authority—she went out to the carriage. Soon she was once more being ushered into Lady Rexford's pink plush parlor by the grim-faced Hettie.

The parlor looked exactly as it had the previous day, with curtains drawn and alabaster lamps burning. Lady Rexford looked much the same, too. The dress she was wearing was of velvet rather than sarcenet, but of an almost identical shade of pink. Instead of looking nervous, however, her round, rosy face was wreathed in smiles, and she made Claudia welcome in the warmest way, pressing cakes and tea upon her and urging her to take off her bonnet and pelisse.

"I hope you'll forgive my bringing you here so early, my dear. But I was wishful to see you and afraid we might miss each other if I left it to chance. I'm going out later today, you see, and might not be back till evening. I've a deal of business to do, getting ready for this Yorkshire trip." Lady Rexford grimaced as she spoke these last words.

"Yes, I know you are busy," said Claudia, pleased to have this opening to bring forward her own business. "And it works out nicely that you should have summoned me here this morning, for I was wanting to talk to you, too, Lady Rexford. You see, I have thought of a plan which might make your stay in Yorkshire more comfortable." To Hettie, who had lingered to hear the opening exchange of greetings and was now preparing to withdraw, she added, "I wish you would stay, ma'am, and hear what I have to say along with Lady Rexford. My plan depends on all three of us working together. If you agree to undertake it, we must begin right away to make our preparations."

She then went on to describe the idea that had occurred to her the night before. Lady Rexford and Hettie listened with obvious interest, but with equally obvious sensations of doubt and skepticism.

"I don't mind letting you and Hettie do all the talking, for I can see it would be better than my trying to do it myself. In fact, that's partly why I hired you in the first place, Miss Chambers," said Lady Rexford, at the conclusion of Claudia's speech. "But this business of my pretending to be a grand lady—well, I'm afraid it won't fly, my dear. I don't know how it is, but people seem to know right away that I'm not to the manor born, as the saying is."

"But I think that has a great deal to do with how you present yourself, Lady Rexford," said Claudia, striving to be diplomatic. "If we were to put you in different clothes, give you the right props, and see that you deported yourself in the proper manner, I don't believe anyone could possibly guess you weren't Lord Rexford's equal when you married him."

Lady Rexford looked pleased but still dubious. "Do you think so?" she said wistfully. Then her face changed, and she shook her head with an air of stubborn determination. "I'm sure it's kind of you to say such things, my dear, but you know I've never pretended to be anything I'm not, and I don't intend to start now. That was one of the things Lord Rexford liked about me, you know. He said there wasn't an ounce of pretense about me."

"Oh, but I am not suggesting that you pretend to be something you are not, Lady Rexford. We will make no attempt to pass you off as a noblewoman by birth. But you *are* a noblewoman by marriage, and it's only right you should enjoy the perquisites that go with your position. Anyone would admit that, for you know a woman always takes her husband's position in life, be it higher or lower than that to which she is naturally entitled."

At this juncture, Claudia acquired an unexpected ally in the form of Hettie. "Aye, you know I've said the same thing myself, Lucy, many a time," she said with a nod. "You don't make half as much of your position as you've a right to, and that's the truth."

"Perhaps you're right," admitted Lady Rexford. For a moment or two she sat biting her lip, indecision written large on her face. "But still I hate to put on fine-lady airs. I am sure Lord Rexford would have disliked it extremely."

"He'd dislike seeing you trampled underfoot a deal worse," retorted Hettie. "And you know that's what's likely to happen if you don't take a strong hand with this precious nephew of his from the beginning."

"Besides, taking control is not the same as putting on airs," added Claudia. "Lord Rexford did leave you his estate, after all, so it's to be assumed he meant you to take control of it. Likewise, we must assume he meant you should take whatever steps were necessary to manage it properly."

Lady Rexford sat silent a moment or two longer, then nodded reluctantly. "There's something in what you say. I suppose I might try your plan, Miss Chambers, but I'm sure I don't know if I'll be able to do what you want me to."

"As to that, you would really have to do very little," said Claudia, pleased to see her idea gain acceptance. "Hettie and I would handle most of the real work. Your role would merely be to look the part of the character we give you—and perhaps, occasionally, to say a few words to confirm something we have already said."

"That doesn't sound so very difficult," said Lady Rexford, looking relieved. "What would I do to look the part, Miss Chambers? I know you said something earlier about different clothes."

This was the area in which Claudia had anticipated the most difficulties. She sought to make her speech as diplomatic as possible. "Yes, I think it would be necessary for you to dress in a different style if you are to create the proper impression. The costume you are wearing now is very lovely and becoming, ma'am, but—well, I think you would carry more authority if you wore plainer dresses in a darker color."

Lady Rexford looked down at her pink velvet dress. "Indeed?" she said blankly. "Do you mean I ought to wear rose color instead of this light pink?"

"No, I mean a darker color altogether," said Claudia. "Black would be best, but—"

"Black?" said Lady Rexford in dismay. "Oh, but I don't care for black, Miss Chambers. I am sure it makes me look at least ten years older."

"Nevertheless, black would be best," said Claudia, her voice apologetic but firm. "My Great-Aunt Ermintrude never wore anything but black dresses, and I don't think anyone could command more authority than she did. Besides—and forgive me if I'm being indiscreet—aren't you still in mourning for your husband? You spoke yesterday as though he had died comparatively recently."

"Just a little over a year ago," agreed Lady Rexford readily enough. "But I've never worn mourning for Lord Rexford. He didn't want me to and told me so many and many a time in the years we were married. 'Lucy,' he said, 'pink's your color, and I hope you won't ever change it—no, not even when the time comes for me to stick my fork in the wall. I don't believe I could rest easy in my grave if I knew you were consigned to widow's weeds for the rest of your life.' " Lady Rexford paused to wipe away a tear produced by this moving recollection.

"I see," said Claudia, endeavoring once again to be diplomatic. "Still, I am sure Lord Rexford would understand if you changed your style of dress temporarily, just for the space of this visit. You know the world is apt to be a censorious place, and people will look askance at you if you appear in colors so soon after your husband's death. You wouldn't have to wear mourning necessarily—but some handsome black silk dresses would serve both to ward off people's criticism and at the same time give you an air of elegance and authority."

The thought of having an air of elegance and authority seemed to console Lady Rexford somewhat. She said she would consider buying some black dresses since Miss Chambers seemed so set on it. "You might consider buying a cane, too," suggested Claudia, a trifle diffidently. "I know you don't need one to walk, of course—"

"I should hope not!" said Lady Rexford indignantly. "A cane at my age! I may be a trifle stout, but my legs are perfectly sound."

"Of course they are," soothed Claudia. "It is only that a cane can be a useful prop as well as a physical support. Great-Aunt Ermintrude used to carry a black ashplant, and whenever she grew angry at what she considered impertinence on someone's part, she would bring it crashing down on the floor. I don't think anyone was ever impertinent twice to Great-Aunt Ermintrude!"

"But carrying a cane makes a body look so old," said Lady

Rexford disconsolately. "And ashplants are such common things. My own grandfather used to carry one, and though he was a very worthy man, I'm afraid he wasn't in the least genteel."

As Claudia was debating what to say in reply to this, Hettie once more came to her aid. "As I see it, it ain't necessary that you carry a common ashplant, Lucy," she said. "It looks to me as though any cane would do the trick. You just want something to lend you consequence, as Miss Chambers says. I've seen some real handsome gold-topped canes in the shops on Bond Street."

"Why, yes, so have I now that you mention it," said Lady Rexford, perking up at once. "A gold-topped cane would be very genteel and ladylike. Hettie, bring me paper and pencil, if you please. I must write all this down."

Hettie obligingly fetched paper and pencil, and Lady Rexford sat down to make a list. "Black dresses. Gold-topped cane," she said as she painstakingly inscribed the words on the paper. Then she looked expectantly at Claudia.

"You might put down a quizzing glass, too. A *gold* quizzing glass," said Claudia, forestalling the protest that Lady Rexford was opening her mouth to make. "I hadn't thought of it before, but my godmother Lady Worley often wears a quizzing glass. And she has a way of looking through it that is very quelling indeed."

What was good enough for Lady Worley was evidently good enough for Lady Rexford. She wrote down, "Quizzing glass— gold," without a word of protest.

"Anything else, my dear?" she asked, looking at Claudia.

"I think that will do to start with," said Claudia. "Once we have your props and costumes, we can concentrate on studying your role."

"I tell you what, Miss Chambers: You'd better come shopping with me this afternoon," said Lady Rexford, as she folded up the list and placed it carefully in her reticule. "That is, if you can spare the time. You know better than I what's proper, and I could use your help in choosing these things you say I need."

"Certainly I can spare the time," said Claudia with pleasure. "Let me send a note to my brother and sister-in-law so they will not worry, and then I will be happy to accompany you."

The note was written and dispatched; and as soon as Claudia, Lady Rexford, and Hettie had assumed their bonnets and wraps, they set out for Bond Street.

What followed was one of the most enjoyable afternoons of Claudia's life. She had never before enjoyed the luxury of shopping with untrammeled taste and unlimited credit. Lady Rexford followed her advice slavishly in everything and even insisted on buying several things for her as well. "For it looks as though you'll be playing a role same as me in this business, Miss Chambers," she said shrewdly. "And I'm sure you need the clothes for it just as I do."

"That is true," said Claudia, wistfully surveying the model of a bronze green morning dress and matching pelisse that a dressmaker had just presented for her inspection. "But you have been so generous to me already, Lady Rexford! I hate to allow you to do anything else."

"Nonsense, my dear," said Lady Rexford firmly. "It gives me pleasure to buy you pretty things, especially since I'm doomed to buy nothing but black dresses this trip myself. In any case, I haven't the figure to wear most of these modern styles. It's as good as a play to have somebody young and pretty to buy clothes for." Waving aside Claudia's further protests, she turned to the dressmaker and said firmly, "Miss'll take the bronze green and the gold taffeta afternoon gown and that ivory satin. Also the yellow sprig muslin. Just charge them all to my account, if you please, and have them delivered to my house in Bridges Street."

From the dressmaker's, they proceeded to a milliner's establishment, where Claudia helped Lady Rexford choose several impressive black hats and bonnets in the style of Great-Aunt Ermintrude. Lady Rexford then went on to buy Claudia a chip-straw bonnet trimmed with flowers and a bronze green hat ornamented with plumes that matched her new pelisse and morning dress to a nicety.

"But no caps!" she told Claudia with a shake of her finger. "I never could abide caps, and I hope you'll humor me by not wearing one while you're working for me, Miss Chambers. Hettie insists on wearing hers in spite of everything I say." She shot a look of humorous forbearance at her friend and servitor. "She says caps save a deal of hairdressing, and I suppose that's true. But I've never cared for them myself."

It was no sacrifice for Claudia to forswear the wearing of caps in Lady Rexford's employ. She did so willingly, and Lady Rexford was so pleased by her ready acquiescence that she bestowed an additional bonnet on her—a high-crowned French creation that the milliner swore was straight over from Paris. The party then returned to Bridges Street to look over and talk about their new purchases.

"I must say I do feel a deal more confident when I'm holding this," said Lady Rexford, looking with pleasure at the handsome gold-topped cane she had just purchased. "I feel like the Queen herself, all tricked out with her state robes and staff!"

"You must strike your cane on the floor whenever you give an order or whenever you wish to give emphasis to your words," said Claudia, smiling. "Try it now, Lady Rexford. Say, 'Miss Chambers, I asked you to bring me the parcel with my eyeglass in it. Kindly bring it to me at once!' "

Lady Rexford obediently repeated these words, rapping her cane on the floor as she did so. Both voice and rap were rather feeble, but after Claudia had made her repeat the maneuver two or three times, she was able to wield her new prop with an impressive effect.

"My, don't I sound a perfect Tartar!" she said, laughing. With a mischievous look at Hettie, she added, "Hettie, I am perishing with thirst. Kindly bring me some tea and a bite to eat, *if* you please!" She emphasized the words with a rap of her cane so ferocious that it set the bric-a-brac in a nearby cabinet rattling on its shelves.

"I can see somebody's going to be insufferable to live with if this keeps on," said Hettie darkly, but she went to fetch the tea nevertheless.

While she was busy with this errand, Claudia and Lady Rexford experimented with the latter's new quizzing glass.

"I never thought the day would come when I'd be wearing an eyeglass, but I can see it does give you some advantage," confided Lady Rexford, surveying Claudia experimentally through that instrument. "Why, with this and my stick to support me, I almost feel I could face Master John without quaking. Almost, but not quite," she concluded, laying down the quizzing glass with a sigh.

Claudia was glad this subject had come up of its own accord. "Is Master John really so formidable as all that?" she asked. "I know you said you were reluctant to meet him, but I had supposed that was only because he made himself so disagreeable about his uncle's marriage."

"Oh, no! To be sure, I was not inclined to make a bosom-bow of him after the way he spoke about me and Lord Rexford, but that is not the only reason I would rather not meet him. For I already *have* met him, you see—or at least had him pointed out to me when he was in Town a couple of years ago. And I assure you that his looks gave me no desire to ever further the acquaintance!"

"What does he look like?" said Claudia curiously.

Lady Rexford shuddered. "A great, scowling, black-browed creature, more like a prizefighter than a gentleman. He must take after his mother's family, for I am sure the Rexfords in general were very distinguished-looking people. My Lord Rexford, in particular, was accounted a most handsome man."

"I am sure he was," said Claudia mechanically. Inwardly she was considering the information Lady Rexford had given her. It was little enough to go on, but even that little was enough to show her that, of all the possible adversaries she might meet in Yorkshire, Master John was likely to be the most formidable.

However, that was no more than she had suspected before. And though Lady Rexford might tremble at the prospect of meeting him, Claudia reminded herself that at least a week must elapse before that fateful meeting could take place. That would surely be enough time to bolster Lady Rexford's courage and fit her with the skills she would need to triumph against her disagreeable nephew.

In the days that followed, Claudia had reason to be gratified by her protégé's progress. Lady Rexford was an excellent pupil: attentive, obedient, and anxious to please. As the day approached for the party's departure for Yorkshire, she confided to Claudia that she believed she was going to enjoy the trip.

"I'm actually looking forward to using some of these tricks you've taught me, my dear. Indeed, I already used them the other day when I went to be fitted for my new furs at the furrier's. They tried to fob me off with a set of second-rate sables at first-rate prices, but I just looked them in the eye and told them I wasn't having any of it. And they ended by giving me a set of first-rate sables for less than they tried to charge me for the other ones!"

"Good for you!" said Claudia. "I believe you *are* ready for Yorkshire, Lady Rexford. Hettie and I are ready, too, I think. In any event, we will have plenty of time to rehearse our roles while we are on the road. Staying in inns will be excellent practice for us. I've been thinking it might be a good thing for you to bring your own bedsheets along with you. I remember my godmother talking of one of her friends who does that whenever she passes a night in an inn, and it sounds very grand and uncompromising, just the sort of thing a lady like our new Lady Rexford would do!"

"It does, doesn't it?" said Lady Rexford, obviously enchanted by this picture of herself. "I'll do it, upon my word! I'll tell Hettie to have the housemaids pack my own bedlinens, and I believe I'll tell her to put in my own tea and spirit lamp, too. I've heard it's very difficult to get a decent cup of tea at posting houses."

Claudia approved this idea, and the next two days were devoted to putting Lady Rexford's possessions in proper shape for the journey.

Claudia's own packing was a relatively easy matter. Her possessions were few and her wardrobe scant, apart from the new clothes Lady Rexford had showered upon her. These had remained at Bridges Street and were to be packed in one of Lady Rexford's trunks, in accordance with that lady's own suggestion.

Claudia was grateful to fall in with this suggestion. She knew the appearance of a new and rich wardrobe would cause a stir in her brother's household. Even the thirty-pound advance had created a certain amount of controversy. Edmund had looked solemn and said he hoped Lady Rexford was as respectable as she was generous, while Anthea said acidly that she wished *she* had thirty pounds to fritter away. Claudia had mollified the former by promising to return home immediately if she found herself in difficulties, while the latter was pacified by a handsome gift of toys and clothing for her children. And so, having bidden farewell to her brother and her small niece and nephew (who were sincerely sorry to see her go) and to her sister-in-law (who made a decent pretense of being so), Claudia left the home that had been hers for the last three years and went forth to begin her new career.

She was a little saddened at the idea of leaving home and family. But her sadness was lightened by Lady Rexford's open-armed welcome. "Ah, here you are, my dear! I declare if I wasn't worrying you might change your mind at the last moment. But Hettie here said you'd be as good as your word, and of course she was right as usual. Just let my men put your trunk in the boot, and then we'll be on our way."

The trunk was duly stowed in the boot of the carriage, and Claudia took her place inside with Hettie and Lady Rexford. She observed that Hettie looked much as usual, though her apron had been replaced by a traveling pelisse and her habitual cap supplemented with a battered straw bonnet. But Lady Rexford cut an unexpectedly sleek and genteel figure in a dress of black lutestring, severely tailored and worn with a veiled bonnet impressive in both dimension and trimming. Claudia praised her lavishly on her appearance.

"Do you know, I think I *do* look rather good," said Lady Rexford, looking complacently down at her silk-clad figure. "Black's not as unbecoming to me as I supposed. It's slimming, at any rate, and that's something." She fingered the quizzing glass that hung from her neck and looked at the gold-topped cane that stood in a corner of the carriage. "I declare, I feel more and more ready to deal with Master John!"

"I hope you *are* ready, Lady Rexford. We'll see how you manage when we stop for luncheon. Remember, Hettie and I will do most of the talking, but if you *are* obliged to speak to anybody—because they've asked you a direct question, for instance—make sure you look them in the eye. Wait a moment before answering, and just tap your cane on the floor two or three times as you stare at them through your quizzing glass. I guarantee that will overawe them if anything can."

This plan was followed when the party stopped for luncheon, and it enjoyed a fair success. Claudia and Hettie swept into the inn, followed at a little distance by Lady Rexford. This latter lady stood tapping her cane gently on the floor and looking around her with a critical eye while Claudia made her demands to the innkeeper, a burly man in his forties.

"Lady Rexford will require a private parlor and a luncheon of at least two courses," she told him. "I trust you received my letter some days ago in which I detailed her specific requests."

"Oh, yes, miss," said the landlord, glancing with curiosity at Lady Rexford's black-clad figure. "The parlor's all ready, with the fire made up and the table laid, just as you requested. I'll tell my missus you're here, and she'll have luncheon on the table in two shakes."

During the meal, Lady Rexford deported herself magnificently. She consumed the landlord's excellent luncheon with a critical air, condescended to praise the gooseberry tart, and remarked that the pullets were not ill dressed. There *was* an awkward moment when, in a burst of overconfidence, she proposed sending back a dish of cutlets that she claimed were underdone.

"Nonsense, my lady," said the landlord's wife, a sharp-featured woman who had been waiting on them during the meal. "Them cutlets is done as done could be. I cooked 'em myself." She regarded Lady Rexford with a belligerent eye.

Lady Rexford, obedient to Claudia's training, attempted to raise her quizzing glass to her eye. But she was so nervous that her fingers could not even find the chain on which it was suspended. Claudia, seeing her difficulties, threw herself into the breach.

"Lady Rexford prefers her cutlets to be less rare," she said in a calm, clear voice. "We would appreciate it very much if you would take them back to the kitchen and cook them a few minutes longer."

The landlady protested a little more, but finally consented to return the dish to the kitchen for further cooking. After she was gone, Lady Rexford looked apologetically at Claudia. "My dear, I am sorry," she said. "I'm afraid I bungled that business dreadfully."

"Not at all," said Claudia cheerfully. "It was only a minor mishap, and as you see, we were able to carry our point nonetheless. Next time you will do better, I have no doubt."

"Perhaps so," said Lady Rexford, picking disconsolately at her gooseberry tart. "But I am afraid I shall always find it difficult to look people in the eye. Particularly people as disagreeable as that old alewife!"

"Well, if you really find it impossible to look people in the eye, don't look at them at all," said Claudia. "Addressing people while not looking at them is nearly as good as staring them out of countenance, I do believe. And later, when you are more comfortable, you can use the cane and quizzing glass as we have practiced."

Lady Rexford, however, vowed she was comfortable enough now to use the more advanced technique. "It was only that I let my nerves get the better of me this time," she told Claudia. "Next time we stop, I'll do better, Miss Chambers. Just you wait and see."

Claudia praised this plucky attitude, but inwardly she was a little worried lest her pupil might again overreach herself. As it developed, however, her worrying was needless. Lady Rexford covered herself with glory that evening by overawing not only their landlord and his wife, but an elderly Irishwoman, an itinerant wine merchant, and three young gentlemen who also happened to be staying at their inn.

"I do believe I'm getting the hang of this," she told Claudia jubilantly as they relaxed in her sitting room that evening. "It's really quite simple once you learn the way of it. But of course I couldn't do it without you and Hettie. Why, when I hear you going on and on about Lady Rexford demanding this and Lady Rexford desiring that, I forget sometimes it's me you're talking about. It's almost as though I really were a great lady used to having her own way in everything!"

Claudia quite understood Lady Rexford's feelings. There had been moments that day when she, too, had become caught up in her performance and begun to feel as though she were living her role rather than merely acting it. When she told the landlady that my lady Rexford desired her morning chocolate at eight o'clock precisely, she forgot her employer was an elderly ex-housekeeper of timid disposition. Instead, she found herself visualizing a much more formidable lady—a grande dame on the order of Great-Aunt Ermintrude, who was quite capable of throwing the whole house into disarray if her chocolate were delivered five minutes past the hour.

Likewise, when one of the chambermaids asked in an awestruck tone if Lady Rexford always traveled with her own sheets, Claudia was able to answer, "Oh, yes," without any sense that she had told a falsehood. And when she assured this same chambermaid that Lady Rexford was a terribly strict and demanding mistress, she found herself believing her own words and trembling at the notion of incurring this fictional Lady Rexford's displeasure.

Altogether, Claudia had reason to be pleased with the success of her scheme. Lady Rexford was daily gaining in dignity and self-confidence, while she and Hettie worked as a well-oiled team to smooth all possible obstacles from her path.

Three days and two nights on the road were sufficient to give them all a reasonable experience in their new roles. When at last they reached Rexford Park, late in the afternoon of the third day of their travels, Claudia hoped they were ready now to face the more formidable challenges that undoubtedly awaited them there.

Four

Rexford Park proved to be a large Tudor mansion set in the midst of extensive grounds. Lady Rexford's face was pale with excitement as the carriage turned between a pair of towering gateposts bearing the Rexford coat of arms. Claudia felt excited, too. She looked out the window, taking in the splendor of their surroundings. Just beyond the gates was the Gatehouse—a three-story brick building that was larger and finer than many a rich man's mansion. As Claudia was gazing at it respectfully, a man came out of the Gatehouse. He stopped dead when he saw the carriage and stood watching as it rattled past. Claudia supposed he must be the gatekeeper or some other menial attached to the estate. She observed in an absent way that he was tall, dark, and not bad looking in a rough way, but she was too much occupied in surveying the scenery to pay much attention to a mere man. A moment more and he was lost to view as the carriage turned a corner of the drive.

"Dear me, but I'm nervous," announced Lady Rexford, looking wildly around her. "There's the house, just as Rexford always described it—and oh, dear, whatever will I do? They've got every servant in the place lined up to meet me!"

"No!" exclaimed Claudia. She half rose from her seat to look out the opposite window of the carriage. To her dismay, she saw that Lady Rexford's statement was quite correct. Several dozen people were assembled before the stately red brick mansion with its entrance tower and parapets. That they were

servants was evident from their uniforms, consisting largely
of liveries for the men and caps and aprons for the women;
that they were hostile was apparent from their faces, which
wore looks both curious and critical as they watched the carriage draw to a stop before the entrance. Lady Rexford
clutched Claudia's arm.

"I can't do it, my dear! Indeed, I can't. If it were only a
couple of servants I'd manage well enough, but coming all at
once this way—no, I can't do it. I'd sooner drive all the way
back to London." In a despairing voice, she added, "This is
Master's John's doing, I don't doubt. Blast the man! He's intent
on making this business as uncomfortable for me as possible!"

"Is he? Then we shall foil his intentions," said Claudia resolutely. "There's no reason you must undergo such an ordeal
as this right now, Lady Rexford. Just leave it all to me, and
we'll get the best of Master John yet."

As soon as the footmen had opened the door and let down
the steps of the carriage, Claudia got out and walked over to
where the servants were standing. She did her best to act calm
and unruffled, but inwardly she found it unnerving to be surveyed by forty or fifty pairs of curious, critical, and hostile
eyes. It was comforting to reflect that she was wearing her
new bronze green pelisse and hat and that her appearance was
irreproachable. "Fashionable clothes may not be everything,
but they're a great comfort when one is feeling nervous,"
Claudia told herself with an inward laugh.

Having reached the steps where the servants were standing,
Claudia paused to consider her next move. The servants were
still looking at her, but their faces were less hostile now, and
many of them looked merely curious. It was evident that they
were wondering who she was and what her approach might
herald. "Good afternoon," said Claudia in a brisk and businesslike voice. "I wonder, is one of you the housekeeper
here?"

Her eyes had already singled out an elderly woman in the
front row as a likely choice. The woman was tall and lean with

scraped-back gray hair and a hatchet face. She wore a black bombazine dress, and there was an air of authority about her person, coupled with a hostility that was singular even in that notably hostile group. The woman met Claudia's eyes, hesitated, then nodded. "I'm Mrs. Fry," she said in a grating voice. "And who might you be, miss?"

"I am Miss Chambers, Lady Rexford's companion. Lady Rexford is feeling very unwell after her journey, and she desires to go to her rooms immediately. Is everything in readiness for her?"

"Aye, everything's ready. We got your letter saying she'd be arriving this afternoon, and we've been waiting this hour to greet her."

There was a hint of spiteful triumph in Mrs. Fry's voice that betrayed what kind of greeting she had prepared for her mistress. Claudia merely smiled, however, pretending to take her words at face value.

"Why, that is very kind of you, Mrs. Fry. But I'm afraid Lady Rexford isn't up to the fatigue of making any formal greetings today. Please order the servants to disperse for now and assist me if you please in showing her ladyship to her rooms. You might also instruct the cook to send up some tea and a light repast."

Mrs. Fry's face was a study in conflicting emotions. "Aye, to be sure," she said. "But begging your pardon, miss, I think Lady Rexford might take the time to say good afternoon to us all, seeing we've been waiting an hour for her."

"Do you?" said Claudia gently. "That shows that you are not acquainted with Lady Rexford's state of health. It is essential that we get her to her rooms as soon as possible. Shall you dismiss the servants or shall I?"

Mrs. Fry gave Claudia a resentful look, then turned and dismissed the servants with a few brusque words. Having done this, she followed Claudia out to the carriage.

Claudia approached the carriage a little nervously, fearing Lady Rexford might still be in a state of hysterics. She was therefore overjoyed to be greeted by a sharp voice. "There you are at last, Miss Chambers! I've been waiting an age for you, I vow and declare." The words were accompanied by a loud rap of Lady Rexford's cane.

"I'm very sorry, my lady," said Claudia, concealing her delight at this heroic effort. "I'm sure I hurried as quick as I could. This is the housekeeper, Mrs. Fry. She will help see you to your rooms."

"She will, will she?" Lady Rexford surveyed Mrs. Fry briefly through her quizzing glass. Mrs. Fry returned the look defiantly, but Claudia thought she looked slightly taken aback.

At last Lady Rexford let the quizzing glass drop from her eye and nodded dismissively. "Very well. She may take my left arm and you my right, Miss Chambers. Hettie, you bring my jewel box and dressing case. The footmen can bring the rest of the bags, but see they don't dawdle about it. I want my things sent to my room immediately so I can undress and lie down until dinner."

"Certainly, my lady," said Claudia, taking Lady Rexford's right arm and bestowing a surreptitious squeeze upon it. "Well done, ma'am!" she whispered. "Keep it up till we get to your rooms, and I believe you will carry the day."

Thus encouraged, Lady Rexford kept her act up admirably, all the way to the suite of rooms that had been prepared for her. She scolded Claudia for walking too fast and Hettie for unspecified clumsiness and even ventured to reprove Mrs. Fry when that lady went to open the windows of her bedchamber. "Close those windows if you please, Mrs. Fry. That draft would be the death of me in my condition."

Mrs. Fry, looking offended, shut the windows again. "I hope these rooms meet with your satisfaction, my lady," she said stiffly. "We hadn't much notice of your coming, or we would have tried to do better."

Lady Rexford glanced around the bedroom with its dimity hangings and light oak furniture. "It will do for now, I suppose," she said. But her voice held no conviction.

Claudia, fearing that the interview was being prolonged beyond her capabilities, addressed the housekeeper with a smile. "Thank you very much for your help, Mrs. Fry. I believe Lady Rexford's maid and I can manage things from here. We'll let you know if she requires anything else." Gently but firmly she escorted the housekeeper to the door.

As Claudia was shutting the door, Lady Rexford made a last, noble effort. "Miss Chambers, come here this instant," she barked, striking her cane on the floor. "I can't find what you have done with my vinaigrette, you stupid girl."

"Coming, my lady," called Claudia. With an apologetic smile, she shut the door firmly in the housekeeper's face.

As soon as the door was shut, Lady Rexford collapsed limply on the bed. "Oh, my, I never realized how hard it was to be a great lady! Do forgive me for calling you stupid, Miss Chambers. It was the only thing I could think of on the spur of the moment."

"And it worked splendidly," said Claudia, giving her a hug. "If Mrs. Fry does not yet fully respect you, I think she has at least gained a proper respect for your temper! But I'm afraid we will never cozen her into serving you for love. She looks a most sour, distempered old creature."

"Aye, that she does," agreed Lady Rexford as she removed her bonnet. Looking around the room, she added, "And if she hasn't fobbed me off with one of the second-best bedchambers, I'll be a Dutchman! These shabby little rooms were never the mistress's chambers, I'm thinking."

"No, although I wouldn't precisely call them shabby," said Claudia, also looking around at the handsome oaken furniture and dainty white hangings. "However, I'm sure we can do better in such a house as this. I'll see about having your rooms changed later, ma'am. Is there anything else you want me to see to?"

Lady Rexford said she could think of nothing offhand, but would leave it all to her dearest Miss Chambers. A warm smile accompanied her words. Claudia smiled back, then tripped off to do battle once more with Mrs. Fry.

She found that dame sulkily directing the unloading of Lady Rexford's baggage and conversing with a gentleman in a frock coat, who appeared to be the butler. "Putting on airs and ordering us about like she was a lady born," Mrs. Fry was saying vengefully. "She's no more a lady than what I am! You know she was naught but a housekeeper before his late lordship married her."

The butler laughed. "That sounds like jealousy, Sukie," he said slyly. "Maybe you think his lordship would have done better to marry his Yorkshire housekeeper rather than his London one?"

"No, indeed!" said Mrs. Fry with a toss of her head. "I'm sure I know *my* place. If other people only knew theirs—"

"I beg your pardon," said Claudia gently. Both Mrs. Fry and the butler jumped.

"Oh, it's you, miss," said the housekeeper in some confusion. "I didn't hear you come up."

"Evidently not," said Claudia more gently still. The butler, murmuring something about seeing to the plate, discreetly took himself off. Claudia watched him go, then turned to the housekeeper. "I wished to talk to you about Lady Rexford's rooms, Mrs. Fry," she said, still in a gentle voice.

"What about 'em?" said Mrs. Fry, eyeing Claudia suspiciously. "You're not saying they're not clean, I hope. I saw to their cleaning myself only yesterday."

"Oh, yes, they are admirably clean. But Lady Rexford would prefer a larger set of rooms such as befits the mistress of the house."

At these words, Mrs. Fry's jaw tightened. "She's got the largest rooms that are fit for her to stay in," she said truculently. "And I should think they'd be good enough for the likes of *her.*"

Claudia made no immediate answer to this speech. She merely looked at Mrs. Fry without speaking. Mrs. Fry tried to return her look defiantly, but could not help fidgeting slightly. "What do you mean, Mrs. Fry?" said Claudia, still in a gentle voice.

Mrs. Fry fidgeted some more, started to speak, then turned away, biting her lip. "Nothing," she said sullenly. "I'm sure I didn't mean nothing." Over her shoulder she added, "But there's no other rooms Lady Rexford *could* stay in, miss. The ones she's in are the best in the house."

"Are they indeed?" said Claudia. "Well, unfortunately she has taken a dislike to that particular set of rooms, so we must look about for some others. If you would kindly lend me your keys, I will do a little exploring to see which would suit her best."

Claudia was pleased to see several strong emotions cross Mrs. Fry's ill-tempered face in succession. "Oh, that's not necessary, miss," she said, in a voice that struggled to be conciliatory. "If she's really taken a dislike to those rooms, then I'll see to finding her some others."

"Thank you, but I think you had better let me do it," said Claudia. "I know her likes and dislikes better than anyone else, and I would not want you to waste your time preparing a second set of rooms that might be as unsuitable as the first."

Mrs. Fry did not argue with this speech, but her face was resentful as she led Claudia upstairs. "I'm sure I hoped those rooms would suit Lady Rexford," she said. "It's a pity to make the housemaids go to the work of preparing them for nothing."

"Oh, it needn't be for nothing," said Claudia cheerfully. "Those rooms will do very well for me, Mrs. Fry. I'm not nearly so particular as Lady Rexford."

"It's to be hoped not," said Mrs. Fry. She spoke emphatically, but there was a hint of curiosity in her eyes as she regarded Claudia. "Just who are you, miss? I don't quite place you in this business."

Claudia smiled. "Oh, I told you earlier what my place was, Mrs. Fry. I am Lady Rexford's companion." Making her voice solemn, she added, "And if I am to retain that place, I must see that she is made happy in her surroundings. I shall need your help with that, Mrs. Fry, and the help of the other servants."

Mrs. Fry sniffed, but could not resist asking a further question. "Is she as particular as all that then, miss?"

"Oh, very particular!" said Claudia. Searching her mind for an appropriate illustration, she happily remembered an exploit of her Great-Aunt Ermintrude's. "I believe once she turned off all the servants in her house en masse because she felt they were shirking their duties."

"Well, she'd best not be trying that here," said Mrs. Fry, tossing her head. "This is my Lord Rexford's house, not hers. She wouldn't get far trying to turn off the staff!"

Claudia regarded the housekeeper unbelievingly. "But Lord Rexford is dead!" she said. "Unless you mean—oh, I daresay you are speaking of Master John. Of course he would be Lord Rexford now. But I understood this house was left to Lady Rexford, not to him—or at least that she has a life interest in it."

"That's as may be," said Mrs. Fry with another toss of her head. "But as far as me and the other servants are concerned, it's Lord Rexford who's master here. We don't care much what the lawyers say."

"Is that so?" said Claudia with a pleasant smile. "Well, I am sure lawyers can be very tiresome, but I'm afraid in this case we can't entirely disregard them. Lady Rexford *is* mistress here at present, and as long as she is, I fancy she can do pretty much as she likes about firing and hiring servants. It would be very awkward if you were all obliged to find new places." She paused to let the words sink in.

"We'll see about that," was Mrs. Fry's grim-voiced response. Under the circumstances, Claudia thought it best to let the remark go unanswered.

They had reached the upstairs hall by this time. Mrs. Fry at once set off rapidly toward its farther end, but Claudia lingered to look at the doors on either side. "Just a moment, Mrs. Fry," she called. "What are these rooms here?"

"That's the book room there, miss," said Mrs. Fry. She stood waiting impatiently as Claudia peeped inside the book room. "And that's the cedar parlor there beside it."

"And this room?" said Claudia, trying the door opposite the cedar parlor. "It seems to be locked, Mrs. Fry. Have you the key for it?"

Rather reluctantly, Mrs. Fry produced a key from the ring at her waist. "But you don't want anything in there, miss," she protested as Claudia set about unlocking the door. "It's only an old bedchamber what's never used anymore."

A glance was sufficient to show Claudia that the room was both larger and grander than the one Lady Rexford was presently occupying. "Oh, but this will suit Lady Rexford admirably, Mrs. Fry. Please have the maids make up the bed immediately so we may move her things here as soon as possible."

Mrs. Fry's face was mutinous. "She can't have that room," she said. "That's the master's room—Lord Rexford's that was, I mean. It'd be his nephew's room now. And it isn't fitting that anybody else should stay there, let alone a jumped-up—"

"I'm afraid I must be the judge of that," said Claudia, intervening firmly in this speech. "This is the room Lady Rexford would prefer. Please see that it is made ready for her immediately."

The only answer she got was a hostile look. Claudia repeated her request in a louder voice. "My, how bold I am getting!" she marveled to herself. "I never would dare to defy this old harpy on my own account, but in Lady Rexford's service I can be brave as a lion."

Her bravery had its effect. Mrs. Fry muttered sullenly that she would order the maids to make up the room before Lady Rexford was ready to retire for the night.

Delighted with her victory, Claudia turned to go. "I must be getting back to Lady Rexford now," she said. "I trust she is feeling better after her journey. But still I doubt she will be well enough to eat downstairs tonight. Please tell the cook to have dinner served in her room."

Up came Mrs. Fry's chin in immediate protest. "That's not possible, miss. Cook's already got dinner laid out in the dining room. I meant to tell you earlier that dinner's served here at four o'clock."

"Indeed?" said Claudia in amazement. She had heard of country hours, but four o'clock in the afternoon seemed an absurd hour to dine.

Mrs. Fry bridled at her amazement. "I'm sure I don't know why you're surprised, miss. Dinner's always been served at four o'clock here at Rexford Park. The present Lord Rexford prefers to keep up the custom."

Claudia was by this time very tired of hearing about the present Lord Rexford. "I doubt Lady Rexford will have the same preference," she said shortly. "As tonight's dinner has already been prepared, I suppose we must eat early this once, but after this it would be better to have dinner served at a later hour—say, six o'clock."

Mrs. Fry merely eyed her with dislike. "Do you understand, Mrs. Fry?" asked Claudia. "Tonight's dinner is to be served in Lady Rexford's rooms as soon as the dishes can be conveyed there. I will let you know her preferences for tomorrow night, but you can tell the cook that dinner should be served at six o'clock rather than four. Will you tell her, please?"

"I'll tell her," said Mrs. Fry. It was an ungracious assent, but an assent it undoubtedly was. Claudia felt that was all that mattered. Wishing the housekeeper a good day, she then returned to Lady Rexford's rooms to give her and Hettie an account of her triumph.

"It seems to me you did wonderfully well, my dear," was Lady Rexford's admiring comment when Claudia had related to her all that had passed between her and Mrs. Fry. "That was a good notion of yours, to have dinner served in my rooms tonight. However, I doubt I'll feel like swallowing much dinner at four o'clock in the afternoon! To think of dining at such an hour! Why, Lord Rexford and I always dined at eight in London."

"Yes, but this is the country, you know, and they do keep earlier hours here than in London," said Claudia. "That's why I told Mrs. Fry to have the cook serve dinner at six after this. It seemed a good compromise between our way and theirs. However, if you prefer to dine at eight o'clock—"

"No, it's no matter, my dear. I daresay six will do well enough. Indeed, I'm sure I may as well keep early hours while I'm staying here. I don't know how I shall fill half my days as it is, and that's a fact."

That afternoon and evening passed pleasantly enough, however. Dinner was served in Lady Rexford's rooms in accordance with Claudia's instructions. The footmen who brought up the trays of food showed some tendency to linger, perhaps merely out of curiosity or perhaps because they expected to wait on their new mistress; but Claudia told them firmly that their services were not needed and sent them away again. She and Lady Rexford and Hettie then enjoyed a merry and relaxed meal around the fire, drinking a good deal of wine and praising each other for the clever way they had carried off their roles thus far.

They were full of food and wine and courage by the time Mrs. Fry tapped at the door to say that Lady Rexford's new rooms were ready. Lady Rexford, mantled once more in her new dignity, nodded graciously at the news and ordered Claudia and Hettie to be quick about packing up her things. The transfer was then accomplished in a stately and ceremonial manner, which reminded Claudia of nothing so much as a royal procession.

Lady Rexford led the way, holding her cane as though it were a scepter. Next came Claudia and Hettie, carrying her dressing case and other small personal effects. Last of all came the footmen struggling with the trunks and heavy baggage while Mrs. Fry served as a grim-faced escort.

Once Lady Rexford had been installed in her new quarters, the footmen and Mrs. Fry were dismissed once more, and the three conspirators were free to while away the evening with small-talk and piquet.

"We've been successful so far," Claudia told herself as she made herself ready for bed that night in the chambers Lady Rexford had vacated. "Indeed, today was the crucial test, and we all came through with flying colors. From now on, things can only get easier."

Claudia might not have been so confident of this if she had known what trials awaited her on the morrow. But since she did not know, she went to bed quite cheerfully and proceeded to sleep the sleep of the just.

Five

The new day began without any sign of trouble. Lady Rexford breakfasted privately in her room, as she and Claudia had agreed would be best.

"Of course you must eat your dinner downstairs," said Claudia as she helped herself to a cup of tea. "But I don't see why you can't take your other meals in your room if you want to. I've been thinking, Lady Rexford, and it seems to me that it's in your interests to keep your contacts with the Rexford Park servants to a minimum. As long as you hold yourself aloof, you'll be too much an unknown quantity for them to be openly rude."

Lady Rexford, whose success the day before had done much to bolster her courage, took exception to this tame advice. "Ah, but I don't want to spend all day in my rooms, Miss Chambers," she said. "Let the servants be rude to me if they dare. I'll settle 'em!" She thumped her stick on the floor with a martial air.

Claudia was pleased by her protégé's spirit, but she could not help fearing she was venturing too much, too soon. "Well, of course it is your decision, Lady Rexford," she said. "If you feel equal to it, you may certainly take all your meals downstairs. But I still think we would do better to go cautiously, especially here at the beginning."

Lady Rexford pooh-poohed this advice, however, and declared her intention of avoiding conflict no more. "I am quite able to hold my own, I think, as long as you and Hettie back me up. Right after breakfast I shall summon Mrs. Fry and ask her to—"

Just then came a tap at the door. Claudia instructed the caller to enter, and all three ladies rearranged their faces into their most forbidding expressions. The caller was one of the Rexford Park maidservants. She entered the room at Claudia's command, looking very shy and scared at this foray into unknown territory.

"Begging your ladyship's pardon, ma'am," she said, curtsying nervously again and again as she spoke. "There's someone to see you downstairs—that's to say, it's Lord Rexford to see you, my lady. He's in the drawing room." Having spoken these words, she dropped a final curtsy and fled.

The three ladies regarded each other wide-eyed. "Lord Rexford!" said Claudia. "What can he mean by calling at this hour?"

"Lord Rexford!" repeated Lady Rexford, clutching her dressing gown across her bosom. "Oh, but I cannot see *him,* my dear. Why, I'm not even dressed! And even if I were—no, I can't possibly see him. Oh, Miss Chambers, what should I do?"

This speech, coming from a lady who had been declaring her valor a moment before, made Claudia smile inwardly. "I'll put him off, of course," she said. "I am dressed, and I can go down and tell him to come back later today. Eight in the morning is hardly a decent hour for calling, after all."

"Oh, don't have him come back today!" gasped Lady Rexford, clutching her dressing gown even tighter. "Say I mean to keep to my rooms until tomorrow. I can't possibly see him until then—and even tomorrow I doubt I'll be ready."

"I'm afraid you must see him *sometime,*" said Claudia gently. "That is the reason you came to Yorkshire, after all. But there is certainly no reason why it need be today. I'll go down and tell Master John—Lord Rexford, I mean—that you are still unwell after your journey and mean to keep to your rooms today."

"Yes, tell him that," said Lady Rexford. "I'm sure it's quite true, for I do feel most unwell." She pushed her plate of toast and eggs away from her. "My appetite is quite spoiled at the thought of seeing that odious man."

As Claudia went downstairs to the drawing room, she was prey to equal parts of curiosity, indignation, and apprehension. At last she was to meet Master John—the same Master John who had implied that the innocent and good-natured Lady Rexford was an unprincipled adventuress. Claudia felt all the indignation toward the young viscount that such conduct merited. At the same time, however, she could not help remembering that he *was* a young viscount, the successor of a long line of landed noblemen. Claudia had had few dealings with the nobility in her life, but she had an inborn and instinctual respect for rank and title that caused her to regard even this errant nobleman with a certain awe.

These sensations were magnified by all she had heard of this particular nobleman. Lady Rexford obviously regarded him with fear and trembling. Claudia refused to admit to any such craven emotions herself, but her heart was beating uncomfortably fast as she resolutely opened the drawing room door.

Lord Rexford (or Master John, as Claudia persisted in thinking of him) was standing in front of the fireplace, frowning up at the portrait above the mantel. Claudia was astonished to recognize him as the same man she had seen at the Gatehouse the day before. She had only caught a glimpse of that man, but he was not a person to be easily forgotten. Well over six feet tall, with a figure broad in proportion to his height, he seemed to dwarf the delicate gilt furnishings of the drawing room.

He turned quickly as Claudia came in, the scowl deepening

on his face. Claudia, viewing him critically at this close range, decided he was not at all handsome. She was, however, forced to admit that he possessed the other two traditionally masculine attributes: being very tall and dark. Indeed, darkness even more than height seemed to be Master John's distinguishing characteristic. His hair was black and so were his eyes; his strongly-cut features were dominated by a pair of heavy black brows; and his complexion had a swarthy cast that gave a Gypsyish look to his whole countenance.

As Claudia looked into that scowling, black-browed face, it flashed through her mind how right Lady Rexford had been to describe her nephew as looking more like a prizefighter than a gentleman. Master John certainly did not resemble any gentleman she had ever seen before. The difference lay as much in the way he was dressed as in his more personal attributes. Knowing his position in the world, Claudia had unconsciously expected him to be arrayed like the beaux whom she had often seen parading along Bond Street. But Master John was clearly no Bond Street beau. His olive green coat looked as though it had seen several years of hard service, and his hat was a low-crowned affair that any self-respecting beau would have scorned to be seen in. His unstarched neckcloth was carelessly knotted about his swarthy throat, and his legs were adorned by a pair of mud-splattered breeches and top-boots.

Having taken in all these details, Claudia's eyes returned to Master John's face. She observed that his scowl had abated somewhat, having been replaced by a look of surprise. "Who are you?" he demanded, looking her up and down.

Claudia reflected that this was just the kind of behavior she would have expected from Master John. No polite "How do you do?" or "Good morning" for him, oh, no, indeed! Only a brusque "Who are you?" accompanied by a blank stare.

"It's a good thing *I* am seeing him instead of Lady Rexford," Claudia told herself. "I daresay she would be frightened into tolerating his rudeness, but I won't be. He shan't intimidate *me* with his black-browed scowls!"

Raising her chin slightly, Claudia looked at Master John a moment without speaking. At last she said gently, "I beg your pardon?"

She was pleased to see that he was enough of a gentleman to feel the rebuke. A darker color flooded his swarthy cheeks. "I beg your pardon, ma'am," he said, sounding confused. "I didn't mean to be rude. It's only that I was expecting someone else."

"You were expecting Lady Rexford, I daresay," said Claudia with a nod. "That's why I am here. She sent me to tell you that she is not feeling well enough to receive callers today. If you could return tomorrow, perhaps she might feel equal to seeing you."

These words made John's black brows snap together once more. "Indeed!" he said. "And what guarantee have I that she would not put me off with the same excuse if I return here tomorrow?"

"None, to be sure," said Claudia cheerfully. "You will merely have to hope that your luck—and her health—will be better."

"Well, I like that!" he said in some dudgeon. "So I am to kick my heels here day after day on the off chance my aunt will have fifteen minutes to spare me?"

"Not necessarily," returned Claudia. "If there is any message I can relay to her or any matter that needs her immediate attention, I would be more than happy to act as your go-between."

Once more John subjected Claudia to a searching scrutiny. "Oh, you will, will you?" he said. "But that brings me back to my original question, ma'am. Just who *are* you? You aren't—" He hesitated. "You aren't my aunt's daughter, by any chance? I never heard she had any children."

Claudia laughed. "Oh, no, I'm not Lady Rexford's daughter.

I am her companion, Miss Chambers." She smiled sweetly at John. "And who might you be, sir?"

A reluctant answering smile appeared on his face. "If you know as much of my aunt's affairs as you seem to, then you must know I am John Rexford," he said. "But you are quite right to reprove me, Miss Chambers. Of course I ought to have introduced myself properly, back at the beginning of our interview."

Claudia was pleased by this frank acknowledgment of wrongdoing. She decided Master John was not quite the boor she had first supposed. "Well, I am very pleased to make your acquaintance, my lord," she said with a curtsy. "Now that we have that taken care of, perhaps we can discuss your aunt's business and see if there is some way we might settle it between us. I would save you a fruitless trip tomorrow if I could." Seating herself on the sofa, she indicated a chair opposite. "Will you please to be seated?"

He sat down readily enough, settling his long limbs with some difficulty amid the profusion of embroidered footstools and little tables that littered the room. Once seated, however, he seemed reluctant to resume the conversation. He merely sat regarding Claudia with a searching gaze.

"I assure you, my lord, that your aunt has done me the honor of making me her confidante," said Claudia, thinking it must be some such concern that tied his tongue. "No matter the nature of your communication, you may rely on my absolute discretion."

"I am sure I may," he replied, still regarding her searchingly. "If I seem to be taken aback, it is only because I did not expect to find someone like you in my aunt's employ. She seems to have shown unusual taste and discernment in her choice of companions."

Claudia could not help feeling flattered by this speech, which was spoken in a tone of simple earnest more gratifying than any amount of gallantry or flirtation. Yet gratifying as his words were, they were also something of a slight to her employer. Claudia had not missed seeing the derisive twist to his mouth when he had spoken of his aunt. And for the sake of Lady Rexford, whom she had come to sincerely love and esteem, she was not about to put up with slights and derision.

"I thank you for your compliment, but I don't think I quite understand you, my lord," she said, looking him in the eye. "Why would you not expect to find someone like me in your aunt's employ?"

She had expected him to show signs of discomfort, but he returned her look imperturbably. "I suppose it is because you are so obviously a lady of quality, Miss Chambers," he said. "I find it surprising that you would choose to work for a woman who is no lady at all."

Claudia's ire was raised by these words and by the cool way John spoke them. "By all I have ever heard, you have never even made the acquaintance of your aunt," she retorted. "That being the case, it seems to me that it ill becomes you to declaim upon her character."

John's black brows drew together at her rebuke. Claudia waited rather nervously, expecting he would make some blistering retort.

But as suddenly as his brow had clouded, it cleared again, and he gave a rueful laugh. "Come, I don't mean to pull caps with you, Miss Chambers," he said. "I can see you are a strong partisan of my aunt's, and I am sure that is very much to your credit. But surely even you, with all your partisanship, must admit that my aunt is a queer sort of viscountess?"

"She is not a conventional one perhaps. But she has been so kind to me that I would be the most ungrateful wretch imaginable to find fault with her," said Claudia earnestly.

John looked at her searchingly once again, but made no reply. Claudia went on, still in an earnest voice. "Indeed, I wish you would not judge your aunt so harshly, my lord. She is a very kind, generous, warmhearted lady, and I am sure she has no wish to be on bad terms with you. Cannot you let bygones be bygones?"

At these words, John's brows drew together again with a snap. "That is easier said than done, Miss Chambers," he said. "Call me unreasonable if you like, but I find it difficult to feel amity toward the person who has robbed me of the greater part of my inheritance!"

He looked and sounded so fierce as he made this speech that Claudia was half afraid of him. But then she remembered Lady Rexford and the duty that was owing her. It was vital that Claudia endeavor to soften John's mood before his aunt had to face him. So she answered him with a composure that surprised even herself, "As I understand it, my lord, it was not precisely a robbery. Your aunt did inherit a life interest in the property, but I have been given to understand that that state of affairs came about through your own agency and not hers. You offended your uncle by insulting both his wife and his understanding—and so he elected to leave the property away from you."

John glared at her speechlessly. Claudia looked back at him with outward defiance but inward trembling. At last he drew a deep breath. "Well!" he said. "So you have been given to understand that it is my own fault that the property was left in this damnable way, have you, Miss Chambers?"

"Yes, I have," said Claudia. In an apologetic voice she added, "Of course it is possible that I have been misinformed. I have heard only Lady Rexford's opinions on the subject, and I know well enough that one never learns all the facts without hearing all sides of the argument." She paused and looked at him inquiringly.

John looked back at her in amazement. "And you seriously expect I should now deliver myself of what you call my side of the story in order to satisfy your curiosity, Miss Chambers?" he demanded.

"Not if you do not like to," said Claudia with some embarrassment. "But you know it is not solely curiosity that prompts me to ask these questions, my lord. I am sincerely attached to Lady Rexford, and I think it in her best interest that she should make up her quarrel with you if she can. So far, it seems to me that the balance of right is on her side, but if there are circumstances I am not acquainted with, of course that would change the situation." Again she paused and looked at him inquiringly.

He was silent a moment, looking first at Claudia and then down at his own folded hands. At last a slow, rueful smile appeared on his lips. "No, you have heard the circumstances pretty accurately, Miss Chambers," he said. "I did insult both my uncle's wife and understanding and was punished accordingly. But look at the matter from my point of view. I was my uncle's acknowledged heir; he had long declared his intention of living and dying a bachelor. Suddenly, at the age of eight and sixty, he writes me a letter in which he proposes to marry his own housekeeper! Can you wonder that I said some unkind things?"

"I don't wonder that you were a little upset," acknowledged Claudia. "But still, I don't see why your uncle shouldn't have married if he wanted to. Even if he proposed to marry his housekeeper—and even if he were eight and sixty. In fact, his waiting so late to marry ought to have been a comfort to you rather than the reverse. Lady Rexford is rather elderly herself, you know, and so there was no question of their producing a son to disinherit you or anything of that nature."

"No, but there was a question of the family honor," said John hotly. "No man likes the thought of acknowledging a low and vulgar serving woman as his aunt. And with all due respect to you and your mistress, Miss Chambers, that is exactly what my aunt is."

"You are mistaken," said Claudia in a calm voice. "Lady Rexford may not have the most exalted of pedigrees, but from all I have been able to find out, her birth is perfectly respectable. Unless you know something about her that I do not?"

"I know nothing of my aunt's birth," said John shortly. "I only know that she used to be my uncle's housekeeper. That in itself would be enough to condemn the match in my eyes."

"Oh, I see. It is because she worked for her living that you do not approve of her. I thought it was because she was low and vulgar." Claudia spoke gently, but there was a perceptible edge to her voice.

John gave her a look both furious and frustrated, then suddenly began to laugh. "Miss Chambers, you are a devil!" he said. "Now you are trying to twist my words into an insult to yourself. I give you my word that such was not my intention."

"I am very glad to hear it," said Claudia sweetly.

John gave her another look of rueful amusement. "And since you drive me to it, I will admit that I have no concrete reason for believing that my aunt is low or vulgar. I had merely assumed that she must be, coming from such a situation. What you tell me of her birth reassures me that she is not low, at least—and if you say so, I am prepared to believe she is not vulgar as well." He looked curiously at Claudia. "*Is* she not vulgar?"

Claudia, uncertain of his criteria for vulgarity, thought it better to avoid answering this question directly. "I would rather you met her for yourself and made your own judgment, my lord. It is a pity she is indisposed today, but I should think by tomorrow she would be well enough to receive you." In a thoughtful voice, she added, "I know she is eager to get this business of the estate settled. It has been troubling her very much."

John smiled incredulously. "I find that difficult to believe, Miss Chambers. She has certainly taken her time in coming north to deal with the situation." Rather bitterly, he added, "In her absence, my hands have been most effectually tied. And they will continue to be tied in the future unless she is prepared to settle here permanently. I cannot repair a barn or replace a fence or renew a tenancy without her approval."

"Please believe the situation suits Lady Rexford as little as you, my lord," said Claudia gently. "She cares nothing for barns and fences and tenancies. I think she would much prefer to have no share in such a troublesome inheritance." Seeing that John still looked incredulous, she added, "Of course, that is only my own opinion. But you might bear it in mind when you meet with Lady Rexford later this week. And if nothing else results from your meeting, you might at least come to an understanding regarding the general management of the property in the future."

"That would be a help," admitted John. He began to rise to his feet. Claudia rose also, supposing he meant to leave. But instead of leaving, he walked over to the fireplace and began once more to study the picture hanging over the mantel.

"That is a very handsome portrait," said Claudia, more to be saying something than because she really admired it.

John nodded morosely. "Yes, but I must confess that I prefer the one that used to hang here. The Rexford Rembrandt, you know. Up till a few years ago it hung over the drawing room fireplace, and I always thought it suited the room admirably."

"A Rembrandt!" said Claudia with interest. "Did your uncle indeed have a Rembrandt? I wish I could see it."

John shot her a quizzical look. "I should suppose you *had* seen it. Wasn't it hanging in my aunt's London house? I always understood my uncle had taken it to Town with him."

Claudia thought doubtfully of the landscapes and crayon portraits she had seen in Lady Rexford's house. "I don't think I remember seeing a Rembrandt there," she said. "But I am afraid I am no authority on art. It is possible I might not recognize a Rembrandt when I saw one."

John shook his head decisively. "You would remember this if you had seen it. A portrait of an elderly woman, quite small." In the air, with his hands, he traced a rectangle about ten by fourteen inches. "But there is a quality about it that makes it unmistakable. Even when I was a boy I admired it, long before I knew its value."

Claudia shook her head. "I'm quite sure I have seen no such picture at Lady Rexford's Town house. But that doesn't mean it's not there! She has a multitude of objects in that house, and I don't pretend to have studied them all. I will ask her about the Rembrandt if you like—and I would also be happy to discuss with her anything else on which you might need an immediate decision. It wouldn't take me a minute to run upstairs and then run down with her answer."

A smile flashed across John's swarthy face. "No, I won't ask you to do any running on my behalf, Miss Chambers. I have nothing to say to my aunt that cannot perfectly well wait until tomorrow."

Claudia smiled back, thinking how much a smile improved him. "Very well, my lord. I trust she will be well enough tomorrow to receive you."

"I trust so, too. At what hour would you suggest I call to maximize my chances of being admitted?"

"Well, not so early as today," said Claudia, striving to be diplomatic. "Of course I know things are done differently in the country, but your aunt is not used to receiving callers at eight o'clock in the morning!"

"Eight o'clock is not so early," said John defensively. "I've been up since five, helping the men over at the Home Farm."

"Ah, that explains it," said Claudia, looking at his mud-splattered boots and breeches.

She meant the remark innocently, but a faint flush rose to John's cheeks. He turned away as though angered or discomfited. "Yes, I'm afraid I did not give much thought to my appearance today. I promise to do better when I call tomorrow, Miss Chambers. Would two o'clock be a suitable hour?"

"Yes, I expect two o'clock would do very well," said Claudia. She eyed John nervously, fearing that she had somehow offended him. But he set her fears at rest by flashing her another of his oddly attractive smiles.

"Very well then, Miss Chambers. I shall call with all due formality at two o'clock tomorrow, and you will see I am not quite the savage I appeared to you today. Please give my compliments to my aunt if you please. It was a pleasure to make your acquaintance." And having smiled once more and executed a bow of more elegance than Claudia would have expected from him, he took himself quickly out of the room.

Six

As John Rexford rode back to the Gatehouse, he found himself reflecting on the interview he had just enjoyed with Claudia.

"Enjoyed" was the proper word. He had taken pleasure in talking to Claudia, though there had been some awkward moments, too. Ruefully he remembered that moment when Claudia, regarding him with limpid brown eyes, had inquired whether it might not have been his own fault that his uncle had denied him full control of his rightful inheritance.

"And she said it just as if butter wouldn't melt in her mouth!" he told himself with a mixture of amusement and exasperation. "She's a cool little devil, that one."

He thought none the worse of Claudia for her deviltry. If anything, his admiration was increased. So many people seemed to have a mealymouthed habit of beating around the bush; one would almost think they were afraid to speak their minds, John reflected, quite overlooking the fact that his own title, rank, and formidable appearance might have had something to do with their reticence. If such an idea had been suggested to him, it would have only made him admire Claudia's conduct the more. *She* had not been afraid to speak the truth. She had laid the blame where he had always known in his heart that it belonged: squarely on his own shoulders.

The thought made John sigh and hunch his shoulders, as though seeking to rid them of an invisible burden resting there.

Ever since his uncle's death, when he had first been notified of the conditions that had been imposed on his inheritance, he had been in a state of controlled fury. It was not that he resented his uncle's marrying, or the propriety of his leaving a life interest in his estate to his widow. That would have been bearable if only old Lord Rexford had married a different type of woman. From the time John was a small boy, he had known he was heir presumptive to his uncle's title and estate, but he had likewise known and recognized the uncertainty of his position. At any moment he might be supplanted in the succession if his uncle chose to marry and produce a son.

John perfectly recognized his uncle's right to do both these things. Being of a cautious and longsighted temperament, he had prepared himself for that possibility, but he had never prepared himself for the possibility of his uncle's marrying his housekeeper. That news, when it had come, had seemed like the worst kind of betrayal. It did not even matter that the new wife was too old to produce a son to disinherit him. Bred to take a vicarious pride in the position that might one day be his, John could not forgive his uncle for an act that seemed to dishonor it. And his anger and disillusionment had led him to speak the words that had later recoiled upon him so disastrously.

Again John sighed and hunched his shoulders, recalling his feelings when the terms of the will had been read to him. It was bad enough to endure having his inheritance encumbered in such a way, but far worse was the realization that the encumbrance had come about through his own agency. So bitter had that realization been that he had instinctively looked about for another culprit on whom to fasten the blame—and a suitable culprit had not been far to find.

Of course it must have been his new aunt who had convinced his uncle to tie up the estate in such a way. John was already certain that she was a conniving creature, bereft alike of breeding and principle. He therefore had no difficulty believing her guilty of this and even worse crimes. Indeed, he had allowed his anger and frustration toward her to build until she had become a veritable monster in his eyes. Had it been possible, he would have much preferred to have nothing to do with her, but the terms of the will required his aunt's consent before any but the smallest and simplest repairs and alterations could be made to the Rexford Park property. And thus far, she had refused absolutely to give her consent without seeing for herself the necessity of the repairs and alterations he proposed to make.

So John had accepted the necessity of meeting with his aunt during her visit north. But though it might be necessary to meet her, John had vowed that no power on earth would make him render to her the smallest sign of affection or respect. And so he had come to Rexford Park that morning, at an hour he knew to be an affront, deliberately neglecting his appearance so as to make the insult all the greater.

Yet this action, too, had recoiled upon him. Instead of meeting his monstrous aunt, he had instead been received by one of the most charming young ladies it had ever been his privilege to meet. And this young lady had informed him that his aunt was not a monster at all, but rather a kind and respectable woman who was as frustrated as he by the terms of his uncle's will.

Regarding this last issue, John preserved a certain skepticism. He had thought of his aunt as a conniving creature for so long that he could not quite rid himself of the belief that she must be enjoying her position as mistress of Rexford Park. But for the first time, he admitted to himself his own role in promoting her to that position. And having done this, he felt suddenly a good deal more tolerant toward his aunt than had ever been the case before.

"We are relatives now, like it or not. That being the case, I may as well swallow my pride and behave like a gentleman," John told himself. "When I call on her tomorrow, I'll wear my new coat and put on my best drawing room manners. Perhaps I'll even bring her some flowers."

As long as he was making conciliatory gestures, he decided he would bring Miss Chambers flowers, too. She was a charming girl, and he regretted now that he had shown her the rough side of his personality so early in their acquaintance. To be sure, he had apologized for his roughness before taking leave of her, but still Miss Chambers must have thought him an uncouth sort of man: the kind of man who would call on ladies in muddy breeches and topboots at eight o'clock in the morning.

He could not help wincing when he recalled the way Claudia had looked at his disreputable garments. "Not that she actually came out and criticized me," he told himself ruefully. "She is too much a lady for that. But I am sure she must think me a complete Yahoo."

John was surprised to find how much this thought disturbed him. He hardly knew Miss Chambers, and it was ridiculous that her opinion should mean so much to him. Likewise, it was ridiculous that he should be looking forward so much to seeing her again. "Of course, she's a charming girl and a very pretty one, too," he acknowledged to himself. In his mind's eye he saw again Claudia's neat and graceful figure; the glossy chestnut hair arranged in a chignon at the back of her head; the brown eyes that had looked so frankly and fearlessly into his own; and the sweet, smiling lips that had managed to coax him from a state of hostility into one of complete submission.

"She's an attractive little witch, and if I weren't as good as engaged to Barbara Brock, I might be tempted to get up a flirtation in that direction," John told himself. "As it is, though, it's out of the question."

Of course any man fortunate enough to enjoy Barbara Brock's favor would never look twice at an obscure and probably penniless hired companion. No matter if she were a very pretty girl with a witching way about her! Barbara was a pretty girl, too, though the word "handsome" was perhaps more suitable to her style of stately good looks. The niece of an earl and the daughter of the richest landowner in the county, Barbara was tall and blond, Junoesque in figure and secure in her position as the belle of the neighborhood. Yet despite her popularity, she had always indicated quite clearly that John, future Viscount Rexford, was the man on whom she intended to bestow her hand, heart, and handsome inheritance.

John had naturally been flattered by this partiality. There was no other woman in the neighborhood who could match Barbara in pedigree or consequence or any who possessed the same degree of attractions both tangible and intangible. When people spoke of a marriage between Barbara and him as a foregone conclusion, he was inclined to be gratified rather than offended. But though he was happy to sit with Barbara at parties and dance with her at balls and assemblies, he had thus far shied away from making her the offer she so clearly expected from him.

It was not that he disliked the idea of marrying Barbara, as John assured himself. She was a handsome, wealthy, well-connected girl, and he could not expect to do better for a wife. But somehow he shrank from the idea of marriage at the present time. Someday he would be ready to take a wife, and then he would propose to Barbara, but at present he was entirely satisfied with the status quo.

So John reflected as he rode along the drive toward the Gatehouse. This was his home for the present, though he might equally well have occupied the modest estate in the north of Yorkshire that had come to him through his father. Still, he preferred living at Rexford Park since it was much more central and convenient. He had also preferred it because it seemed such an effective rebuke to his aunt. Here he was, the proper heir, reduced to living at the gates of his own property while an interloper enjoyed the luxury that should have been his by right.

Yet today he felt almost ashamed at having conceived such a childish revenge. He frowned at his groom, who had come forward to take his horse and who was, as usual, lamenting that he was obliged to use the small stable attached to the

Gatehouse rather than the much larger facility belonging to Rexford Park.

" 'Tis a great pity—aye, a great pity, your lordship. Here ye are, obliged to house your cattle in yon flaysome shed when there's a stable with sixty stalls standing all but empty not a hundred rods away. I never pass t' house yonder without shaking my head over how ye was done out of your rights." He paused and cocked an expectant eye at John, expecting him to join in his denunciation as usual. His surprise was great when John merely advised him to hold his tongue.

"I was not done out of my rights, as you put it, Ted. It was my own fault that the property was left to my aunt instead of me. Really, I have no right to complain."

"My lord!" gasped Ted, his mouth agape. "Ye don't mean it."

"But I do mean it," said John. He smiled into the groom's surprised face. "I know I have been in the habit of blaming Lady Rexford for the disposition of the property—"

"And who should ye blame better?" said Ted warmly. "If your uncle hadn't married *her*, the property would've been yours when he cut up."

"Yes, but I am convinced it would have been mine even in spite of my uncle's marriage if I had not offended him by insulting his wife. It's a judgment on me—that's what it is, Ted. Take my advice and never try to thwart the course of true love. I'm convinced now it doesn't pay." Leaving Ted to gape after him in amazement, he strolled into the Gatehouse.

He was met by Mrs. Meeks, the elderly dame who served as cook and housekeeper in his diminutive household. "Miss Barbara's here, my lord. She called just a few minutes ago, and when I said I thought you'd be back afore too long, she said she'd wait. Your lordship'll find her in the little parlor."

John frowned. He disliked it when Barbara came to the Gatehouse, which she did very frequently and on the flimsiest of pretexts. He supposed he was unreasonable for disliking these visits. After all, he was very fond of Barbara, and he had been thinking of her only a few minutes before with considerable satisfaction. But he much preferred when he could choose the time and place of their meetings rather than being obliged to take time from the midst of a busy workday. So his expression was less than welcoming as he entered the small parlor.

"There you are, Rexford!" Barbara rose to meet him with an affectionate smile. As always, she was dressed in the height of fashion though her frilly gown with its flounces and ruffles was not really suited to her statuesque figure. But the face beneath the bonnet of twilled sarcenet was certainly a handsome one, if a trifle square jawed and strong browed for beauty. John found himself comparing it to Miss Chambers's pretty, witching countenance as he took her hand in his.

"Good morning, Barbara," he said. "What are you doing here?"

Barbara laughed and squeezed his hand with an air of playful reproach. "Oh, Rexford, how can you ask? You must know how fast word travels in such a small place as this. I heard rumors last night that your aunt had arrived at Rexford Park, and so of course I came around first thing this morning to see if it was true."

"Yes, it's true," said John shortly. "I have just got back from waiting on my aunt."

Barbara looked sympathetic and squeezed his hand again. "I know what an ordeal that must have been. Believe me, Rexford, I feel for you. Is your aunt as bad as you supposed?"

"I did not see my aunt," said John more shortly still. "She was indisposed after her journey, so I made arrangements to call again tomorrow."

Barbara was warmly indignant at this treatment. "Well, that is a pretty way to use you, Rexford! If you had not already a disgust of the woman, I am sure such conduct would be enough to give you one. Indisposed, indeed! I would not have expected such airs from a common housemaid."

Although John had himself thought much these same things

at the time, he now found himself perversely inclined to defend his aunt. "She was not my uncle's housemaid but rather his housekeeper," he said. "And whatever her failings may be, she is my aunt now, Barbara. I will thank you not to abuse her in my hearing."

Barbara looked at him with astonished indignation. "Well, this is a change, I must say, Rexford!" she said. "You were ready enough to abuse her yourself not a week ago."

"The more shame to me then," returned John. "It was very improper of me to criticize my aunt and very unjust, too. She has done nothing to injure me."

"Oh, how can you say so, Rexford? When you know she has robbed you of your inheritance!"

"She did no such thing," said John flatly. "It was my own injudicious tongue that robbed me of my inheritance. I had no right to criticize my uncle's marriage, and when I did criticize it, he very justly punished me by leaving the estate to his wife rather than me for the duration of her lifetime."

Barbara gazed at him in amazement. "I've never heard you say such things before, Rexford," she said.

"I suppose that's because I didn't care to think about them before. It's not comfortable to own that one has injured one's self through one's own foolish conduct."

"Well, I shall continue to think your aunt is the party to blame," said Barbara, with calm authority. "It's really iniquitous that such a fine estate should be left to a common, vulgar—oh, pardon me, Rexford. I had forgotten you did not wish to hear your aunt criticized. But it *is* iniquitous, and I can tell you that Mama thinks it iniquitous, too. She says she does not mean to call on your aunt while she is staying in Yorkshire."

"That should punish her," said John, hiding a smile. Privately he thought his aunt ought to rejoice at being spared a call from Barbara's mother. A stout, overbearing woman with a great idea of her own consequence, Mrs. Brock was an unpopular figure with most of the local populace. John always avoided her whenever he could and was glad Barbara did not resemble her in looks or temperament.

Yet listening to Barbara smugly describing the snub her mother meant to deliver to his aunt, he was struck by how much she did resemble Mrs. Brock. And when he looked at her seeking to banish this absurd fancy, he was alarmed to detect a faint but perceptible resemblance in her person as well. The arrogant angle at which she bore her chin, the complacent lines about her mouth and even the settled solidity of her figure were all strongly reminiscent of Mrs. Brock. Barbara was not so stout as her mother, to be sure, but her figure was clearly tending in the same direction despite its present and undeniable allurements.

This idea so much unnerved John that he completely lost track of what Barbara was saying. It was only when she paused and looked at him that he pulled himself together. "I beg your pardon," he said. "Did you ask me a question?"

Barbara frowned. "Oh, Rexford, don't say you were not listening! I was telling you about the trip Mama and I mean to make to Scarborough in August. We were hoping you might be able to accompany us there since Papa finds it necessary to stay on his estate this summer."

John could hardly repress a shudder at the idea of traveling with Mrs. Brock. "I'm afraid not," he said with more haste than gallantry.

Again Barbara frowned. "Oh, Rexford, why ever not? You must know I had counted upon you to be our escort. I'm sure it's the least you can do, considering."

"Considering what?" asked John.

Barbara flushed slightly and looked down at her feet with an air of maidenly modesty that contrasted strangely with her usual self-assured demeanor. "Why, considering what our relationship is. You know people have been expecting for years that we would marry. They will think it very strange if you let me go off to Scarborough by myself—unless, of course, we had become engaged previous to my going."

She swept John a glance from beneath her lashes. John sat immobile, stunned by this bold and unexpected frontal assault. His brain was working frantically, however, and a little reflection was sufficient to show him that Barbara had put him into an uncommonly awkward position. He had no wish to marry her at present, nor did he desire to end all possibility of marrying her—at least not until he had had time to think it over and decide what he really wanted to do.

So he took refuge in evasion. "I'm afraid that, like your father, I shall find it impossible to leave my estate this summer," he said formally. "I should like to accompany you to Scarborough, of course"—he carefully made no mention of Mrs. Brock—"but I must give all my time and attention at present to settling this business between my aunt and me. You see how it is, I hope."

He hoped fervently that Barbara *would* see and that she would not embarrass him with any further references to an engagement. To his relief she did not, but it was evident from her expression that she was disappointed by his refusal and more than a little displeased.

"Really, Rexford, I am becoming quite cross with this aunt of yours. It's bad enough that she should cheat you out of your just inheritance—for that she did cheat you I am quite convinced, in spite of your very gentlemanly denial. But now I find that she means to deprive me of your company in Scarborough as well! Still, it may be that she will not care to linger in Yorkshire for more than a few weeks. I am sure that if Mama and I have anything to say about it, her sojourn in the neighborhood will be a short one!"

John murmured an assent to this speech, but reflected with inward amusement that he now had a reason to be grateful his aunt had come to Yorkshire that summer. She had spared him a trip to Scarborough in the company of Mrs. Brock, as well as provided him with an unimpeachable excuse to postpone discussing marriage with Barbara. It was enough to make him feel quite well disposed toward the woman he had formerly despised. As he bade farewell to Barbara, he found himself looking forward to making his aunt's acquaintance on the morrow—and of furthering his acquaintance with her companion, the charming and spritely Miss Chambers.

Seven

After bidding farewell to John, Claudia returned upstairs. She found Lady Rexford awaiting her in a fluttered state of nerves.

"Oh, Miss Chambers, was it very bad? I have been feeling terribly guilty since you left, thinking I ought not to have sent you alone to deal with that dreadful man."

"But he wasn't dreadful," said Claudia, smiling. "Master John was a little cross at first, to be sure, because he was expecting to see you instead of me—"

"I don't doubt it!" said Lady Rexford with a shudder.

"But when I had explained that you were indisposed, he quite understood. Indeed, once he had got over his first crossness, I found him very pleasant and agreeable."

"No!" exclaimed Lady Rexford, regarding her with disbelief.

"Yes, I did," said Claudia. "Mind you, his manners are a little rough. But I think you will find him not at all formidable when he calls on you tomorrow."

"Tomorrow!" said Lady Rexford, cast into a flutter of nerves once more. "Does he mean to come tomorrow then, Miss Chambers? Oh, but I can't see him—I can't, I can't."

"Indeed, I think you must see him, Lady Rexford," said Claudia in her most authoritative voice. "It would be very rude to put him off again. Not only that, it would likely put him in an ill temper so that your acquaintance would be started on the wrong foot."

"Our acquaintance is already started on the wrong foot," asserted Lady Rexford tearfully. "Such dreadful things as he said about me! If I had my way, I would rather not see the man at all. Oh, Miss Chambers, could you not put him off till the day *after* tomorrow? I think by then I might be ready to face him. But tomorrow is much too soon. I need time to settle my nerves."

Claudia, however, refused to admit this plea. She felt that the sooner Lady Rexford gathered her courage together and faced her nephew, the better it would be for all concerned. Putting the meeting off until another day would only prolong the ordeal. Claudia also suspected that if allowed Lady Rexford would put off the meeting indefinitely, thus negating her whole reason for coming to Yorkshire and destroying any chance of an amicable relationship with John.

"We have till tomorrow afternoon to prepare," she said soothingly. "Two o'clock is the hour he means to call. I told him you did not care to receive visitors any earlier than that, and he took it like a lamb. I really think he is trying to be accommodating, Lady Rexford. You must try to be accommodating, too, without compromising your dignity, of course."

"I'll do my best," said Lady Rexford with a resigned sigh. "How do you recommend I go about it, Miss Chambers?"

"Well, let's see. First impressions are very important, so we want to establish you as a person of authority right from the start. It would be best, I think, if you received him in the drawing room downstairs. That's a very formal room, and I noticed today there was a dais at one end. We can take the biggest chair in the room and put it on the dais and have you sitting there with your cane and eyeglass when Hettie and I show Master John in. That will give you a commanding presence if anything can. Although I'm afraid even with the dais and the chair you will be shorter than Master John." Claudia sighed at this reflection. "He is a very large man. But that can't be helped, so we must do what we can to counter it."

"Aye, he looked like a young giant when I saw him in London," agreed Lady Rexford with a reminiscent shiver. "I never saw a more ogreish-looking fellow."

"Yes, but I don't believe he is so ogreish as he looks. You must keep that firmly in mind, Lady Rexford, and not let his appearance overawe you."

"He doesn't seem to have overawed you anyway," observed Lady Rexford as they went downstairs to inspect the drawing room for the scene that was to be played there on the morrow. "I believe you actually like the man, Miss Chambers!"

"Do you know, I think I do," said Claudia with an air of discovery.

Claudia spent the rest of the morning and part of the afternoon rehearsing Lady Rexford and Hettie in their roles for the following day. Hettie was soon letter perfect, but it took all her and Claudia's combined efforts to bring the principal actress into a state of readiness.

"And even now, I don't doubt but that I'll botch it somehow," said Lady Rexford dolefully as they relaxed together in her sitting room that afternoon. "I know you said to let him start the conversation, but what if he doesn't start it? It'll be very awkward if nobody says anything at all. I know I'll feel obliged to say something just to break the silence—and once I start talking I won't be able to stop. I always talk too much when I'm nervous."

"Don't you worry. If there are any awkward silences, I'll take care of breaking them," said Claudia. "You just sit there and look dignified, Lady Rexford. I think it will all go off splendidly. That black silk lutestring with the veil and beaded headdress makes you look like a queen."

"It *is* a handsome toilette," agreed Lady Rexford, looking a little brighter. "A pretty penny it cost me, too, but I must say it's worth it. Having the proper clothes does make me feel more confident."

"You'll do splendidly," Claudia assured her. As she was speaking, there came a scratching at the door. Claudia went to answer it and found Mrs. Fry standing there. The housekeeper dropped a curtsy, a defiant yet triumphant look on her hatchet face.

"Begging your pardon, miss, but I just came up to say dinner's ready," she said. Having made this speech, she swung around and trotted off again at a swift pace.

"Dinner?" said Claudia blankly. "But surely it can't be six o'clock already!"

She spoke to empty air, however. Mrs. Fry had already vanished. But as though eager to confirm Claudia's suspicions, the long-case clock in the hall chose that moment to strike the hour. It tolled four slow, sonorous strokes, then stopped with an air of finality.

"It's only four o'clock!" said Claudia. A wave of anger swept over her. She turned to face Lady Rexford and Hettie, both of whom were regarding her with inquisitive faces.

"What was that about, my dear? Surely she did not say dinner was ready?" said Lady Rexford.

"She did indeed," said Claudia in a tight voice. "And then fled like a thief afterward."

"But I thought dinner was to be at six," said Hettie, looking puzzled. "Didn't you say you'd told her we wanted it at six?"

"I did tell her. But obviously she has seen fit to ignore my instructions. I can see I shall have to have another talk with Mrs. Fry."

"I will talk to Mrs. Fry, too, if you like," offered Lady Rexford. "I may be afraid of Master John, but I'm not afraid of her—much. She's only a housekeeper after all, and I used to be that myself."

Claudia considered. "I think it would be best if you let me deal with her for now, ma'am," she said. "We can bring you into it later if we find it necessary to proceed to open warfare.

But I hope it doesn't come to that. I shouldn't think so, for Mrs. Fry stands to lose much more than you do."

"That's true," said Lady Rexford, looking pleased. But Hettie shook her head gloomily. "I misdoubt you'll move her by talking, Miss Chambers. She looks to me like a spiteful old body. And if spite's her motive, even the threat of losing her job likely won't make her change."

"Well, I can try at any rate," said Claudia, turning resolutely toward the door. "Wish me luck, everyone, for I expect I shall need it."

She found Mrs. Fry downstairs, hovering near the door of the dining room. The housekeeper looked self-conscious as Claudia approached, but managed to greet her with a calm manner and even an attempt at a smile. "Ah, there you are, miss. I hope Lady Rexford will be down soon, for Cook tells me everything's dished up."

"Then it shall all have to be undished again," said Claudia, not mincing words. "Lady Rexford desires that dinner be served at six o'clock as I plainly informed you yesterday. What do you mean by serving it at four again?"

A spark of defiance glinted in Mrs. Fry's eye. "I'm sure you told me no such thing, miss," she said.

"And I am very sure that I did—and that you remember my doing so," said Claudia, barely keeping a rein on her temper. "Really, this will not do, Mrs. Fry. If you will not relay Lady Rexford's orders to the cook, then I shall have to give her the orders myself."

Mrs. Fry protested that she was quite willing to relay Lady Rexford's orders, but that she was certain no such order had ever been given. This statement Claudia received with an incredulous smile. "It's no matter. You and I both know what was said, Mrs. Fry—and if you failed to pass the order on yesterday, then you must do so now. Tell the cook to have the dinner re-served at six o'clock."

"Upon my word, miss, that can't be done," protested Mrs. Fry, looking really discomposed for the first time. "There's ducklings for dinner—and Spanish fritters, too. They'll be spoiled if they ain't ate right away."

"Then the cook will have to prepare new ones," said Claudia with gentle firmness. "Lady Rexford wants her dinner at six, and if you value your position, Mrs. Fry, you had better see that her wishes are respected."

Instead of being cowed, Mrs. Fry was merely incensed by these words. "My position!" she repeated with a snort. "I ain't dependent on *her* for my position! This is Lord Rexford's house, and it's him I work for. You may tell my Lady Rexford so, with my compliments."

"This may be Lord Rexford's house, but Lady Rexford is managing it at present," countered Claudia. "And it is quite within her power to dismiss any servant who fails to please her."

This threat, too, failed to impress Mrs. Fry. "I'd like to see her try," she scoffed. "As I said, this house and everything in it belongs to Master John—to Lord Rexford, I mean. And he'll never let me nor any of the other servants be dismissed by the likes of *her.*"

Claudia was on the verge of retorting that she and the other servants had better take refuge with Master John, then. "And very welcome he is to you, too!" she added silently, looking into Mrs. Fry's crabbed and triumphant face. But she acknowledged to herself that such a remark would not serve her employer's best interests. Lady Rexford would find it inconvenient if the whole staff of Rexford Park quit and moved to the Gatehouse. "And I'll wager Master John would find it inconvenient, too," she told herself with an inward smile. "Indeed, when it comes to such a servant as Mrs. Fry, I doubt he wants her any more than we do!"

This thought had no sooner crossed Claudia's mind than it gave rise to an unscrupulous plan. Why should not John Rexford have Mrs. Fry if he wanted her? And if he did not want her, why should he not help to keep her in line? "I'll talk to him tomorrow," Claudia told herself gleefully. "If I approach him in the right manner, I expect I can enlist his help without too much difficulty. In the normal way one doesn't care to appeal to one's enemy for assistance, but in this case it will be quite enjoyable! Besides, since meeting Master John, I can't think of him as an enemy anymore. He seems really quite human and pleasant—and he has a sense of humor, too. I wouldn't have expected it of him, but he does."

Claudia resolved to speak to John on the morrow and enlist his aid in her struggle with the Rexford Park servants. In the meantime, however, it was necessary to do something with Mrs. Fry. Turning to the housekeeper, Claudia summoned a smile to her lips.

"Of course, if you prefer to work for Master John—for Lord Rexford, I mean—then you certainly may. I have nothing to say to that, though I am sure Lady Rexford and I should be very sorry to see you leave Rexford Park. But if you will not obey Lady Rexford's orders, I suppose there is no alternative. She is the owner of the property at present, you know, not Master John." She paused to let the words sink in.

Mrs. Fry muttered something about foreigners and impostors, but her faith seemed a little shaken. "I came to Rexford Park thirty-three years ago, as a girl of sixteen," she told Claudia in a belligerent voice. "I've no intention of leaving now."

"Wonderful! Then I'm sure you will take care of this business about the dinner for Lady Rexford," said Claudia. "Please have it re-served at six o'clock." And she hastily left the room before Mrs. Fry could reply.

"How did you make out, my dear?" Lady Rexford asked eagerly as Claudia reentered the sitting room.

Claudia shook her head. "Not too well, but I think I got the message across that you're not to be trifled with. Still, I have no idea what kind of dinner we'll get this evening. We must be prepared for the worst. Mrs. Fry has already threatened me with warmed-over fritters and dried-out ducklings."

Hettie sniffed. "You'd think the cook in a great house like this would have more pride than to serve a meal like that," she commented dourly. "But there's no saying what people'll do when they set their minds to act like fools. I tell you what, Miss Chambers: If you find the dinner tonight's not edible, just you ring for me. I'll go down to the kitchen and see about fixing us a proper bite and sup. I haven't forgotten so much about cookery that I couldn't."

"I'm sure you could," said Claudia, smiling. "That is a very generous offer, Hettie, and Lady Rexford and I will hold it in reserve in case Mrs. Fry serves us something quite inedible. But I think—I hope—that it won't be that bad. And after tonight, I have a plan that should ensure Mrs. Fry complies with my orders a little more enthusiastically."

Lady Rexford was curious to know the details of this plan, but Claudia evaded her questions. She felt it would be better to make her appeal to John without his aunt's knowledge. By way of distracting Lady Rexford from the subject, she began to instruct her on what her behavior should be that evening at dinner.

"Very stately, very reserved, and just the least little bit critical. Don't be afraid to speak up if a dish is really bad. We cannot let that sort of thing go unremarked, or we shall get nothing but bad dishes the whole time we are here. But I think it would be better to say nothing if it appears the cook has really tried. I have an idea that Mrs. Fry is responsible for tonight's misunderstanding, and it would be unfair to visit her sins on anyone else. If, however, we get another mediocre dinner tomorrow night, then we shall have to close with Hettie's offer to cook for us!" She smiled at the maidservant.

"I'll do it and welcome," responded Hettie. "In fact, I don't mind saying I'd a deal rather cook than dine with Mrs. La-di-da Fry in the housekeeper's room!"

"Yes, I don't blame you. However, you might be able to do

some good there, so we shall try the experiment this once. Keep your eyes and ears open, and try to build up Lady Rexford's reputation all you can. And whatever you do, don't let the other servants bully you!"

"Trust me for that," said Hettie, smiling grimly. "There'll be no bullying of me, nor I won't stand to hear Lady Rexford abused neither. The first one as tries it will be sorry he opened his mouth, believe me!"

Claudia did believe her, and she watched Hettie go off to dinner in the housekeeper's room with a serene and untroubled heart. She felt somewhat less serene and untroubled where Lady Rexford was concerned, however. It was true that she and Lady Rexford would be the only ones eating in the dining room that evening, but they would do so before a critical audience: the butler, the footmen, and perhaps Mrs. Fry and some of the maids as well. And considering the hostility Mrs. Fry had shown even at the mention of Lady Rexford, Claudia feared no good could come of letting the two meet.

But she need not have worried. Mrs. Fry was mercifully absent during the meal, which was as well cooked as could be expected, considering its largely warmed-over nature. The service, too, was quite tolerable, though the butler tried initially to fob the two ladies off with a very inferior and much watered wine. Claudia, who was no judge of wine, would have drunk it uncomplainingly and never known the difference, but Lady Rexford was having none of that. Fired with a desire to show Claudia that she, too, could manage these servants, and secure in the knowledge acquired during fifteen years in the household of a wealthy bon vivant, she set down her wineglass with a bang.

"This wine is scandalous," she said severely. "Perfectly scandalous. Don't you think it's scandalous, too, Miss Chambers?"

Claudia, who had noticed nothing amiss, supposed her mistress was merely staging a scene for the servants' benefit. That being the case, she thought it her duty to play along. "Perhaps it is a little weak," she ventured.

"A *little* weak! Why, there's more of the rain barrel than the grape about it." Raising her quizzing glass to her eye, Lady Rexford regarded the butler imperiously. "You, there! Go down to the cellar, if you please, and bring us up something worth drinking. Miss Chambers, you might go with him. You know my tastes, and you'll see I'm not fobbed off with watered-down vinegar like this again." She pushed her wineglass away from her with a disdainful air.

The order suited Claudia as little as it did the butler, but she had no choice but to obey it. It was not that she minded being sent off to the wine cellar on a menial errand. That was merely part of her role, and she was glad to see Lady Rexford entering so enthusiastically into her own part. But she did wish her mistress had rehearsed this particular scene with her ahead of time. As she followed the butler along the corridor and down the steps to the wine cellar, she wished fervently she had thought to study a little on the subject of wine before coming to Rexford Park.

Once in the cellar, she looked helplessly around her at the racks of bottles. "You'll be wanting a claret, I suppose," said the butler sullenly. "The best of 'em are in those racks over there."

Claudia walked over to inspect the racks he had indicated. The bottles all looked alike to her; and the cryptic labels tacked here and there on the racks meant nothing to her. She chose a bottle at random, pretended to study it, and put it back. "Haven't you anything better than this?" she asked.

"No, I haven't," said the butler with great firmness. "Not in the way of clarets, I haven't. Those are Burgundies over there," he added hastily as Claudia walked over to examine some adjacent racks. "Her ladyship wouldn't care for them."

His anxiety to keep her away from the Burgundy racks aroused Claudia's suspicions. "Her ladyship is very fond of

Burgundy," she said firmly. "Let us have a bottle of that if you please. Which do you consider the best?"

More sullenly than ever, the butler indicated a row of bottles at the very bottom of the rack. "That'd be the Chambertin, I suppose. His late lordship laid it in some dozen years ago. But I wouldn't bother with it if I were you, miss. It's poor, thin, washy stuff, not fit to be compared with a good claret."

The way he spoke made Claudia more certain than ever that he was deliberately steering her away from the Burgundy. "There's only one way to tell, I suppose," she said. "Let us taste it."

"Taste it, miss?" said the butler, staring.

"Yes, taste it," said Claudia firmly. "Fetch us a corkscrew and a couple of glasses if you please."

With obvious reluctance, the butler fetched corkscrew and glasses. "This is very improper, miss," he protested. "It ought to be decanted first."

"I suppose it ought, but we will dispense with that nicety this once," said Claudia, studying the fluid in her glass. It looked all right, and a cautious taste showed it to taste all right, too. It was, in fact, surprisingly pleasant stuff, Claudia decided, taking another, larger sip. Of course there was no saying that Lady Rexford would agree with her taste, but if she did not, it would be an easy matter to fetch up another bottle.

"This will do, I think," she said with authority. "Take it upstairs if you please, and we'll see what Lady Rexford thinks."

What Lady Rexford thought was not immediately apparent from her face. Her eyes widened slightly when Claudia explained what vintage she had obtained for her, but she merely nodded a curt assent when the butler offered to pour her a glass. When Claudia asked anxiously how she liked it, she merely said, "A very fair wine, Miss Chambers." But she drank two and a half glasses of it, and when she and Claudia and

Hettie were alone later that evening, she gave her real opinion, interspersed by fits of reminiscent chuckles.

"Lord, my dear, you do have a pretty taste in wine, don't you? It was all I could do to keep from laughing out loud when you brought up that Chambertin. Of course it deserved to be drunk with a better meal than that one, but I can't deny it made those warmed-over ducklings go down a deal easier!"

"That was all an accident, I'm afraid," said Claudia, smiling. "I really don't know anything about wine. I could see the butler didn't want me to choose one of those particular bottles, so I thought it must be something good. He looked quite nonplussed when I insisted on tasting one!"

"Aye, I'll wager he did! I don't doubt the old rogue was hoping to keep the best of the cellar for his own use. Well, we'll thwart him in that. You must tell him to set a bottle of the Chambertin on the table at every meal, Miss Chambers. We might as well have the pleasure of drinking it."

Claudia promised to do this, and Lady Rexford leaned over to pat her hand. "You're a treasure, Miss Chambers. I feel sometimes I oughtn't to take advantage of you the way I do. It don't seem right ordering you about when you're twice the lady I am."

"I don't mind a bit," said Claudia, smiling. "It's what we've been rehearsing, you know, and I am glad to see you are now so comfortable in your role that you feel free to improvise as you did this evening. Only I hope you will tutor me a little on the subject of wine if you plan to send me down to the cellar again! It was only an accident that led me to get so lucky this evening."

Lady Rexford shook her head seriously. "No, it wasn't," she said. "You said yourself that you could tell the butler was trying to steer you away from those particular bottles, so that's what you chose. Well, that's a simple enough thing, but it's what one person in a hundred wouldn't think of doing if they even noticed what the old fox was up to in the first place. I tell you, you've a real gift for that sort of thing, Miss Chambers. I don't know what I should do without you, and that's a fact."

"Aye, you've made a fair job of it, miss, seemingly," said Hettie, adding her dour measure to this encomium. "The servants at dinner tonight had more good than ill to speak of you, and that's saying something, seeing as how they aren't exactly happy to have any of us here. Even Mrs. Fry allowed as you were very genteel and ladylike."

This tribute brought a warm glow to Claudia's heart. "I'm afraid I can't return Mrs. Fry's compliment, but I am sure I am much obliged to her for it," she said, laughing. "And I am glad if I have helped smooth things over for you, Lady Rexford. But you know we mustn't start congratulating each other yet. The biggest challenge still lies ahead of us, after all."

"Master John," said Lady Rexford with a shudder.

"Yes, Master John. But though he *is* our biggest challenge, I don't intend to let him intimidate me. Just you wait and see, Lady Rexford. I'll get the best of Master John before the summer's out, or my name isn't Claudia Chambers!"

Eight

At two o'clock precisely the following afternoon, John Rexford presented himself at the Rexford Park manor house. He was admitted by Mrs. Fry, whose sour face lost much of its sourness when she saw him.

"Oh, it's you, my lord! Come in, come in." Relieving John of his hat and gloves, she continued speaking in a confidential voice. "I don't hardly need to tell you how glad I am to welcome you back, my lord. But it's sorry I am that I'm not welcoming you back to your own home—as Rexford Park should be and as all of us here consider it *is*. For it's a fact, my lord, that we don't care a groat for her ladyship upstairs—Lady Rexford, as she calls herself, though lady she is not and never will be to my way of thinking."

"Is that so?" said John in an absent voice. He was hardly aware of Mrs. Fry's diatribe. In his left hand was a posy of roses and fern, which he had brought for his aunt, and in his right was a second, smaller posy, which he intended for Claudia. He had hoped he might have the opportunity to bestow this token on Claudia privately, along with an apology for his behavior the day before. But to his disappointment, she appeared to be nowhere about. Probably she was sitting with his aunt, winding wool or reading aloud or brushing lapdogs or doing one of the hundred and one other tiresome activities that were the usual lot of hired companions.

Mrs. Fry, meanwhile, had noticed his floral burden. "What's

that?" she demanded, regarding the roses with an incredulous eye. "Don't say you're bringing flowers to that woman? After the way she's robbed you of your inheritance?"

John reddened. "She didn't rob me," he said. "It was my uncle's decision to leave the property as he did, and now that I have had time to reflect a little, I see the justice of his decision. As for the flowers, I thought they would be a nice token, a way of welcoming my aunt and—er—Miss Chambers to the neighborhood."

"Miss Chambers!" exclaimed Mrs. Fry in a much tried voice. "Don't talk to *me* of Miss Chambers. If you had as much to do with her as I have!"

"Why, what has she done?" said John in surprise. "She seemed to me to be a very pleasant, well-bred young lady."

Mrs. Fry sniffed. "You wouldn't think so if you had to take orders from her," she said sourly. "It's 'Lady Rexford wishes this' and 'Lady Rexford prefers that' all day long until the rest of the staff and I don't know where to turn. Why, just yesterday—you'll hardly credit it, my lord, but it's every word true—Cook had only just got dinner on the table when she comes to me and says, 'Lady Rexford wishes dinner put back until six o'clock.' Two full hours! Cook wasn't half put out."

"Well, you know, Mrs. Fry, many people do dine later than four o'clock nowadays," said John, trying to soothe the irate housekeeper. "I know the Brocks dine at six and sometimes even later when they have company."

"That's all very well for the Brocks. They're gentry and can do as they like in their own home, I suppose. But here at Rexford Park we've always dined at four o'clock, and I don't see any reason why we should change that because of the whim of a jumped-up ex-housekeeper."

"A what?" said John in a voice that startled Mrs. Fry.

"Goodness, my lord! All I said was that I didn't care to take orders from a jumped-up ex-house—oh, very well, my lord. I'll call her Lady Rexford if you prefer it. But I tell you, it goes sorely against the grain with me to call her that. When

I remember old Lady Rexford, your sainted grandfather's wife—"

"You had much better give over your reminiscing and settle yourself to obeying the orders of the present Lady Rexford," said John. "She is your mistress now, like it or not. And if you want to keep your position—"

"Not if it means obeying the likes of *her,*" said Mrs. Fry venomously. "That's what I told Miss Chambers last night, and that's what I'm telling you now. The other servants all say the same. It's you we're working for, my lord, and we don't intend to let her ladyship—oh, there you are, miss. You came up so quiet I didn't hear you."

John looked up and saw Claudia regarding Mrs. Fry with an inscrutable expression.

"No, evidently not," she said. "I came downstairs to see if Lord Rexford were here." Shifting her gaze to John, she added, "Your aunt is expecting you, my lord. If you will please to step this way? Mrs. Fry, I don't think we need *your* services any longer."

Mrs. Fry, looking discomposed, curtsied, and took herself off with a confused speech about seeing to John's hat and gloves.

John felt a little discomposed himself as he followed Claudia toward the drawing room. "Look here, Miss Chambers," he said, "I don't know how much you overheard of what Mrs. Fry was saying, but I wouldn't want you to get the wrong idea. I wasn't encouraging her to criticize my aunt or anything of that nature."

Claudia turned to look at him. "Were you not?" she said.

John thought there was skepticism in her voice. Despite his best efforts, he found himself flushing. "No, I was not," he said emphatically. "She cornered me as soon as I came through the door and started pouring a lot of nonsense in my ear about my being the real master of Rexford Park and all the servants being determined not to obey my aunt's orders. I don't know what she meant by it, for heaven knows *I* have no authority here."

Again Claudia gave him an inscrutable look. "Don't you?" she said.

"None at all, though you may not choose to believe it, Miss Chambers. And though you may not choose to believe this either, it happens that after I talked with you yesterday, I came to the conclusion that it is better so. Here, these are for you." Abruptly, he thrust the smaller bouquet at Claudia. "I was rather short with you yesterday, and I'm sorry for it. I hope you'll accept these as a token of my regret and try to forget your first impression of me. I'm not quite such a Yahoo as I may have seemed." He gave her a diffident smile. Claudia appeared taken aback by the flowers, but John thought she also looked pleased.

"Oh! Why, I'm sure I took no offense at your manner yesterday, my lord. It was quite understandable, given the circumstances. But I shall forgive you all the more readily since you've made such a handsome reparation. What lovely roses!"

"I am glad you like them. You see, I have also brought some for my aunt." John showed her the other bouquet. "I am trying to do this thing properly, Miss Chambers."

"I see that you are." Claudia's eyes traveled over the shining Hessians and immaculate biscuit-colored pantaloons that replaced the mud-spattered breeches and topboots he had worn yesterday. They went on to consider briefly his well-cut blue topcoat, the snowy expanse of linen above his waistcoat, even the unobtrusive knot that finished his neckcloth. "You look very much improved, my lord. Quite handsome, in fact."

The words were spoken grudgingly, yet they gave John a curious satisfaction. "Thank you," he said. "I might return the compliment. You look very handsome yourself, Miss Chambers."

"Thank you," Claudia said, and gave him another look, both pleased and surprised.

As she led him toward the drawing room once more, however, John felt dissatisfied with his compliment. "Handsome" was simply not the right word for Miss Chambers. Pretty, yes—she was distractingly pretty in her dress of antique gold brocade with its square neck and tiny, tucked-up sleeves. Pretty likewise were her long-lashed dark eyes, the rich chestnut hair drawn smoothly into a knot at the nape of her neck, and the smile that had peeped out once or twice during their conversation.

But she was not handsome. "Handsome" was a word he associated with a different type of woman. Barbara Brock, for instance, was an indisputably handsome woman. Everyone said so, and no one more frequently or emphatically than Barbara herself. "I believe I am the handsomest girl here tonight," she had been known to observe complacently when she and John attended a party together. Heretofore John had always agreed with her. Yet it occurred to him now to wonder how she would compare if she were placed side by side with Miss Chambers. Barbara's majestic figure, blond hair, and highly colored complexion were certainly more eye-catching, but there was something appealingly feminine and graceful about Miss Chambers's appearance all the same. In fact, it seemed to John that she made Barbara appear overblown and a little coarse.

He pushed the reflection away from him hastily, but it recurred to him as Claudia glided gracefully along the hall in front of him, revealing now and then a glimpse of a dainty ankle or a pretty profile. Altogether he was in a distracted state by the time he reached the drawing room where his aunt was waiting.

Claudia was in a distracted state, too. Her emotions had undergone several rapid changes since the moment she had come downstairs in search of John.

She had been full of contempt and indignation to find him in conversation with Mrs. Fry, apparently inciting the housekeeper to further acts of rebellion. But his disclaimer afterward had disarmed her, as had the flowers he had given her. Claudia looked with bemusement at the posy of roses and fern in her hand. Who would have expected John Rexford to make such a gallant gesture? And who would have expected him to look so elegant and gentlemanly after the gauche appearance he had made the other day?

When she had told him he looked handsome, she had not been overstating the case—or at least not by much. He would never be a conventionally handsome man, but there was something very attractive about his appearance today. Especially when he smiled. Claudia found herself responding to that smile, in spite of the fact that he was her employer's sworn enemy and most outspoken critic.

With a sense of guilt, she recalled herself to her duties. Lady Rexford was awaiting her in the drawing room, gowned in her most impressive black silk, equipped with her cane and quizzing glass, and attended by the faithful Hettie. But it would not do to make her wait too long for her nephew's appearance. Kept in limbo for an excessive time, she might lose her nerve, as she had already threatened to do a dozen times that day. Mrs. Fry had already delayed things some minutes by waylaying John on the way in, and John had unwittingly delayed them even longer with his apology and gift of flowers. By now, Lady Rexford must be in an almost unbearable state of nerves, assuming she had not already given way to them and fled the drawing room.

This did not prove to be the case, however. When Claudia reached the drawing room door and tapped nervously for admittance, a stately voice at once responded, "Come in." Heartened, Claudia swung open the door.

"It's Master—I mean, it's Lord Rexford, my lady," she said with a deep and reverential curtsy. "He has called to speak with you, as I informed you yesterday."

"Ah, yes." With a superbly negligent air, Lady Rexford raised her quizzing glass to her eye. "Do come in, my lord. I am delighted to make your acquaintance."

"As I am yours, ma'am," responded her nephew. His voice was reserved, but Claudia was relieved to see that his manner was perfectly polite. He even condescended to salute the hand that Lady Rexford carelessly extended to him. "I was sorry to hear you were unwell yesterday, my lady. But you appear to be recovered in health today, to judge by your looks."

"Yes, thank you," said Lady Rexford. She was bearing up well under the ordeal thus far, Claudia was happy to see. It was true that her cheeks were pinker than usual, but her nephew could not be expected to know that—though he was scrutinizing her very narrowly, Claudia observed. But she thought his interest natural. He was meeting his aunt for the first time, under circumstances that rendered their meeting more than usually interesting. Besides, anyone might have been forgiven for staring at Lady Rexford as she appeared that afternoon.

Her dress of heavy black silk was faultless in cut and distinguished by a total lack of ornament. Its elegant severity served to diminish the plumpness of her figure and invest it instead with a queenly dignity. Her snowy hair was arranged atop her head in a complex arrangement of braids, half hidden by a fascinating edifice of black lace and jet beads, which added several inches to her height.

Nothing could make so small a lady look really tall, of course. But seated atop a thronelike chair and further elevated by a foot-high dais, she made altogether an impressive figure. Certainly she looked neither common nor vulgar. On the contrary, with her cheeks flushed with excitement and her blue eyes wide and slightly dilated, she looked not merely impressive but very lovely. Claudia thought it no wonder that the late Lord Rexford had been so taken with her. She only hoped his nephew would be similarly affected.

It appeared that he was. A smile suddenly softened his harsh countenance, and he executed a second bow, still holding Lady Rexford's hand in his. "Forgive me for staring, ma'am. I did not mean to be rude, but the fact is you are not at all what I expected."

"Well, you're not what I expected either," responded Lady Rexford, returning his gaze with an interest equal to his own.

She spoke in quite a natural voice. Claudia, fearing she was forgetting her role, hurried to intervene. "Only see what Lord Rexford has brought me, my lady!" She displayed her bouquet. "Did you ever see such lovely roses?"

"Yes, and I have some for you, too, ma'am," said John, presenting Lady Rexford with the other bouquet. He was still smiling, but his voice was serious as he added, "There have been differences between us in the past, I know, but I have come to regret the part I played in them. I hope that we may now be able to work together for the good of the estate and that our differences may be a thing of the past."

Lady Rexford looked at him as though scarcely believing her ears. She threw one brief look at Claudia, conveying a mixture of amazement and respect. "Why, my lord, that's very kind of you!" she said. "I'm sure I hope the same as you—and I'm sure I thank you very much for the roses. Pink roses, too! Miss Chambers must have told you pink's my favorite color."

"No, indeed!" said Claudia quickly. "That was merely a lucky guess on Lord Rexford's part. I am sure I told him nothing of your likes and dislikes."

There was a warning note in her voice, for she feared Lady Rexford was once again forgetting her role and betraying too much of her natural self.

But Lady Rexford went on, unheeding. "Well, lucky guess or not, I'm sure I'm much obliged to you for the flowers, my lord. Your uncle often used to bring me roses like that."

"I'm glad I resemble my uncle in that regard, though I'm afraid that's as far as the resemblance extends," said John, smiling. "He was always accounted a very good-looking man."

"Aye, that he was, but you're not so unlike him as I first thought, my lord. That's what I meant a minute ago when I said you weren't what I expected. Now that I see you up close, I can see you've something of his cast of countenance—though to be sure, you're a fair bit taller than he was and a deal darker, too."

John laughed. "Yes, I'm afraid I am. But you do me great honor in comparing me to him, ma'am, and I thank you very much."

Claudia had listened in some dismay to this exchange. The conversation was not going at all as she had expected. With every passing moment Lady Rexford was losing more and more of her grande dame hauteur and relapsing into her naturally frank and friendly manner. Still, it did not seem as though her nephew was disgusted by this circumstance. On the contrary, he was that moment welcoming her to the neighborhood with a smile of perfect affability. Observing this miracle with wide eyes, Claudia decided it might be as well not to interfere while matters were going so well.

Matters continued to go well throughout the interview. John accepted a chair at Lady Rexford's request, and before long, they were plunged in a deep and earnest conversation about the Rexford Park property and its ambivalent legal status.

"Aye, there's no doubt but that it's an awkward business, my lord," said Lady Rexford with a sigh. "I don't mean to say a word against your uncle, who was in general as wide-awake a man as you could ever wish to see. But sometimes I wonder what he was about, yoking the two of us together in this harum-scarum fashion. As far as I can see, the whole property might go to the dogs with neither of us able to say yea or nay to anything without being contradicted by the other."

"It *is* awkward," agreed John. "We must hope we can agree on some kind of general policy about the way the property should be managed in the future. And I see no reason why we may not. I confess that I was disappointed by my uncle's will, but even so, I should not care to see the family property go to the dogs."

"That's very fairly spoken, my lord, and nothing would suit me better than an agreement such as you speak of. And in the meantime, perhaps we can clear away some of these other matters you wrote about, concerning fields and barns and fences and such."

"Of course. If you like, I would be happy to take you out sometime these next few days and let you inspect the property so you can see exactly what needs doing. I am sure you would feel more comfortable about giving your approval if you had verified matters for yourself."

"That's very kind of you, my lord, and I suppose I wouldn't mind looking around the property sometime if it was convenient. But as for giving my approval—why, I'm sure you could show me every field and barn and fence on the place and I should be none the wiser." Lady Rexford gave a deprecatory chuckle. "I'm a Londoner, you know, not a countrywoman, my lord. You may as well go ahead and do whatever you think proper. I'll trust you not to cheat me."

Claudia, listening in alarm, thought this was entirely too much trust to be given on such short acquaintance. John was certainly showing himself more amiable and easygoing than she had dared hope, but still business was business, and it was her business to see that her employer was not taken in. She addressed Lady Rexford in a loud but respectful voice.

"Excuse me, my lady, but you know it might be as well if you did take a look at the property before giving your consent to any repairs or alterations. If nothing else, it would give you some acquaintance with the place so you would know better in the future what concerns might arise and what might need doing."

Both John and Lady Rexford turned to look at her in surprise. "There's something in what you say, my dear," acknowledged Lady Rexford. "Still, I don't know what good it would do if I did look at the property. As I said before, I don't know much about farming matters."

"Even so, it wouldn't hurt to take a look about," repeated Claudia. She was conscious of John's gaze upon her, but she meant to hold her ground, even at the risk of offending him.

He was still Master John as far as she was concerned, and his goodwill had yet to be proven.

To her surprise, however, he immediately agreed with her statement. "Miss Chambers is right," he said. "It wouldn't hurt for you to look about the place, Lady Rexford, even if you trust me to make the necessary changes. It would make me more comfortable if you approved my plans firsthand—and I think it would make Miss Chambers more comfortable, too." With a mischievous look at Claudia, he added, "If I mistake not, she is the kind of lady who likes to see every i dotted and every t crossed."

"Yes, she is a very clever, conscientious girl," said Lady Rexford, regarding Claudia with pride and affection. "She keeps me up to the mark in everything, and I don't know what I would do without her. Why, it's she who ought to look at the property with you, my lord, and approve the necessary repairs. I'd trust her to do a better job than I would myself, and that's a fact."

"What about it, Miss Chambers?" said John, smiling at Claudia. "Will you consent to play the part of Lady Rexford's bailiff as well as her companion? I have no doubt you would fulfill the one role as admirably as you do the other."

Claudia hesitated before answering. She knew it to be her duty to perform whatever task Lady Rexford assigned her—and she was obliged to admit that, in this case, the task sounded quite an interesting one. It was, moreover, a task that she could probably perform better than her employer, just as Lady Rexford had said. But Claudia was still a little wary about John, in spite of his roses and compliments and apparent amiability. Accepting this commission would undoubtedly require her to spend some hours *tête-à-tête* with him, and that was a not entirely comfortable thought. She looked indecisively at John, who smiled back at her.

"On my honor, Miss Chambers, I don't bite," he said. "I won't deny I have a fearful bark on occasion, but you've already shown yourself impervious to that. Do say yes, and let us call the matter settled."

Another smile accompanied this plea—a smile of such charm that it wrung an impulsive yes from Claudia's lips before she had well considered what she was doing. In the back of her mind, a small voice whispered that she was behaving imprudently, but she shut her ears to its warning. John was smiling at her, Lady Rexford was smiling at her, and even Hettie was regarding her with a look of dour approval.

"That's settled then," said John, briskly rising to his feet. "And now I suppose I had better be taking my leave. I've already stayed far longer than is really proper for a first call. But you will forgive me for that, I hope, Lady Rexford. You know I have several years of neglect to make up for."

"Ah, you mustn't think of that, my lord," said Lady Rexford, also rising to her feet and extending her hand to him once more. "What's past is past, is what *I* say, and seeing that we're both sensible people, we'll do better to live in the present. You're welcome to come here whenever you like, my lord— and I hope that'll be often. This place is as much yours as mine, after all."

"You are very kind," said John, saluting her hand. Claudia observed, however, that a crease had appeared between his brows. She waited until he had said his farewells, then followed him out of the drawing room.

"One moment, if you please, my lord. I needed to talk to you privately for a few minutes."

"Certainly, Miss Chambers," he said, halting and turning around again to face her. He spoke courteously enough, but she saw the line was still between his brows.

"Forgive me if I am detaining you," she said coldly. "I can see you are in a hurry to go. What I have to say can wait until another time."

He regarded her with surprise. "What makes you think I am in a hurry to go?" he said. "I assure you that such is not the case, Miss Chambers."

"The expression on your face says otherwise," retorted Claudia. "I noticed it before when you were saying good-bye to Lady Rexford. You looked rather as though you had eaten something that disagreed with you!"

A look of rueful amusement appeared on John's face. "You are very perceptive, Miss Chambers," he said. "Yes, something did disagree with me just now, but it had nothing to do with my digestion. It was merely that comment of my aunt's about Rexford Park's being as much mine as hers. It hit me in what is still rather a tender spot, I'm afraid. But I hope you will give me credit for at least trying to conceal my feelings. I don't think my aunt noticed anything amiss even if you did."

"No, I don't think Lady Rexford noticed anything amiss," said Claudia. She hesitated a moment, then went on carefully. "You behaved very well toward her this afternoon, my lord. I was pleased to see it, and I know she was pleased, too. May I ask what you thought of her?"

Another smile appeared on John's face. "Well, chiefly I was relieved to find her so presentable! She is a very attractive woman and not entirely without breeding either. My uncle appears not to have been so amiss in his judgment as I supposed. Really, she is much better than I expected."

This praise was not as enthusiastic as Claudia would have liked, but she decided to let it pass. "I thought you would be agreeably surprised in her, my lord," she said. "When you come to know her better, you will find she has other good qualities, too."

John merely looked amused at her words. "Indeed?" he said.

Claudia was irritated by his amusement. "Indeed, yes," she retorted. "I will admit there are ladies who are Lady Rexford's superior in manners and breeding, but none who surpass her in kindness or generosity or any of the other really important human virtues. You may smile at that if you like, Master John, but I assure you it's true!"

The name slipped out before Claudia could catch herself. She looked at John guiltily. He was regarding her with astonishment but not, she thought, with anger. "What did you call me?" he asked.

"Master John," said Claudia in a humble voice. "Forgive me, my lord. I know I ought to call you Lord Rexford, but somehow I always think of that name as belonging to the *other* Lord Rexford—to Lady Rexford's husband, you know."

"As a matter of fact, so do I," said John. A reluctant smile was hovering around his lips. "Still, it was quite a shock to hear you call me Master John just now! For a moment there, I imagined I was back in short coats, being dressed down by my nurse for some childish misdeed!"

Claudia was blushing. "Do forgive me," she said again. "I can't think how the name slipped out, my lord. I promise it won't happen again."

There was a distinct twinkle in John's eye now. "Oh, well, it's no great matter," he said. "Now that I'm over the shock, I confess I rather enjoyed the novelty of hearing myself called Master John by a pretty young lady. You may call me that if you please, Miss Chambers—but if you do, I must insist on calling you by your Christian name, too. I think that is only fair. What is your name?"

"My name is Claudia," said Claudia in some confusion. "But—"

"Claudia? Well, that is a very pretty name and not just in the common style either. I think it suits you, Miss Chambers. For you are not just in the common style either if I mistake not."

He looked down at her in an appraising way. Claudia found herself blushing more deeply than ever. Desperately she sought for a way to change the subject. "I thank you very much for the compliment, my lord, but indeed it was merely a silly slip of the tongue that made me call you by your Christian name. I had heard Mrs. Fry do so earlier, you see, and I suppose that is what made me think of it." By now she had regained her composure, and she went on in a businesslike voice. "And that reminds me, my lord. There was something I wished to discuss with you regarding Mrs. Fry. That is why I wanted to speak to you in the first place."

"Oh, yes?" he said, looking wary. "What about Mrs. Fry? I assure you, if you are referring to the nonsense she was spouting earlier—"

"Yes, I am referring to that, my lord. I agree with you about its being nonsense, for it was my understanding that Lady Rexford has control over the household staff as well as the house itself. And that means she may discharge any servant whom she finds unsatisfactory. Isn't that true?"

"Yes, it is true," said John, his brows drawing together. "But I should be very sorry to hear of her doing such a thing. Most of the servants at the Park are old family retainers who have worked here for years and years."

"Yes, I thought as much," said Claudia, pleased to see him playing so neatly into her hands. "And I assure you that Lady Rexford would regret discharging them quite as much as you would. But if they will not obey her orders, what else can she do?"

"Do you mean they are *not* obeying her orders?" said John, looking incredulous. "I know Mrs. Fry said something of the sort earlier, but I confess I thought she was talking through her hat."

"No, she was not talking through her hat, my lord. From the very first, her attitude has been hostile and uncooperative. Of course that is understandable, for she is an old family retainer as you say, and naturally she would resent taking orders from anyone whom she considered an outsider. But it leaves Lady Rexford in a very difficult position. Mrs. Fry seems to have a great deal of influence over the other servants, and as long as she incites them to insolence and disobedience, your aunt can hardly be blamed for not wanting to keep her in the household." Claudia paused, looking at John.

"I suppose not," he said grudgingly. "But really, I cannot believe it is as bad as you say, Miss Chambers. After all, my aunt has only been here for how long—two days? I am sure if you give Mrs. Fry time she will settle down and accept the situation."

Claudia shook her head. "I am afraid it's more serious than that, my lord. It is not a mere unwillingness to obey Lady Rexford that I am speaking of, but an absolute refusal. And whenever I have tried to point out to her that her behavior is putting her job in jeopardy, she merely says that she is working for you, not Lady Rexford. She told me only last night that you would be happy to take her in if Lady Rexford is dissatisfied with her work."

"*I* take her in?" said John in a startled voice. "How, pray tell, does she expect me to do that? At present I am living in the Gatehouse with a staff of exactly three: my valet, my groom, and old Mrs. Meeks, who does the cooking and cleaning for us all. I don't have any need of a housekeeper there, and even if I did, I should have more regard for the feelings of Mrs. Meeks. She has considered the Gatehouse as her own personal property for more than forty years, and I shudder to think of the fur that would fly if I tried to put a housekeeper over her. Besides, Mrs. Fry isn't the most congenial person with whom to live—" He broke off, looking guiltily at Claudia.

"Exactly," said Claudia with false affability. "Yet you seem eager for us to keep her on here at Rexford Park in spite of her uncongeniality."

John reddened. "That's different," he said. "Mrs. Fry has been housekeeper here for nearly as long as Mrs. Meeks has been taking care of the Gatehouse. And though her personality may leave something to be desired, I do think so many years of faithful service are worthy of some consideration."

"Of course," said Claudia sweetly. "But please remember that her years of service have been devoted to you and your family, my lord, and not to outsiders like Lady Rexford and me. So far we have been able to obtain very little service from her indeed. And since she seems willing to leave here and go work for you at the Gatehouse, I thought that might be a very good solution to the difficulty."

"Well, it isn't!" said John. "We must find some other solution." He thought deeply, running a hand through his hair in
a distracted manner. "Look here, Miss Chambers," he said at
last. "Suppose *I* have a word with Mrs. Fry? Of course I haven't any real authority over her, but as long as she thinks I
do, I might be able to make her settle down and see reason."

"Why, that would be an excellent solution, my lord!" exclaimed Claudia, just as if she had not been angling for this
offer all along. "I am sure both Lady Rexford and I would be
much obliged to you if you were able to convince Mrs. Fry
to do her job."

John promised to go and have a word with the housekeeper
before he left, but he showed no immediate signs of leaving.
"I think Mrs. Fry is in the housekeeper's room right now,"
hinted Claudia. "Shall I send her to you? Or would you prefer
to go to her?"

"Oh, I will go to her, Miss Chambers. There's no difficulty
about that. You needn't trouble yourself in the matter." He
looked ruefully at Claudia. "You seem in a great hurry to get
rid of me."

"Not at all," protested Claudia, trying to hide her amazement at this unexpected statement. "I would be very glad to
have you stay, my lord, but—"

"But you are eager to get all the i's dotted and the t's
crossed," finished John with a wry grin. "Very well, Miss
Chambers. Only don't forget, there's another i that will take
our joint efforts to dot. You haven't forgotten you are commit-
ted to making a tour of the property with me so that you may
approve the necessary repairs, have you?"

"No," said Claudia, surprised. "But I supposed there was
no hurry about that, my lord."

"Nevertheless, I should like to see the matter settled. Shall
we say tomorrow at two o'clock?"

"I do not know if Lady Rexford would find it convenient
for me to go tomorrow, my lord," hedged Claudia. "Perhaps
it would be better to say the day after tomorrow. That would

give me time to make my arrangements and put Lady Rexford's affairs in order before I go."

John gave her a long look, then suddenly smiled—an unwilling smile, it appeared to Claudia, but a genuine one nevertheless. "I would consider that statement most commendable, Miss Chambers, only I have an uneasy feeling that one of those affairs you speak of arranging is myself! However, you manage me in a most adroit and painless fashion, so I'll say no more. Let me go and talk with Mrs. Fry, as I promised, and I'll plan to see you again the day after tomorrow."

Nine

Before leaving Rexford Park, John went down to the house-keeper's room. He had promised Claudia he would have a word with Mrs. Fry, and since he was a man who kept his promises he did have a word with her—a great many words, as it happened. But it was only with the greatest difficulty that he was able to convince the housekeeper to give over the campaign of rebellion and insurrection she had plotted against Lady Rexford.

"Why, Master John—my Lord Rexford, I mean—you're never saying you want me to take orders from that underbred huzzy?" she exclaimed in a dudgeon. "She has no right here at Rexford Park—no right at all. I don't care what the lawyers may say. The place ought to be yours, and I'd have thought you, if anybody, would agree with me."

There was a reproach in her voice that made John uncomfortable. He shook his head, trying to smile. "No, I'm afraid not, Mrs. Fry. Like it or not, my aunt has a life interest in Rexford Park, and so it is she whom you must obey. I hope you will do it for my sake, if not for hers—but I should prefer you to do it for hers. She appears to be quite a worthy woman, and she *is* my uncle's widow, you know. That in itself ought to entitle her to your respect."

Mrs. Fry gave him the disillusioned look of one whose idol has proven to have feet of clay. "That I should live to hear you say so, Master John!" she said, lifting up her hands. "You, who ought to be master here this minute! I do believe that woman's bewitched you. She's done the same to you as she did to your uncle."

"No, she has not done the same to me as she did to my uncle," said John, irritated by this speech. "Lady Rexford is an amiable and attractive woman, I'll admit, but I would not let myself be swayed by anything she could say or do. I am merely looking at the facts of the case, and the plain fact is that my aunt is now mistress of Rexford Park. That being so, she is entitled to your full obedience and respect, Mrs. Fry. I should be sorry if you were to withhold either out of any idea of mistaken loyalty to me."

Mrs. Fry gave him another long look of disillusionment, which slowly kindled into a vindictive anger. "I know what it is!" she exclaimed. "You've let yourself be talked over by that minx Miss Chambers! I saw her with you earlier, smiling and coaxing and looking as though butter wouldn't melt in her mouth. I should have known then what she was about, the scheming little cat! Don't you be taken in by her, my lord. She may choose to put on the airs of a fine lady, but birds of a feather flock together, you know. No real lady'd work for an upstart like your aunt unless she was by way of being the same thing."

John found himself irrationally incensed by this speech. "That will be enough, Mrs. Fry," he said sharply. "You do yourself no credit by speaking in such a manner. And I do not think you do Miss Chambers credit either. She *is* a lady, whatever you may think, and it is not your place to criticize her. Nor is it your place to criticize my aunt, if it comes to that. I told you earlier today that I did not like it."

In a whining, self-justifying voice, Mrs. Fry said she couldn't help disliking to see outsiders in the place of her beloved Master John. "Of course I'll obey Lady Rexford if you ask me to, my lord. But it's only because *you* ask me to. I wouldn't lift a finger for her sake any more than I would for that Miss Chambers."

Looking into her spiteful face, John felt a rush of revulsion. "She really is a most disagreeable old beldame," he thought, before catching himself with a feeling of guilt. Of course he ought not to criticize Mrs. Fry. She had been his most earnest supporter ever since the terms of his uncle's will had become known. Her spite toward Lady Rexford and Claudia was merely an expression of her loyalty to him, and he ought to be grateful for a loyalty so unwavering. But still there was a touch of reserve in his voice as he responded to Mrs. Fry's speech.

"Very well, Mrs. Fry. I will trust you and the other staff to make my aunt's stay here at Rexford Park as pleasant as possible. I'll check in from time to time to see how things are going."

"Aye, and right glad we'll be to see you here, my lord," said Mrs. Fry, passing over the first part of his speech and responding to the last with a beaming smile. John went away from this interview feeling he had not accomplished as much as he had hoped.

"But there, I suppose it was unrealistic to imagine I could settle things so easily," he told himself. "When you're dealing with women, even the simplest matters have a way of becoming complicated."

Women! It seemed to John as though his affairs were complicated by far too many of the sex. Ruefully he thought of his aunt and Mrs. Fry. They stood like Titans ranged on opposite sides of a mighty conflict, in which it seemed only too likely that he would be expected to play a mediator's role. And everyone knew that a mediator's role was very nearly as thankless—and every bit as perilous—as that of the bringer of bad news.

Then there was Claudia. To all appearances, she too was a mediator in the conflict between his aunt and Mrs. Fry. But Mrs. Fry appeared to have taken her in dislike, judging from the wild accusations she had made against Claudia's character that afternoon. Such accusations were ridiculous, for no one in their senses could suppose such a pretty, genteel, and well-bred young lady was a scheming adventuress.

"Yet she does have a way with her," John owned to himself. He thought again of how pretty Claudia had looked that afternoon, and how cleverly she had maneuvered him into speaking with Mrs. Fry. "I strongly suspect she had that as her goal from the beginning, though it seemed at the time as though it were all my own idea. And how quickly she dismissed me once she gained what she wanted!"

This last thought, especially, tended to rankle John. He could think of no good reason why Claudia should want him for anything besides his influence with the servants, but he nonetheless felt hurt that she should make her uninterest so clear. He was, after all, a tolerably well-off, wellborn, good-looking man, and he had gone to unusual lengths to make himself agreeable that day. The least she could have done was flirt with him a little, John told himself. "But I might have been one of the footmen for all the personal interest she showed in me! Ah, well, we are engaged to go driving around the estate the day after tomorrow. Perhaps she will be more forthcoming then."

At this point John began to indulge his imagination in thoughts of how that interview might go if Claudia ever forgot her businesslike detachment. And so engrossed did he become in these imaginings that he completely forgot about the fourth woman in his life. But he was reminded of her speedily when he returned to the Gatehouse to find a pointed message awaiting him there.

"Miss Barbara called. She says not to forget you're expected at the Towers for dinner tonight," Mrs. Meeks told John. "Six o'clock, and mind you're not late."

"I am not in the habit of being late for dinner engagements," said John testily. It struck him that Barbara's message was brusque to the point of being insulting. It also struck him that a great many of her recent communications had been lacking in that tenderness and tact one would have expected from one's affianced bride.

"And we aren't even engaged yet," John fumed as he went upstairs to his room. "I must nip this sort of thing in the bud, or God knows where it will end. Barbara has no excuse for treating me like a half-wit who can't be depended on to remember a dinner engagement. I've never forgotten one of her dinners yet—though I'm tempted to give this affair tonight the go-by, by Jove. That would show her!"

In the end, John decided against demonstrating his independence in such a drastic manner. But he did go so far as to wait until ten minutes past six before presenting himself at the Towers. It was Barbara herself who opened the door to him. She was looking very handsome in a dress of cherry-colored sarcenet, with her golden hair coiffed *à la sappho* and her cheeks as rosy as her dress. But it was clear from her expression that she was displeased by John's tardiness.

"You're late," were the first words out of her mouth. "Mama has been in a perfect fret, worrying that dinner would be spoiled. It isn't like you to be so inconsiderate, Rexford. Didn't you get my message?"

"I got *a* message," said John. He waited till the butler had relieved him of his hat and gloves; then he spoke again, deliberately. "A very insulting communication I thought it, too. But perhaps Mrs. Meeks did not recall it quite correctly."

"All I told her was to be sure to remind you to be here at six," said Barbara impatiently. "A simple enough message, I would have thought!"

"Too simple for my taste," returned John. "I don't care for being ordered about like a servant—or a fool."

Barbara gave him a look of mingled surprise and irritation. "Nobody thinks you're a fool, Rexford," she said. "It's only that this is a very special dinner, and I wanted you to be sure to be on time. Sir Lucas is dining with us tonight. He has just got back from Italy."

"What?" exclaimed John. It had been his intention to make

more of an issue of Barbara's message, but these words made him forget all about it. "You don't mean to say that popinjay is back in Yorkshire? I thought when he left for Italy this last time he planned to stay there for good."

"No, he is back at Pinehurst again. For heaven's sake don't talk so loud, Rexford." Barbara lowered her own voice to a murmur. "He'll hear you and be offended."

"I don't care if he *is* offended," said John, raising his voice higher. "In fact, I hope he is so offended that he decides to leave the house. You know I can't abide Sir Lucas Davenport, Barbara."

"Yes, I know, but surely you can put up with him for this one evening," said Barbara, casting a nervous look over her shoulder. "Come along, Rexford. It's too late to make difficulties now. Mama will be frantic if she has to delay dinner much longer."

John was tempted to retort that it was not too late to make difficulties and that he would rather go without dinner than dine with Sir Lucas Davenport. But by making a heroic effort, he managed to keep his tongue between his teeth. Mr. and Mrs. Brock were expecting him; their servants had seen him enter the house; and to leave now would be a very pointed insult, which would undoubtedly give rise to gossip and speculation throughout the neighborhood.

Under the circumstances, it seemed better to go ahead and dine with Sir Lucas just this once. John was the less reluctant to do this because he was not without a certain curiosity to see Sir Lucas again, even in spite of his avowed dislike. If nothing else, it would be interesting to see how Sir Lucas would reconcile his return to Yorkshire with certain well-publicized statements he had made two years ago about the insupportability of life in northern England.

So John accompanied Barbara to the drawing room, where the rest of the company were waiting. Sir Lucas was conversing with Mrs. Brook, languidly waving one white hand as he talked and laughing now and then his affected laugh, which was one of the things John disliked most about him.

John surveyed him grimly. As usual, Sir Lucas was dressed in an exquisite, not to say dandified, fashion. His satin knee breeches were dazzling in their whiteness, his waistcoat was tastefully embroidered with cornflowers, and his azure blue coat had silver buttons as big as crown pieces. At first glance, he might have been taken for a man of John's age, but a closer inspection would have revealed him nearer to fifty than thirty. Yet his auburn hair was as luxuriant as ever, swept back from his noble brow in Byronic style, and his handsome profile with its aquiline nose and pouting lips was only a little marred by the ravages of time.

That profile was turned to John as he came in, but a moment later Sir Lucas became aware of his presence and swung round to greet him with a beaming smile. "Well, if it isn't my old friend John Rexford!" he exclaimed. "Or no—I ought rather to say *Lord* Rexford, oughtn't I? I heard you had recently attained to your uncle's dignities. Dear, dear, I must be very careful in giving you the precedence this evening, or I shall find myself at *point non plus*."

"Good evening, Sir Lucas," said John shortly. Sir Lucas always made a point of professing great friendship for him, even though he must have sensed John's dislike. It was John's suspicion that Sir Lucas derived amusement from provoking him in this manner, and his suspicions were strengthened by Sir Lucas's next remark.

"Lord Rexford of Rexford Park! It sounds very good, upon my word. Only I heard there had been a difficulty concerning the Rexford Park property. Barbara was telling me about it before you arrived—something about its being left to your uncle's relict instead of to you? How vexing that must be, and how revoltingly unfair. All your friends must unite in thinking you ill used."

Sir Lucas's voice was sympathetic, but his gray eyes sparkled maliciously as he regarded John. John was spared answer-

ing by Mrs. Brock, who broke in with small ceremony upon
Sir Lucas's mocking expression of sympathy.

"Now that we are all here *at last*"—her eyes lingered disapprovingly on John as she spoke—"we had all better go into
the dining room and sit down. Rexford, you may take me in.
Sir Lucas can follow with Barbara."

John accepted Mrs. Brock's plump arm with a polite smile,
but inwardly he was less than pleased by this arrangement. He
was even less pleased to hear Sir Lucas paying extravagant
compliments to Barbara as he escorted her into the dining
room. "Ah, I declare it is worth losing the precedence to have
the privilege of partnering so much beauty! You look a veritable rose tonight, Miss Brock—a blooming English rose."

Barbara accepted the compliment complacently as she took
her place beside Sir Lucas. Mrs. Brock was at the foot of the
table, and the fifth member of the party, Mr. Brock, sat at its
head. His position, however, was a mere sinecure. Everyone
in the neighborhood knew that Mrs. Brock was the real head
of the Brock family, while Mr. Brock, a small, mild-looking
man, was commonly held to have sacrificed all pretense of
authority in order to secure domestic peace.

"Will you have soup?" he said, addressing the company with
a deprecating smile. Everyone said they would have soup except his wife, who advised him sharply to never mind talking,
but to serve the soup before it was stone cold. Mr. Brock
obediently served forth the soup and spoke not another word
for the rest of the meal.

His silence was hardly noticeable, however, thanks to the
flow of chatter emanating from Sir Lucas. "A delightful meal,"
he gushed as the soup and fish were replaced by a roast of
beef. "You can't imagine how homesick I have been for good,
honest English fare, Mrs. Brock. There are things to be said
for Italy and Italian cooking, of course, but after a time I found
myself longing—absolutely longing—for a nice, bloody roast
of English beef."

"Oh, so it was the lack of English roast beef that drove you out of Italy?" said John with a sardonic smile. "I recall your saying two years ago that Italy was the only place for civilized living and that nothing could compel you to return to such a barbaric country as England."

Sir Lucas waved these remarks aside with an indulgent smile. "I daresay I did say something of the sort. But that was two years ago, and I have discovered in the meantime that I have, after all, a soft spot in my heart for old England. The English food—the English countryside—and of course, the English girls." A smirk at Barbara accompanied these words— a smirk that made John long to hit him.

"I have always said there is no place like England," said Mrs. Brock, as though that settled the matter. "We are glad to see you back at Pinehurst, Sir Lucas. I always thought it a most charming house."

"Yes, it's good enough, I suppose. But of course it cannot compare to *your* home, ma'am, or to Lord Rexford's." Sir Lucas threw another sly look at John. "But there, I'm forgetting, aren't I? Rexford Park is in the hands of the enemy."

"Indeed, it is most unjust," said Barbara warmly. "I declare I quite detest that woman. I hope I shall never be obliged to meet her, for I'm sure I could not treat her with even common courtesy."

"It is not likely that you ever *should* meet a person of her sort, my dear, said Mrs. Brock. "Of course she does not mean to mix socially while she is staying here. That would be a little much, I think!"

She spoke with a decided air that grated on John's nerves. "Why do you say so, ma'am?" he said. "I should think my aunt has as much right to mix socially as anyone in the neighborhood."

These words made everyone look at him in amazement, even Mr. Brock. It was Barbara who spoke first. "You cannot mean it, Rexford!" she said. "A woman like that? I am sure she is perfectly impossible."

"Not at all impossible," said John. "She seems a very pleasant and unexceptionable person. I greatly enjoyed talking to her this afternoon."

"So you have met her, have you?" said Sir Lucas, raising his eyebrows. "I confess that I am surprised to hear it, Rexford. I would not have envisioned you—er—consorting with the enemy in that fashion."

John was not about to explain the terms of his uncle's will, and in any case, he was irked by Sir Lucas's comment. "I do not consider her to be my enemy," he said. "She came by the property honestly, and I would be the last to begrudge it to her."

"Well, I'm sure you're an example to us all, Rexford," drawled Sir Lucas, raising his eyebrows once more. "If I were in your position, I doubt I would be so forgiving."

"I'm sure *I* should not be," said Barbara, surveying John with disfavor. "I declare, I do not understand you, Rexford. You spoke as strongly against this woman as anyone a few weeks ago."

"Perhaps I did," said John. "But I have learned my lesson since then, as you can see. My aunt is quite welcome to Rexford Park."

"Still, it must go against the grain to think of its being in another's hands," said Sir Lucas, regarding him with some curiosity. "Of course the place was rather antiquated, but the grounds were quite decent, and there were some first-rate pieces of art. That Rembrandt your grandpapa brought back from his Grand Tour, for instance. I wouldn't mind owning that myself."

"Yes, it was a fine piece," said John, frowning a little. "At present, it seems to have been misplaced. I must be sure to ask my aunt about it next tine I see her."

"I daresay she sold it so as to enrich herself at your expense," said Barbara viciously. "Nothing would surprise me in such a woman as that."

John merely looked at her. She colored a little under his gaze. "Of course I don't mean to speak ill of your aunt, Rexford—though she is only your aunt by marriage, after all! But you know if the painting is missing, then she is by far the most likely person to have taken it."

"I must say, it does sound suspicious to me," agreed Sir Lucas. "Bad luck for you if it is so, Rexford. That Rembrandt really was a most exquisite painting, though in general I prefer the works of the Italian masters to the Dutch."

John shook his head. "I am sure my aunt had nothing to do with the Rembrandt's disappearance," he said. "I daresay it is only stored away in a box room somewhere and will turn up one of these days."

The others accepted his tacit dismissal of the subject, though Mrs. Brock said darkly that she, for one, would be much surprised if the present Lady Rexford had nothing to do with the painting's disappearance. However, she was soon lured into a discussion of Italian fashions initiated by Sir Lucas. This conversation lasted for the rest of the meal. When dinner was over, the ladies retired to the drawing room, Mrs. Brock adjuring the gentlemen not to sit too long over their port. Since John and Sir Lucas had nothing to say to each other, and Mr. Brock had nothing to say to either of them, they were not loath to follow this advice. As John entered the drawing room with the other gentlemen, Barbara seized his arm and drew him off into a corner.

"I have been thinking, Rexford, and I really believe you are taking this matter of the missing Rembrandt much too coolly. You must ask your aunt about it next time you see her. Don't let her put you off with any denials. As far as I can see, there's no one but she who *could* have taken it. If she is proven to have sold or stolen it, that might possibly give you grounds for setting aside your uncle's will. I would investigate the matter very thoroughly if I were you."

John had every intention of questioning his aunt about the missing Rembrandt, but he was annoyed by Barbara's assumption of authority in the affair. He was also annoyed by her presumption of his aunt's guilt. "But you know you are not me, Barbara," he said curtly. "I am afraid you will have to allow me to handle the situation in my own way."

"And so I would, Rexford, if I thought you would handle it properly," retorted Barbara. "But you seem so unconcerned! I don't understand at all why you have had such a change of heart about your aunt. It's almost as though she has bewitched you."

It was the second time that day that someone had accused John of being bewitched by Lady Rexford. He was both amused and irritated. "Don't be ridiculous, Barbara," he said. "Of course my aunt has not bewitched me. But I think I am a pretty good judge of character, and after seeing and speaking to her, I find it hard to believe she would behave dishonestly."

Barbara laughed harshly. "Well, if she has not bewitched you, she seems to have made a conquest of you nonetheless. Take care, Rexford! I'll wager that this famous show of honesty was all staged for your benefit."

"And I'll wager that it was not," said John coldly. "But even if it was, I fail to see what motive my aunt could have for taking the Rembrandt. She receives a generous jointure under my uncle's will—"

"A foolishly generous one, by all I have heard," interposed Barbara.

John ignored the interruption. "And I don't know when she would have had the opportunity to take the Rembrandt, even if she had wanted to. So far as I know, it has always hung here at Rexford Park. And my aunt has never even been in Yorkshire until this visit."

"Oh, I daresay she inveigled your uncle into bringing it to London with him," said Barbara. "She probably has it hanging in her house right now."

"Not according to Miss Chambers. She has never seen it there, and she thinks it unlikely that such a picture should appeal to my aunt's taste."

This speech caused Barbara to look at him very hard. "Oh, indeed!" she said. "And who, may I ask, is Miss Chambers?"

"She is my aunt's companion," said John. He spoke the words self-consciously and had hard work to repress a blush. Yet why should he feel self-conscious about speaking of Claudia? There had been nothing in their relations that Barbara or anyone else could object to. Still, he found himself reluctant to elaborate on his single, bald statement of fact. But a single, bald statement of fact did not satisfy Barbara, who went on looking at him with narrowed eyes and suspicious mien.

"So your aunt thinks it necessary to have a companion, does she? That is putting on airs with a vengeance! I suppose this Miss Chambers is some poor, dried-out old maid too stupid to get her living any other way?"

John thought to himself that no description could have been more unlike Claudia. The thought of calling such a vibrantly lovely young lady a "poor, dried-out old maid" was enough to make him laugh out loud. "No, I wouldn't say that," he said, with as straight a face as he could muster. "For one thing, Miss Chambers seems not stupid at all, but on the contrary quite astute. My aunt appears to think highly of her judgment, at any rate. She has deputed to her the job of inspecting and approving the repairs that are pending on the estate."

"Indeed!" said Barbara. She meditated a moment, still looking at John very hard. "I suppose you will find it tiresome driving an elderly spinster about the estate?"

"I hope I should do my duty by her, no matter how elderly she might be," said John, hiding a smile. But either he did not hide it well enough or the ambiguity of his statement had made Barbara suspicious. She pounced on him immediately.

"Rexford, you are being very evasive. Just how old *is* this Miss Chambers?"

"As to that, Barbara, I have no way of knowing. But if I had to guess, I should say she is a few years younger than yourself."

"Younger than me?" exclaimed Barbara, looking deeply displeased. "Why, she must be a mere babe then! *I* am only two and twenty, after all."

John, who knew her age to be at least two years older than this, preserved a discreet silence. Barbara, meanwhile, went on with her musings. "You say she is young and somewhat clever, Rexford. I suppose, then, that she is very plain? Clever girls are so often plain, I have observed."

"I wouldn't exactly call her plain," said John cautiously.

"But of course she is not a *pretty* girl, is she? She could hardly be very pretty, or she would not have been reduced to taking a position as a hired companion."

Pinned down in this manner, John felt he had no choice but to speak the truth. "As to that, I could not say. But I thought her a very pretty girl."

"Who's a pretty girl?" said Sir Lucas, overhearing this last statement. "You know I am always ready to make the acquaintance of a pretty girl, Rexford. I beg you will introduce me to this paragon!"

"We were speaking of my aunt's companion, Miss Chambers," said John shortly. "And I doubt I shall have any opportunity to introduce you to her, Sir Lucas. As far as I know, my aunt does not mean to go into society while she is here, and so there is little chance you will meet Miss Chambers unless you go to Rexford Park."

A wicked smile appeared on Sir Lucas's handsome face. "Well, if Mohammed will not go to the mountain, then the mountain must go to Mohammed," he said. "I hope you won't resent it, Rexford, but now I think of it, I believe it is really my duty to call upon your aunt and welcome her to the neighborhood."

"Suit yourself," said John with a shrug. "I've already said I hold no grudge against my aunt. You may certainly call on her if you like."

He spoke in an indifferent voice, but inside he was feeling a good deal less indifferent. The idea of Sir Lucas and Claudia meeting was a disturbing one. Even if Sir Lucas's goal was merely a harmless flirtation—and John knew Sir Lucas well enough to be sure he would not be satisfied with a harmless flirtation if there was a chance of its becoming something more—it was still a disturbing idea. He scowled at Sir Lucas as the latter smiled at him sweetly. "Many thanks, Rexford. Of course I could not be easy in my mind if I knew it would displease you to call on Lady Rexford."

"Oh, certainly," said John ironically. He waited till Sir Lucas had moved out of earshot; then he spoke his real thoughts. "Of all the insufferable mountebanks!"

Barbara made no reply to this speech. It was apparent that her thoughts were still absorbed by John's earlier remarks. "So Miss Chambers is a young and pretty girl. A young and pretty and _clever_ girl. Aye, I've no doubt that she's clever! As clever as her mistress, I'll warrant, and quite as unprincipled."

John was by now thoroughly tired of the whole subject. He spoke with emphasis. "I've told you that I dislike hearing you abuse my aunt, Barbara. If you cannot do otherwise, at least pay me the compliment of not doing it while I am within hearing."

"That's all very well," retorted Barbara, with a flash of anger in her eyes. "But you cannot expect me to sit silent while a couple of unprincipled women make a fool of you, Rexford. This Miss Chambers, now—she seems to have wormed her way wonderfully into your confidence, considering you have only met her once."

John was by this time so irritated that he spoke the truth quite regardless of possible consequences. "As a matter of fact, I have met her more than once," he said. "I spoke with her yesterday as well as today."

"Oh, yes?" demanded Barbara on a rising note. "And what did you speak about during these meetings?"

"About a great many things, Barbara, but none that would interest you. Today we chiefly spoke about the staff at Rexford Park and about when would be most convenient to make a tour of inspection of the estate. We are engaged to go out driving the day after tomorrow."

We'd Like to Invite You to Subscribe to Zebra's Regency Romance Book Club and Give You a Gift of 4 Free Books as Your Introduction! (Worth $19.96!)

If you're a Regency lover, imagine the joy of getting 4 FREE Zebra Regency Romances and then the chance to have the lovely stories delivered to your home each month at the lowest prices available! Well, that's our offer to you and here's how you benefit by becoming a Regency Romance subscriber:

- 4 FREE Introductory Regency Romances are delivered to your doorst
- 4 BRAND NEW Regencies are then delivered each month (usually befor they're available in bookstores)
- Subscribers save almost $4.00 every month
- Home delivery is always FREE
- You also receive a FREE monthly newsletter, *Zebra/Pinnacle Romanc News* which features author profiles, contests, subscriber benefits, bo previews and more
- No risks or obligations...in other words you can cancel whenever you wish with no questions asked

Join the thousands of readers who enjoy the savings and convenience offered to Regency Romance subscribers. After your initial introductory shipment, you receive 4 brand-new Zebra Regency Romances each month to examine for 10 days. Then, if you decide to keep the books, you'll pay the preferred subscriber's price of just $4.00 per title. That's only $16.00 for all 4 books and there's never an extra charge for shipping and handling.

It's a no-lose proposition, so return the FREE BOOK CERTIFICATE today!

Say Yes to 4 Free Books!
Complete and return the order card to receive this
$19.96 value, *ABSOLUTELY FREE!*

If the certificate is missing below, write to:
Zebra Home Subscription Service, Inc.,
P.O. Box 5214, Clifton, New Jersey 07015-5214
or call TOLL-FREE 1-888-345-BOOK
Visit our website at www.kensingtonbooks.com.

FREE BOOK CERTIFICATE

YES! Please rush me 4 Zebra Regency Romances without cost or obligation. I understand that each month thereafter I will be able to preview 4 brand-new Regency Romances FREE for 10 days. Then, if I should decide to keep them, I will pay the money-saving preferred subscriber's price of just $16.00 for all 4...that's a savings of almost $4 off the publisher's price with no additional charge for shipping and handling. I may return any shipment within 10 days and owe nothing, and I may cancel this subscription at any time. My 4 FREE books will be mine to keep in any case.

Name _____

Address _____ Apt. _____

City _____ State _____ Zip _____

Telephone ( ) _____

Signature _____ RN040A
(If under 18, parent or guardian must sign.)

Terms and prices subject to change. Orders subject to acceptance by Zebra Home Subscription Service, Inc. Offer valid in U.S. only.

PLACE
STAMP
HERE

‖‖₁₁‖₁₁‖‖₁₁₁‖₁‖₁₁‖₁₁‖₁₁‖₁₁‖₁‖‖₁₁‖₁₁‖₁‖₁₁₁‖‖₁₁‖

REGENCY ROMANCE BOOK CLUB
Zebra Home Subscription Service, Inc.
P.O. Box 5214
Clifton NJ 07015-5214

"Indeed!" said Barbara, her eyes snapping. "Well, I forbid you to do any such thing, Rexford."

John looked at her in amazement. "You forbid it?" he said. "What makes you think you have the right to forbid me to do anything, Barbara? I think you forget yourself."

Barbara's already red cheeks grew redder at these words. When she spoke again, her voice was calmer, but it was obvious she was struggling to control her temper. "And I think you have forgotten all that has passed between us, Rexford. We have, if I mistake not, an understanding, and that understanding certainly entitles me to express my wishes. It is my wish that you have nothing further to do with this Miss Chambers."

"I'm sorry, Barbara, but that cannot be. Indeed, I think you are being unreasonable to request it. It is necessary that I meet with Miss Chambers, seeing that she is my aunt's delegated authority."

At these words, Barbara's temper broke completely. "Well, then, go on and meet with her! Since my wishes mean nothing to you, go and do what you like. It's obvious you prefer Miss Chambers's company to mine—"

"I didn't say I preferred her company to yours," protested John.

"Oh, yes. You've made it perfectly clear, my lord. And that being the case, you needn't bother calling *here* anymore. Go call on Miss Chambers instead. Call on her tomorrow, if you like. I'm sure *I* have no objection."

John stared at her a moment, then got to his feet. "Thank you. I believe I will," he said and left the drawing room abruptly.

Ten

Claudia came away from her interview with John feeling very well pleased with herself.

She felt very well pleased with him as well. It had been unexpectedly easy convincing him to talk with Mrs. Fry, and her only concern now was whether such a talk would do any good.

"Of course we cannot count on his influence having any effect," she warned Lady Rexford, having recounted the substance of her conversation with John. "It will not do to get our hopes too high. When four o'clock comes around, Mrs. Fry may very well try to serve us dinner again."

"I declare I almost don't care if she does," said Lady Rexford. She had been in a euphoric mood ever since her meeting with John, and she laughed aloud now with sheer delight. "I'm just so pleased that I've got this business of meeting Master John over with. And to have it turn out so well, too! I was in a regular quake beforehand, supposing he'd be terribly stiff and toplofty, but nothing could have been further from the case. Did you not think him very amiable, my dear?"

"He *seemed* amiable," said Claudia cautiously. "But it is hard to be sure what he is really like on such short acquaintance. However, I was pleased to see him behave so properly toward you, ma'am."

"He did behave well, didn't he? Now that it's over, I tell you truly that I did not expect him even to be civil, let alone bringing me flowers and paying me compliments and making apologies for the way he behaved before. It fair took my breath away—that I can tell you. And I owe it all to you." Laughing once more, Lady Rexford enveloped Claudia in an exultant hug. "I know full well that things wouldn't have gone half so smooth if you hadn't met Master John first and prepared the ground for me, so to speak. I never did a better day's work than the day I hired you, and that's a fact."

"Well, it is very kind of you to say so, ma'am," said Claudia, laughing also and returning the hug. "But you know it remains to be seen if Lord Rexford's good conduct will last."

"Oh, it'll last," said Lady Rexford confidently. "I'm sure it'll last. We got on like a house afire—didn't you notice? I found myself forgetting he was Master John and treating him just like he was one of us."

"Yes, I noticed," said Claudia. She hesitated, then went on, choosing her words with care. "Indeed, ma'am, I did not like to see you behave *quite* so freely with Lord Rexford. He was very friendly and polite this afternoon, to be sure, but remember that not so long ago he was your enemy. It would not hurt to hold him in reserve until we are sure he means to behave."

Lady Rexford waved aside the idea of such cautious conduct, however. "Oh, I don't think we need trouble ourselves about that, my dear. I'm sure Master John means to behave himself now. Why, only consider this business of his talking to Mrs. Fry for us! Wouldn't you say that proves he's friendly and well disposed?"

"It would *seem* to prove it," said the cautious Claudia. "But the proof of the pudding is in the eating, you know—and until we know if our pudding will be served at four or six o'clock tonight, we will not know if Master John's talk was of any use!"

It seemed to have been of use. Dinner was announced at six o'clock and was rather better cooked and served than on the previous evening. And though Mrs. Fry's mien could hardly have been described as friendly, she did obey those orders that

Claudia and Lady Rexford saw fit to issue her that evening.
It was, as Claudia acknowledged afterward, a powerful indication of John's goodwill and influence.

"I wish I could thank him," she reflected to herself as she
lay in bed that night. "I am afraid I was rather cool with him
this afternoon and did not show myself so grateful as I ought
to have done. But I will be seeing him the day after tomorrow,
at least, so I can thank him then. I wish I had agreed to go
out driving with him tomorrow so I might thank him the
sooner."

Claudia was thus both surprised and pleased when John's
arrival was announced the following afternoon. She hurried
down to the drawing room, not even pausing to relay the news
to Lady Rexford first.

"Oh, my lord, I did not expect to see you until tomorrow!"
she exclaimed. "That is when we were engaged to go out looking at the property, was it not? I was sure we had agreed on
tomorrow and not today."

"Oh, yes, it was tomorrow we had agreed on," said John.
He had risen to his feet as she came into the room, and now
he stood looking down at her.

It struck Claudia that his manner was rather odd. But she
was too pleased at having an opportunity to express her gratitude to spend much time speculating about the oddness of
John's behavior.

"Well, I am very glad you called anyway, my lord," she
said, extending her hand to him with a smile. "I wanted to
thank you for talking with Mrs. Fry yesterday. Your words
seem to have worked wonders. I cannot tell you how grateful
I am for your intercession, and Lady Rexford is very grateful,
too."

John looked down at her outstretched hand. At last he took
it in his and bowed over it. "You're very welcome, Miss Chambers," he said. "I'm glad I could be of service to you and my
aunt."

He spoke stiffly, and Claudia observed that he seemed to

have trouble looking her in the eye. Again she thought this odd, but she supposed he was merely preoccupied with other affairs. "I suppose you would like to see your aunt," she said encouragingly. "Let me go upstairs and tell Lady Rexford you are here. She will be glad to see you, I know. Won't you please be seated?"

"Yes, thank you," he said, but made no move to take a chair. Claudia, shaking her head inwardly, hurried upstairs to tell Lady Rexford that her nephew had come to call.

As she had anticipated, Lady Rexford was delighted by the news. "I'll see him, and with pleasure," she declared. "Just let Hettie tidy my hair a bit, and I'll be right down. Why do you suppose he came calling again so soon, Miss Chambers? I know you said you'd made arrangements to look at the property with him, but I thought that wasn't until tomorrow?"

"Yes, it was tomorrow," said Claudia. "I don't know why he called today. It seems to me, however, that his manner is rather odd. We had both better be on our guard until we learn what this is all about."

But when they joined John in the drawing room, they found him as friendly and eager to please as on the previous afternoon. Indeed, if anything, he seemed even more eager to please. Before an hour had gone by he was laughing and joking with Lady Rexford as if they had been lifelong acquaintances. And though his manner toward Claudia was slightly more reserved, he was perfectly friendly. But his friendliness underwent a slight check when a second caller was announced.

"Sir Lucas Davenport," intoned the butler, bowing low as he ushered that gentleman into the room.

Claudia looked wonderingly at Sir Lucas. He made a strange and unlikely-looking figure as he minced into the room with his auburn forelock waving and a complacent smirk on his handsome face. Claudia recognized his towering shirt points, bulky neckcloth, and pinched and padded topcoat as being of the very highest and most radical kick of gentlemen's fashion. This recognition would have pleased Sir Lucas, but he would have been less pleased by Claudia's accompanying thought—namely, that he looked rather old to be dressed in such an extreme fashion. But fortunately her thoughts were unguessed by Sir Lucas, and so he smirked around the drawing room with perfect self-possession.

"Well, well," he said as his eyes fell upon John. "I did not expect to find you here today, Rexford. But your presence is quite fortuitous. I had feared I must introduce myself to the ladies—a sad deviation from proper etiquette, you know. But now you can perform the introductions for me."

Claudia observed that John looked displeased by this speech. However, he bowed and said shortly, "Lady Rexford, Miss Chambers, allow me to introduce Sir Lucas Davenport. Sir Lucas, this is my aunt Lady Rexford, and this is Miss Chambers."

Sir Lucas acknowledged his introduction to Lady Rexford with a dramatic, "My lady!" accompanied by a sweeping bow. Claudia he likewise acknowledged with a bow, but there was a wolfish gleam in his gray eyes as he surveyed her. "So this is Miss Chambers!" he said. "I am very pleased to make your acquaintance, my dear."

Both Claudia and Lady Rexford murmured that they were pleased to make his acquaintance, too, but neither could guess who he was or why he should be calling on them. Sir Lucas himself was no help in this regard. He had disregarded the usual formalities of visiting and was now engaged in paying both ladies fulsome compliments. It was John who came to their rescue. "Sir Lucas owns a property in the neighborhood not far from here," he told Claudia and Lady Rexford. "I happened to meet him yesterday at the home of a mutual friend, and when I mentioned you were visiting Rexford Park, he declared his intention of calling upon you."

"And I am very glad I did," said Sir Lucas, his eyes drifting toward Claudia once more. "Dear Lady Rexford, allow me to welcome you to the neighborhood. And you, too, Miss Chambers. If there is anything I can do for either of you while you are here, I beg you will let me know of it."

"That is very kind of you, Sir Lucas," said Lady Rexford. She spoke in her best grande dame manner, raising her quizzing glass to her eye and surveying Sir Lucas with a calm, critical gaze.

Claudia was relieved to see that she did not mean to gather Sir Lucas to her bosom as she had done with her nephew. It was, in Claudia's reckoning, a risky enough business to trust John. To trust an unknown Sir Lucas besides would be, she felt, foolhardy in the extreme. Still, Sir Lucas seemed a pleasant, polite gentleman. Claudia thought it only right to thank him for her share of the compliment.

"Yes, Sir Lucas, you are very kind," she said with a smile. "I trust Lady Rexford and I will have no need of your assistance, but it is good of you to offer it."

To her surprise, John immediately agreed with this speech. "Indeed, I trust you will have no use for Sir Lucas's services, Miss Chambers," he said. "Please remember that Lady Rexford is my aunt. Any assistance that either of you might require would more properly come from me."

Claudia stared at him in amazement. Sir Lucas merely smiled. "I am sure your present devotion to your aunt is very commendable, Rexford," he drawled. "But perhaps Miss Chambers is remembering—as I am—a time not so very distant when you were not *quite* so dutiful a nephew."

Seeing that this remark had deprived John of speech, Claudia hurried to fill the breach. "Indeed, Sir Lucas, Lady Rexford and I are very glad you have called," she said. "It is a pleasure to make the acquaintance of our neighbors."

"The pleasure is all mine," returned Sir Lucas, looking her up and down with bold-eyed admiration. "And I would obtain even greater pleasure from furthering the acquaintance. Would you and Lady Rexford care to accompany me to an assembly at our local village rooms next week? I would that I could offer you something better in the way of society, but unless one of the neighbors chooses to give a party, we have little besides the weekly assemblies at Lockbridge to look forward to."

"Why, I don't know," said Claudia, surprised by this proposal. "I don't believe Lady Rexford and I had planned to do much socializing while we are in Yorkshire, Sir Lucas."

Lady Rexford supported this statement, albeit in a wistful voice. "I'm sure your invitation sounds very diverting, Sir Lucas. But I think we must decline it all the same. As Miss Chambers said, we did not plan to do any socializing while we are here."

"Well, if you ever change your mind, feel free to call on me as an escort," said Sir Lucas. He remained a little longer, talking on inconsequential subjects, but finally got up to take his leave. "It was charming meeting you both—and I must say, I was glad to get an opportunity to see Rexford Park again. It looks as magnificent as ever, though I see the Rexford Rembrandt no longer hangs in its old place." His eyes rested innocently on John. "Rexford was saying something about that yesterday, as I recall. Something about your having taken it to London, Lady Rexford."

"I said I supposed the painting must be in storage somewhere," said John, scowling at him. "The suggestion that it had been taken to London was not put forward by me if you will take the trouble to recall the conversation properly, Sir Lucas."

"Ah, yes, it was Miss Brock who suggested it, wasn't it? Well, I suppose the fair Barbara would naturally have a stake in wishing to keep the treasures of Rexford Park together."

"Who is Miss Brock?" said Lady Rexford, looking lost. "And what's this about a painting?"

Rather reluctantly, John explained about the missing Rembrandt. "I mentioned something about it to Miss Chambers when I called the other day," he added, looking at Claudia.

"As for Barbara Brock, she is one of our local belles," put in Sir Lucas. "I would suppose Lord Rexford would have mentioned her, too, when he was calling here, Miss Chambers. Oh, did he not? Well, well, that is very surprising, considering the extent of the friendship between him and Miss Brock." He threw John a malicious smile. "All of us in the neighborhood have been expecting the news of their engagement any time these past five years."

Claudia observed that John did not deny this speech, but merely brushed it aside with an impatient gesture. "At any rate, after thinking it over, I have come to the conclusion that the Rembrandt must still be somewhere here at Rexford Park," he said. "It seems inconceivable that my uncle would have taken it with him to London. You don't recall seeing it there, do you, Lady Rexford?"

Lady Rexford shook her head vigorously. "Not if it's like what you described: 'A small, dark picture of an elderly woman.' No, I'm sure there's no such picture in our London house. I'd have noticed it if there was, for Rexford let me furnish the place new after we were married. I did away with a lot of the old paintings—dingy old things they were—and bought some new ones that had a little life and color to them. And Rexford never made any objection when I bundled up all the castoffs and sold them to a secondhand dealer."

"Well, that seems to settle that," said Sir Lucas. He went on to take his leave of the party with a promise to call again in the near future and a last, languishing look at Claudia.

"What a very curious man," observed Lady Rexford as soon as the door closed behind Sir Lucas. "I suppose it was kind of him to call on us, but just the same I can't say that I was much taken with him. For all his bowing and scraping and pretty compliments, I should say he was a troublemaker."

"He *is* a troublemaker," said John forcefully. Both ladies looked at him in surprise. He gave them a rueful smile. "However, I fear I am slightly prejudiced as regards Sir Lucas. I have never cared for him from the time I first made his acquaintance years ago. And the feeling appears to be mutual. At any rate, he takes pleasure in needling me whenever he can. Some of his needling is on the mark, I'll admit, but the rest is completely off target. His comments about the Rembrandt, for instance. I assure you I never said or implied you were responsible for its disappearance, ma'am."

"Oh, I don't doubt you, my lord," Lady Rexford assured him. "It's easy to see Sir Lucas was merely trying to stir up trouble." With a mischievous smile, she added, "I notice, however, that you don't deny his accusations concerning this Miss Brock! Ought we to congratulate you, my lord?"

Claudia thought John looked almost ludicrously dismayed by this speech. "Oh, no, nothing of that sort," he said hurriedly. "Miss Brock and I are friends, nothing more." He glanced at Claudia, then away again.

Lady Rexford shook her head. "Well, all I can say is that if you do ever mean to be more than friends with this Miss Brock, then mind you don't keep her waiting too long for a proposal. If she's the belle Sir Lucas says she is, she's probably got plenty of other suitors."

"Dozens of other suitors," said John, still looking at Claudia.

"There you are, then," said Lady Rexford triumphantly. "You mustn't dawdle, or you'll find yourself cut out."

John thanked her for this advice, but gave no indication whether he meant to follow it. Instead he began talking about leaving. "I've already stayed far longer than is decent. It's after five now, almost time for you and Miss Chambers to be thinking of your dinners."

"Aye, that it is," said Lady Rexford, looking at the clock. "However, that's no reason for you to go rushing off, my lord. Why don't you stay and take dinner with us? Miss Chambers and I would enjoy the company, wouldn't we, Miss Chambers?"

"Certainly," said Claudia. She was a little provoked by the way John had snubbed her that afternoon, but she was determined not to show it. After all, his manners toward Lady Rexford were the chief thing, and these could scarcely have been improved on. She was as pleased as her employer when John declared himself quite willing to stay to dinner, and she smiled upon him graciously as she went to relay the order to the cook.

When dinner was announced, John rose and gave his right arm to his aunt. After a brief hesitation, he offered his other arm to Claudia. "If you will, Miss Chambers?" he said.

"Thank you, my lord," said Claudia, accepting the arm with a cool smile. She surveyed his face covertly as he escorted her and Lady Rexford into the dining room and seated them at the table. His expression was impassive, even a little forbidding, but it changed to one of amazement when he took the first sip from his wineglass.

"Good God!" he exclaimed, lifting his goblet to survey the ruby fluid within. "What is this? Surely it's not claret?"

Lady Rexford laughed delightedly. "No, it's Burgundy, my lord—some Chambertin your uncle laid down. A very fair vintage, isn't it?"

"Very fair indeed," said John, taking another, longer drink. He shook his head in wonderment. "If this is Burgundy, then all I can say is that I've never tasted Burgundy before. This is more like the nectar of the gods."

"Aye, it's something out of the ordinary," agreed Lady Rexford. "Miss Chambers found it down cellar the other day, and we've been enjoying it every night at dinner." She looked at John a trifle guiltily. "I hope you don't mind, my lord. Now I think of it, it's your wine as much as mine, the same as everything else in the house. And it wouldn't do for us to drink all of it. I'll give orders that the rest of the Chambertin isn't to be touched."

"You needn't do that," said John quickly. "As you say, it's your wine as much as mine. Indeed, I have no claim at all to it at the moment. And if you put off drinking it until I do have a claim to it, it might be past its peak." He looked wistfully down at his glass. "I must say, however, that I envy you the duty of drinking it! No duty could ever be sweeter, I am sure."

"You're right there," agreed Lady Rexford. "But still, I can't like depriving you of your share of it, my lord. I tell you what: Why don't we save the Chambertin for those evenings we're together? That way, we'd each get our share, and everything would be square and aboveboard. Of course it would mean your dining with us a great deal," she added rather dubiously. "Perhaps you'd rather just take half the bottles and be done with it."

John looked at her, then at Claudia. An odd little smile appeared on his lips. "No, I like your first idea best, ma'am," he said. "I will be very happy to dine with you whenever you like."

This arrangement being equally agreeable to Lady Rexford, the matter was solemnized by a formal toast. "To the vineyards of Chambertin and an equal sharing of their bounty," declared John, lifting his wineglass on high.

"I'll drink to that," said Lady Rexford cheerily, raising her wineglass likewise.

"And I," said Claudia. She was aware of John's eyes upon her as she took a sip from her wineglass. He took a drink from his own glass, then lifted it once more.

"Now we must drink to Miss Chambers and her intrepidity in discovering the wine," he said. "I propose to you Miss Chambers!"

Claudia was embarrassed by this tribute, but Lady Rexford endorsed it enthusiastically. "To Miss Chambers!" she said, smiling at Claudia. "Bless you, my dear, and you needn't look so shy. I'm sure you deserve it, and more besides."

"I am sure she does," agreed John, regarding her with quizzical dark eyes.

Claudia was glad when his attention was diverted to the fish course, which a footman had just presented to him with a bow. The fish course was succeeded by a leg of lamb with peas and carrots, a raised rabbit pie, and some turkey poults with eggs.

Throughout the meal, John and Lady Rexford laughed and chatted and addressed each other like old friends. The Chambertin flowed so copiously that a second bottle had to be opened, and it was during this second bottle that the subject of the village assemblies once more arose.

"I used to be a great one for dancing when I was younger," said Lady Rexford wistfully. "Even now, there's nothing I love more than a party. But I suppose these assemblies really aren't the thing for someone in my position."

John, who was in the midst of refilling Claudia's wineglass against her earnest protestations, paused to regard his aunt with surprise. "Why should you say so?" he asked. "A great many of the gentry hereabouts attend the Lockbridge assemblies. Of course they attract a somewhat mixed crowd, but I for one should consider them unexceptionable."

Lady Rexford flushed. "I don't mean they're exceptionable in any way, my lord! No, indeed. It was my own position I was talking about. You know, none better, that I wasn't born to my present station in life, and I'm sure there're those who would criticize me if I made so bold as to show my face at a public assembly. No, don't protest, my lord. You know it's so, and there's naught to be done about it."

"I suppose there might be those who would criticize," acknowledged John. "But I think the majority of people hereabouts would be glad to welcome you to the neighborhood if you went the right way about it."

"What way is that?" said Lady Rexford, looking incredulous. "You don't think I should accept Sir Lucas's invitation, do you?"

John vetoed this suggestion forcefully, but with a hint of abstraction in his manner. "A private party would probably be better than a public assembly as far as making you known to the right people," he said. "In fact . . . I don't suppose you'd be interested in giving a party of your own?"

Both Claudia and Lady Rexford looked at him in surprise. "A party of my own?" repeated Lady Rexford. "You mean I should give a party here at Rexford Park?"

"Not if you did not want to, of course," said John. "But

you must know that at one time it was the custom to hold a fete at Rexford Park every summer. Everyone was invited—the tenants, the villagers, and all the neighboring gentry."

"Indeed?" said Lady Rexford with amazement. "These fetes of yours must have been very large affairs, my lord!"

"Yes, we used regularly to entertain five or six hundred people. Of course it has been some years since the custom was discontinued. But even now people still talk about how much they enjoyed the Rexford Park fetes and how much they would like to see us hold another one. If you cared to go to so much trouble, nothing could more surely impress the neighbors in your favor. But of course it would be a great deal of bother and a great deal of expense, too."

"I don't care for that," said Lady Rexford. "But to give a party for five or six hundred people! I can't imagine how one would set about it."

"Mrs. Fry could help you, I'm sure. She has supervised many such parties in the past, and I expect she knows exactly how everything ought to be managed. You could probably leave the whole business in her hands if you wanted to."

The notion of leaving everything in Mrs. Fry's hands clearly did not set well with Lady Rexford. "No, indeed!" she said emphatically. "If I'm to hold a party, I should prefer to plan out the details myself. All I need to know is what is usual at these fetes of yours. Is there dancing?"

"Yes, but nothing very formal. Country dances mainly, with perhaps a cotillion or two for the fashionable folk. Usually there are two tents for dancing: one for the gentry and one for the farmers and villagers."

"I see, I see," nodded Lady Rexford, making a mental note. "And a sit-down supper after the dancing, I suppose—or would a running supper be better? Naturally one would have refreshments all through the party, but I would not like to be thought shabby."

Claudia, who had listened in consternation as these plans were tossed back and forth, thought it time to intervene. "Dear

Lady Rexford, I do not think you have considered how much time and expense such a party would entail," she said. "Remember you are a stranger in the neighborhood. Why should you give a party for hundreds of people you have never met?"

"Why, in order to meet them, of course, Miss Chambers," said John as Lady Rexford looked doubtful. "I would have thought that leaped to the eye!"

"Yes, of course *that* leaps to the eye. But I still question whether Lady Rexford has a duty to entertain five or six hundred perfect strangers," said Claudia, eyeing him with resentment. "You must know her health is very delicate." Looking significantly at Lady Rexford, she added, "Indeed, ma'am, I think you have forgotten what a *strain* you find it to meet *strangers*. I am afraid you would find the whole business an *ordeal* rather than a *pleasure*."

"You have forgotten that Lady Rexford possesses a perfectly good nephew to help her bear the *strain* of the *ordeal*," returned John in mocking imitation of her own accents. "I would make sure she was properly introduced to people and did not stand for too long at a time."

Claudia ignored him and kept her eyes fixed on Lady Rexford. "Indeed, ma'am, are you certain you wish to undertake such a laborsome task just now?" she said. "I cannot think it at all necessary."

Lady Rexford looked at her, then at John. He gave her an encouraging smile. "Miss Chambers is quite right in saying it is not necessary, ma'am," he said. "But if you would like to do it, you may count on me to lend my assistance."

Lady Rexford drew a deep breath. "I believe I'll do it," she said. "That's to say, I *shall* do it. I have quite made up my mind—with all due apologies to you, Miss Chambers." She looked apologetically at Claudia. "You are quite right in saying it will be a great deal of work, but I think—I am sure—that I am equal to it."

"Very well," said Claudia. She spoke in a resigned voice, but privately resolved to argue the case further as soon as she and Lady Rexford were alone. She waited with impatience for John to take his leave.

He was very slow about doing this, however. Even after dinner was over he remained a considerable time, chatting freely with Lady Rexford and somewhat less freely with Claudia. But at last he rose to go.

"I'll show you to the door, my lord," said Claudia with the semblance of a polite smile.

John seemed to sense her offer was more than mere politeness. His face wore a wary look as he followed her into the hall.

"Have I done something amiss, Miss Chambers?" he asked. "It isn't this business about the fete, by any chance, is it?"

"Yes, it is," said Claudia. "Why are you so set on Lady Rexford giving a party, my lord? It seems odd to me that you should promote such a scheme."

John raised his eyebrows. "Do you think so? I assure you I was only trying to please my aunt, Miss Chambers. She seemed to like the idea, and I could not see any reason why she should not give a party if she wanted to."

"Perhaps *you* could see no reason!" retorted Claudia. "But I can see several reasons why she should not think of such a thing. I am afraid you persuaded her into it against her better judgment."

John looked at her keenly. "I think you mean I persuaded her into it against *your* better judgment, Miss Chambers," he said. "It seems to me you are the one who is really opposed to the idea."

"So I am," said Claudia warmly. "And so would you be, too, if you had Lady Rexford's best interests at heart."

John regarded her in silence for a long moment. "It may come as a surprise to you, Miss Chambers, but I think I do have my aunt's best interests at heart," he said. "What makes you think I do not?"

Claudia regarded him with skepticism. "Come, my lord. Your memory cannot be as short as all that!" she said. "Remember the conversation we had that first morning you called here. It did not seem to me then that you were so strongly concerned with your aunt's welfare!"

"No, I wasn't then, of course," agreed John. "It wasn't until you talked to me that I became convinced I hadn't been doing my aunt justice and swung round to your viewpoint."

This speech took Claudia's breath away. "You cannot be serious!" she said after a moment's silence.

"Indeed, I *am* serious," said John. "Why should you be so surprised that your arguments convinced me, Miss Chambers? You believed in them yourself, didn't you?"

"Yes, of course. But—"

Here Claudia paused, at a loss for words. A faint smile appeared on John's face. "But you didn't expect *me* to believe them," he said. "In fact, you expected me to cling to my own opinion in a perfectly pigheaded manner, with no regard for logic or justice."

"Yes," said Claudia baldly.

John laughed. "Well, it's easy to see you haven't a very high opinion of me, Miss Chambers," he said. "But I assure you that I am not so bad as you suppose. Indeed, I hope I may convince you that I am *not* so bad—and I only hope I may be as persuasive in my arguments as you are in yours."

Claudia looked at him, startled by something in his voice. He averted his eyes quickly, however, and began to speak again in a different voice—a voice quite ordinary and businesslike.

"I suppose I should be leaving now, but I shall see you tomorrow afternoon, Miss Chambers. We have still an engagement to look over the property tomorrow, have we not?"

"Yes, I suppose so," said Claudia, bewildered by this sudden change of subject. "But—"

"I shall come by for you tomorrow afternoon, then. Will two o'clock be suitable?"

"Two o'clock will do very well," said Claudia. "But—"

"Until two o'clock tomorrow, then, Miss Chambers. *Au revoir.*" With a suddenness that caught Claudia off guard, he took her hand in his, raised it to his lips and kissed it. *"Au revoir, Miss Chambers,"* he said again and strode away down the hall, leaving the bewildered Claudia staring after him.

Eleven

"He must be mad!" said Claudia.

She had reached this conclusion after a sleepless night spent puzzling over John's behavior. Truly, his behavior did seem wildly inconsistent. He had paid her scarcely any attention at dinner, speaking only to snub her and otherwise treating her as though she were of only perfunctory interest. Yet as soon as they were alone, he had suddenly paid her several bewildering compliments, hinted in a dark and mysterious fashion that he hoped to improve his acquaintance with her someday, and culminated matters by kissing her hand.

"Can it be that he means to get up a flirtation with me?" wondered Claudia as she reflected on these actions. "I haven't much experience with flirtations, but I wouldn't somehow have pictured Master John as a flirtatious sort of man. Not like Sir Lucas—*he* was a flirtatious man if you please! I felt quite uncomfortable every time he looked at me."

Claudia spent a little time reflecting disapprovingly on Sir Lucas's looks. But thoughts of Sir Lucas recalled to mind some of the things that gentleman had said or hinted about John, and this soon brought her thoughts back to their original subject.

"Sir Lucas spoke of his being engaged to some local girl—a local girl who's supposed to be a great beauty. Barbara Brock was the name, wasn't it? Yes, that was the name. John may have denied there was anything between him and this Miss

Brock, but he looked very self-conscious when he denied it. I daresay he does have an interest there. Well, it's nothing to me if he does, but I think it very bad of him to try to flirt with me if he is engaged, or nearly engaged, to another girl. But there, perhaps he wasn't trying to flirt with me at all. Perhaps he was merely trying to assure me that his intentions toward Lady Rexford were good. But then why did he kiss my hand? And why did he look at me that way—as though he thought me something very rare and wonderful? He must be mad!"

She repeated this conviction to Hettie and Lady Rexford over breakfast, but found neither of them inclined to agree with her. Hettie merely opined that Master John was "a deep 'un," while Lady Rexford, whose head was full of plans for the upcoming fete, laughed to scorn the idea that he could be mad and advised Claudia to think no more about his odd behavior.

"Depend on it, my dear. He is as sane as you or I. I wish you would turn your mind instead to the question of when we're going to give this party of ours. I can't decide what date would be best."

Claudia obediently bent her thoughts to this problem. But as soon as she and Lady Rexford had settled on the night of the next full moon, so as to make the drive home easier for the party guests, Claudia reverted once more to the subject of John.

"Upon my word, ma'am, I wish you would think twice about the idea of giving this party," she told Lady Rexford. "I don't trust Master John's motives one bit. Why should he be so friendly all at once? I asked him that very question, and he had the nerve to say it was all my doing! He said that I had quite convinced him with my arguments the other day and that he is now perfectly reconciled to your inheriting Rexford Park! Did you ever hear anything more unlikely?"

"Ah, my dear, you're much too modest," said Lady Rexford, giving her a fond smile. "Why shouldn't you have convinced him? I've seen you do many a thing just as clever in the time I've known you. I daresay it happened just as Master John said, and if that's the case, then I'm sure I'm much obliged to you. You're a treasure and no mistake."

"Yes, but—" began Claudia.

"No buts," said Lady Rexford firmly. "I'm convinced that Master John means to be friendly now and that we needn't worry ourselves about his doing us a disservice. So if you'll give your attention to this matter of the fete, my dear, I'll be very grateful. We've a hundred questions to settle before the invitations go out."

Claudia tried to give her attention to the fete, but even as she discussed music, dancing, and refreshments with Lady Rexford, she found her thoughts straying back to the subject of John. Today was the day she was to accompany him on a tour of the estate. How would he conduct himself during the drive? Would he be brusque and distant or embarrassingly warm and complimentary as he had been last night? Claudia decided that she would keep her own manner cool and businesslike so as not to be embarrassed however he might behave.

"I shall not let him fluster me this time," she vowed. "I must remember that this is a business meeting and conduct myself accordingly. Even if Master John is an attractive man— and he *is* attractive, even if he's not precisely handsome—it simply won't do to let my head be turned by his attentions."

John, meanwhile, was making a similar resolution. He had taken leave of Rexford Park and Claudia in a most giddy and exalted mood, but by the time he had reached the Gatehouse he had begun to chastise himself for his behavior.

"She must think me a lunatic or a fool," he told himself disgustedly. "And by God, I begin to think I must be one or the other. What the deuce did I mean by kissing her hand like that? Of course she's a pretty girl and a devilish taking one, too, but she's also my aunt's hired companion. And she's made it clear she hasn't much opinion of me. It can't be that I'm developing a *tendre* for her, can it?"

The thought was a disquieting one, but John told himself firmly that such could not be the case. It was merely that Barbara had put his back up, inspiring him to pay court to Claudia out of defiance. The fact that he had not once thought of Barbara while he was with Claudia rather discredited this theory, however, as did the exaltation he had felt as he touched his lips to her hand.

She really was an attractive girl—and a very principled one, too. Barbara had said that she was an adventuress selfishly actuated by motives of greed and self-interest. But John felt convinced that Barbara was mistaken. So far Claudia's attitude toward him had been more wary than encouraging, and she had demonstrated a most commendable loyalty toward her employer. Indeed, it seemed to him that Barbara had shown more greed and self-interest in her behavior than Claudia had done in hers.

"Perhaps it's just as well I broke with Barbara," he told himself. "I didn't plan on doing it, but the way she pushed me about this business with Miss Chambers was simply intolerable. No self-respecting man could have put up with such behavior. And I have no intention of sacrificing my self-respect for the privilege of marrying any woman even if she is niece to the Earl of Brockhurst! Yes, perhaps it's for the best that Barbara and I are through, but that doesn't mean I need rush myself into a love affair with the next decent-looking girl I meet. I must be on guard with Miss Chambers after this and treat her with no more than common civility."

Accordingly, he prepared himself to meet Claudia with caution and common civility. This did not prevent him from spending an inordinate amount of time on his toilette, however. His valet was astonished when he was requested to shave his master a second time in one day and to assist him in tying his neckcloth. But he concealed his gratification at these unusual requests and sent John off to Rexford Park in fine style.

Claudia was waiting for him there. John had just brought his curricle to a halt when she came hurrying out of the house. He greeted her in a cool, businesslike manner, but could not help thinking how pretty she looked in her dress and pelisse of bronze green with a fetching little matching hat perched atop her glossy chestnut head. She returned his greeting in a voice as cool as his own, however, and seemed as determined as he to keep things on a business footing.

John felt both relieved and disappointed. Of course it was better that there should be no personal complication between them. Undoubtedly it was better, but still he could not help feeling chagrined that Claudia should indicate her uninterest so plainly. In spite of himself he was piqued. He found himself casting frequent sideways looks at her profile as he drove along. "I thought we would look at the Home Farm and hot-houses first," he said. "Then we can go on to visit some of the tenants and perhaps some of the cottagers as well if we have time. Most of our cottages are in such terrible shape that a strong wind would blow them down."

"Perhaps we had better look at them first then," suggested Claudia, her eyes fixed perseveringly on the road ahead. "I should think it would make more sense to inspect first those things most needing repair."

"Just as you like," said John. He spoke calmly enough, but inwardly he was nettled. Of course it did not matter what part of the property they looked at first. Likewise, he was obliged to admit that it made sense to inspect first those things most needing repair. But it stung his pride that Claudia should have been the one to suggest it. He eyed her resentfully as he drove the curricle toward the huddle of cottages arranged around the margin of a distant field.

Claudia, however, seemed intent only on business. She swept the cottages with a keen, appraising glance as they approached, and she willingly accepted John's offer to show her through one of the dwellings.

"This is Mrs. Sparks," he said, introducing Claudia to a tiny, much wrinkled woman who was seated on the cottage door-step, calmly smoking a pipe. "Mrs. Sparks, this is Miss Chambers, an emissary of my aunt's. Do you mind if I show her about your cottage?"

Mrs. Sparks grinned, showing a set of hideously blackened teeth. "Help yourself, my lord," she said. " 'Tis little enough for t' young lady to see, I trow."

This was, alas, no more than the truth. Claudia looked wide-eyed around the single small room, which, with a lean-to adjoining the rear, comprised the cottage's interior. "Why, there isn't even glass in the windows!" she exclaimed.

"Nor ever has been that *I* can remember," volunteered Mrs. Sparks, taking another drag on her pipe. "I puts me old cloak over t' windows when t' weather turns cold. It keeps t' worst of t' wind and rain out, but it makes t' place mortal dark."

"I should think so!" said Claudia. Having looked around a little more, she politely thanked Mrs. Sparks for allowing her to inspect her home. Mrs. Sparks returned an amicable nod to these thanks and went on smoking her pipe as Claudia and John left the cottage. Once they were seated in the curricle again, Claudia said in a decided voice, "I shall certainly recommend that Lady Rexford have these cottages rebuilt. Why, I wouldn't think of sheltering pigs in such a place, let alone human beings!"

"It hasn't been within my power to make any major renovations on the estate," said John defensively. "I would have had those cottages pulled down a year ago, but without my aunt's consent it was impossible."

Claudia gave him a surprised look. "Oh, to be sure! I wasn't blaming you, my lord. Only it is terrible to think of people living in such squalor. We must do all we can to remedy the situation as quickly as possible."

John agreed in a reserved voice, but he could not help feeling more charitable toward Claudia for sharing his own opinions. He was still more in charity with her after their next call. This was to the home of a prosperous farmer,

Robert Burke, who was one of the principal tenants of the Rexford Park estate.

Claudia did not complain at being taken on an extensive tour of the farm by Mr. Burke. Nor did she betray anything but interest at the succession of fields, fences, and outbuildings that he showed her and John. She consented cheerfully to drink tea with his wife and daughters afterward, and her manners were so friendly and gracious that the Misses Burke begged her to visit again whenever she could.

"I should like to very much," Claudia told them with a smile. "And perhaps when I come again you will do me the honor to play for me on your pianoforte. Such a handsome instrument! I have been admiring it all the time we have been drinking our tea, and I am sure it must be well worth hearing."

"Aye, that it is, miss," said Mrs. Burke, swelling with pride. "We bought it not a year ago, and Emily and Clara are coming along nicely in their lessons." Lowering her voice, she added, "Robert thinks it a silly extravagance, but I'm determined my girls should be brought up like ladies."

She eyed Claudia rather anxiously after making this speech, obviously fearing her guest might laugh at or disapprove of her ambitions. Claudia responded sympathetically, however, causing Mrs. Burke to vow that her daughters should take her as a model of what a lady's manners ought to be.

"I'm sure I'm much obliged to you, ma'am," Claudia laughed, and took a friendly leave of all the Burkes. John made his own adieux, then silently accompanied her outside to the curricle.

Claudia did not seem to notice his silence. "They seem to be a most worthy family," she said in a musing voice. "I shall certainly recommend that Lady Rexford renew their lease. And if Mr. Burke wants to rent that other farm he was talking about, I see no reason why he should not be allowed to. Do you?"

"No, certainly not," said John. He meant to say no more, but could not resist adding a grudging compliment. "You conducted yourself very well back there, Miss Chambers. And at

Mrs. Sparks's cottage, too. I can see that my aunt is justified
in trusting you to handle her business."

Claudia shot him a quizzical look, but merely said, "Thank
you, my lord."

John nodded and relapsed into silence. To himself, however,
he acknowledged that he had been impressed by her tact and
discretion, as well as by her quick grasp of the essentials of
the business they were discussing. He would not have supposed a young lady could have shown so much acumen about
a subject that was obviously unfamiliar to her.

"She wouldn't make a bad bailiff with a little more training,"
he grudgingly admitted to himself. "Assuming it was the custom
to have lady bailiffs, that is!" The thought made him smile, but
the next moment the smile vanished from his face. A solitary
rider had just come into view, cantering along the lane that led
from the Burke farm to the manor house. And though John could
not be sure of the rider's identity at this distance, the horse she
was riding looked remarkably like Barbara Brock's favorite sor-
rel mare.

"But it can't be Barbara," he told himself incredulously.
"Why, the last time we spoke, she told me in no uncertain
terms that she was through with me. What would she be doing
here now?"

Nevertheless, the rider proved to be Barbara. She was splendidly clad in a trailing habit of blue cloth with a lace jabot at
her throat and a high-crowned cork hat atop her blond head.
She rode directly up to the curricle and reined in her mount,
directing a brief, hostile look at Claudia before smiling sweetly
at John. "Ah, Rexford, there you are," she said. "I knew you
must be somewhere hereabouts."

John did not return her smile. "I am surprised to see you
here, Miss Brock," he said. "Have you come to call on my
aunt? I believe she is at home this afternoon if you care to
pay your respects."

Barbara's face grew red, but whether with anger or embarrassment he could not guess. "I came to see you and not your

aunt, Rexford, as you must know," she said. "You mentioned you would be out looking at the property today—you and Miss Chambers." She threw another hostile look at Claudia. "Won't you introduce us, Rexford?"

John did so, albeit reluctantly. Claudia was regarding the newcomer with interest, and he felt sure she must be remembering Sir Lucas's insinuations about him and Barbara. "Miss Brock, this is Miss Chambers. Miss Chambers, this is Miss Brock. Her family owns a property not far from here."

Claudia acknowledged the introduction with a smile and a civil "How do you do, Miss Brock?"

To this greeting Barbara returned no answer, merely favoring Claudia with a stare before dismissing her with a contemptuous nod. "I thought you would enjoy having some company during your errand, Rexford," she said, addressing herself to him as though he were alone. "So I had Regina saddled up and came over to join you."

John was angered at her behavior, which was both rude toward Claudia and uncomfortably proprietary toward himself. He raised his eyebrows. "I must say I am surprised, Miss Brock," he said. "After our conversation yesterday, I would not have expected you to favor me and Rexford Park with your company."

This pointed speech failed to discompose Barbara. "You must know I was not in earnest yesterday, Rexford," she said with a laugh. "Let us say no more about it. Here I am, and here I mean to remain as long as you need me."

"But I don't need you," said John. The words came out more bluntly than he had intended, but still Barbara was not discomposed.

"It's not as though I have anything pressing to do today, Rexford. I would quite enjoy accompanying you and Miss Chambers." She flashed Claudia another look of dislike.

John was irritated, but it was clear that Barbara could not be dissuaded from accompanying them without some very plain speaking on his part. He was reluctant to undertake the necessary plain speaking in front of Claudia. Even though he had been trying all afternoon to convince himself that he cared nothing for Claudia or her opinions, he found himself anxious now to appear good in her eyes. Not for any personal reason, of course, as he assured himself. It was merely because he regretted that Barbara had been so rude to her and wished to spare her any additional unpleasantness. But this did not explain why he found himself resenting so deeply the addition of Barbara to their party.

John found himself resenting Barbara's presence more and more as the afternoon wore on. She talked incessantly, ignored Claudia completely, and addressed him with a familiarity that set his teeth on edge. When they stopped to visit the home of another of Rexford Park's principal tenants, she was patronizing to the farmer and his wife and openly critical of their possessions.

"Lace curtains!" she exclaimed, regarding these objects with shocked disapproval. "I should think muslin curtains would be good enough for persons of your station, ma'am. At the Towers, none of our tenants are allowed to have such extravagances. Mama and I feel that it is quite unfitting that the lower orders should be allowed to ape their betters."

"Happen that depends what you mean by your betters, miss," drawled the farmer's wife. She might have gone on to say something even more pointed had not Claudia taken her aside to praise the exquisite neatness of her kitchen garden. This pleased her so much that she insisted on presenting Claudia with a basket of asparagus and a large cabbage.

"I'll give you a piece of advice, my lord," the farmer's wife told John in a low voice as they were leaving. "If you're trying to make up your mind between them two gels, why, just you go and offer for that one." She nodded toward Claudia. "T' other's a handsome creature, I don't deny, but you'll have no peace if you marry her. My sister-in-law was just such another, and a sorry dance she led my poor brother. I've often thought he took the ague and died just to get away from her."

John was too taken aback by this advice to administer the snub that it undoubtedly merited. He merely wished the woman good day and followed Claudia and Barbara out to the curricle.

It was clearly undesirable to make any more calls while Barbara was a member of their party. Canvassing his options, John decided to spend the remainder of the afternoon on a tour of the Home Farm and the hothouses. Of course he and Claudia could not escape Barbara on this tour; nor could they escape the constant flow of advice and criticism that flowed from her lips as she accompanied them around the property. John found himself growing angrier and angrier as they went along. And he also found himself comparing Barbara's behavior with Claudia's, much to the former's disadvantage.

These thoughts were not apparent to Claudia, however. When John announced brusquely that they had seen enough for one day, her sensation was one of relief mingled with a faint regret.

"I'll wager he doesn't kiss my hand when he takes leave of me this time," she told herself as she bade him farewell at the doorstep of Rexford Park. Nor did he; but he assisted her down from the curricle very carefully and lingered a moment to speak to her even as Barbara was calling impatiently for him to hurry and come along.

"I'm sorry, Miss Chambers," he said in a low voice. "Forgive me if you can. Today has not gone quite as I planned it."

Claudia did not know exactly what to reply to this speech and so she thought it better not to allude to it at all. "Thank you for showing me around the property, my lord," she said instead. "I shall speak to Lady Rexford about the changes we spoke of and see about getting her approval."

"Yes . . . yes. I would be very grateful if you would do that." Claudia thought there was a trace of wistfulness in John's eyes as he looked down at her. "Well, good afternoon, Miss Chambers. Give my regards to my aunt if you please, and tell her I will soon wait upon her."

"Of course," said Claudia. With a smile and a bow to him and another to Barbara (who did not return it), she went into the house.

Twelve

The next few weeks went by swiftly for Claudia. She had not only her usual duties to keep her busy, but also the business of planning Lady Rexford's fete. Lady Rexford leaned on her as heavily in this matter as in all others, and if Claudia had not possessed a conscientious spirit, she might easily have ordered the party to suit herself rather than her mistress.

John was notably absent during this time. To be sure, he occasionally called to pay his respects to his aunt or to leave some offering of fruit or flowers, but Claudia generally managed to keep out of his way during these visits. She told herself that she had no desire to see him again. But this was not true, for she had in fact a strong and persistent desire to see him again. Yet her own common sense told her she was better off avoiding his company. He was, after all, the affianced husband of Barbara Brock, who was undoubtedly the most offensive, obnoxious, ill-natured woman she had ever met. And any man who could wish to marry such a woman must be himself seriously flawed in character.

"And he *is* flawed in character," Claudia reminded herself. "He has rough manners, a great deal of pride, and a hasty temper. I should know, for I got a taste of all three the first time he called here!"

Yet Claudia was obliged to admit that not only had John apologized for his behavior on that occasion, he had since then done his best to make amends for it. He obviously had some

redeeming qualities. Claudia almost wished he had not, for
then she would not have felt so bad about his being engaged
to Barbara Brock.

"However, it's no affair of mine," she told herself. "I'm sure
he can marry any girl he likes and welcome." This being the
case, Claudia determined to think no more on the subject of
John and to concentrate her efforts on the upcoming party.

There was certainly plenty to be done in this regard. Claudia
threw herself with enthusiasm into the work and so did the
other residents of Rexford Park, even Mrs. Fry. Reluctant she
might be to serve Lady Rexford, but her reluctance was out-
weighed by the prospect of resurrecting the traditional mid-
summer fete at Rexford Park. "Besides, it's Master John's
party quite as much as my Lady Rexford's," she told Claudia
triumphantly. "I hear he's been around to all the neighbors
telling them he'd be greatly pleased if they found themselves
able to come. A good thing, too, for if he hadn't, I doubt you'd
have got a single acceptance."

"Perhaps not," said Claudia shortly. She was irritated by the
mention of John's name and hurried to change the subject.
"Please tell the cook about the date and the menu we have
decided upon, Mrs. Fry. And let me know if any problems
develop. I'll be glad to lend my assistance if needed."

Mrs. Fry, however, intimated that she and the cook could
manage very well without Claudia's assistance. Claudia,
snubbed, returned to Lady Rexford, who was deep in an earnest
consultation with Hettie about her toilette for the great occasion.

"Hettie thinks I ought to wear black for the party, Miss
Chambers," she told Claudia sadly. "I had hoped I might wear
colors just this once—but she says not. What do you think?"

"I think you would make a better impression in black," said
Claudia, trying to be tactful. "Of course you can wear what
you like, ma'am, but Hettie is quite right in saying black would
be best."

Lady Rexford heaved a deep sigh. "Black it is then," she

said. "Still, I can't help thinking it dull to wear naught but black all the time. I wish I were a young thing like you, Miss Chambers. I'll wager *you* don't mean to wear black to the party!"

"I hadn't thought what I was to wear," said Claudia, knitting her brows. "I suppose I might wear my gold silk again. Only it seems a bit showy for the occasion."

"Not a bit of it," Lady Rexford declared. "But you mustn't wear your gold silk, Miss Chambers. Pretty as that is, it's only an afternoon dress, and you need something a good deal finer for an occasion like this. And I know just the thing," she continued, regarding Claudia's figure with a meditative eye. "I saw a picture of it in the last number of *Ackerman's.*"

"But I don't need another dress, ma'am," laughed Claudia. "I would think myself wickedly extravagant to buy another new dress after all the lovely ones you bought me in London."

Lady Rexford looked roguish. "Bless you, my dear. Who said anything about your buying it? I'll stand the expense of this dress, just as I did the others. And I won't consider myself wickedly extravagant either! I'm sure it's not extravagant to want to see a pretty girl suitably dressed. Just look at this dress here and see if you don't think it's the loveliest thing you ever saw."

Claudia looked at the elegant confection of lace and watered silk that Lady Rexford held up for her inspection. "Lovely, but hardly suitable," she said dismissively. "Remember, ma'am, I am your hired companion. It's not right that I should be so finely dressed."

"You may be my companion, but that's no excuse for you to look like a dowdy," Lady Rexford retorted. "I declare, it quite puts me out of patience to see such a pretty girl make so little of her looks. You let me buy this dress for you, Miss Chambers. It's an investment in your future, as you might say. No, you needn't laugh, for I assure you I'm quite in earnest. Wearing a dress like this, you're sure to catch some gentleman's eye—and if you play your cards right, you might even end by getting a proposal! I daresay you'd like being married a deal better than being a companion to an old woman like me."

"Indeed, I should not," said Claudia decidedly. "You must not think of getting me the dress on that account, ma'am. I cannot allow it."

Lady Rexford drew herself up to her full height of four feet ten. "Miss Chambers, are you questioning my authority?" she said sternly. "I am telling you that I mean to buy you this dress. And if you don't choose to wear it, you'll have no choice but to leave my employment."

Claudia regarded her in blank amazement, then burst into peals of laughter. "Oh, ma'am, that was very well done!" she said. "Almost I believed you meant it."

"I did mean it," said Lady Rexford, her stern manner abating not a whit. "If you feel you can't wear this dress as my companion, why then I'll fire you—that's all. Then you can wear it without any scruples!"

"That won't be necessary," said Claudia, choking back her laughter. "Of course I will wear the dress if you insist, ma'am. But if it results in anyone making me a proposal of marriage, I hope you will forgive me if I don't accept it! Indeed, I want no husband."

Lady Rexford smiled shrewdly. "Time enough to decide that when you see who's proposing," she said. "If you get any proposals you don't want, just you turn 'em down, Miss Chambers. I'm sure I turned down a dozen proposals before I accepted Lord Rexford."

This matter being decided, Lady Rexford lost no time in writing to her London dressmaker. "I've no opinion of provincial dressmakers, my dear," she told Claudia. "Better to send to London and have the business done right."

Done right it was, too, and in an incredibly short time. Hardly a week had elapsed before the dress, fitted to Claudia's measurements, was delivered by special messenger.

It came at a time when a host of last-minute details was

absorbing Claudia's attention. She had scarcely time to try the dress on, observe that the fit was perfect, and set it aside until the day of the fete.

That, too, came with astonishing rapidity. Before Claudia knew it, the great day had dawned—a day that seemed likely to fulfill their fondest hopes as regarded the weather. And likewise before Claudia knew it, it was afternoon and time to bathe, arrange her freshly washed hair, and put on the dress, which was patiently waiting for her in her wardrobe.

"Oh, dear," said Claudia weakly, gazing at her reflection in the mirror.

As might be expected, the dress that her mistress had bestowed on her with such a high hand was pink, Lady Rexford's favorite color. But to merely call it pink hardly did it justice. It was fashioned of watered silk shading from a pale apple blossom at the corsage to a deep rose at the hem of its heavily flounced and ruched skirt. The dress was further enriched with yards and yards of snowy lace that ornamented its pink silken splendor like frosting flourishes on a wedding cake. The dressmaker had included a circlet of pink silk roses to be worn in the hair, and the overall effect was both extravagant and ridiculously feminine. "Oh, dear," said Claudia again. "It's certainly a pretty dress, but I don't look at all like myself in it. I wonder if I dare wear it."

"You'd better, miss," said Hettie, who had been helping Claudia dress and arrange her hair. She paused to insert a hairpin, then continued in a sober voice. "It'd hurt Lucy's feelings something terrible if you didn't wear that dress tonight. She's set her heart on your making a fine appearance." In a lighter voice, she added, "And I must say, you do look pretty as a picture, miss. I shouldn't be surprised if Lucy's right and you haven't gentlemen falling in love with you left and right."

"I shouldn't think so," said Claudia. She was annoyed to find that John's face had popped into her head at Hettie's words. Of course he was almost the only gentleman she knew in the neighborhood apart from Sir Lucas, so perhaps it was not surprising that his image should have been summoned to mind. But Claudia was quite sure John would be very cool to her that evening, if he condescended to speak to her at all. Of his falling in love with her, she had no expectation. Her annoyance with herself was all the greater because she could not help feeling disappointed that this was the case.

The fete officially began at five o'clock, just as afternoon was giving way to evening. The sun was starting to slip toward the west, painting long shadows on the lawn and gardens and highlighting the preparations that had been made for the expected influx of guests. Two dancing pavilions had been erected—one for the country folk and a second, more elaborate structure for the gentry. Refreshments were available at both sites and also at the large tent where the country folk would take their supper. Supper for the gentry was to be served on the terrace, with dozens of little tables situated amid the flower beds and fountains. Claudia, who had supervised their placement, surveyed them with contentment as she accompanied Lady Rexford out onto the lawn.

"It all looks lovely, ma'am," she said. "And you couldn't have asked for a nicer day. The weather is perfect for an alfresco party."

"Yes, it is," agreed Lady Rexford. She was wearing a gown of black crepe over sarcenet, slightly softened with a fichu of white lace. A handsome turban of black crepe trimmed with black and white plumes crowned her head, and her quizzing glass hung on a gold chain around her neck. She twisted it nervously between her fingers as she looked around her. "Upon my word, I do hope everything goes well. I'm just a little nervous about greeting so many strangers. I hope Rexford gets here before people start to arrive."

"He already is here, ma'am," said a cheerful voice behind her. Both she and Claudia turned and found John standing behind them.

He was wearing a severely tailored black evening coat and pantaloons that served to make his impressive figure look yet more impressive. His neckcloth was neatly knotted and his black hair smoothly swept back from his brow, though there was a suggestion of a rebellious wave here and there to show that this was not its natural state. Claudia noted all these things automatically and noticed, too, that he looked very attractive in this formal array. The next moment, however, she was startled by the change in his expression. He had been smiling as he spoke, but as his eyes moved from his aunt to her, the smile froze on his face. "Miss Chambers?" he said.

There was blank disbelief in his voice. Its significance was not lost on Claudia, who became more certain than ever that her dress was both unbecoming and inappropriate. However, it was too late to change it now. Lifting her chin defiantly, she dropped a deep and deliberate curtsy. "Lord Rexford," she said. "How pleasant to see you again."

To her indignation, he did not immediately respond to her greeting. He seemed to be thinking of something else, though his eyes were certainly fixed on her. But at last he bowed and said gravely, "Good afternoon, Miss Chambers. You are in such gorgeous array that I hardly recognized you."

Claudia looked at him suspiciously, but could not decide whether he were quizzing her or not. She was glad to see a group of people in festive attire wending their way across the lawn. "It looks as though the first of your guests have arrived, ma'am," she told Lady Rexford. "We had better move over by the terrace so we can greet them as they come in."

"By the refreshment tent would be a better place," said John. "That's where we always received guests in the past."

"Your aunt does not care what was done in the past," said Claudia. She was annoyed at being contradicted and determined to do a little contradicting herself. "Lady Rexford is more concerned with what suits her in the present, my lord. And that happens to be the terrace."

"But I don't mind where I greet the guests, my dear," protested Lady Rexford with a look at John. "It really doesn't matter to me one way or another. And if the receiving has always been done by the tent in the past, perhaps I ought to respect the tradition."

Claudia said nothing more, but eyed John resentfully as she accompanied him and Lady Rexford to the tent. By the time she had been there an hour, greeting guests and making small talk, however, her resentment had faded a good deal. There were so many other things to see and think about that her irritation with John had taken a backseat in her thoughts.

The residents of the neighborhood, motivated partly by curiosity and partly by John's urgings, had turned out in force to meet the new chatelaine of Rexford Park. Lady Rexford and Claudia were introduced to literally hundreds of people. Most of them showed themselves quite friendly to the two ladies with the open warmth and easy manners typical of rural society. The Brocks were an exception. They came sweeping in after most of the other guests had already arrived, Barbara flamboyant in orange crepe with a green satin bodice; her mother large, square, and uncompromising in ruby red sarcenet; and Mr. Brock small and insignificant in black and white evening clothes.

Claudia observed that John scowled when he saw them making their way across the lawn. She wondered at this, supposing he would be pleased to see his bride-to-be. She had no way of knowing that the appearance of the Brocks had come as a surprise to him—and a very unwelcome surprise at that.

The last time John had seen Barbara was on the afternoon she had invited herself along on the tour of Rexford Park. He had held his peace as long as Claudia was with them, but as soon as he and Barbara were alone he had let her know in no uncertain terms that she had overstepped herself.

"I would like to know what you meant by your performance today, Barbara. Seeing that you told me just the other day that you wanted nothing more to do with me—"

"I didn't say that, Rexford. What I said was that I didn't want you associating with Miss Chambers. But since you insisted on disregarding my warnings, I thought it better that I should come with you when you met. You are so trusting I am afraid that an unprincipled woman like her could make a fool of you with the greatest ease."

"It was not Miss Chambers but you who made me look a fool, Barbara. Who asked you to appoint yourself my nurse-maid?"

Barbara's face took on a hurt look. "Why, don't say you're angry with me, Rexford," she said plaintively. "I only did it for your own good, I assure you."

"The deuce you did!" said John, speaking out of the depths of experience. "I think we both know better than that, Barbara. It was jealousy that prompted you to come here today, not concern for my well-being."

"Jealousy!" exclaimed Barbara. In an instant her expression had changed from one of hurt to one of unbridled fury. "I, jealous of a little milk-and-water schoolroom miss with hardly a word to say for herself? I promise you that you are quite out there, Rexford! I, Barbara Brock, niece of the Earl of Brockhurst, jealous of a hired companion? Jealous of a girl of little breeding and less countenance? You make me laugh, Rexford."

John, regarding Barbara's inflamed face, thought she looked very far from laughter. But he ignored this and went on in an uncompromising voice. "Be that as it may, I will not tolerate interference in my affairs, Barbara. Your coming here as you did today was quite unnecessary and—I may as well say it—very offensive to me as well. I can certainly conduct my business with Miss Chambers without the presence of a chaperone."

Barbara regarded him with flashing eyes. "And this is how you behave after I was good enough to overlook the way you spoke to me yesterday!" she said.

"Nobody asked you to overlook it," returned John. "But I don't recall saying anything so terrible to you yesterday. It was you, if you remember, who objected to a simple business meeting with a respectable young lady. And it was you who gave me a most unreasonable ultimatum about either eschewing her company or yours."

Barbara started to speak, then stopped. "This discussion is pointless," she said coldly. "I see no use in prolonging it. We will talk of this another time, Rexford, when you are able to discuss the matter rationally. Good day." And she had spurred her horse in the opposite direction.

It had been John's hope that Barbara would let the matter go and that her threat of renewing their discussion at a later time would prove an empty one. Week had succeeded week with no word from her, and he had allowed his hopes to strengthen. But he saw now that he had been too sanguine. Here was Barbara, accompanied by both her parents, swooping down on him with a smile that did not disguise the determination in her eyes. Yet was it possible he was doing her an injustice? It was an amazing concession for her to appear at his aunt's party at all. Perhaps she intended it merely as a way to make amends for her earlier behavior. He wondered why the idea stirred him with so little enthusiasm as he bowed to Barbara and her parents.

"Mrs. Brock—Miss Brock—and Mr. Brock. Allow me to introduce you to my aunt, Lady Rexford, and to Miss Chambers. Lady Rexford, Miss Chambers, these are the Brocks, near neighbors of ours."

He was pleased to see that his aunt acknowledged the greeting with a dignified smile and bow, quite as though she were to the manor born. Indeed, it was the Brocks who came off looking underbred. Mr. Brock smiled and bowed politely enough, but Mrs. Brock merely gave both ladies a cold stare and a frigid nod, and Barbara ignored them entirely to concentrate upon John.

Tucking her arm beneath his, she smiled up at him sweetly. "Oh, Rexford, you see I could not withstand your invitation," she said. "Here I am, and I expect you to repay me for my concession by engaging me for the first dance."

This speech infuriated John, implying as it did that Barbara was here at a personal invitation from him rather than a general one from her hostess. He was angered, too, by her rude manner to his aunt. "I'm afraid that is impossible, Miss Brock," he said in a clear, deliberate voice. "You see, I had planned on dancing the first dance with my aunt if she is willing."

He smiled at Lady Rexford, who smiled back at him with surprised pleasure. "You are very kind, Rexford," she said. "Of course I should be delighted to dance with you."

Barbara looked displeased by this exchange, but summoned up a short laugh. "Yes, I suppose you must do your duty by your aunt if she insists. But the second dance I shall expect you to dance with me."

The minatory tone of this speech was too much for John. Without stopping to reflect, he spoke out boldly. "I am afraid that is impossible, too, Miss Brock. I am engaged to Miss Chambers for the second dance."

He felt rather than saw Claudia start at these words. Turning to her, John fixed her with a beseeching gaze. "It was for the second dance that we were engaged, was it not, Miss Chambers?" he asked.

Claudia was astounded by this turn of events. She could not imagine why John should be so reluctant to dance with his bride-to-be, but reluctant he obviously was. There was no mistaking the appeal in his eyes as he regarded her. Somehow, she could not bring herself to refuse that mute appeal.

"Why, yes, I believe we were, my lord," she said slowly.

These words brought Barbara's eyes upon her, a mixture of amazement and contempt in their depths. "Why, it's Miss Chambers!" she said. "I almost did not recognize you in your—finery." Her eyes traveled scornfully from Claudia's rose-colored silk sandals to the wreath of flowers atop her head. "Upon my word, when I look at you, I am tempted to believe that fine feathers do indeed make fine birds!"

Mrs. Brock, who had been listening to this exchange in frowning silence, now spoke for the first time. "Miss Chambers?" she said. "The name seems familiar, but I cannot immediately place it. Who is this young lady, Barbara?"

"She's Lady Rexford's hired companion, Mama," said Barbara with a short laugh. "It's a new thing for the host of a party to prefer to dance with one of the servants rather than with his guests, isn't it? Ah, well, I doubt not I can find someone who will dance with me. Here is Sir Lucas approaching now. *He* will certainly not prefer a servant's company to mine." And without vouchsafing a word of farewell to Claudia or Lady Rexford or even to John, she walked over to join Sir Lucas, who had just appeared in the garden entranceway.

Thirteen

"I don't think much of that young lady's manners, do you?" whispered Lady Rexford to Claudia after Barbara had stalked off. "Imagine making a scene like that in public! I may not be a lady born, but even I know better than that."

"I don't think Miss Brock feels obliged to follow the constraints practiced by us lesser mortals," said Claudia with a dry laugh. "Of course I don't know her very well, but from what I have seen of her, she appears to have a very high opinion of herself."

"Aye, so she does, my dear. It surprises me that Rexford should choose such a woman for his bride. You know he himself is quite easygoing and pleasant and not a bit toplofty."

Claudia stole a glance at John, who was greeting a young gentleman who had just joined their party. "Do you think Lord Rexford and Miss Brock are engaged?" she inquired diffidently. "I know Sir Lucas said so, but it seemed to me that he was not especially friendly toward Miss Brock just now."

"Ah, you mean because he chose to dance with you instead of her! That did look peculiar, but I daresay there's an explanation for it. Perhaps they've had a falling out, and he was trying to make her jealous. I remember once, when I was a girl, one of my beaux got mad at me for dancing with another fellow at a party. He spent the rest of the evening flirting with my biggest rival. But it was me who he walked home with just the same, and I daresay it'll be the same tonight with

Rexford and Miss Brock. No doubt we'll see them dancing
together before the evening is over."

Claudia, thinking this over, was obliged to admit it seemed
only too likely. She felt resentful, however, that John should
have chosen her as his instrument of jealousy. She could not
even consider it a compliment that she had been chosen rather
than another, for she had been the only young lady standing
nearby at the critical moment. The appeal she had read in
John's eyes was simply a hope that she would play along with
his farce.

"How dare he embroil me in his affairs?" she thought indignantly. "I wish now I had denied I was engaged to dance
with him. That would have made him look no how! Well, I'll
put him off when the time comes, but I daresay he had no
intention of dancing with me anyway. What a fool I am. I
ought to know better than to let Master John take advantage
of me in such a way!"

Claudia continued to fulminate about John's behavior as the
afternoon faded into evening and the orchestra began to tune
up, preparatory to the start of the dancing. For the first dance,
as promised, John led out Lady Rexford. Claudia watched with
mingled emotions as her employer, smiling and with cheeks
pink as a girl's, took her place at the top of the line opposite
her nephew. At that moment Claudia felt a touch on her arm.
Turning, she found herself confronted by a young gentleman
with very fair hair and very blue eyes. He addressed her with
a shy smile.

"Begging your pardon, miss, but I wondered if you'd care
to stand up with me for the first dance? I'd be very much
honored if you would."

Claudia recognized her would-be partner as Mr. William
Williams, the owner of a small freehold property in the neighborhood. From words that had been spoken while they were
being introduced, she had gathered that he farmed his land
himself, which technically put him more in the category of
yeoman than gentry. But his manners seemed good, and he

had a gentlemanly appearance that inclined Claudia in his favor. Smiling, she bowed her consent to his proposition. "It's Mr. Williams, isn't it?" she said, as he escorted her onto the floor. "I remember Lord Rexford introducing you earlier this afternoon."

"That's right, miss," said Mr. Williams, looking pleased. "I wouldn't have supposed you'd have remembered, seeing how many people you've met tonight. But I remember *your* name right enough. It's Miss Chambers, though I won't presume to call you by it and never you fear it, miss."

"Why should you not call me Miss Chambers?" said Claudia, amused. "I should think there could be no objection to your using my name."

Mr. Williams looked pleased but dubious. "Well, I will if you don't mind, miss—Miss Chambers, I mean," he corrected. "Only I didn't like to presume, you know. I felt I was presuming something terrible anyway, asking the prettiest lady at the party to dance with me."

Claudia laughed. "You do me too much honor, Mr. Williams," she said.

"Indeed, I don't," said Mr. Williams warmly. "I'm very much obliged to you for dancing with me, miss." He hesitated a minute, then went on, blushing slightly. "Tell me, miss— Miss Chambers, I mean. Is it true you work for the old lady there?" He jerked his head in the direction of Lady Rexford. "Somebody said as you was a servant of hers, but I couldn't hardly believe it."

Claudia felt pretty sure who this somebody was, and it did not increase her charitable feelings toward Barbara Brock. "I am not a servant of Lady Rexford's, but rather her companion," she told Mr. Williams. "My position is more that of a guest in her home than a servant, although it's true she does pay me a salary."

"Aye, I thought that'd be the way of it," said Mr. Williams, nodding with satisfaction. "Anyone can see you're a lady born and not a serving girl, whatever people may say. But it's a great shame that a girl like you should have to work at all. You ought to be mistress of your own home rather than running an old lady's errands."

This was flattering, but a little too personal for Claudia's taste. She decided to change the subject. "You are very kind, Mr. Williams, but I assure you I am quite content in my position. I wish we would talk about you instead of me. Have you lived in this neighborhood long?"

Mr. Williams was nothing loath to talk about himself, and he entertained Claudia with a full description of his past, his present situation, and his hopes for the future. "There's a parcel of land I'd like to buy from the Rexford Park estate if I could," he said wistfully. "It'd round out my place very neatly and give me enough pasturage to graze another hundred head of sheep. You don't suppose Lady Rexford would be willing to sell, would you?"

Regretfully Claudia explained about the terms of the late Lord Rexford's will. "I don't think Lady Rexford could sell any part of the estate even if she wanted to. You had better approach Lord Rexford about it. The estate will be his someday, you know, and it is just possible that you might be able to buy the property of him sooner if both he and his aunt were willing."

Mr. Williams received this advice with a doleful sigh. "Sounds like I'd be better off making a bid on old Dawson's place," he said. "It's what folks have been advising me to do ever since he put it up for sale, but his land's not so good as the Rexford Park land. However, it's not tied up in legal knots either." He sighed again, then smiled at Claudia. "But there, I don't mean to bore you with my troubles, Miss Chambers. You've listened to me like an angel, and I'm sure I'm much obliged to you. It looks as though our dance is almost over. I don't suppose—it's probably presuming something terrible— but do you think you might care to stand up with me again?"

Claudia thought of John and of his stated intention to dance the second dance with her. Part of her felt a sneaking desire to keep their engagement, but she ridiculed this desire as irrational. John had only asked her to dance because he wanted to annoy Barbara Brock, whereas Mr. Williams sincerely wished to dance with her. She smiled at him. "I think I am free for the next dance, Mr. Williams," she said. "And I would be very pleased to dance with you again."

As they were waiting on the floor for the music to start again, however, Claudia saw John making his way purposefully in her direction. She averted her eyes, but was not really surprised when she felt a touch on her elbow a moment later. "I believe we were engaged to dance this set together, Miss Chambers?"

"Were we?" said Claudia. She looked John full in the face.

He nodded, looking surprised. "Yes, I asked you a couple of hours ago, don't you remember? Back when we were receiving guests. The first dance I was naturally obliged to dance with my aunt, but now I am free."

"Well, I am *not* free," said Claudia, her voice betraying a hint of triumph. "Mr. Williams has been kind enough to ask me to dance this dance with him, so you need not feel obliged to stand by our agreement, my lord. I am sure there are plenty of other ladies with whom you would rather dance than me."

John looked at her gravely. "No, there are not. It is you with whom I wish to dance, Miss Chambers. I am sure Mr. Williams will excuse you, seeing that ours was an earlier engagement."

Mr. Williams, perhaps thinking of the advantages of appeasing the future owner of Rexford Park, was quick to resign his own claim in favor of John's. Claudia was annoyed at this—at least, she told herself that she was annoyed. But in some small, inner corner of her mind, she could not help feeling gratified. It was not John's statement that there was no other young lady he wished to dance with more than her; that, of course, was mere flattery. But she thought better of him for standing by their agreement, even if he would rather have been released from it.

Having settled John's motives satisfactorily in her mind, Claudia waited to see what he would say to her. She was determined to let him open the conversation, seeing as he had been so determined to dance with her (though only for politeness' sake, of course). But for several minutes he seemed content merely to dance in silence. Claudia was just wondering whether she ought, after all, to open the conversation when he spoke. "I hope you are not disappointed about my preempting Mr. Williams's place, Miss Chambers. You know there will be many more dances this evening which you can dance with him if you choose."

Claudia shook her head. "No, I'm afraid not, my lord," she said gravely. "Not unless the manners of Yorkshire differ greatly from those prevailing in London. There, you must know, it is the gentlemen who choose when and with whom to dance, and not the ladies!"

A slow smile dawned on John's face. "Ah, you are quizzing me, Miss Chambers!" he said. "Of course you are quite correct, but I had taken Mr. Williams's willingness in the matter as a foregone conclusion. To speak truth, I should not wonder at any man's willingness to partner you. You look very handsome tonight—no, not handsome. I would say rather that you look beautiful, Miss Chambers."

His eyes gravely appraised her face. Claudia found herself coloring. "That's only because of what I am wearing," she said lightly. "Your aunt was kind enough to present me with this dress—and to insist on my wearing it, though I told her it was not suitable for a hired companion. Indeed, my lord, you must not think I would willingly have invited criticism by dressing so finely."

John was silent for a moment. "I would hope none of our guests would be so rude as to criticize you for dressing finely," he said at last. "But if they do, I beg you will let me know about it, Miss Chambers. I'll take care they don't repeat the performance."

Claudia wondered if he was talking about Barbara Brock.

She dared not ask him outright. But to her surprise, it was he who broached the subject of his fiancée.

"I am afraid you must have been offended by Miss Brock's comments earlier this evening. She prides herself on always speaking her mind—which to my way of thinking is not always a positive trait. A little polite self-restraint makes the world go round a deal smoother in my opinion." A sudden smile lit up his face as he looked down at Claudia. "Now call me a hypocrite if you dare, Miss Chambers! I know you are thinking that I did not scruple to speak my mind during *our* first interview!"

"I wasn't thinking it," Claudia assured him truthfully. "Indeed, my lord, I had almost forgotten that interview."

"Had you? I haven't—nor ceased to regret it either. But your saying you have almost forgotten it makes me feel a little easier in my mind."

Claudia looked at John in surprise, not quite knowing how to take this remark. His expression surprised her, too, being curiously serious and intense. But when he spoke again, it was merely to offer a commonplace remark about the evening being a very fine one. Claudia agreed that it was, and they finished out the dance in the exchange of polite nothings.

As soon as the music ended, Mr. Williams came hurrying over to beg Claudia to dance with him again. She hesitated a little before consenting, with a glance at John to see if he would have any objection. He made none, however, though his face was more grave than ever as he relinquished her to Mr. Williams.

"It was a pleasure dancing with you, Miss Chambers," he said. "I hope—"

What he hoped, Claudia was never to know. Barbara Brock came hurrying up just then, cutting in upon the conversation with her habitual lack of ceremony.

"There you are, Rexford," she said, taking his arm possessively. "I hope there is no reason why you may not dance with me now? Sir Lucas has been good enough to take your place for these first two dances, but I told him you and I were engaged for the third."

"Then I must not contradict you, must I?" said John. Claudia thought there was an edge to his voice, but he allowed Barbara to lead him off without further dispute—and also without finishing his question to Claudia. Claudia was left with Mr. Williams and also with Sir Lucas, who had strolled over with Barbara and had remained to make a leisurely inspection of Claudia's figure through his quizzing glass.

"Excuse us, Sir Lucas," said Claudia, incensed at this behavior. "Mr. Williams and I are engaged to dance this next dance together."

Her statement caused Sir Lucas to briefly transfer his scrutiny to Mr. Williams. What he saw evidently did not interest him, however, for he soon switched his gaze back to Claudia. "Charming, charming," he murmured. "You are *au fait de beauté*, Miss Chambers. May I hope that when you are done dancing with—er—Mr. Williams, you will consent to dance with me?"

This request did not suit Claudia, but she could think of no polite way to decline it. "Of course I will dance with you if you like, Sir Lucas. But please do not feel obliged to ask me merely because of my connection with Lady Rexford."

Sir Lucas looked amused. "My dear Miss Chambers, I do not concern myself with dances of obligation," he drawled. "In fact, it is a point of honor with me never to do anything from a sense of obligation. I only do what suits my own pleasure at a given moment. And at this particular moment, it suits my pleasure to dance with you."

This speech suited Claudia no better than his previous one. She made up her mind that she would on no account take the floor with Sir Lucas, even if she found it necessary to plead a sprained ankle and sit out the rest of the dances that evening. Giving him only a noncommittal smile by way of reply, she took Mr. Williams's arm and hurried him out onto the floor, where the dancers were already taking their places for the third dance.

This passed agreeably enough, though Claudia was so busy thinking up strategies to evade Sir Lucas that she paid only faint heed to her partner's conversation. Mr. Williams did not seem to notice her preoccupation, however.

"I wish those dashed musicians hadn't finished up so quick," he said wistfully at the conclusion of the dance. "It seems to me I've never danced a shorter country dance. I don't suppose you'd care to dance with me a third time?"

Claudia, who had no wish to make herself conspicuous in this manner, politely declined Mr. Williams's invitation. Looking disconsolate, he wished her a good evening and meandered sadly away in the direction of the refreshment tent.

He had scarcely gone when Sir Lucas presented himself with an unctuous smile. "Here I am, you see, Miss Chambers. I assure you, duty could be no more punctilious than pleasure warmly anticipated!"

It gave Claudia much satisfaction to inform him that she was too weary to dance the next dance with him. But great was her horror when Sir Lucas, finding her adamant on this point, insisted on sitting out the dance along with her.

"No, indeed, you must not think of doing such a thing, Sir Lucas," said Claudia with would-be vivaciousness. "Sitting out the dance with me would be duty in its dreariest form, and you have already told me how you abhor duty!"

"But I will be looking at you while I sit, and that will be a pleasure," he responded without missing a beat. "May I get you something to drink, Miss Chambers? Lady Rexford's champagne appears to be drinkable though not so good as my own."

Claudia accepted the offer of champagne, supposing it would rid her of Sir Lucas for at least the time it took him to go to and from the refreshment tent. But he merely flagged down a passing footman, ordered him to fetch two glasses of champagne, and took Claudia's arm with a satisfied smirk.

"Shall we find somewhere to sit down, Miss Chambers? I saw a pleasantly secluded bench over behind the rose garden."

"No, I would rather stroll about if you please," said Claudia, who distrusted the idea of a rose garden *tête-à-tête* with Sir Lucas. "I helped Lady Rexford plan this party, you know, and it's my duty to make sure all is going well."

Sir Lucas consented to this plan, although he shook his head over the word duty. "You should have nothing to do with that ugly word, Miss Chambers, any more than I do," he told her as they strolled amid the crowds on the lawn. "Living for pleasure is a thousand times more amusing."

"Yes, but not nearly so profitable," retorted Claudia. "Of course you may pursue such a policy without hindrance, Sir Lucas, seeing that you are fortunate enough to possess independent means. But those of us who work for a living must concern ourselves with duty whether we like it or not."

Sir Lucas gave her another of his unctuous smiles. "That is because you are taking the wrong way to earn a living," he said. "A pretty girl like you could surely find some more pleasant and profitable enterprise than laboring as an old lady's companion."

This speech, spoken in a tone of innuendo, rendered Claudia temporarily speechless. Sir Lucas went on, his voice low and insinuating. "I, for one, can think of several ways you might support yourself without reference to duty, Miss Chambers. If you were interested in discussing them with me sometime—"

"Thank you, no," said Claudia, finding her voice at last. "No doubt you mean well, Sir Lucas, but my situation with Lady Rexford satisfies me entirely."

Sir Lucas raised an incredulous eyebrow at these words, but to Claudia's relief, he allowed the subject to drop. "At any rate, you do look a delectable morsel tonight, Miss Chambers," he said, letting his eyes rove over her face and figure. "I do not think I am exaggerating when I say that you are quite the most enticing thing at this party."

"Thank you, Sir Lucas, but I am a person, not a thing,"

said Claudia coolly. "What's more, at this moment, I am a person with several pressing duties. I think you had better excuse me while I attend to them."

Sir Lucas smiled and shook his head. "No, you said you would give me this dance, and I intend to extract a full dance's worth of your company," he said. "You really ought to come and see the rose garden with me, Miss Chambers. It wouldn't take a minute, and then you could attend to your unpleasant duty."

Hoping to get rid of him in this way, Claudia consented to take a look at the rose garden. There were several other couples strolling there, so she had no fear of Sir Lucas's behaving inappropriately. Still, she took care to avoid the more secluded paths and to keep the conversation on strictly impersonal subjects. "I suppose this cannot compare to the gardens of Italy, but it seems to me a lovely place," she said as they strolled along the paths. "What wonderful roses!"

"They're good enough for England," said Sir Lucas with a disparaging glance around him. "But you ought to see the gardens of the Palazzo Doria or the villas of Frascati, Miss Chambers. I would that I could show them to you."

These last words, and the look that accompanied them, convinced Claudia that she had been long enough in the rose garden with Sir Lucas. "I think we had better be going back to the pavilion now," she said with finality. "It's getting rather dark."

"Yes, but the moon will soon be rising," said Sir Lucas, catching hold of her hand. "You'll stay here and watch it rise with me, won't you?"

"No, indeed," said Claudia, trying to pull away from him. "I must be getting back to the pavilion. Lady Rexford will be wondering what has become of me."

Sir Lucas gave it as his opinion that Lady Rexford could go hang. "Stay with me just a little longer, Miss Chambers," he urged, trying to slip an arm around her waist. "I'll see you don't lose by it. By God, I hope the old lady does fire you!

You deserve better than to wear away your life in the service of an ungrateful dowager."

Sir Lucas was stronger than his dandified appearance would have suggested. Claudia found it no easy task to escape his embrace. As she struggled to free herself, she observed with a sensation of disquiet that the garden was now almost deserted. Most of the couples had left some minutes ago when darkness first began to fall. Altogether, she was quite relieved when she saw John making his way across the rose garden in her and Sir Lucas's direction.

Fourteen

While Claudia had been warding off the attentions of Sir Lucas, John had been enduring attentions of a similar kind from Barbara Brock.

She had made no further comments about his dancing with Claudia, contrary to John's expectations. Instead, she seemed determined to make herself agreeable—as agreeable as it was possible for Barbara Brock to be.

"It's been far too long since I've danced with you, Rexford," she said, smiling up at him as they went down the line of dancers. "And even longer since I've danced with you at Rexford Park. We shared our first dance together here at one of your uncle's parties years ago. Do you remember?"

John did remember, but the memory brought little pleasure. The event Barbara spoke of seemed to have taken place in another lifetime. He found himself curiously reluctant to talk about it and so let Barbara's question go unanswered. "It's a beautiful night for dancing," he said instead. "My aunt chose an excellent night for her party."

Barbara made a little moue of distaste. "Don't call it *her* party, Rexford! I'm sure it's your party much more than your aunt's. If you had not been good enough to support her in her social aspirations, I am sure she might have looked in vain for her guests tonight."

John said nothing. Barbara rattled on, oblivious to the clouds gathering on his brow. "Goodness knows it was hard enough to convince Mama that we should attend tonight! I hope you are properly grateful to me, Rexford."

"Grateful?" said John, raising his eyebrows. "Why should I be grateful, Barbara? Generally, you know, it is the guest who expresses gratitude to the host, not vice versa."

Barbara stared at him, then laughed. "Are you fishing for compliments, Rexford? Very well, I will pay you a very pretty one. You have succeeded in making your aunt appear quite respectable this evening. I am sure that merely looking at her one would never suspect what a common background she comes from."

"You are very kind, Barbara, but I am afraid your compliment is misplaced," said John coldly. "I have nothing to do with my aunt's manners and appearance tonight or at any other time."

Barbara gave him an indulgent smile. "It is very chivalrous of you to say so, Rexford, but you know I can scarcely believe that. Someone must have given her a hint on how to dress and conduct herself, or else how would she know what was proper in such a situation?"

John looked at her steadily. "Perhaps she has the instincts of a lady even if she has not the birth and background of one," he said. "I suppose such a thing is possible—just as it is possible for a lady bred and born to disgrace herself by her conduct."

Barbara shook her head with calm assurance. "Oh, no, Rexford, you are wrong there," she said. "Everyone knows that blood must tell. Your aunt appears good enough, but she is of common blood, and as such, she can never possess the instincts of a lady."

John said nothing, but merely looked at Barbara. He looked at her so long and hard that his gaze finally pierced her iron self-assurance.

"What's wrong, Rexford? Why are you looking at me that way?" she asked.

John spoke with cold deliberation. "You say my aunt can

never have the instincts of a lady. Well, I begin to wonder whether *you* have them, Barbara. I had always believed it was bad form to criticize one's hostess—and never more than when one is actually enjoying her hospitality."

An angry flush rose to Barbara's cheeks. She stopped dead on the dance floor, nearly causing a collision with a couple coming down the line. "And because I choose to speak my mind, you think your aunt's manners superior to mine?" she said in a rising voice. "Upon my word, Rexford, this is effrontery indeed! I said nothing before about your snubbing me in order to dance with Miss Chambers—though some people might have said I had a better claim on your attention than a milk-and-water miss who must work for her bread. But now you have not only snubbed me—you have insulted me. I tell you I won't stand it, Rexford. You owe me an apology."

John was acutely conscious that Barbara's behavior was attracting the attention of those around them. Nonetheless, he spoke up boldly. "You want me to apologize for speaking the truth?" he said. "I thought you were an advocate of speaking one's mind on every occasion, Barbara. Or is that a privilege you reserve to yourself?"

"Insolence!" hissed Barbara, fairly gnashing her teeth. "I shall never forgive you for this, Rexford. Already I have been far too forgiving, but this is the final straw. I do not care to remain in the company of a person who could behave toward me as you have. As far as I am concerned, you are free to spend the rest of the evening with your aunt—and with Miss Chambers."

"I ask nothing better," said John.

For answer, Barbara turned on her heel and stalked away. John, murmuring an apology to those around him, left the dance floor and went in search of Claudia. Although embarrassed by the scene in which he had just taken part, he felt oddly exultant, too. There could be no doubt now that he and Barbara were finished. And though he supposed he might later regret his rashness in casting off the heiress of the house of

Brock, he felt now rather as though he had been relieved of an intolerable burden.

He did not analyze the impulse that sent him looking for Claudia as soon as he was free. If asked, he might have said he was merely following Barbara's suggestion. Yet the thought of Claudia had been haunting him all evening. How lovely she had looked in that pink dress—and how pleasant her conversation had been when they had danced together.

There could be no doubt that Miss Chambers was a pretty, intelligent, well-bred girl. But John felt this bare catalog of virtues did not do her justice. There was a streak of wit in her conversation and a wicked sense of humor lurking beneath her ladylike demeanor that lent her character a delightful piquancy. It struck him that Barbara had never shown much sense of humor. "Really, it's almost as though the scales have fallen from my eyes," he told himself with bemusement. "And all I see now is Claudia Chambers. Can it be . . . ? No, I won't think about it yet. It's too soon to tell. All I wish to do right now is find her and talk with her and perhaps dance with her once more. The future can take care of itself."

It took him some time to find Claudia, however. He inquired of his aunt, who was happily chatting with some new acquaintances near the refreshment tent. But all she could say was that she had last seen Claudia dancing with Mr. Williams.

John, nothing daunted, set out to find Mr. Williams. From that gentleman, he learned that Claudia had gone off somewhere with Sir Lucas. "And I don't doubt she's with him yet," added Mr. Williams gloomily. "All the ladies seem crazy about that fellow. For my part, I think he's a regular rum one and a Bartholomew Baby to boot. Every time I see those frilly shirts and purple gloves of his, I'd like to take him off by himself and thrash him."

John wholeheartedly sympathized with this desire, but he merely thanked Mr. Williams for his information and went off to look for Claudia and Sir Lucas.

He came upon them in the rose garden just as it was growing

dark. Sir Lucas had his arms around Claudia—at least, he had one arm around her and was trying to draw her closer with the other. The sight of the two of them in such an intimate position seemed to trigger some violent and unsuspected madness in John. For a moment he was seized with an urge to kick Sir Lucas's satin-clad posterior into the nearest rosebush. But a second glance showed him that Claudia was by no means encouraging Sir Lucas's embraces, and this realization restored him to sanity. He strode forward with a frown gathering on his brow.

Claudia did not even see the frown. She merely saw John, arrived in the nick of time to rescue her from Sir Lucas—and she hailed him with open arms.

"Lord Rexford! Oh, my lord, thank heaven you are here. Would you be kind enough to take me back to the party?"

"Of course I will," said John. He was so disarmed by the warmth of her welcome that he came near to forgetting Sir Lucas. With difficulty, he recalled himself to a sense of duty. "But are you sure there is no other service I can perform for you, Miss Chambers?" He looked pointedly at Sir Lucas, who had released his hold on Claudia and was now standing with his arms at his sides, looking extremely foolish. "It appeared as though you were in difficulties when I came up."

"Yes, I was," said Claudia. She, too, looked pointedly at Sir Lucas. "You must know that Sir Lucas wished me to stay and see the moon rise, my lord. So much did he wish it, in fact, that he refused to take me back to the party when I asked him to. But your arrival nicely resolves the dilemma. *You* can take me back to the party now, and Sir Lucas can stay here and watch the moon as long as he wants."

Sir Lucas, recognizing defeat as inevitable, set about recovering his position. "Ah, it will not be the same without you, Miss Chambers," he said gallantly. "I had not realized you so much wished to return to the party, or of course I would have respected your wishes. I hope you realize that?" He bared his teeth in what was meant to be a winning smile. "I would not have this incident spoil our friendship in any way."

Claudia did not even deign to answer him. "Good evening, Sir Lucas," she said shortly. John gave her his arm, and together they started back toward the cluster of tents on the lawn.

As they walked arm in arm along the gravel path, John cast frequent looks at Claudia. Although disarmed by the way she had welcomed him, he could not help wondering how she had ended up in the rose garden with Sir Lucas in the first place. At last, unable to repress his curiosity any longer, he decided to make a few discreet inquiries. "I hope my appearance on the scene did not embarrass you, Miss Chambers," he said. "But you looked to be in difficulties, so I thought I had better intervene."

"I am very glad you did, my lord," she said warmly. "I didn't suppose Sir Lucas would have behaved that way, or I would not have gone walking with him in the first place, I assure you."

"How came you to be walking with him in such a secluded spot?" John asked. "Not that I mean to criticize, Miss Chambers. But you must know that to be alone with a man like Sir Lucas is practically an invitation to bad behavior."

Claudia looked offended. "You forget that Sir Lucas is practically a stranger to me, my lord," she retorted. "He seemed to be a gentleman, so I thought there could be no harm in accepting his invitation to walk in the garden. And it's not as though we were all alone there, at least not in the beginning. There were a dozen other couples in the garden when we first arrived, but they must have left soon after we got there. I didn't realize we were alone until Sir Lucas became . . . offensive."

This explanation quite satisfied John. He gave Claudia a smile at once reassuring and apologetic.

"Forgive me, Miss Chambers," he said. "I didn't mean to sound critical. I only wondered how you came to be alone with Sir Lucas. He does appear to be a gentleman, as you say, and I can quite see how you might have accepted his invitation in good faith."

Claudia accepted this apology with a reserved smile, and they walked on in silence for a little while. John was very conscious of her arm resting lightly on his and of her figure beside him, lovely and feminine in its silken draperies. He admired the way she held herself, with an upright grace and dignity, and the confident tilt of her glossy chestnut head. But he felt also gloomily conscious that she was annoyed with him. Before he knew what he was doing, he blurted out a second apology. "Please, please forgive me, Miss Chambers. I was a fool to suppose you were encouraging Sir Lucas. Indeed, I was very sure you were not, but when I first spied you together in the garden I rather lost my head, don't you know."

He stopped walking to regard Claudia with great earnestness. She looked back at him, her expression smiling but also a bit surprised. "To be sure I will forgive you, my lord," she said. "I can readily believe that appearances were against me." In a rueful voice, she added, "If I seemed annoyed just now, it was only because I feel myself that I was imprudent to invite a *tête-à-tête* with Sir Lucas. I felt from the beginning that he was not trustworthy. If he tried to kiss me, it was no more than I deserved."

John cleared his throat. "Well, as to that—" he began, then stopped.

"As to what?" said Claudia, looking up at him inquiringly.

John hesitated a moment, then went on with sudden recklessness. "As to that, I can hardly blame Sir Lucas for wanting to kiss you. It happens that other men at this party share the same desire, myself included."

Claudia merely regarded him with raised eyebrows. Following the same reckless impulse, John leaned down and touched his lips to hers. "You look very lovely, Miss Chambers—and very sweet," he said in a low voice. "I think you must be the sweetest girl in the world."

"Well!" said Claudia in a faint voice.

John regarded her anxiously. She did not seem to be angry, but already he was cursing his imprudence. "Forgive me, Miss Chambers," he said humbly. "I didn't mean for that to happen. I'm afraid I lost my head again."

Claudia regarded him wordlessly for a moment. "It seems to me that you might keep that head of yours under better control, my lord," she said. "On what do you blame your madness this time—Sir Lucas or the moonlight?"

"I have heard that moonlight often has an unsettling effect on people," offered John.

"Very well, let us blame it on the moonlight," said Claudia. She began walking toward the tents once more, but again John stopped her.

"You're not angry, are you, Miss Chambers?" he said. "I meant no disrespect by kissing you, I assure you."

"Of course not. On the contrary, you did it to demonstrate the depth of your respect for me, I suppose," said Claudia with an incredulous smile. John nodded seriously.

"That's it exactly. I am glad to find you so quick of understanding, Miss Chambers. But then I always had a very high opinion of your understanding, together with your many other admirable attributes."

Claudia rolled her eyes. "If this keeps up, I shall be expecting you to make me an offer of marriage next," she remarked.

"Why not?" said John, smiling equably. "I had intended to wait a little longer before broaching the subject, but since you mention it—"

Claudia put her hands over her ears. "No, no, my lord! I am sure now that it is neither my charms nor the moon that has prompted this display, but rather your aunt's champagne. So let us be agreed that you kissed me as a mark of respect and say no more about it."

"No, I won't. Not tonight, at any rate," said John. Claudia made no reply. Neither of them said any more as they walked back to the lawn, where the other guests were making merry under the light of the moon and the thousands of colored lanterns that were strung beneath the tents and neighboring trees.

As soon as they caught sight of Lady Rexford holding court at the far end of the refreshment tent, Claudia hastily excused herself to John and went over to join her. She flattered herself that her manner appeared quite as usual, but in truth she was badly shaken. She had been kissed once or twice by gentlemen in the past, but never with quite that combination of tenderness and masculine determination. The mere thought of it seemed to turn her weak in the knees. Even more disturbing were the remarks John had made after the kiss, in which he had seemed to imply that his intentions were serious.

"But that cannot be when he is engaged to Barbara Brock," Claudia told herself. "At least, I suppose he is engaged to her. His greeting to her tonight did not appear much like it, to be sure, and neither did the way he spoke about her when we were dancing together. But even in spite of those things, I could easier believe him engaged to Miss Brock than believe him serious about offering for me. He must have been joking—that's all. But it's a queer kind of joke, and I wouldn't have thought he was the sort of man to behave in such a way. He looked and sounded quite serious."

So serious had John looked and sounded, in fact, that Claudia's peace of mind was profoundly disturbed for the rest of the evening. She stayed close beside Lady Rexford, refusing to dance in spite of the earnest urgings of half a dozen would-be suitors. Sir Lucas was among these suitors, and though Claudia had no compunction about refusing *him,* her refusal lacked the indignation it might have contained previous to her interview with John. Sir Lucas went away from the interview feeling quite buoyant, convinced that Miss Chambers had forgiven him his faux pas and would someday succumb to his charms.

Claudia was unconscious of having given this impression to Sir Lucas, however. She was, indeed, conscious of little that happened after that kiss and conversation with John—until the moment that Barbara Brock came up to her and formally begged the privilege of having a word with her in private.

"Indeed, it will not take a minute, Miss Chambers," she said, fixing her pale-lashed blue eyes on Claudia's face. "I would regard it as a great favor if you would allow me to say a few words to you apart from the others." She cast an expressive glance at Lady Rexford.

Claudia eyed Barbara askance, trying to guess what her request could mean. For a moment she wondered guiltily if Barbara knew about that kiss John had given her and had come to revile her for it.

But though Barbara's voice and manner could not have been called friendly, they were not openly hostile. In fact, she appeared more humble than Claudia had ever seen her before. Curious to know what could have prompted such an uncharacteristic mood—and curious also to know what Barbara could wish to say to her in private—Claudia consented to walk with her into the far end of the dancing tent, where only a few bored-looking chaperones sat yawning on their benches.

Once they were alone, Barbara lost no time in getting down to business. "Miss Chambers, I thought I should say a few words to you, lest you misunderstand the situation between Lord Rexford and me." She fixed Claudia with a meaningful gaze. "It has not escaped my notice, nor the notice of others, that you have been spending a great deal of time in his company."

"I would not call it a *great* deal of time," said Claudia, hoping she was not blushing. "We have been obliged to meet several times for the purposes of business, but that can hardly be counted as keeping company with him, Miss Brock."

Barbara laughed dryly. "Come, Miss Chambers," she said. "I and everyone else here tonight saw you dancing with him. I think you can hardly call that a business meeting."

"He *asked* me to dance with him," said Claudia defensively.

"I don't doubt it, Miss Chambers. What I question is your motive in accepting his invitation."

"Why should my motive for accepting Lord Rexford's invitation be any different from my motive for accepting Sir Lucas's or Mr. Williams's?" said Claudia, who was beginning to be irritated by Barbara's manner. "All three of them asked me to dance, you know."

"Sir Lucas asked you to dance?" said Barbara, momentarily distracted from the subject of John. "I was not aware of *that.*"

Claudia thought she looked offended. But Barbara did not long allow herself to be sidetracked from the matter at hand. "Ah, well, I have nothing to say to your dancing with Sir Lucas, though as a friend I would advise you to be on guard with him," she told Claudia. "You must know that a man in his position can have no honorable motive in pursuing a girl whose station in life is so far beneath his own. And the same is true for Lord Rexford. I hope you have not allowed yourself to entertain hopes in that direction, for if you do it will certainly be my duty to crush them."

"Your duty as a *friend,* I suppose," suggested Claudia with just the slightest bit of sarcasm in her voice.

Barbara took the words at face value, however, and nodded solemnly. "Yes, it is as a friend that I have come to you tonight, Miss Chambers. In fact, if you will promise not to let it go any further, I shall tell you a secret that I have told none of my other friends—not even those whose position would seem to warrant such a privilege more than yours."

She paused, looking impressively at Claudia. "You are too kind, Miss Brock," said Claudia, who was beginning almost to enjoy herself. "But you know I would not be comfortable receiving any information as privileged as that. My position as companion to Lady Rexford requires a most perfect frankness between me and my employer. Perhaps you had better tell your secret to one of your more deserving friends instead of me."

"That would hardly answer the purpose, Miss Chambers. It is you who need this information, you see." Barbara thought for a moment, her brow deeply furrowed. "I suppose it would be all right if you tell Lady Rexford what I am about to tell you," she said. "But make sure she knows that the information must go no further."

"I really cannot undertake to dictate conditions to Lady Rexford," said Claudia coldly. "If you choose to make me a confidante, you will simply have to trust in her discretion as well as mine."

"I think I can trust in her discretion. She appears to dote on her nephew. So when I tell you that he and I are engaged but have not yet publicly announced our engagement, I am sure she will cooperate with us in keeping our secret."

Barbara brought forth this speech with an air of triumph. So triumphant was she, indeed, that Claudia was puzzled. "But surely that is an open secret, Miss Brock," she said. "Sir Lucas told Lady Rexford and me weeks ago that you and Lord Rexford were on the verge of becoming engaged. And I have heard other people speak of it as well."

"Have you?" said Barbara. She gave Claudia a penetrating stare. "Perhaps this talk has been unnecessary then. But I thought I had better speak to you, Miss Chambers, lest you fancy that Lord Rexford's attentions toward you meant more than they did."

Claudia was suddenly weary of Barbara's condescension. She felt weary of nearly everything at that moment, and her weariness was compounded by a bitter disillusionment. Nothing Barbara had told her had come as a surprise, yet to have her suspicions confirmed in such a manner had been unexpectedly painful. That kiss John had given her earlier, so sweet and unexpected at the time, had been changed by Barbara's words into something sordid and shameful. Pain and anger caused Claudia to speak bluntly.

"And it does not bother you, his paying attentions to other girls?" Claudia said. "If I were engaged to a man, I think I would find it humiliating to have to explain his behavior to every girl he danced with."

Barbara looked undecided whether to receive this speech

with anger or indulgent laughter. She decided on the latter course. "It's evident you know nothing about men, Miss Chambers," she tittered. "Even an engaged man may indulge himself in a flirtation with another girl—especially when that girl has encouraged him to the top of her bent."

"I, encourage him?" said Claudia, growing angry in her turn. "You are mistaken, Miss Brock. I have not encouraged Lord Rexford in the slightest. If you do not want him paying attention to me in the future, you had better drop a hint in *his* ear. I assure you it would be more efficacious."

Barbara smiled (an odiously complacent smile, Claudia thought it). "I think letting you know the facts of the case will be efficacious enough. I depend on its being so, at any rate." Still smiling, she turned to go. "I won't keep you from your duties any longer, Miss Chambers," she threw over her shoulder. "Good evening to you, and please give my thanks to Lady Rexford for a very pleasant evening."

Fifteen

When Claudia finally went to bed that night (at an hour that might more properly be called morning), she had resolved in her heart that from now on she would have as few dealings with John Rexford as she could possibly manage.

She could not decide whom she resented most, him or his fiancée. Certainly Barbara Brock had been the more openly offensive of the two. Yet Claudia was obliged to own that Barbara's offenses had also been the more forgivable. It was natural that a lady should resent her lover paying undue attention to another lady. What was not natural was for a man, supposedly engaged, to deliberately kiss another lady while calling her the sweetest girl in the world.

"And I didn't encourage him to do it either," Claudia told herself fiercely. "It must be that he is merely a shameless flirt like Sir Lucas. But how odd that he should have responded as he did when I brought up the subject of marriage! Breach of promise suits have been founded on less, as Edmund could tell him. I suppose he was merely joking, but I feel even more strongly than I did before that it's a nasty kind of joke. And I would rather not have anything more to do with a man who would joke on such a subject."

In the days that followed, Claudia made a point of avoiding John insofar as she was able. This was not very far, however. Being attendant on Lady Rexford, she was forced to see him often whether she wanted to or not. She always took care never to be alone in his company, however.

But it happened one day that she found herself alone with him, even against her will. On a sunny morning about two weeks after the day of the fete, Lady Rexford found she had run out of the beautifying lotion with which she maintained her still admirable complexion.

"Shall I run to the village and see if I can buy you some more, ma'am?" offered Claudia. "I would be more than happy to do so. It's a lovely day out, and I wouldn't mind a little exercise."

"Why, that would be very kind of you, my dear, if you're certain you really don't mind. But I beg you won't feel obliged to walk all the way into Lockbridge. I am sure my carriage is quite at your service."

Claudia refused the carriage, however, and set off on foot, a wide-brimmed straw bonnet on her head and a shopping basket on her arm. She had worn her lightest dress, a pale yellow sprig muslin with a broad ribbon sash of deeper yellow, and she had the pleasant consciousness of being both attractively and suitably dressed. She walked along the lane, admiring the blue of the sky overhead and the starlike blossoms of woodbine and jessamine that sprinkled the hedges on either side.

By the time she reached Lockbridge, the small village that lay not far from the gates of Rexford Park, she was warm and ready to rest for a while in some shady spot. The well in the center of the village marketplace seemed to offer a suitable refuge, shaded as it was by the roof of the well house. Claudia refreshed herself from the dipper that hung beside the well, then seated herself on the well's broad rim to watch the residents of Lockbridge going about their business.

There was plenty to see, though nothing of a very exciting nature. The blacksmith leaned against the doorway of his shop, chatting with a gentleman clad in the smock and leggings of a farmer. A small girl with sunburned legs drove a flock of geese along the high street. A stout woman with a market basket emerged from the butcher's shop and walked briskly down the street, followed at a distance by a couple of hopeful-looking dogs.

It was a peaceful bucolic scene, and Claudia found enjoyment in surveying it. For the first time since the night of the fete, she came close to forgetting the kiss John had given her that fateful evening and the betrayal it represented. She was therefore much annoyed when she perceived John's tall, broadshouldered figure strolling along the shady side of the high street.

Claudia turned her back on him and pretended to be studying a calico cat lazing in the window of the house opposite. To her annoyance, she found her heart beating uncomfortably fast and her body trembling with excitement.

"Fool!" she scolded herself. "It's foolish to get so excited about a man who's engaged to another girl. What if he did kiss me at the fete? He's probably kissed dozens of girls, and one more hardly makes any difference. Why, he probably hasn't given me a second thought since—"

"Miss Chambers?" said John's voice in her ear. Claudia started. This caused her to lose her balance on the well curbing, and if John had not reached out and caught her, she would have tumbled into the water.

"Oh!" said Claudia, now flustered in good earnest.

"I'm sorry," said John, looking hardly less flustered than she was. "I didn't mean to startle you, Miss Chambers. Are you all right?"

"Quite all right," said Claudia. She tried to pull away from his grasp. But John did not release her, even after she had gotten to her feet and moved a few feet away from the well. Claudia was embarrassed by her situation and even more embarrassed when she looked up to confront John's worried gaze.

"I'm sorry," he said again. "Truly I didn't mean to surprise you like that, Miss Chambers. I thought you must have heard me approach. But apparently not. Your thoughts must have been very absorbing ones to occupy you so completely."

There was a faint question in his voice. "Yes," agreed Claudia. She did not mention that it was he whom she had been thinking about. Giving herself a mental shake, she once more sought to disengage herself from John's hold. He released her this time, but continued to survey her with a searching expression.

"You are obviously still shaken, Miss Chambers," he said. "Perhaps you had better sit down for a moment until you have recovered yourself. Or can I give you a ride somewhere? I have my rig with me."

He pointed down the street, where a curricle harnessed to a magnificent team of gray horses was being tended by a liveried groom. "What beautiful horses," said Claudia, moved to involuntary admiration.

John smiled. "My one extravagance. I've always had a weakness for horseflesh." His mouth twisted ruefully. "It's a weakness for which I've been criticized. Sir Lucas stopped me last week and inquired with exaggerated surprise if the Four-in-Hand Club had relocated from Hanover Square to Lockbridge!"

"Oh, Sir Lucas," Claudia began, and then fell silent. She was remembering the last occasion on which they had discussed Sir Lucas. John looked at her quizzically.

"Of course we both have small reason to think of Sir Lucas with affection. He has not harassed you any more since the night of the fete, I hope."

"No," said Claudia. The earnest way John was looking at her made her uncomfortable. It also made her feel faintly resentful. Why should he be so critical of Sir Lucas when he himself had behaved just as badly? Indeed, he had behaved worse than Sir Lucas, for Sir Lucas had not been engaged to another lady at the time he had tried to kiss her.

John seemed unaware of this irony, however. He went on looking at her earnestly. "I am very relieved to hear it, Miss

Chambers," he said. "If he bothers you again, you must let me know. I'll be glad to have a word with him."

This was too much for Claudia. "It's very kind of you, my lord, but I am quite able to manage my own affairs," she said, looking at him steadily. "The only reason Sir Lucas was in a position to harass me before was because I made the mistake of trusting him. Now that I know his true character, I shall never do so again."

"I am glad to hear it," said John.

Claudia noted with resentment that his voice and manner were perfectly calm. It was evident that he had not felt her words had any personal application and that it was not only Sir Lucas whom she had ceased to trust. She decided to make her message a little clearer.

"Indeed, my lord, you surprise me. I had not supposed from your behavior at the party that you had any objection to promiscuous kissing!"

It was evident from John's face that these words had brought him to attention. When he spoke again, however, his voice was as calm and composed as ever. "On the contrary, Miss Chambers," he said. "I do not approve of promiscuous kissing at all. Why should you think it?"

This was an awkward question. Much as she wanted to, Claudia could not bring herself to allude directly to that kiss he had given her. She laughed shortly. "If you don't remember, then I shall not remind you!" she said. Turning away, she added, "I beg you will excuse me now, my lord. I have an errand for your aunt to discharge."

To her annoyance, John fell into step beside her. "Have you? Perhaps you will not mind if I accompany you, Miss Chambers. There were one or two things I've been wanting to ask you. Now is as good a time as any."

"What sort of things?" said Claudia, shouldering her basket and heading toward the chemist's shop. "Your aunt is quite well if that is what you mean."

"No, though that is good news, of course. But what I wanted to ask really concerns you rather than my aunt."

"Oh, yes?" said Claudia, shooting him a suspicious look. "What do you want to ask?"

"Any number of questions, Miss Chambers. To start with, the direction of your brother in London. My aunt mentioned you had a brother there who is your nearest relative."

"Yes," said Claudia, amazed by this statement. "But why do you want Edmund's address, my lord? Did you want to consult him about some legal matter?"

"Yes, in a manner of speaking." There was a slight pause before John spoke again. "Your brother is an attorney?"

"A barrister, my lord. He works out of Gray's Inn."

"I see," said John. With a smile, he added, "I ought to have guessed you had some connection with the legal profession. If your brother is half as clever and persuasive as you, I daresay he is a force to be reckoned with."

Although Claudia suspected this was mere flattery, she could not help being pleased by it. "Yes, Edmund is a wonderful barrister," she said. "He has done very well for himself, especially this last year or two. If things continue as they are going, he will be able to pay off the mortgages on Ashdown Grange several years before we anticipated."

Again John paused before replying. "I suppose Ashdown Grange is your family home?" he said.

"Yes, it's been in the family for ages. But we haven't lived there since my father died."

John seemed very interested in this statement. So interested was he that before long Claudia found herself explaining all about her family and background: how the Chambers family fortunes had declined through the years and how Edmund was working diligently to build them up again.

"I wish I could do something myself toward paying off the mortgages," she concluded wistfully. "I thought when I took this position I might be able to help, but Edmund refuses to accept any part of my earnings unless it's in the form of gifts for his children."

"He sounds like a most estimable brother," commented John. "And you sound like a most estimable sister, Miss Chambers. I expect he was sorry to see you leave his home."

"Yes, but his wife wasn't," said Claudia candidly. "That is the main reason I decided to look for a position, my lord. And I can't tell you how wonderful it is to be where I am really wanted and needed. Your aunt is so good to me. She treats me more like a friend than an employee."

John nodded, but seemed disinclined to talk. Claudia, glancing sideways at him, thought he was regarding her thoughtfully—almost, she thought, respectfully. "But I won't be taken in by *that* again," she told herself. "I still remember how he tried to convince me he kissed me that night at the party only because he respected me so much!"

The thought made Claudia harden her heart toward John once more. Her manner became appreciably more chilly, but to her annoyance he hardly seemed to notice. He accompanied her silently as she went from shop to shop, apparently absorbed in his own thoughts. Piqued, Claudia decided to put an end to the interview. "I thank you very much for your company, my lord, but I must take leave of you now," she said, accompanying the words with a stately bow. "I am finished with my errand for your aunt and ought to be returning to Rexford Park."

"You must allow me to drive you there, Miss Chambers," he said at once. "It would be my pleasure, I assure you."

"Thank you, but I will not put you to so much trouble, my lord. Indeed, I would rather walk."

"I have just told you that it will be no trouble, but on the contrary a pleasure, Miss Chambers. If you will wait here while I fetch my curricle—"

"I don't want to ride in your curricle," said Claudia in exasperation. "I tell you that I would rather walk, my lord!"

As she was speaking, she saw a gentleman in a stanhope drive by and look intently in her direction. Claudia looked back in some puzzlement, whereupon the gentleman's face brightened with recognition and pleasure.

"Why, it's Miss Chambers!" he exclaimed, pulling his horses to a stop. "How d'ye do, Miss Chambers? I thought it was you, but I couldn't be sure till you looked up just now. You remember me, don't you? William Williams, at your service. We danced at the party t'other night."

"Yes, certainly I remember you, Mr. Williams," said Claudia, smiling and bowing warmly. "How do you do?"

"Very well—very well indeed. I've nothing to complain of, at any rate." He returned Claudia's bow and then, recognizing John, ventured another, more tentative bow in his direction. "How d'ye do, my lord? Fine day, isn't it?"

"Very fine," said John shortly.

Quashed in this manner, Mr. Williams was glad to turn his attention back to Claudia. "What brings you to Lockbridge this afternoon, Miss Chambers?" he asked. "Been doing some shopping?"

"Yes, I had an errand to run for Lady Rexford. But I am done with it now and was just on the point of starting back."

"In that case, perhaps you'll let me give you a ride home?" There was a hopeful look on Mr. Williams's ingenuous face as he regarded Claudia. "You didn't drive here on your own, did you?"

"No, I walked. I suppose you might give me a ride home if you liked." Claudia did not dare look at John as she made this statement. "If you're sure it won't be too much trouble, Mr. Williams?"

Mr. Williams assured her jubilantly that it was no trouble at all. Getting down from the stanhope, he assisted Claudia in mounting that sporting vehicle; then he got in beside her. She risked a brief look at John once she was seated beside Mr. Williams.

"Good afternoon, Lord Rexford. It was pleasant seeing you again."

"Good afternoon to you, too, Miss Chambers," he returned

gravely. He remained standing where he was, looking after her as she and Mr. Williams drove off.

All the way back to Rexford Park, Claudia could not rid herself of a sensation of guilt.

Of course John was a libertine—and a presumptuous libertine at that. She had certainly done right to depress his pretensions. But still she could not help feeling that she had been unnecessarily harsh in her manner of doing so. It would have been enough to have refused his offer of a ride without accepting Mr. Williams's as a way of emphasizing it. She could not forget the grave, almost grieved, look on John's face as he had bid her good afternoon. It haunted Claudia on the way home so much that she heard almost nothing of Mr. Williams's artless chatter. It was only when they were almost to the gates of Rexford Park that two sentences penetrated her thoughts.

"Well, what do you say, Miss Chambers? Willing to give it a go?"

"I beg your pardon?" asked Claudia, dragging her thoughts away from John. "Willing to give what a go, Mr. Williams?"

"Marriage," he said simply. "I'm asking you to marry me, Miss Chambers." As Claudia stared at him, he went on with a touch of diffidence. "I hope you won't think it's presuming. But the fact is, I've been crazy about you since the first time I saw you. You're a dashed pretty girl and smart as a whip, too. As I see it, you're just the kind of girl who'd make me a bang-up wife."

"I don't think—" began Claudia.

Mr. Williams hurried on anxiously. "Please don't say no until you've thought about it, Miss Chambers. I know you've got more breeding than I do, but I've done very well for myself in the farming line. Anyone living hereabouts will tell you the same. I could give you a good home and 'most anything else you wanted. And I do care about you—as much as a man ever cared for a woman, I trow. I'd treat you like a queen if you'd say you'd marry me."

Claudia wanted to laugh, but it was clear that Mr. Williams's sentiments were genuine, even if a bit awkwardly expressed. She spoke gently, hoping to spare his feelings. "I am sure you mean all you say, Mr. Williams, but I'm afraid it's not possible for me to accept your very flattering offer. I have no thought of marriage right now."

"I've taken you off guard, I expect," said Mr. Williams with an understanding nod. "That's natural enough, but you know you needn't answer me right away, Miss Chambers. Take your time and think it over. I'm willing to wait weeks—months if necessary."

"You are very generous, but I'm afraid that would only be giving you false encouragement, Mr. Williams. Indeed, I cannot marry you."

Mr. Williams looked crestfallen. "Why not?" he said. "Don't tell me some other fellow's beaten me to the punch?"

Claudia was annoyed to find that John's image had sprung unbidden into her head at these words. "Certainly not," she said sharply. "It is no reason such as that which causes me to refuse you, Mr. Williams."

"Then what is the reason? Is it that I'm not quite in your class? I know I'm not, but I do care for you, Miss Chambers. And though I may not be a nob with a dozen carriages and a grand house in town, I can at least make it so you won't have to work for your living."

Claudia was happy to seize on this excuse. "But I enjoy working for Lady Rexford," she said. "And indeed, I think she has come to depend on me, Mr. Williams—not merely as an employee but as a friend. It would make her very unhappy if I were to leave her employ."

Mr. Williams meditated. "I'll have a talk with her," he said at last, nodding with a satisfied air. "If she's as much your friend as you say, then she'll see the reason of your marrying and gaining an establishment of your own. I'll explain to her all I mean to do for you—and if she has any justice in her at all, I think she'll agree that you're better off marrying me. Not to brag, but I'm considered a pretty warm man in these parts."

Claudia was taken aback by this proposition. "You mustn't say anything to Lady Rexford!" she exclaimed. "Really it's not at all necessary, Mr. Williams. I am sure she will not hear of my leaving her."

"She's bound to hear of it, for I'm going to tell her," said Mr. Williams with a determined set to his jaw. "Just leave it all to me, Miss Chambers. I'll go bail I can make the old lady see reason." In a softer voice, he added, "Mind you, I don't blame her for not wishing to see you go. I'm sure anybody'd feel the same that was lucky enough to have you around in the first place."

"Not necessarily," said Claudia, thinking of Anthea. But she said no more, for it was clear that Mr. Williams was determined to talk to Lady Rexford. The only way to dissuade him from doing so would be to tell him flatly that she did not and never could care for him, and Claudia was too softhearted to do that. Mr. Williams seemed like a pleasant, respectable, well-intentioned young man. It was not his fault that she could not care for him as he deserved. It might be cowardly to blame her refusal on Lady Rexford, but Claudia felt such a refusal would be less painful for him than a more personal one. And it would also fit in nicely with the reputation Lady Rexford was seeking to establish in the neighborhood: that of a determined woman who ruled her household with a rod of iron.

As soon as they reached Rexford Park, she showed Mr. Williams into the drawing room, then hurried off to find Lady Rexford. She found her in her sitting room, where she was engaged in a friendly game of piquet with Hettie. "My dear ma'am, you must help me," she cried, shutting the door and sinking down on an upholstered settee. "There's a gentleman who's here to ask you to let me marry him, and you must tell him you can't spare me at any price."

"No, to be sure I cannot," said Lady Rexford, blinking a

little at this speech. "But who is this gentleman, my dear? Do I know him?"

"Yes, you met him at the fete. His name is William Williams, and he has a property not far from here." Rapidly Claudia explained the circumstances of Mr. Williams's proposal. "I'm sorry to make you do the refusing for me, ma'am, but indeed he would not accept my excuses. If you could tell him you cannot part with me, I think it would convince him I was serious without making the rejection a personal one. Do you mind?"

"No, to be sure I do not, my dear," said Lady Rexford, rising to her feet. With a whimsical smile, she added, "I doubt not it'll be good for me to refuse somebody something. Since Rexford talked to the servants, they've all been so agreeable that I've nothing to do but smile and say 'If you please' and 'Thank you.' I'll tell this young man that I won't hear of your marrying him—and indeed, my dear, it'll be nothing more than the truth. Just leave it all to me. I'll send him away with a flea in his ear!"

Lady Rexford sailed downstairs to deal with Mr. Williams, and Claudia went to her own room. Her mood was a little pensive. Softheartedly, she found herself regretting the disappointment that lay in store for Mr. Williams. But of course it was necessary to refuse him, just as it had been necessary to snub John. And with this reflection Claudia tried to comfort herself as she changed her dress and waited for Lady Rexford to return with news of Mr. Williams's rout.

The process took much longer than she would have believed possible. It was a good hour before Lady Rexford returned and even then her face did not reflect the unmixed satisfaction that Claudia had anticipated.

"You did refuse him, ma'am, didn't you?" said Claudia, regarding her with alarm.

"Oh, yes, I refused him," said Lady Rexford in a gloomy voice. "I told him I could not do without you, just as you said."

"That's good," said Claudia with relief. "It's all settled then?"

"Well, no . . ." Lady Rexford regarded Claudia with indecision. At last she seemed to make up her mind. Dropping down in a nearby chair, she took Claudia's hand between her own. "I wonder, my dear, if you have really thought this over," she said. "Are you quite sure you wish to refuse this young man?"

"Quite sure," said Claudia with annoyance. "I was never more sure of anything in my life."

Lady Rexford shook her head. "In general, my dear, I think your judgment very sound. But I hope you will pardon me if I say that in this case, I think you are being a bit hasty. I spoke to Mr. Williams for a good time this afternoon. Really, he seems a most estimable young man, and he seems to care for you quite sincerely, too. I think you could do much worse than marry him."

"No doubt I could, but that is quite beside the point, ma'am. I don't wish to marry Mr. Williams. I would rather stay with you."

"Yes, but I cannot like to see you sacrifice your prospects this way, Miss Chambers. I'm sure I appreciate your wishing to stay with me—don't think that I don't. But it's as I've told you before: Such a pretty girl as you should have a home and family of her own. According to Mr. Williams, he can do very well for you, and I'm sure you'd be a deal happier with a handsome young husband than with an old woman like me."

"I wouldn't be," said Claudia stubbornly. "I don't want a husband. At least—no, that's quite correct, ma'am: I don't want a husband. And if you have encouraged Mr. Williams to dangle after me, then you have done both of us a disservice."

"I didn't go so far as that, my dear. I told him plainly that your marrying him was out of the question, but he just stood there cool as cool and told me he wouldn't give up hope until he saw you married to somebody else. I declare, I quite admired his spirit. I think you might have been impressed, too, Miss Chambers, if you had seen and heard the way he talked."

"He sounds to have had more determination than I would have expected," admitted Claudia. "But still I could not think of marrying him, ma'am."

"Well, if you ask me, you *should* think of it, my dear. Such a chance may not come your way again, you know. Just you give it some thought. Mr. Williams doesn't look likely to change his mind anytime soon, so you can take your time and think it over at your leisure."

Claudia's response was to say again that she could not think of marrying Mr. Williams. It was a response she was obliged to repeat many times in the days that followed. Lady Rexford never wearied of pointing out the advantages of the match, and such was her eloquence that Claudia soon began to wonder whether she might, after all, do well to consider Mr. Williams's offer.

"It's true that I would rather not be a hired companion all my life, even for such a mistress as Lady Rexford," she owned to herself. "Nor would I care to go home and live at daggers drawn with Anthea again. But I cannot like the idea of marrying a man I don't love."

It was not, she assured herself, that she cherished any romantic notions of marrying for love. She had outgrown such fantasies years ago when she had ceased to be a girl in her teens. Still, she greatly feared that even at the mature age of two and twenty she was capable of behaving foolishly. This was demonstrated by the way John's face kept popping into her head at the most inopportune moments—just when she had almost convinced herself that she ought to accept Mr. Williams's offer, for instance. Such foolishness was very vexing. Still more vexing was the strange thrill that went through her when she recalled that kiss he had given her at the fete.

"All the more reason I ought to accept Mr. Williams's offer," she told herself. "Marrying without love may not be the ideal, but it would be better than developing an infatuation for a libertine who is engaged to another girl."

Claudia reached this conclusion on a hot morning in July while she was out cutting roses for Lady Rexford in the rose garden. Absently she snipped half a dozen gorgeous crimson blooms, her thoughts absorbed in the painful dilemma that faced her. So absorbed was she that she inadvertently snipped her finger at the same time. The resulting rush of purely physical pain drove all else from her mind.

"Oh, dear," said Claudia, looking at her hand in dismay. The cut was not a deep one, but the blood was flowing freely, and she had nothing on hand to staunch it. "I'd better go back to the house," she decided aloud. Picking up the basket of roses in her uninjured hand, she turned around—and found herself face-to-face with John.

Sixteen

Since the day Claudia had driven off with William Williams, John had been in a disturbed frame of mind.

Of course he had not expected the course of his love affair to run perfectly smooth. At the moment, however, it did not seem to be running at all. He visited regularly at Rexford Park, but Claudia was so seldom to be seen during these visits that he came to suspect she was purposely avoiding him. This made him reluctant to accept Lady Rexford's friendly invitations to stay, eat dinner, and drink a bottle (or two) of Burgundy with her.

On those occasions he did stay to dinner, he got scant satisfaction from it. Claudia took little part in the conversation, refused to look him in the eye even when he addressed her directly, and always excused herself from the table as soon as possible.

John was not accustomed to abandoning his goals in the face of adversity. On the contrary, a touch of adversity generally only increased his determination to get his way in the end. But he came close to despairing now. Ever since the night of the fete, Claudia seemed to have made up her mind that he was persona non grata. His decision to kiss her that evening had been partly prompted by impulse and partly by a conviction that the time had come to tell her how he felt about her. But instead of advancing his cause as he had hoped, he appeared to have dealt it a deathblow.

He did not consider Barbara Brock to be a factor in this outcome. As far as he was concerned, his relationship with Barbara was a thing of the past. He had not seen her since the night of the fete, and though it was awkward to be on the outs with one's neighbors, John thought it better to appear rude rather than risk being misunderstood. Accordingly, he refused all invitations to the Towers and took care not to attend any other parties where Barbara was likely to be present. By taking these measures, he felt satisfied that he had demonstrated to everyone that he was no longer one of Barbara's suitors.

It was unfortunate that it had taken him so long to have his eyes opened about Barbara. It was even more unfortunate that this event should have taken place at the same time he was falling in love with Claudia. But in his mind the two events, though concurrent, were unrelated. He had always been slightly dissatisfied with the idea of marrying Barbara. This was demonstrated by his reluctance to formally propose to her, even after five or six years of the most lavish encouragement.

He felt no such reluctance with Claudia. Even after knowing her only a day, he had been impressed by her sweetness, spirit, and common sense. Now that he had known her a month and a half, he was impressed to the point of fervor. He admired her loyalty to his aunt, a woman she might easily have despised. He admired the quiet competence with which she discharged her duties. He admired the independence that had led her to seek employment in a stranger's house rather than remain in a household where she felt unwanted. He admired everything about her, and sometimes it seemed to him that he could not wait another day to tell her so.

But the one time he had tried to do so, on the evening of the fete, his assurances had been so coolly received that he hesitated to make another attempt. It was evident that she had been offended by his kissing her. He had probably frightened her by being too precipitate. John thought it better to try to rewin her trust before making another such attempt. There was no hurry, as he reminded himself. Lady Rexford now spoke of remaining in Yorkshire all summer, and John was confident that in the month or two that remained to him, he ought to make at least some headway in his courtship.

It therefore came as a great shock when he heard of William Williams's proposal.

He heard the rumor first in the village, where he was engaged in an errand at the saddler's. The saddler, an elderly man known equally for his magnificent waist-length beard and his love of gossip, volunteered the information as he attended to John's business. "I do be hearing summat interesting about young Williams up at Grove Point Farm," he told John. "Summat very interesting indeed. But mayhap you've heard it yourself already, m'lord, seeing your aunt lives at t' Park."

"No, I can't say I have," said John, regarding the saddler with surprise. "What has Mr. Williams to do with my aunt?"

"Nary a thing with her, my lord, but a good deal with t' young lady that's staying with her if all I hear be true."

"What's that?" John said so sharply that the saddler looked at him in amazement.

"Why, they say poor Will's quite nutty upon t' young lady. A very pretty young lady she is, by all accounts, and wonderful genteel, too. Somebody told me he'd gone for and proposed marriage to her, but I don't know as I put much credit in that. There's been no banns posted, as you'd expect if he'd really asked her to marry him. But wisht, you never know. Being as she's a young lady and hails from London (as I do hear), mayhap she's too nesh for banns. Like as not she'd want poor Will to put up t' brass for a license, so they could be married in t' evening like city folk." He shook his head disapprovingly. "I don't approve of such starts myself. Banns and a morning wedding, with a nice breakfast afterward, is good enough for anyone—that's what *I* say." He paused and looked at John expectantly.

John knew he was meant to agree with this statement, but small talk was quite beyond him at that moment. "Excuse me. I must go," he said rapidly. "See that my harness is sent to the Gatehouse as soon as it is done." With these words he strode out of the shop, leaving the saddler gaping after him.

He had chosen to walk into the village so that he was obliged to walk all the way back to Rexford Park in a fever of speculation. Could it be possible that William Williams had proposed to Claudia and that she had accepted him? Could it be that the woman he loved was now promised to marry someone else?

By the time he reached the Park, his anxiety had reached an unbearable pitch. So anxious was he that he eschewed the drive, took a short cut across the lawn, and happened upon Claudia just as her accident took place.

"Claudia!" he said and never knew he had called her by her first name.

Claudia did not hear him because she was intent on cutting roses. An instant later, however, John heard her give a soft exclamation. Thinking she must have seen him and must be meditating a hasty retreat, he hastened his steps to intercept her. "Claudia!" he said again, then froze as he perceived the blood on her hand. "My God, what's happened? Are you injured?"

His voice was so horror-struck that Claudia could not help smiling. "Yes, but my injury is a very slight one, my lord," she said, holding out her hand for him to see. "I was cutting roses, but foolishly made the mistake of cutting myself instead."

John caught her hand in his and looked at it closely. "Yes, it is only a scratch," he said with relief. "Still, it ought to be seen to. Here, wrap your hand in my handkerchief and let us go into the house."

Claudia accepted the handkerchief and allowed John to take the basket of roses in its stead. As they walked across the lawn together, she glanced shyly at his profile. He looked very stern and distant, she thought, not at all like a man who would presume on the intimacy of calling a young lady by her first name. Yet that was what he had done a moment before. Claudia decided it must have been a mistake, a mere slip of the tongue. He had probably been so shocked at the sight of blood on her hand that he had been betrayed into addressing her informally. Claudia was the more sure that this was the case when he spoke again, this time in a tone of the utmost formality.

"I trust your hand is no worse, Miss Chambers?"

"No, it is a great deal better," said Claudia, looking down at the injured member. "It's not even bleeding any longer, my lord. Your handkerchief has done all that was necessary."

"Nevertheless, it ought to be properly dressed," he said firmly. "As soon as we get to the house, I'll send one of the servants after the doctor."

"Indeed you shall not, my lord," said Claudia with equal firmness. "I am persuaded the doctor would laugh at me for consulting him about such a scratch as this. Let me hear no more about it if you please. Shall I call your aunt for you?"

They were nearly to the house as Claudia asked this question. John stopped, looking down at her. "No, thank you, Miss Chambers," he said. "As it happens, I called today to see you rather than my aunt. If you are sure that you will not consult a doctor about your hand—"

"Quite sure," said Claudia firmly.

"Then we may as well stay out here and talk."

"If you like," said Claudia, a little warily. She pointed to a nearby arbor containing a weather-beaten wooden bench. "Shall we sit there to talk?"

"That will do very nicely," said John. He sat down on the bench, and Claudia seated herself at the opposite end, as far away from him as possible. He promptly slid closer. "Tell me, Miss Chambers. Is it true what I have heard?" he asked, looking into her eyes.

In spite of her embarrassment at finding herself in such proximity to John, Claudia was amused by this question. "Why, that depends on what you have heard, my lord," she said, smiling. "You may have heard any number of rumors that I am in no position to verify."

John did not return her smile. "You can verify this one," he said. "I understand William Williams has made you an offer of marriage."

Claudia felt her color rise. "Yes, I may say that you have understood correctly, my lord," she said, striving for composure. "Mr. Williams has indeed done me the honor you speak of."

"And do you mean to accept him?" said John, looking steadily into her eyes.

Looking back at him, Claudia was swept by a wave of anger. What right had he to look at her like that and to ask such personal questions when he was himself engaged to another girl? She spoke with cold deliberation. "I will be glad to answer that question, my lord, when you can prove to me that my private affairs are any business of yours."

She observed with satisfaction that John's color had also risen. Still, he went on, looking steadily into her eyes. "I suppose most people would say your affairs were none of my business," he said. "But that is because they do not realize how I feel about you. You, on the other hand, do know—at least I hope you know by now. I thought I made my feelings fairly clear on the night of the fete."

Claudia heard these words in disbelief. It was bad enough that he had dared to allude to that disreputable incident at the fete; now here he was, implying that he had serious feelings for her! Yet he must know she was aware of his engagement to Barbara Brock. Was it possible he supposed she would be amenable to some kind of illicit relationship? Really, there could be no other explanation. He was a dog in the manger, not interested in marrying her himself, but eager to prevent her marriage to anyone else.

This idea made Claudia lose her temper entirely. It was either that or burst into tears, and she reckoned anger was the safer emotion.

"You made your feelings quite clear the other night, my

lord," she said fiercely. "The more shame to you that it should be so!"

He seemed startled by her warmth. "I don't consider it any shame to care about you, Miss Chambers," he said. "Why should I? You are a beautiful, intelligent, charming young woman with a character as admirable as your appearance. You come from a family that is at the very least respectable and—if I read between the lines correctly—even exalted. I should be proud, not ashamed, to make you my wife."

"Your wife!" exclaimed Claudia, staring at him. "Don't pretend you want to make me your wife, my lord!"

His eyebrows rose. "Certainly I want to make you my wife, Miss Chambers," he said. "I thought I had made that clear at the fete. But in case I did not, I would be happy to elaborate on the statement."

Before Claudia could guess his intention, he had gathered her into his arms. She had time only to note that his dark eyes were aglow with laughter—and, perhaps, a warmer emotion—before he kissed her.

At the touch of his mouth on hers, Claudia's anger melted away as though it had never been. She felt only surprise and wonderment, combined with a strange rising rapture. It felt wonderful to be enveloped in the warmth and strength of John's arms—wonderful to feel the firm yet gentle pressure of his lips on hers. It was a pressure that seemed to coax rather than demand, and it would have been all too easy to yield to that pressure, to give him what he evidently desired.

But what did he desire? The thought came stabbing through the warm haze of pleasure that was engulfing Claudia. Her eyes flew open.

As though sensing the changed tenor of her thoughts, John ceased kissing her, but he continued to look down at her with what appeared to be his whole heart in his eyes. "Oh, Claudia," he said. "I do love you."

Claudia drew sharply away from him, gazing at him in revulsion. "Don't!" she said. "Don't, my lord! You mustn't—indeed you must not."

"No?" said John. He said it smilingly, but his smile faded when he saw her evident distress. "What is it, Claudia?" he asked gently. "What's wrong?"

Claudia continued to stare at him, disregarding both questions. "I would not have supposed it possible," she said in a low voice. "I would not have believed you could be so iniquitous. Have you no shame at all?"

"That is the second time you have implied I should be ashamed of myself," said John with an edge in his voice. "Pray tell me, Miss Chambers, what cause have I for shame? I had not supposed there was any shame in proposing marriage to the woman I love."

"None at all, assuming you are free to follow through on your proposal," retorted Claudia. "But a very great deal when you are already engaged to another woman!" She turned her face away, fighting back the urge to cry.

If she had not been looking away, she would have seen John's thunderstruck expression. "Engaged to another woman!" he said. "What nonsense is this? Who told you I was engaged to another woman?"

"Miss Brock herself, my lord! But I had heard it from others even before she told me. I should think you would have known you could never succeed with such a deception in a small neighborhood like this one."

By now the truth had begun to dawn upon John. He was torn between amusement and irritation. "You have heard of that old business between me and Barbara Brock, I suppose," he said. "I ought to have told you of it before, perhaps, but I thought it better to wait until we had reached an understanding."

"Yes, I daresay you did," agreed Claudia with awful sarcasm. "Poor Miss Brock! I wonder what she would say if she could hear you refer to your engagement with her as 'that old business.' I assure you, my lord, that in spite of how you may choose to regard the matter, she regards it as sufficiently real and binding."

John was looking very grim. "Does she?" he said. "And you believed her?"

"What choice had I, my lord? Ever since your aunt and I arrived here, we have heard from various people that you were engaged or about to become engaged to Miss Brock. I could hardly disbelieve a story that had such wide credence, could I?"

John opened his mouth, then closed it again. It would have been so easy to deny that any engagement existed between him and Barbara. But Claudia's words had given him pause.

Of course Barbara had no right to go around telling stories that were not true. But was it not partly his own fault that her stories were so readily believed? He had been a longtime suitor of hers, and there had been a time when he himself had supposed they would one day be husband and wife. He had done nothing to contradict people when they spoke of his and Barbara's marriage as an eventual certainty.

It might be technically true that he owed no loyalty to Barbara, seeing that he had never made her a formal proposal. But their relationship had been such a long-standing one that John felt he did owe her at least a chance to save face in the matter. She was a prominent person in the community, and her reputation would suffer if it were whispered that she had been jilted. It would be better if she were given a chance to personally refute the rumors that were flying about before he took matters in his own hands and refuted them himself.

And that meant he had a responsibility to speak to Barbara one more time before he said anything further to Claudia. John admitted this responsibility reluctantly. It was frustrating to have to keep silence when he wished to assure Claudia that he had never loved or proposed to any woman but her. It was worse than frustrating to let her believe he was a blackguard when he had been, at worst, only thoughtless and shortsighted. But he was a gentleman, and gentlemen did not shirk their duties toward ladies, even ladies who had behaved in a less than ladylike manner. He must square matters with Barbara before he would be free to tell Claudia the whole story.

Claudia, looking at him, could see the struggle he was undergoing. Her heart sank. In spite of what Barbara and others had told her, in spite of what she herself had told John a moment before, she had been hoping that he would deny his engagement. But it was clear now that he could not deny it. That meant there was nothing for her to do but accept the truth and deal with it as best she could. Once more Claudia felt a smarting of tears behind her eyes, but she was determined not to give way to them—not as long as she was in John's company at any rate. Blinking furiously, she rose to her feet.

"I see you have no answer, my lord. I suggest it would be better if we forgot this conversation ever took place. If you will excuse me now, I must take these flowers in to Lady Rexford."

"Wait!" said John. Claudia waited, though she felt the futility of the gesture. What could he say that could possibly change things? If he could not deny his engagement to Barbara Brock, what was there that he *could* say?

What he actually said was, "I am sure all this must have a very irregular appearance, Miss Chambers. But I beg you will believe that my behavior is not so bad as it appears. I promise I will tell you the whole story as soon as I am at liberty to do so."

This sounded like an evasion to Claudia. Disillusioned and downhearted as she was, she managed a skeptical smile. "Is there anything else, my lord?" she asked with just the slightest touch of irony in her voice.

"Yes. Don't marry William Williams," he said. Taking her face between his hands, he pressed a fervent kiss on her brow, then turned and strode away.

Seventeen

After John had left, Claudia picked up her basket of roses and walked slowly into the house.

She felt dazed by what had just happened. Strange and unexpected as it had been to receive a proposal from Mr. Williams, this was a thousand times more strange and unexpected. It was not every day, she told herself wryly, that one received an offer of marriage from an eligible viscount. Even if that same viscount was proven to be already engaged to marry somebody else, it was still a memorable event. Claudia thought it best to rationalize John's proposal in this manner, because she knew there was not the slightest possibility of her ever forgetting it. It was engraved on her memory in characters too deep to be effaced, and she very much feared it was graven on her heart as well, though she tried to deny it.

"It's not possible that I love him," she told herself. "After the way he has behaved today, I ought to regard him with the utmost contempt. But I don't—I don't—I'm terribly afraid I don't. Even in spite of knowing the truth, I find myself wanting to believe in him—wanting to believe that he loves me and wants to marry me—wanting to believe that speech he made at the last when he assured me he could explain everything. If only he could! But it's futile to hope for such a thing. He is merely an unprincipled wretch with a talent for dissembling. He ought to be on the stage instead of wasting his talents on a foolish hired companion in Yorkshire."

The vision of John, tricked out in actor's garb and earning accolades behind the footlamps, brought a dreary smile to Claudia's lips. For the rest of the day, by dint of concentrating very hard on John's iniquities, she was able to keep her spirits from sinking quite out of sight. But they were low enough in spite of all she could do. Mrs. Fry remarked acidly that "she seemed to have had the ginger taken out of her," while Hettie and Lady Rexford hovered over her anxiously, suggesting remedies as diverse as sal volatile, brandy, and burned feathers.

"No, thank you," said Claudia to all these remedies. She knew well enough that only time could cure the malady that was afflicting her.

She went to bed that night in a mood of blackest depression. Yet her depression was a little eased when she reflected that the worst of her ordeal must now be behind her. Disillusionment on such a grand scale could happen only once, Claudia reasoned. Having once accepted that John was a faithless scoundrel, she ought to be that much closer to forgetting him. Tomorrow would bring her yet closer to that ideal state, and the next day closer still, until at last her heart ceased to ache altogether and she was able to regard him with complete indifference.

Yet the morrow did not bring the relief Claudia had expected. Nor did the following day, or the day following that. It was not until a full week had gone by that Claudia began to realize the insidious nature of her complaint. In spite of her common sense and better judgment, in spite of the undoubted wisdom of putting all thought of John aside and going on with her life, Claudia found she had not yet reached the point where such a thing was possible. She could not expunge all her John-related hopes and dreams and desires from her heart until she had spoken to him once more and heard the explanation he had promised. That this promise was almost certainly a sham to save face did not matter. Claudia's heart chose to believe in him, even if her head did not. Each day found her waiting anxiously for his promised visit, and each day found her bitterly disappointed when he did not come.

This was naturally a frustrating situation. Claudia did her best to hide her state of mind from her employer, but Lady Rexford could not help noticing her uneven spirits, her sudden start every time a knock sounded on the door, and her strange unwillingness to leave Rexford Park for so much as an hour.

"I don't understand it, my dear, not in the least. Now that we've got our foot into the local society as you might say, why should you wish to sit moping here at home when you could be out dancing or dining or playing cards? I'm sure that here lately we've been getting invitations enough that we might go out every night if we chose. Of course I don't care to rake it so hard as that, and I quite agree that it's better if we keep ourselves a bit exclusive, especially here at first when we're still more or less strangers to everybody. But a little society now and then is a good thing, as you surely must admit, my dear. Why don't you care to go to this rout Mrs. Falconer's holding? It sounds very diverting."

"I'm sure it is. And I'll go if you want me to, ma'am," said Claudia, forcing a smile. "It's only that I don't care to go on my own account."

"And why on earth not? When I was your age, I'm sure I would have jumped at the chance to go to a party—especially a party where my beau was likely to be."

"What beau? What do you mean?" said Claudia. She spoke more sharply than she had intended, for her thoughts, as always, had flown immediately to the subject of John. For a guilty moment, she felt certain Lady Rexford must have learned of his proposal.

Lady Rexford, however, smiled and shook her head. "What beau do I mean? Why, Mr. Williams, to be sure. Bless the girl, she's so many beaux she can't keep track of them all! And it's no wonder, I'm sure, for when I went to the Desmonds' the other night, I had at least half a dozen young fellows sidle up to me and ask sheepish like if you was planning to come later on. Sir Lucas asked about you, too. But you may be sure I didn't give *him* any encouragement." Lady Rexford thinned her rosebud mouth to a disapproving line. "He may be a fine gentleman with a handle to his name, but the plain fact is I don't care for him or his manners. Even if you could bring him up to scratch (which I take leave to doubt, my dear), I'd say you'd do better to marry Mr. Williams."

"My dear Lady Rexford, at the moment there is as much chance of my marrying the one as the other—which is to say, no chance at all."

Claudia's voice and manner were very firm as she made this statement. Lady Rexford looked wistful, but experience had taught her the futility of arguing with her companion in this mood. "Well, I'm sure I think it's a great pity," she said with a sigh. "But if you can't care for him, my dear, then you can't—and that's all there is to it."

Claudia was relieved to see that her mistress appeared resigned to the situation. "I am so glad you understand, ma'am," she said, giving Lady Rexford a grateful smile. "And I hope you will understand also that I would rather not go to Mrs. Falconer's tonight. I'm simply not in the mood for a party."

"Well, if you don't wish to, I shall not press you, my dear. But I hope you've no objection if I go without you? The thing is that I met Rexford today when I was in the village, and he said he was going to the Falconers' tonight, too. It's been almost a week since I've seen the dear boy, and I wished to consult him about one or two matters that have come up in connection with those cottages we are building."

The mention of John made Claudia's heart give a little leap. She scolded herself for her foolishness, however, and schooled her features into an expression of mere polite interest. "So Lord Rexford is to be at the Falconers', too, is he?" she said. "I am relieved to hear it, ma'am. If you have your nephew for company, I can be assured that you will not want for mine."

"But I will, my love. You know I would rather have both you and Rexford with me if I could pick and choose. Are you sure you won't come to the Falconers'? I am afraid you will be very dull if you stay home, for you know this is Hettie's night off."

"I intend to keep too busy to be dull," said Claudia with forced cheer. "I thought I would amuse myself this evening by looking for the Rexford Rembrandt. You know we have done nothing toward locating it, ma'am, and by all accounts it is a very valuable painting."

Claudia had formulated this excuse during the small hours of the previous night, feeling that Lady Rexford would more likely excuse her from attending the Falconers' party if she had a positive reason for staying home. Nor was she wrong, for Lady Rexford heartily approved her initiative.

"Indeed, I have been thinking for quite a while that we ought to be looking for that old painting," she said with a shake of her head. "And I am sure that you can find it if anyone can, Miss Chambers. Only don't wear yourself out with too much looking. If it doesn't come to light straight off, just you wait, and Hettie and I'll join you in making a proper search for it tomorrow. I'm sure we ought to be making a push to find it, for though Rexford hasn't said any more about it since that first day, I don't want him to think that I had anything to do with its disappearance. And I can see it looks suspicious, the painting disappearing about the time his uncle and I were married."

She left for the Falconers' soon after this. Claudia bade her good-bye, then commenced immediately upon her search.

She began at the top of the house in the box rooms and attics, intending to work her way down. It proved a not wholly congenial task. The day had been a hot one, and the rooms under the roof were very warm as well as being replete with dust and cobwebs. Still, Claudia persevered. She had an interest in achieving her task, even apart from her motive of pleasing Lady Rexford.

It was, after all, John who had been the first to speak of the Rembrandt. It was he who seemed to value it most, both as an heirloom and a work of art. To find it would certainly please him. Claudia would not admit it to herself, but the idea of pleasing John held a strong attraction for her. She might not be able to marry him, but she could at least restore to him his missing family property. And in years to come, he would look at the Rembrandt and perhaps remember Claudia Chambers, the young lady who had played a small role in restoring it.

This romantic idea fueled Claudia for more than two hours. She poked through trunks and boxes, peered into packing crates, and sorted patiently through what appeared to be several centuries' worth of accumulated rubbish. She found several pictures, but none that could possibly be the missing masterpiece.

" 'A small picture, rather dark, depicting an elderly woman,' " quoted Claudia, shaking her head as she looked around the box room she had just searched. "I'm sure there's no such thing up here. I'll move down a floor and start looking in the unused bedchambers."

Here she encountered a problem, however. Those bedchambers not in use were all locked, and it was necessary to demand the keys from Mrs. Fry.

"What do you want the keys to those rooms for?" demanded Mrs. Fry, looking at Claudia suspiciously, as if she suspected her of planning to ransack the house for valuables. "There's not a thing in them apart from the furniture, you know."

"Likely not, but I want to look anyway," said Claudia as politely as she could. "If I might please borrow the keys?"

With visible reluctance, Mrs. Fry surrendered the keys. It was clear she was still suspicious of Claudia's motives, however, for during the next hour she made half a dozen trips to the upper story to "look in" on the search and assure Claudia that there was nothing of value to be found in any of those old rooms. Claudia found this exasperating enough, but she was really incensed when, on her seventh trip upstairs, Mrs. Fry announced that Sir Lucas Davenport was downstairs waiting to see her.

"Sir Lucas!" exclaimed Claudia. "Whatever is he doing here? Well, I can't see him—that's for certain. My dress looks as though I've been using it to sweep the floor. Please tell Sir Lucas I am indisposed."

"That'd be a lie, miss," said Mrs. Fry virtuously. "You know it's against my principles to tell lies. Anyway, you'll have to see Sir Lucas, for I told him you'd be right down. You wasn't doing anything of importance as far as I could see, and I supposed you'd be glad of some company."

Gritting her teeth, Claudia left the bedchamber she had been searching and went down to the drawing room. Outside the door, she paused to remove her apron and dust off her dress as well as she could. She then squared her shoulders, pinned a simulated smile on her lips, and entered the room.

"Good evening, Sir Lucas," she said briskly. "What can I do for you?"

"Merely allow me to look at you," returned Sir Lucas with a gallant bow. "You are a refreshing sight as always, Miss Chambers. I confess, I am relieved to see you in such evident good health. When I learned from Lady Rexford that you had chosen to stay home this evening, I feared it must be some indisposition that kept you away. And so I called to see if there was any service I could render you."

"No, I am quite well," said Claudia, keeping her voice as brisk and discouraging as before. "It was kind of you to be concerned, Sir Lucas, but you see your concern was needless. You may return to your party now with an easy mind."

"Ah, but I would rather stay here with you," returned Sir Lucas. Not waiting for an invitation, he dropped down on the sofa and smiled at Claudia with would-be charm. "It was a dull party anyway, and I saw no point in staying once I learned you were not to be there."

"Unfortunately, you are likely to find it even duller here," retorted Claudia. "I am not a lady of leisure, Sir Lucas. At the moment I am in the midst of some work for Lady Rexford that demands my whole attention. I beg you will excuse me."

Sir Lucas looked disappointed. "What kind of work?" he asked. "Is it something I could assist you with, Miss Chambers?"

"Thank you, but I need no help, Sir Lucas. I am merely looking for something . . . something that one of us has misplaced here in the house."

Claudia was pleased with this explanation, which she felt was sufficient to provide a decent excuse for abandoning Sir Lucas while still vague enough not to arouse his curiosity. But something in her manner must have betrayed her, or else Sir Lucas possessed the gift of reading minds. He leaned forward in his chair with sudden excitement. "It's not the Rexford Rembrandt you're looking for, is it?" he asked.

"Yes, as a matter of fact it is," said Claudia, too surprised to dissemble. "How did you know?"

Sir Lucas smiled, showing a set of wolfish white teeth. "Ah, that was merely a lucky guess on my part. The Rembrandt is the only thing of value that I knew to have been misplaced in the household, so naturally my mind flew to that at once. And in truth, I have been wondering for some weeks why more hue and cry has not been made over its disappearance. That portrait was a masterpiece. My own art collection is not contemptible, but I would gladly exchange any or all of the paintings in it for that one."

Claudia was surprised by the passion in his voice. "Yes, I understand the missing painting was a very fine one," she said. "But I begin to think it must not be here at Rexford Park after all. I have been searching for some hours now and have found no trace of it."

"Where did you look?" asked Sir Lucas.

Claudia told him, rather surprised to be making a confidant of Sir Lucas Davenport. But this was a different Sir Lucas from the gentleman who had just been paying her extravagant and unwelcome compliments. His place had been taken by an authoritative Sir Lucas, who fired off questions one after another and did not hesitate to tell her where she had gone wrong.

"You say you looked for the picture in the attic and most of the upper bedrooms, Miss Chambers. But it sounds as though you were looking for a *framed* picture—and you know it is quite possible that when the Rembrandt was removed from the drawing room it was also removed from its frame. In that case it would only be a flat piece of canvas—or even a roll of canvas, which might fit with ease inside a container no larger than a pencase."

"Oh, dear," said Claudia, quite staggered to think she had overlooked this possibility. "I never thought to look for an unframed picture, Sir Lucas. I suppose now I shall have to go back and search the whole attic over again."

"I'll help you," said Sir Lucas, getting to his feet.

Claudia wondered if she ought to try to stop him. At present he seemed to have abandoned his earlier amorous mood, but there was no saying whether he might not take it up again once he and Claudia were alone in the attics. However, her fears in this regard were banished by Sir Lucas's next speech.

"You had better call one or two of the maids to help us search, Miss Chambers. We can cover ground much faster that way. I can't imagine why Rexford hasn't made a proper search for the painting long before now. By God, if it were my Rembrandt that had gone missing, I would have torn the house apart looking for it."

Judging by Sir Lucas's subsequent actions, Claudia could readily believe it. He swept through the attics like a hurricane, upending boxes and trunks, scattering books, papers, and documents to the left and right, and leaving the dull job of picking up to Claudia and the maid.

This latter, a young and rather bovine-looking girl who rejoiced in the name of Hepsibah, had been grudgingly lent to them by Mrs. Fry after various dire warnings that Claudia must not complain tomorrow if the parlors were not properly swept and dusted. Hepsibah was mightily enjoying this change from her usual routine, but she was also bewildered by Sir Lucas's rapid and destructive progress through the attic.

"What's t' gentleman looking for again?" she whispered to Claudia. "A picture, is it?"

"Yes, a very fine and valuable old painting," said Claudia. "It used to hang downstairs in the drawing room until a few years ago. But for some reason it was removed, and now we are trying to discover what has become of it."

"Ah," said Hepsibah with a shake of her head. "I wouldn't know what painting you mean, miss. I've only been here at t' Park a year come this Michaelmas. In all that time t' drawing room's always been just as it is now." Her voice became tinged with gloom as she added, "And I misdoubt I'll be staying here once my year's up. Mrs. Fry don't think my work's up to snuff, though I'm sure I try hard enough to suit."

Claudia said sympathetically that Mrs. Fry was very hard to please, to which statement Hepsibah returned a heartfelt assent. She and Claudia then turned their attention to picking up a trunkful of old clothes that Sir Lucas had left scattered on the floor.

"I'm glad to hear 'tis a fine and valuable painting we're looking for," said Hepsibah, as she shook out and refolded a brocade sacque. "I'll confess now that, when I heard you and t' gentleman talking about a missing picture, my heart misgave me for a minute that it might be my own picture you was wanting."

"Your own picture?" said Claudia, who was busy sorting through several sets of buckled and high-heeled shoes. "Have you a picture of your own, Hepsibah?"

Hepsibah laughed self-consciously. "Nay, miss—though I like to *think* 'tis my own. But 'tis really only an old one I borrowed, as you might say."

"Oh, yes?" said Claudia politely. She was not much interested in the maidservant's chatter, but it was not in her nature to be rude. "What kind of a picture is it?"

"I don't suppose you'd think it anything much, miss. 'Tis only a little old thing and that dark you can hardly see what 'tis you're looking at."

"What?" Claudia stopped sorting shoes and stared at Hepsibah. "You say it is a small, dark picture? It's—it's not a picture of an elderly woman, by any chance, is it?"

"Why, yes, it is, miss. An old woman wearing a sort of white cap on her head, like what my own grandmother used to wear. That's part of t' reason I took such a fancy to it, I believe. 'Twas my grandmother who raised me from a babe, my own mother not surviving her lying in. And so when Granny passed away a year or two ago—well, I'm bound to say I've missed her something fierce, miss. Having that picture to look at made me feel like I had her with me again if you can understand what I'm saying."

"Yes, I can understand," said Claudia with as much composure as she could muster. "But, Hepsibah, it sounds as though your picture might be the one we are looking for. No, I forgot—you said you had borrowed it."

"Well, in a manner of speaking, miss," said Hepsibah, looking discomfitted. "To speak truth, I found it packed away by itself in a drawer in t' old master's bedroom and took it for myself, not supposing it had any value. Like I said before, 'tis only a little thing and that dark you can hardly see aught but t' old woman's face."

Claudia took a deep breath. "I think we had better have a look at this picture of yours, Hepsibah," she said. "Let me call Sir Lucas, and we will all go look at it together."

It took a few minutes to divert Sir Lucas from the search and make him understand what Claudia had discovered. As soon as he understood, however, his excitement knew no bounds. He was hardly more restrained when at last they arrived in Hepsibah's room, a tiny chamber tucked up under the eaves. Against one wall stood a white iron bed, neatly made; a deal chair and table stood against the other beside a small chest of drawers. But Claudia and Sir Lucas had no eyes for any of these things. It was the picture on the wall above the bed that absorbed all their attention.

As Hepsibah had said, it was a small picture, barely a foot

wide and little more than that in length. Its subject was an elderly woman wearing a fluted white cap. She was not an attractive woman in any sense, and in truth, it would have been more accurate to call her homely. Yet there was something so frank and appealing about her plump face, something so irresistibly lifelike and humorous in the blue eyes that met the onlooker's so squarely that one hardly noticed this defect. Indeed, so skillful had the artist's rendering been that Claudia almost expected the woman to open her mouth and address their company with some rustic witticism.

"Is it the Rembrandt?" she asked, turning to Sir Lucas.

"Yes, it is," he said. Walking over to the picture, he reached up and unhooked it from the wall with reverent fingers. "My God! And to think a valuable thing like this has been hanging in a housemaid's room all this while!"

"I didn't know 'twas valuable," said Hepsibah defensively. " 'Tis such a little thing—though to be sure, 'tis wonderful lifelike. I catch myself talking to her sometimes, just as though 'twas really Granny herself in t' room with me. And bless me if sometimes I don't fancy she's about to answer me back!"

"Yes, it's a wonderful rendering," said Sir Lucas. "Only see how beautifully Rembrandt has captured the nuances of light and shadow upon the canvas, leaving the background dark so as to emphasize his sitter's face. That's one of the hallmarks of his style."

Both Claudia and Hepsibah listened respectfully as Sir Lucas discoursed for some moments on Rembrandt's painting techniques. When he was done, Hepsibah heaved a heavy sigh.

" 'Tis very interesting, sir, upon my word. I'm sure I never realized how wonderful a picture it was. It just looked like Granny to me. But I suppose I'll have to give her up now." She looked wistfully at the canvas in Sir Lucas's hands.

"I'm afraid so, Hepsibah," said Claudia gently. "But as I understand it, the picture used to hang in the drawing room until a few years ago. I expect now that it is found Lady Rexford will wish to restore it to its original place. So at least you will be able to see it now and then, even if you can't have it in your room."

"I suppose 'tis better than never seeing it at all," said Hepsibah with another sigh. "Do you mean to put it down in t' drawing room this minute?"

Claudia pondered for a moment, then shook her head. "No, I think not," she said. "Lady Rexford should be the one to restore it to its proper place. How pleased she will be that it has turned up! I can hardly wait until she gets home to tell her."

Sir Lucas, who had been listening to this conversation in silence, now spoke up. "Why need you wait?" he said. "Let us take it to her now, Miss Chambers. It will be a pleasant surprise for her, as you say, and perhaps it will do something to liven up that very dull soiree the Falconers are giving this evening. It couldn't hurt, at any rate."

On the whole, Claudia liked the idea. She told herself that it was her duty to inform Lady Rexford as soon as possible about the recovery of the Rembrandt. And of course it was her duty to inform John about it, too.

Claudia tagged this last reflection on as if it were afterthought, but in reality it was John's reaction rather than Lady Rexford's that chiefly concerned her. What would he say when he learned she had found the missing Rembrandt? Undoubtedly he would be surprised and pleased. It might even be that in an excess of delight he would try to kiss her again, though this was a liberty Claudia was determined not to allow.

But though resolute against letting John kiss her, she could not resist the larger temptation to see him again. Even after all that had passed between them—and even knowing that he was engaged to Barbara Brock. The temptation was all the more tempting because Claudia had the splendid excuse of duty to justify it. So when Sir Lucas urged her again to take the painting to Lady Rexford, offering to drive her to the Falconers' in his own chaise, Claudia gave way without an argument.

"Let me just change my dress first, Sir Lucas," she told him. "I won't be a minute."

It was more than a minute, but rather less than a quarter of an hour, when Claudia once more presented herself in the drawing room. She had changed her dusty cambric for a pretty evening dress of ivory satin, and she had also washed the dust from her face and hands and tidied her hair. But to her annoyance and embarrassment, she was forced to endure one more encounter with Mrs. Fry before she and Sir Lucas could leave the house.

"And where might you be going at this hour, miss?" demanded Mrs. Fry in a voice rife with suspicion. "It's pretty late to go out driving with gentlemen alone, I'm thinking!"

Claudia swallowed her irritation and forced herself to speak calmly. "Sir Lucas and I are not going out driving, Mrs. Fry," she said. "He is merely taking me to the Falconers'. I find there is something I must discuss with Lady Rexford—something that cannot wait until she gets back."

As Claudia spoke, she glanced involuntarily at the bundle beneath Sir Lucas's arm. At his suggestion, they had wrapped the Rembrandt in one of Claudia's shawls and stowed it in a bandbox, partly to protect it from damage and partly to keep it a secret until they were ready to unveil it to the company. But it seemed to Claudia that these artifices were insufficient against Mrs. Fry's suspicious gaze. Certainly she looked long and hard at the bandbox beneath Sir Lucas's arm as he and Claudia went together out to the chaise.

Once seated in Sir Lucas's chaise, Claudia quickly forgot about Mrs. Fry. Opening the bandbox, she removed the picture from its wrappings and sat studying it with delight as Sir Lucas gave the order to his driver.

"What a masterpiece this is," she said as he joined her in the chaise. "I see more in it every time I look at it. And what irony to find it in a housemaid's room. Poor Hepsibah! I am afraid she is going to miss not having her 'Granny' about."

"Buy her a new bonnet, and she'll soon forget all about it," said Sir Lucas callously. He took the picture from Claudia's hands and surveyed it with gloating eyes. "Yes, indeed! Quite a masterpiece, and most fortuitously discovered. I would not have dared hope for such luck."

Claudia was surprised by the exultation in his voice. Sir Lucas had never struck her as a particularly philanthropic man, but tonight he seemed as pleased by the Rexfords' good fortune as if it had been his own. She thought this quite the nicest trait she had yet seen in him. It could not quite atone for his behavior at the fete, of course, but she found herself warming to him slightly as the carriage continued on its way to the Falconers'.

Yet even as Claudia chatted companionably with Sir Lucas, she was thinking of John. How would he react to her appearance at the party? How would he react to the reappearance of the Rembrandt? And would Barbara Brock be there, or might it be possible that she could see him alone for a few minutes? These questions occupied Claudia so fully that when the chaise slowed and finally came to a stop, it took her a moment to notice. "Are we at the Falconers' at last?" she asked, peering out the window.

Sir Lucas gave an uninterested glance out the window. "No, I believe it is only a tollgate," he said.

"A *tollgate?*" Disbelievingly, Claudia peered out the window once more. "But how can that be? There's no tollgate between Rexford Park and the Falconers'!"

Sir Lucas said nothing. Claudia, casting a glance his way, discerned a guilty smile on his lips. "Sir Lucas, this is not the way to the Falconers'!" she said indignantly. "Where are you taking me?"

Sir Lucas's smile grew broader. "I am taking you to London," he said. "Forgive me for the deception, Miss Chambers, but you must know that the temptation of gaining both you and that magnificent Rembrandt at one stroke was too much for me to resist. So I have decided to elope with you—with the both of you if I may be allowed to put it that way. And I'm sure no man ever eloped with two more desirable companions!"

Eighteen

Although John had intended to return to Rexford Park within a day or two, in order to make a full explanation of his affairs past and present to Claudia, he found himself frustrated in his intentions. He could not make any explanation to Claudia until he had seen Barbara Brock—and seeing Barbara Brock was proving unexpectedly difficult.

He had gone to the Towers immediately after leaving Rexford Park on the day he had proposed to Claudia. He meant to see Barbara and make her understand that he was not engaged to her and had no intention of becoming so. But when he arrived at the Towers, he was informed by a supercilious butler that Miss Brock was "not at home to company, my lord." And she remained not at home to company—or at least not to John's company—for the next week and a half.

John found the delay infuriating. He suspected that Barbara knew his intentions and was purposely avoiding him. But what could he do? He could hardly force his way into the Towers and demand to see her. Nor could he safely entrust such a delicate matter to a note or letter. In order to make Barbara understand his determination not to marry her, as well as to convey his regrets that his past attentions had been subject to misunderstanding, it was necessary to see her in person. And this Barbara seemed determined not to allow.

"But she can't stay 'not at home to company' forever," he told himself. "Sooner or later she must step out of the house, and then I shall have it out with her. If only I knew when that would be! Claudia must wonder why I haven't returned to see her as I promised. If I delay too much longer, she would be perfectly justified in thinking me a lying scoundrel and marrying William Williams instead. Yes, no doubt about it, I must see Barbara and see her soon. I'll drop by the Towers tomorrow and find out if she's decided to show her face."

But when John arrived at the Towers the next day, the door was opened to him by a footman who repeated the now familiar response that Miss Brock was not at home to company. "Well, can you tell me when she *does* mean to be at home to company?" demanded John in exasperation. "She's not sick or anything of that sort, is she?"

The footman, who was young and clearly somewhat inexperienced, looked confused. "No, my lord—at least I don't think so," he said doubtfully. "I did hear as she was going to the Falconers' party tonight—and I wouldn't think she'd do that if she was sick. But there, I wouldn't like to say for certain. Do you want me inquire for you?"

"No, no, don't do that," said John quickly. "It's no matter. I'll call again tomorrow and find out from Miss Brock herself."

As he left the house, he rejoiced over the piece of information he had gained. So Barbara was going to the Falconers' tonight, was she? Well, in that case he would go there, too. He would demand a private word with her, and if she persisted in refusing, he would consider himself free to repudiate their engagement without reference to her feelings.

He had no more made this resolution than he met his aunt, out calling upon a neighbor. Pausing to chat with her for a few minutes, he learned that she, too, was going to the Falconers' that evening. Impulsively he accepted her invitation to make one of her party. Would Claudia also be a member of the party? John hoped so, although he suspected it might be a delicate matter to break off relations with one girl while attempting to convince another to marry him in the course of a single evening. Still, he meant to make the attempt if the opportunity presented itself. He felt he had already wasted enough time settling matters with Claudia, and he dared not risk further delay.

It was a disappointment when Lady Rexford's carriage stopped to pick him up at the Gatehouse that evening and he saw that Claudia was not in it.

"I asked her to go, but she wanted to stay home and work," said Lady Rexford with a shake of her head. "She's that hard-working, is Miss Chambers. I'm sure I never saw her like. But I suppose being a lady born and a member of a great family, she's been to enough parties that missing one isn't any great shakes."

John expressed polite agreement, but felt inwardly that there was probably a different explanation for Claudia's absence. By now, she must be convinced that he never meant to return to Rexford Park at all. Hurt by his neglect and knowing he would be at the Falconers' that evening, she had probably taken this route to avoid him.

The idea disturbed John, but it also strengthened his determination to have matters out with Barbara that evening. And he reflected that it was perhaps just as well that Claudia was not there to observe the process. He could have his talk with Barbara, and whenever Lady Rexford was ready to leave, he could return with her to Rexford Park and there make a formal explanation and proposal to Claudia.

This plan pleased him, and as soon as he arrived at the Falconers', he began looking around for Barbara. He had no great difficulty locating her. Dressed in a showy gown of lavender crepe and lemon satin, she was the center of a noisy group seated around the fireplace. John walked over to join them.

"Good evening, Rexford," she said, hailing him with a gaiety that John felt verged upon impudence. "Upon my word, we are grown quite strangers, are we not? It has been nearly two weeks since I have seen you."

"That is not *my* fault," said John pointedly. "However, I am glad to be able to see you at last, Miss Brock. There is something I was wishing to discuss with you."

"Is there? Ah, but a party is no place to discuss serious subjects, Rexford. You had much better sit down with us and join us in discussing that ridiculous Chinese summerhouse Mrs. Desmond is building in her garden."

"I have something more important than Chinese summerhouses to discuss, Miss Brock," said John, looking her in the eye. "If you would be so kind as to accompany me to the library, I would be very much obliged to you. Of course if you would rather I discussed it here . . ."

This veiled threat had its effect. With a toss of her head, Barbara rose to her feet. "Very well, Rexford," she said coldly. "But I can give you only a few minutes."

"A few minutes is all I need," said John. He stood aside to let her pass, then followed her into the library and shut the door.

Once in the library, Barbara turned to face him with a defiant expression. "Well, Rexford? What is it you wish to say to me?"

"What I wish to say is very simple. From now on, I would appreciate it if you would refrain from telling people that you and I are engaged, Barbara. You must know it is not true, yet Miss Chambers tells me you assured her we were soon to be married."

Barbara's face wrinkled into an ugly scowl. "Miss Chambers!" she said. "How determined she must be to become the next Lady Rexford! I would not have imagined her having the impertinence to tax you with the story."

"And I would not have imagined your having the impertinence to spread it in the first place," returned John. "You know I have never asked you to marry me, Barbara."

Barbara's face reddened, but she tossed her head and looked defiant once more. "Not in so many words perhaps, Rexford. But you know we have been seen together at nearly every social event in the county for the last five-and-a-half years. Everyone takes it for granted that we are to marry, and I am sure I cannot be blamed if I did the same."

"But *did* you do the same?" said John, looking into her eyes. "When you told Miss Chambers we were to be married, did you honestly believe it?"

Barbara said nothing, but looked sullen. After a moment, John went on in a gentler voice.

"I don't mean to put all the blame on you, Barbara. I know I was wrong to let matters drag on as they did without resolving them one way or another. That is why I wished to speak to you before I set the record straight with Miss Chambers and everyone else. You may give your friends and family whatever explanation you choose, but I must insist that you tell them we are not and never have been engaged to marry. Otherwise, I shall be forced to tell them myself. And I don't think you will care for the way I go about it."

Barbara's eyes flashed. "Never fear, my lord!" she said. "I'll merely tell them the truth, which is that I wouldn't marry you if you were the last man on earth! Miss Chambers is quite welcome to you, and I wish her the joy of you." She turned and stomped out of the library.

After she left, John remained standing still for several minutes. He felt positively dizzy with relief. After he had recovered a little, he opened the library door and cautiously appraised his position. Not far away, Barbara was talking to her particular friend, Miss Falconer.

"And I told him, 'Ah, you do me too much honor, my lord, but I'm afraid I cannot accept you,' " she told Miss Falconer. "And oh, he was so taken aback! You should have seen his face. Of course *some people* would regard him as a good catch, but *I* am related to the Earl of Brockhurst, you know. The Rexford title, by contrast, is quite modern—quite modern and descended in a line that is anything but direct. I am sure I can do much better for a husband than a mere parvenu viscount."

John smiled grimly. It was obvious that Barbara was already

spreading the story of their breakup, though hardly in a form
to do him credit. However, he did not grudge her the specious
triumph. On the whole, he felt it was no more than he deserved
for having behaved so thoughtlessly.

His chief preoccupation now was Claudia. He was blessedly
free, and might ask her to marry him as soon as he pleased,
but he could not go to her until his aunt was ready to leave.
And judging by the comfortable way Lady Rexford was chatting with her hostess, that looked to be a considerable time.

John bore it as long as he could. By the time an hour had
gone by, however, he had made up his mind to wait no longer.
In part, this was due to Barbara's behavior. She had been in-
dustrious in spreading the story of her and John's breakup—
her version of the story—and he encountered numerous
pitying, curious, or amused looks from his fellow guests. But
irritating as this was, it was not the only thing that made him
anxious to leave. As the evening wore on, he felt more and
more a nagging sense that he ought to declare himself to
Claudia without delay. So strong did this sense become at last
that he abruptly quit the party, leaving word to his aunt that
he was called away. Then he set out to traverse on foot the
three-and-a-half miles that separated the Falconers' home from
Rexford Park.

All the way to Rexford Park, he castigated himself for being
an idiot. "A nice exercise for a man wearing dancing pumps,"
he muttered as he stumbled over stones in the dark and
splashed recklessly through puddles left by an earlier rain
shower. "What difference would a few hours have made?
Claudia's not likely to marry William Williams in the space
of one evening. I might just as well have waited until my aunt
was ready to go." But still he stumbled grimly on until at last
he reached the Gatehouse.

Having had enough walking for one evening, he paused at
the Gatehouse to change his muddied footwear and order out
his curricle. He then swiftly traversed the short distance to
Rexford Park's manor house. With a fast beating heart, he ap-

proached the front door, wondering what fate awaited him behind that impassive portal.

Claudia, meanwhile, was doing her best to avert the fate
that Sir Lucas clearly intended for her.

Railing at him had proven wholly ineffective. Sir Lucas
merely assured her that she would enjoy being his mistress
once she had accepted the situation. "You shall not find me
ungenerous," he assured her. "I'll rent you a little house in
some quiet neighborhood, and you may have carte blanche as
to decorating it. And as to your wardrobe, why, you may have
carte blanche there, too. I shall take pleasure in fitting you out
as suits a woman of your attractions."

It did no good at all to tell Sir Lucas that she had no intention of becoming his mistress. When Claudia threatened to
get out at the next stop and walk back, he smiled winningly
and said, "I hope you won't force me to physically restrain
you, Miss Chambers. I detest brutality of any sort, and it would
be such a shame to start our relationship on such an unpleasant
note. Far better that you should resign yourself to the inevitable. You must see I could hardly let you go now without leaving
myself open to some painful reprisals."

Finding threats to be useless, Claudia switched to pleas.
"But, Sir Lucas, I cannot simply go off and leave Lady Rexford like this," she pleaded. "You must know she is dependent
on me, and her health is not very strong. If I simply disappear
without a trace, I am sure she will worry greatly and perhaps
even fret herself into a decline. I cannot like to have that on
my conscience."

Sir Lucas patted her hand sympathetically. "What a nice,
thoughtful girl you are, Miss Chambers! But you know Lady
Rexford need not remain in suspense indefinitely concerning
your fate. As soon as we have you established in London, you
have only to write and tell her that I have made myself re

sponsible for your care and that you want for nothing. That ought to set her mind at rest."

Claudia bit back the urge to say sarcastically that Lady Rexford would no doubt be greatly relieved to find her young companion established as the mistress to a thief and blackguard. "But it may be days before we are settled in London!" she pleaded instead. "And in that time, I am sure Lady Rexford will make herself sick worrying about me. If I could only send her word where I have gone, it would be so much better." She made this statement as pathetically as she could and even managed to squeeze out a few tears to accompany it.

"There, there," said Sir Lucas, stroking her arm tenderly. Claudia's flesh crawled at his touch, but she forced herself to endure the caress and even look grateful for it.

"There, there, my dear," he repeated. "Of course it's rather a rude trick to take French leave of the old lady, but you must see that it wasn't possible to give her notice under the circumstances. As soon as we get to London—"

"But that will be days yet," cried Claudia, finding an excuse to pull her arm away from him in order to dab at her eyes. "Dear Sir Lucas, do let me send her word now! I am sure I could not be easy in my mind a moment until I have done that." She gave Sir Lucas a look half shy, half provocative. "Please, please, won't you let me send her a message? You must know I would be happy enough to accompany you to London if it were not that I felt I was injuring Lady Rexford."

Sir Lucas was not proof against this kind of cajolery. "I suppose you might send her a message," he conceded. "We'll stop at the next inn we come to, and I'll fetch you paper and ink so you can write her a letter. Will that satisfy you?"

"Yes, that would be wonderful, Sir Lucas!" said Claudia with an ecstatic smile. To herself, she marveled that such a simple stratagem should have worked. Sir Lucas must be even more of a conceited fool than she had imagined if he thought she would willingly accompany him to London while any chance of escape remained.

But he proved not so much a fool as she had supposed. At the inn, he neither left the carriage himself nor allowed her to leave it, but rather sent his footmen to fetch pen, ink, and other writing materials.

"Of course I must insist on reading whatever you write to Lady Rexford," he remarked casually, as he handed these articles to Claudia. "You will understand I cannot countenance your begging her to rescue you or anything of that kind."

"Of course," said Claudia, concealing her chagrin. She stared at the blank sheet of paper before her, wondering what to say. Clearly Sir Lucas would not permit her to send Lady Rexford an outright plea for help, and even if she were able to somehow conceal such a plea within a more innocuous message, Lady Rexford still might not receive it until it was too late, depending on when she got back from the Falconers' that night.

"And in any case, what *could* I write that would satisfy Sir Lucas and still warn Lady Rexford that I am being carried off against my will?" she thought unhappily. "I might as well say that I am delighted to run off with Sir Lucas and expect to be very happy as his mistress!"

This thought had no sooner crossed her mind than she recognized its essential brilliance. Lady Rexford knew she disliked Sir Lucas. She knew also that Claudia was not the sort of girl to accept a gentleman's carte blanche and run away on the spur of the moment, leaving only a blithe note behind detailing her intentions.

"And to make it even more unlikely, I'll address the note to Mrs. Fry," thought Claudia gleefully. "Lady Rexford will know I would never do that if I were leaving of my own free will. And the wonderful thing is that Mrs. Fry will lose no time in passing the note on to Lady Rexford, because she hates us both so much. She would be glad to see me disgraced and Lady Rexford discomfitted."

Claudia therefore wrote her note, taking care to make it as silly and simpering as possible.

Of course I dislike leaving Lady Rexford like this, but Sir Lucas has promised to take me to London and install me in a home of my own, where I will have every luxury. I am sure I would be foolish to pass up such a marvelous opportunity. Dear Mrs. Fry, do break the news to Lady Rexford gently. I fear it will be a shock to her, but a girl must think of herself, you know. Such a wonderful chance may never come my way again.

Having generously underscored this missive, put in numerous exclamation points, and signed herself, "Hastily, Claudia Chambers," Claudia added a postscript.

Convey also my thanks and compliments to Lord Rexford. He has been most gracious to me during my stay at Rexford Park. The fact that I leave Yorkshire so unceremoniously (!) does not mean I shall not remember with fondness those who made my visit there so enjoyable.

Reading through this epistle, Claudia felt it to be a masterpiece of fatuous sentiment. She hoped Lady Rexford would lose no time in reading between the lines and sending a rescue party after her.

And though rescue in any form would be very welcome, Claudia's secret hope was that it would come in the form of John. It seemed not an unreasonable hope. He had accompanied Lady Rexford to the Falconers', so the chances were good that he would also escort her home. Thus it was that Claudia had been moved to add her postscript, on the chance John might see it and recognize the unwritten plea it contained. He knew her well enough to feel how out of character such a message was, she reflected with hope, as she handed the letter to Sir Lucas and watched him read it through. And even if he did not—well, he had told her he loved her on the occasion of their last meeting. If he had spoken the truth, he would not want to see her run away with Sir Lucas, even if he assumed she had gone of her own free will.

But before John would have a chance to prove the authenticity of his feelings for her, she must first get word to him of her predicament. And that meant getting her letter past Sir Lucas's inspection. Claudia felt a certain anxiety on this score, for she feared not even an egoist like Sir Lucas could believe he had so easily overcome a virtuous woman's scruples. Yet such appeared to be the case. She saw Sir Lucas's lips curl one or twice as he read through her foolish ramblings, but he concealed his contempt fairly well. "That should do nicely," he said, folding up the letter and affixing a wafer to it. "I'll give it to the landlord and tell him to have it posted tomorrow."

"Tomorrow!" said Claudia, barely concealing her dismay. She had no wish to wait twenty-four hours or more for her rescue. Thinking rapidly, she put on her most coaxing manner. "Cannot it be sent by special messenger?" she begged Sir Lucas. "I would be glad to pay the cost myself. I simply cannot bear to think of Lady Rexford spending all night worrying about me and perhaps making herself ill in the process."

Sir Lucas said indulgently that she was a tenderhearted little creature and tried to slip an arm around her waist. Claudia thwarted this maneuver by the simple expedient of bursting into tears. "Sir Lucas, I know it's foolish, but I simply can't be easy in my mind until I've sent Lady Rexford word of what's become of me," she said, burying her face in her handkerchief. "It breaks my heart to think of her waiting and worrying all night long. I'm sure I can't take enjoyment in *anything* until I know her mind has been set at ease."

By dint of stressing this theme over and over, Claudia was able to eventually win Sir Lucas's consent to the idea of a special messenger. She thanked him prettily and watched with satisfaction as the messenger rode off with the precious missive in his bag. Yet beneath her satisfaction lurked an uneasy concern. It was nine o'clock now, and she and Sir Lucas had been on the road for more than an hour. Even if the messenger rode at a flat-out gallop, he could not hope to reach Rexford Park much before ten. It might take an hour more before a rescue party could be organized and sent after her. Altogether, she could not look for help in less than three hours, and already Sir Lucas was showing signs of becoming amorous. Claudia could only hope that she would be able to hold him off long enough for help to arrive.

Nineteen

When John finally presented himself at Rexford Park shortly after the hour of ten o'clock, he was admitted by Mrs. Fry, who appeared to be in a state of great excitement. John scarcely noticed the housekeeper's agitation, however. He was very much intent on his own affairs.

"I need to speak to Miss Chambers," he told Mrs. Fry. "May I see her please?"

Something that might have been consternation but looked more like triumph flickered briefly in Mrs. Fry's eyes. "That you may not, my lord," she said. "Miss Chambers ain't here right now. And it's not likely that she ever will be again from the looks of things!"

The triumph in Mrs. Fry's eyes was unmistakable now. "Why, what do you mean?" asked John in surprise. "I was at the Falconers' just now, and I am sure my aunt told me that Miss Chambers had chosen to stay home this evening and do some work for her."

"And I've no doubt my Lady Rexford believes what she told you, my lord—but it ain't true. Miss Chambers left here nigh on two hours ago. And if ever she sets foot at Rexford Park again, it'll be more than I bargain for!"

John disregarded most of this speech, which he took for mere spite. All that interested him was the fact that Claudia was not there. "So she's stepped out, has she?" he said in disappointment. "How very unfortunate. Did she leave word when she would be back?"

"No, for I'm telling you she won't be back, my lord! Sly she was about it, too, telling me she was going over to the Falconers' to see my Lady Rexford. 'I find there is something I must discuss with Lady Rexford,' she said, in that snippety way of hers. Properly took me in, she did, though I suspected all the while there was something wrong about her. When I seen Sir Lucas carrying that bandbox of hers, I should have known something was up."

John found this speech nearly as incomprehensible as Mrs. Fry's previous one. He chose to concentrate upon the least incomprehensible part. "Sir Lucas?" he said. "What was *he* doing here? You don't mean to say that *he* was taking Claudia—Miss Chambers—to the Falconers'?"

"No, I mean to say he was eloping with her! All that talk about the Falconers' was gammon and nothing more. Oh, I can see how it was clear enough now, though I never suspected it at the time. But I knew that Miss Chambers was a sly one, right from the beginning. *I* wasn't fooled by her fine speeches and ladylike airs."

"That is quite enough, Mrs. Fry," said John coldly. Whatever the housekeeper might be implying about Claudia—and he was still far from clear on the subject—he still disliked to hear her criticized. "What's this nonsense you're talking about Miss Chambers? You don't seriously expect me to believe that she has eloped with Sir Lucas Davenport, do you?"

"Haven't I just been telling you this ten minutes that she has?" said Mrs. Fry in an exasperated voice. "She and him left here together just over two hours ago—*and she took a bandbox with her!* Ah, I should have known as soon as I saw *that* what was in the wind. But being taken up with my own affairs as it happened, I never thought twice about it, except to wonder what it was she might be taking with her. Good gracious heavens, the silver! I'd best be calling Raikes to make a count of it, for there's no telling what she's made off with, the huzzy."

With these words, Mrs. Fry turned to go, but John stopped her. "And you have based this whole rigmarole on the fact that Miss Chambers went off somewhere in Sir Lucas's carriage and took along a bandbox?" he demanded. "Why, I can think of a dozen reasons why she might have done so without bringing elopement into the question."

"No doubt, my lord, no doubt," retorted Mrs. Fry. "But elopement's what she had in mind all the same. Ah, the sly creature! Pretending to be a lady, and her no better than she should have been all along."

"That is *enough*, Mrs. Fry," said John, who was really angry now and more than a little worried about Claudia. "If Miss Chambers has really disappeared, then of course we must make a search for her. If she was going to the Falconers'—"

"You needn't look for her at the Falconers', my lord, nor in any place except Sir Lucas's carriage. Haven't I been telling you she's eloped with him?"

"Yes, and I'm telling you I don't believe it. Not that I'd put it past Sir Lucas to try to make off with her, for I don't think he's to be trusted where women are concerned, and he's already shown that he admires Miss Chambers. Still, I can't believe he would be bold enough to abduct her."

Mrs. Fry snorted. "He wouldn't have to be bold, my lord, for the lady's bold enough for two! If you don't believe me, read this." She thrust a letter into John's hand.

John read the letter, at first with puzzlement, then with growing incredulity. He had to read it twice before he understood it, and even then, he could not believe what he had read. The thing was impossible. Claudia could not have eloped with Sir Lucas and gone to London to be his mistress. Yet that was what the letter stated, not only plainly but proudly.

John's first reaction was one of hurt and bewilderment. His second was a rage of epic proportions. Claudia had betrayed him—betrayed him in a manner that must haunt him all his life. He had judged her a woman of wit, sweetness, and integrity—a woman he would be proud to make his wife. But she had spurned his honorable proposals and accepted a carte blanche from Sir Lucas instead. She was clearly a foolish, heartless, immoral creature who cared only for personal gain; that much was clear from her letter.

Running his eye over those damning paragraphs, John marveled that he could have been so deceived. If it had not been a matter of such tragic personal interest, he would have supposed the whole thing some gigantic, not too funny joke. That postscript, for instance, in which she thanked him for making her stay in Yorkshire "so enjoyable." Could she really have written that with a straight face?

"If she did, then she's not the woman I took her for," John reflected grimly. "But then it seems she is *not* the woman I took her for. If she was, she never would have accepted a carte blanche from Sir Lucas or left me with only that taunting postscript by way of farewell. And she certainly never would have abandoned Rexford Park without notice and left it to Mrs. Fry to inform my aunt of her abandonment!"

Something in this last thought seemed to set off a warning bell in John's mind. Surely even a foolish girl would have known better than to entrust such news to a woman she must know disliked her? He looked at the letter again, carefully reading the paragraph in which Claudia begged Mrs. Fry to break the news to his aunt gently. Enlightenment did not dawn upon him all at once; it came gradually, like a conviction being born in his heart. Claudia could not have written this letter— not without some strong outward influence, at any rate. And once he had reached this stage in his reasoning, it was not hard to guess what that influence must be.

John swore loudly and crushed the letter in his hand in sudden excitement. "Good God! That's it, of course. How could I have failed to guess it?"

Mrs. Fry misinterpreted the cause of his excitement. "Terrible, isn't it?" she said, shaking her head in spurious sympathy. "But you mustn't think you was alone in being fooled, my lord. There'll be plenty who'll look queer when this news gets around. Of course, nobody'll look queerer than your aunt when all's said and done. It was her who brought that Miss Chambers here, you know, and I'm sure it's a judgment on her after the way she robbed you of your—"

"Shut up!" said John. He spoke the words with a ferocity that made Mrs. Fry jump. She regarded him with astonishment.

"Why, my lord, I didn't mean to—" she began.

"Yes, you did mean to!" said John. "And I have told you time and time again that you must not speak that way about my aunt or Miss Chambers."

Mrs. Fry looked more astonished than ever. "But that letter!" she said. "You can't get away from that letter, my lord."

"Yes, I can, and in the easiest way possible. Don't you see that this letter is all a blind?" John struck the letter in his hand. "Miss Chambers is being abducted by Sir Lucas and has taken this way to ask for help. No doubt it was the only way open to her—and now that I understand it, I think it was very clever."

Mrs. Fry took the letter and read it through suspiciously, as though its contents might have changed during the time it was in John's hands. "I don't see it," she objected. "She says right here that she's happy enough to go with Sir Lucas."

"Yes, because Sir Lucas would let her say nothing else. If I can but lay my hands on him! I'll teach him to go abducting young women! And I think I can do it, too. He has a good two hours' start on me, but if he doesn't expect pursuit—and he would hardly allow Claudia to send this letter if he did— then he will not be setting too hot a pace. Thank heaven I'm driving my grays! It'll be a bit of a race, but I'll wager I can catch them before they reach Tuxford."

Mrs. Fry had listened to this speech in growing dismay. "But, my lord, you'll never be going after them?" she protested. "You may say what you like, but nothing'll make me believe Miss Chambers didn't go off with Sir Lucas of her own free will. I saw that bandbox myself!"

"No doubt there is some perfectly reasonable explanation for the bandbox. As for her going of her own free will, I daresay Sir Lucas lured her into his carriage under false pretenses. We'll know the truth soon enough, once I catch up with them." John was already drawing on his driving gloves.

Mrs. Fry's face was a study in dismay and disappointed spite. "The truth!" she said. "I wager you'll hear little enough of the truth if you're depending on Miss Chambers to tell it. Don't you go believing a word she says, my lord. This letter shows plain enough what sort of girl she is. You're a fool if you let her get round you with her cozening ways, the same as my Lady Rexford did to your uncle!"

"That's enough," said John. He spoke in a quiet voice, but with great finality. "Your services are no longer needed here at Rexford Park, Mrs. Fry. Kindly pack your bags and have yourself removed by the time I return with Claudia."

Mrs. Fry regarded him with her mouth half open and her eyes very round, looking like nothing so much as a landed trout. "Wh-What did you say, my lord?" she gasped.

"I said that you're fired," said John. "Impertinence and insubordination are things I will not tolerate, and still less will I tolerate abuse of the lady whom I hope one day to make my wife."

Mrs. Fry looked more like a landed trout than ever. "Your wife?" she gasped. "But my lord, you don't mean to say—it can't be that you mean to marry *Miss Chambers?*"

"Certainly, if she'll have me," said John briskly. "It remains only to find out if she will. Now if you'll excuse me, Mrs. Fry, I must be off. Kindly leave an address with Raikes where I can communicate with you, and I'll see about forwarding your last month's wages."

* * *

Claudia, meanwhile, was finding it increasingly difficult to fend off the advances of her traveling companion.

Like Scheherazade fighting to retain her head, she had tried every stratagem she could think of to postpone the evil hour. She had complained of hunger until Sir Lucas had stopped at an inn and bought her some sandwiches. Then she had complained that the sandwiches had made her thirsty and begged him to get her something to drink. He had obliged with a flagon of wine, whereupon Claudia had promptly claimed a bad case of carriage sickness and demanded that he slow the pace of the carriage to a virtual walk.

This Sir Lucas had consented readily enough to do. Even at a walk, however, the mileposts seemed to fly by. And Claudia knew Sir Lucas would not be content with such a slow pace forever. Every so often, she surreptitiously checked the chaise's rear window to see if there might be a rescue party on their trail. Whenever she spied a coach lamp rapidly approaching from the rear, her heart gave a leap of hope, but it always came crashing down again when the vehicle passed them and continued on its way without a check.

By the time this had happened a dozen times, Claudia was feeling very disheartened. When once again she heard the approaching rumble of wheels and the hoofbeats of four fast horses, she did not even bother to glance round. Sir Lucas's coachman obligingly moved over to let the faster vehicle go by. Claudia noted absently that it was a curricle harnessed to four beautifully matched gray horses. It was not until she heard Sir Lucas's startled exclamation that she looked again, recognized the driver's familiar, broad-shouldered form, and felt a surge of joy within her heart.

"Damn it!" swore Sir Lucas. "It's Rexford! Don't tell me he means to spoil sport! Coachman, don't let him pass. Don't let him pass, I say."

But it was too late for these instructions. The curricle and four had already swept past Sir Lucas's chaise and was now occupying the center of the road. Gradually it slowed its pace,

forcing Sir Lucas's driver to slow likewise or risk a collision.
Finally the curricle drew to a stop slantwise across the road.
Its driver hopped down, tossing the reins to his groom.
Claudia, glancing at Sir Lucas, saw he was very pale. Sweat
was beading his brow, and a low stream of profanity was issuing from his lips. Rising to her feet, she picked up the bandbox and addressed him politely.

"Thank you, Sir Lucas, but I don't think I care to accompany you to London after all," she told him. "On the whole,
I believe I would rather return to Rexford Park with Lord Rexford."

Sir Lucas's response was merely to swear the louder. He
made no effort to stop Claudia as she unlatched the door and
stepped down from the chaise. Instantly she was enveloped in
a pair of strong arms and crushed against a chest that seemed
much like a stone wall to her dazed senses.

"Claudia!" said John. "Thank God you're safe."

"Quite safe," said Claudia, returning the embrace fervently.
"But I am glad you got here when you did, John. I was running
out of excuses to keep Sir Lucas at arm's length!"

She laughed as she spoke, but John's face darkened. "That
damned blackguard!" he said. "I knew well enough who was
at the bottom of this business as soon as I learned you had
gone with him." Releasing Claudia, he took a purposeful step
toward the chaise. "I think I need to have a word with Sir
Lucas before I do anything else. He must be made to understand that he cannot go around abducting with impunity the
woman I love."

These words caused Claudia's already happy heart to soar
even higher. She laughed with pure joy. "Oh, John, never mind
about Sir Lucas," she said. "He did not hurt me in the least,
I assure you. In fact, if you look at the matter from one angle,
I actually owe him a debt of gratitude."

"I don't see it," John said, and took another step toward the
carriage. Claudia caught his arm, however, and held him back.

"No, John," she said. "I know it's tempting, and there's no

doubt he deserves punishment. But leave it till another time. All I want now is to go home, and it will take long enough to get there as it is."

John admitted the truth of this statement, though he was extremely reluctant to let Sir Lucas escape without punishment. At Claudia's urging, however, he finally ordered his groom to move the curricle onto the side of the road so that Sir Lucas might proceed.

This Sir Lucas lost no time in doing. "Drive on, you fool! Faster! Faster!" he shouted to his coachman. The coachman whipped up the horses, and in a matter of minutes, the baronet's chaise had disappeared from view.

John helped Claudia into his curricle, took the reins from his groom, and with that worthy's help soon had the curricle facing northward again.

"I'm afraid we'll have to go very slowly," he told Claudia. "My team is almost blown, and I daren't push them much farther tonight. I'll stop at the next posting house and change them, but I'm afraid that won't be for another few miles."

"Of course you must not push your horses any farther tonight," agreed Claudia. "I only hope they have suffered no injury in coming this far. I would feel quite guilty if I were the cause of damaging so magnificent a team."

"I'm pretty sure they're not damaged," said John. "It wouldn't have been wise to press them too many more miles, but as it was, I think they quite enjoyed the excuse for a race. I'll change them for a fresh team at the next posting house we come to, and my groom can drive down in a day or two to pick them up."

"In the meantime, a slow pace will suit me very well," said Claudia. "There's something I need to tell you, John."

"And there's something I need to tell *you*," he responded. "In fact, I think you had better let me have my say before you have yours. I don't want you to misunderstand me or my intentions a moment longer."

In a few brief sentences, he described all that had passed

between him and Barbara Brock. "I was a fool to let things go on as long as they did between us, without declaring my intentions one way or another" he finished contritely. "Of course it's not a crime to dangle after a girl without proposing, but I'm afraid Barbara isn't completely unjustified in being angry with me. Still, I assure you I haven't given her any serious reason to complain of ill usage. That story she told you about our being engaged, for instance—that was a complete fabrication. I have never asked any woman but you to marry me, Claudia. You do believe me, don't you?"

Claudia nodded. "Yes, I think I always suspected that Barbara hadn't told me the truth that evening. One of you *had* to be lying—and when it came to the point, I could believe it of her much easier than you. But when I charged you with it that day in the garden and you didn't deny it, it gave me a nasty shock. I began to think it was only wishful thinking that made me so sure your intentions were honorable."

"Well, they *are* honorable. I hope you can believe that now. The only reason I didn't explain all this to you sooner was because I wanted to talk with Barbara first. I felt I owed her the chance to be the one to contradict the story of our engagement rather than doing it myself."

"Of course," assented Claudia. Her heart was singing with happiness. John was revealed to be as honorable and upright as he had appeared, and she was ashamed now that she had ever doubted him. "I quite see that now, John. But I kept expecting you to call—"

"Ah, that was Barbara's doing, too. She's been playing least in sight for the last week or two—no doubt because she knew the lie she'd told you would eventually get back to me and that I'd have no qualms about confronting her with it. But it wasn't until this evening that I was finally able to run her to earth. We had the whole thing out between us, and Barbara agreed to contradict the rumors of our engagement—but by that time I was afraid it was too late. Especially when I saw that note you sent to Mrs. Fry!"

Claudia laughed. "It was a terrible note, wasn't it, John? But you know I really hadn't any other means of sending you word."

"Yes, that's what I supposed. I thought it very clever of you, too—once I had recovered from the initial shock of thinking you had run off with Sir Lucas! That was even worse than thinking you were going to marry William Williams."

When John looked quizzically down at Claudia, she blushed. "I am not going to marry William Williams," she said.

"I am heartily glad to hear it, my dear. You are, if I may say so, much too good for him. And though I'm afraid you are much too good for me, too, that doesn't keep me from hoping that you might marry me anyway. Will you, Claudia?"

Claudia was silent a moment or two. "You are kind enough to say I am too good for you, John," she said. "But most people would say the boot was on the other foot." She regarded him with troubled eyes. "I am afraid that if I were to become your wife they would say you had married beneath you."

"Nonsense," said John forcefully. "In what possible way are you beneath me? You've got character and common sense— loyalty and integrity—aye, and the wisdom of Solomon to boot! Not to mention as pretty a face as a man could ever hope to see smiling at him over the breakfast table every morning. I never met a woman like you before, and I'm damned if I'm going to let you slip away from me now I *have* met you."

Claudia laughed tremulously. "You are very kind to say so, John, but you know there is still the little matter of birth and position. And don't bother pretending it isn't important. Why, on our very first meeting you had something to say on the subject of unequal marriages—and none of it was very complimentary, as I recall!"

John smiled wryly. "I might have known you'd throw that in my face," he said. "But indeed, I had come to think differently on the subject even before I fell in love with you, Claudia. Part of it was what you said to me that first day—and then after I had actually met my aunt and found out firsthand what she was like, I couldn't believe any longer that my uncle's marriage had been the mistake I first thought it."

"Well, you know, I don't think it was," said Claudia candidly. "I've lived with Lady Rexford for nearly two months now, and I am sure that no one could be easier or more pleasant to live with. I expect she made your uncle very happy and comfortable during their years together."

"Well, then!" said John triumphantly.

But Claudia shook her head. "The situations are not alike, John. Your uncle was able to please himself in the matter of marriage, because he was an elderly man and his choice did not directly affect anyone but himself. It will be otherwise when you marry."

"Yes, it will. But while you are trying to point out differences between my uncle and me, you might point out one more. His wife, for all her many excellent qualities, has no pretensions to gentle birth. You, on the other hand, are unquestionably a gentlewoman, and I defy anyone to say otherwise. It might even be said that *you* are the one who is marrying beneath you, for by all I can find out the Chamberses are a considerably older family than the Rexfords!"

Claudia smiled and sighed at the same time. "Older, perhaps, but not so exalted," she said. "And very much worse off in a worldly sense! I am afraid my pedigree is less likely to impress people than the fact that I was your aunt's hired companion before our marriage."

"The more fools they then," said John. Shifting the reins to his right hand, he drew Claudia closer with his left. "Any person who chooses to look down upon you because you once worked for your living is a person with misplaced priorities. That being the case, I should have no compunction in disregarding his or her opinion. You may be able to talk me round on most matters, Miss Chambers, but you'll never convince me that in asking you to marry me, I am not making a most prudent, farsighted, and judicious decision."

Claudia shook her head mournfully. "I was afraid you were likely to prove pigheaded," she said.

Laughter sprang up in John's eyes. "That's right, woman," he said. "You had better save your breath to cool your porridge, as the saying goes. Or better yet, save it to say yes to my proposal. I am confident that if you do say yes, our marriage is quite as likely to result in happiness as my aunt and uncle's. Will you marry me, Claudia?"

Claudia took a deep breath. "Well, I think I will, John—seeing that there is no chance of my talking you around to a more rational frame of mind."

"Not a chance in the world," John said, and kissed her resoundingly.

For some minutes after this, Claudia was so occupied that the subject of the Rembrandt quite slipped her mind. It was John who incidentally revived her memory.

"By the by," he said, "I quite accept that you had no intention of eloping with Sir Lucas when you set out from Rexford Park. But I *am* curious as to why you set out with him in the first place. And I am also curious to learn what is in this box." He nudged Claudia's bandbox with his toe. "You must know that, in taking it with you, you gave rise to considerable speculation among the servants. Mrs. Fry, for one, felt it the strongest evidence that you had voluntarily eloped with Sir Lucas."

"My heavens, I forgot all about the bandbox," said Claudia with a gasp of laughter. "Indeed, I meant to tell you, John, but what with one thing and another it quite slipped my mind."

"I cannot think how that could have happened," said John gravely. "However, I will forgive you for the oversight, assuming you are good enough to satisfy my curiosity immediately."

"Yes, I will." Claudia bent to open the bandbox. "Indeed, it is you who *should* see it first, for its contents are by way of being your own property." Triumphantly she lifted the painting from its wrappings. "It's the Rexford Rembrandt, John!"

"Good God!" said John, almost dropping the reins in his excitement. "It *is* the Rembrandt, by all that's wonderful." He looked at Claudia with kindling eyes. "I might have known the efficient Miss Chambers would bring it to light! Is there no end to what I owe you, Claudia?"

"Well, Sir Lucas was partially responsible for finding it," said Claudia scrupulously. "And so was Hepsibah. In fact, she was the key to the whole puzzle."

"Hepsibah?" said John blankly. "Who on earth is Hepsibah?"

Claudia told him the whole story of how the painting had come to light in the maidservant's room. "Indeed, I hope you will not be angry with her, John. She did not realize the painting was of any value; she merely liked it because it resembled her grandmother. Upon my word, I felt sorry to have to take it from her, seeing how much comfort it seemed to give her."

John laughed. "You are such an eloquent advocate, Claudia, that I find myself tempted to return the painting to Hepsibah forthwith, with apologies for having removed it in the first place! But I really would like to see it hanging above the drawing room fireplace once more. Do you think your protégé would be content with a copy? I should be glad to have one made for her—and I think she deserves it, too, as a reward for honesty. After all, if she had not come forward, we might never have discovered the painting's whereabouts."

Claudia said warmly that this would be a wonderful solution, whereupon John kissed her once more and told her he was putty in her hands. "But even you, with all your eloquence, cannot persuade me to reward Sir Lucas for *his* role in discovering the Rembrandt," he added with a laugh. "Seeing that, immediately after finding it, he attempted to abscond with both it and you, I think he has waived all right to a reward. Indeed, I am still not certain I ought not to pursue him to London and demand satisfaction in the form of pistols for two!"

"Well, I hope you will do nothing so foolish, John," said Claudia warmly. "All's well that ends well, and both the Rembrandt and I are perfectly safe. Besides, a duel would entail a risk to you as well as to Sir Lucas. I would be very much annoyed if my husband-to-be were injured or killed."

John admitted that this consideration carried a certain weight. "Besides, after all that's happened, I doubt Sir Lucas will dare to show his face in Yorkshire again!" he added with a grin. "Getting him out of the neighborhood ought to be satisfaction enough for me, especially considering that I have also recovered the Rembrandt and gained you as my wife."

Claudia was so pleased by his sensible attitude that she kissed him, inspiring him to kiss her back and so setting off another round of loverlike billing and cooing. Their arrival at the posting house put an end to this idyll, however, and forced them to concentrate on practical matters instead.

The tired grays were turned over to the ostler with instructions as to their care and feeding. A new team was harnessed to the curricle, and John then devoted himself to covering the remainder of the journey back to Rexford Park with as much speed as possible.

"If I can get you home before the Falconers' party breaks up, so much the better," he told Claudia. "I'm afraid your leaving as you did caused a certain amount of talk among the servants, but I think we can smooth that over easily enough now that Mrs. Fry is gone."

"Mrs. Fry gone!" exclaimed Claudia. "What do you mean, John? Where has she gone?"

"I don't know, and I don't care. I lost my temper with her because she was determined to think the worst of you, in spite of all the proofs I could find to the contrary. And so I sent her packing. You don't mind, do you?" He studied Claudia's profile. "You know I could not tolerate any employee at Rexford Park who did not respect my wife."

Claudia laughed shakily. "No, I don't mind, John. Mrs. Fry has been a thorn in my side from the beginning and a thorn in your aunt's side, too. Lady Rexford will be very happy to learn she is gone."

"Yes, but I fear she will be less happy to learn I mean to

deprive her of her companion," said John, putting his arm around Claudia's shoulders. "I don't know how I'm going to tell her. Upon my word, I have half a mind to play the coward and hole up at the Gatehouse while you break the news to her!"

When the time came, however, he broke the news to his aunt himself in a sufficiently bold and manly fashion. Lady Rexford had apparently been on the watch for John's carriage, for as soon as he and Claudia entered the house, she came hurrying out of the drawing room with Hettie right behind her. A beaming smile spread across Lady Rexford's face when she saw Claudia.

"There you are, my dear!" she said. "Upon my word, I wondered where you had got to. The servants would have had me believe some ridiculous tale about your having eloped with Sir Lucas, but of course I knew that could not be true. Still, it was very worrisome not knowing where you *had* gone—and Mrs. Fry, who seems to have started all the rumors, now appears to have disappeared herself!"

"I'm afraid I'm the one responsible for *her* disappearance," said John. "As for the rest of it—why don't we all go back into the drawing room and sit down? It's a complicated story, and I would not tire you in the telling of it."

Thus adjured, the whole party returned to the drawing room, and Lady Rexford ordered a pot of tea. "Now tell me everything, my lord," she said, folding her plump hands on her lap and fixing him with a look of pleased expectancy, like a child awaiting a bedtime story. "How did you end up bringing Miss Chambers home when the last I knew you were at the Falconers' yourself? I am sure there must be some terrific mystery about it all."

"Not one but several terrific mysteries," said John with a laugh. "But the first half of the tale belongs to Miss Chambers. I'll let her tell her part, and then take over when my part comes in."

With Lady Rexford's and Hettie's eyes fixed eagerly upon

her, Claudia explained how Sir Lucas had come to Rexford Park while she was searching for the Rembrandt and what had happened once they had found it.

"My lands!" exclaimed Hettie, her eyes starting as she regarded Claudia. "You don't mean to say he tried to make off with you and the painting, miss? Why, I always took him for a gentleman!"

"*I* didn't," said Lady Rexford triumphantly. "I didn't, did I, Miss Chambers? I always thought he was a rascal, for all he was so smooth spoken."

"Yes, and you were quite right, ma'am. But his rascality came to nothing, thanks to your nephew." With a smile at John, Claudia described the note she had sent to Mrs. Fry and John's response.

"And so you set off after her and brought her back," said Lady Rexford, regarding John admiringly. "Between the pair of you, you seem to have acted very cleverly. But I must say that if it had been up to me, I wouldn't have let Sir Lucas get off scot-free as he seems to have done. Any man who could behave as he has tonight deserves a horsewhipping, at the very least."

"I quite agree with you," said John. "But Miss Chambers has convinced me to hold my hand—and indeed, much as I regret not having the opportunity to chastise Sir Lucas, I think she may be right. Where a lady's reputation is concerned, you know, the less noise and publicity, the better."

Lady Rexford instantly acknowledged the truth of this. Turning to Claudia, she said with contrition, "My dear Miss Chambers, I feel quite overcome with guilt that such a thing should have happened while you were in my care! If your brother were to learn of it, he would say I was unfit to have the keeping of you—and he would be perfectly right."

"My dear ma'am, you must not feel guilty," said Claudia, smiling. "What happened tonight was my fault, not yours. I knew Sir Lucas was not trustworthy, yet I foolishly went and put myself in his power. You had nothing to do with the matter, and I am sure my brother would say the same."

"Ah, it's very generous of you to take all the blame, my dear. But I know I shall continue to feel guilty about it until we are certain your reputation has not been damaged. We must put our heads together and consider how best we can scotch the scandal."

"As to that, I have an idea or two myself," said John with a self-deprecating cough. "I don't know what you will say to it, ma'am, but the fact is I have fallen in love with your companion. On the way home tonight I asked her to be my wife— and she was kind enough to accept."

John paused, a little embarrassed. He had certainly no reason to complain of a lack of attention on the part of his listeners. Both Lady Rexford and Hettie were regarding him with wide-eyed incredulity. "I hope you won't be too angry with me, ma'am," he continued diffidently. "Please believe that I much regret depriving you of Miss Chambers's services. If there is anything I can do to make the loss easier for you to bear, you have only to name it."

"Oh, dear," said Lady Rexford, drawing a deep, wavering breath. A moment later, however, a smile began to play around the corners of her mouth. "Indeed I will be sorry to lose Miss Chambers, Rexford, and I am afraid that nothing you or anyone else can do will wholly make up for the loss. But to gain her as my niece by marriage will come as close as anything. Upon my word, I must congratulate you upon your choice of wives, Rexford. Now that I know you are not engaged to that Miss Brock, I don't mind saying that I never cared for her. I am glad to hear you never meant to marry her after all."

"Certainly not," said John with an admirably composed face. "That was all a misunderstanding. I admire Miss Brock and wish her well, but I could never consider marrying her after meeting Miss Chambers."

"And that just shows you've a deal of sense, my lord," said Lady Rexford heartily.

Claudia blushed, and her blush grew deeper at her mistress's next words.

"Indeed, my lord, you do not know what a treasure you are getting. Miss Chambers is a very sweet and superior girl, and she comes of an excellent family, as perhaps you may not know. She's so shy about talking about herself that you'd never know half her virtues if you waited for her to tell you about them."

"I know something of her virtues, I think," said John, smiling at Claudia. "And I know something of her family, too, though I am looking forward to becoming better acquainted with them. Her brother has already kindly offered me the hospitality of his home, but—"

"He has what?" said Claudia, regarding John with amazement. "Do you know Edmund, John?"

"Yes, though only through the medium of the post. I wrote him a few weeks ago, informing him of my intentions toward you. Don't you remember my asking you for his direction that day I met you in the village? When one wishes to marry a young lady, you know, it is customary to ask her nearest male relative for permission to pay one's addresses."

"Very right and proper, my lord," said Lady Rexford approvingly. "Though your uncle and I married without our relatives' consent, I agree it's better by far to follow the custom when you can."

"Well, I don't agree," said Claudia, lifting her chin. "In my opinion, that custom is quite antiquated, John. I love my brother, and of course I want you to meet him and the rest of my family sometime. But I do not need his permission to marry!"

John laughed. "As it happens, he said the exact same thing! He wrote that you were quite independent and that while he would be glad enough to receive me as a brother-in-law, the decision to marry must be your own."

"That's all right then," said Claudia, appeased. "For you know I *am* independent, John. And I may as well give you fair warning that I don't mean to give up my independence merely because we are to be married."

"I don't expect it," said John, smiling. "I have no objection whatever to your independence, Claudia. In fact, it's one of the things I most admire about you."

Claudia shook her head, however, with an expression half smiling and half serious. "Ah, but there is a bad side to independence, too," she said. "It's true I have no one to dictate to me, but likewise I have no one to leave me a convenient fortune. If you are imagining I will bring a handsome dowry to our marriage, John, then you will be sadly disappointed!"

John was just assuring her that he imagined no such thing when his aunt interrupted him. "Don't you be so modest, my dear," she told Claudia. "You may not be an heiress born, but I've a plan that'll let you come to your marriage holding your head as high as any princess. What would you say, my dear, if I was to dower you myself?"

"I would say that you were a great deal too kind, ma'am," said Claudia with determination. "Thank you for the offer, but I really could not think of accepting any more from you than you have already given."

"Ah, but you haven't heard what I propose to give you, my dear. I don't really think you can object, for it's something that would have come to you anyway one of these days—to you and your husband, that is. What would you say if I told you I was thinking of deeding Rexford Park over to the pair of you?"

Seeing that both John and Claudia appeared staggered by this proposition, Lady Rexford went on, glancing at Hettie now and then for support. "The fact is that, though I've enjoyed my stay here in Yorkshire well enough, I'd a deal rather live in London. I'm a Londoner born and bred, and I don't know the first thing about managing a place like Rexford Park. Even before the two of you told me you were engaged, I'd about made up my mind to talk to my lawyer and see what might be done about transferring the ownership of the property. Hadn't I, Hettie?"

"That you did, my lady," corroborated Hettie. "We was talking about it just this afternoon."

"That's right. And now it all works out beautifully. On the day you marry Miss Chambers, Rexford, I'll make over the property to you in full, and you'll never have to ask me again whether we ought to rebuild a cottage or renew a lease." She smiled at John. "I know how you've chafed at having to share the ownership of the place. Well, you needn't anymore, and you owe it all to that bride of yours. I'm sure no girl ever brought her husband a more welcome dowry."

"Indeed not," said John faintly. "But are you sure you wish to be so generous, ma'am? You must know I would be glad to take over the day-to-day management of the place if you prefer to retain ownership. Losing Rexford Park would mean a great reduction in your income."

Lady Rexford laughed indulgently. "Bless you, I've all the income I need even without Rexford Park," she said. "I won't be in want. But with your permission, Rexford, I'd like to take this last quarter's rents and outfit your bride in a way that's fitting to her new position." She smiled at Claudia. "It would give me the greatest pleasure to buy her bride clothes, and I'm sure she could use 'em. She'd rather spend her money on other people than on herself."

Claudia protested, but John agreed his aunt's proposal would be a fair and equitable distribution of the rents, and her protests were overruled.

"You mustn't object too much, my dear," Lady Rexford told her, smiling. "I don't make my gift quite without conditions, you see. The fact is, I'm hoping that you'll ask me to come visit you now and then after you're married. Yorkshire's not so wild a place as I supposed, and I think I could quite enjoy a visit here now and then—say, once a year? And perhaps you could come visit me in London now and then when you've nothing better to do."

"I'm sure nothing *could* be better than visiting you, ma'am," said Claudia, embracing her. "I will come see you in London often and with the greatest pleasure. And I should be very glad to see you often in Yorkshire."

"And I, too," said John, also embracing his aunt. There followed a general flurry of hugging and kissing, in which even the dour Hettie joined in. When presently the butler arrived in the drawing room, bearing the tea tray Lady Rexford had requested, he blinked at the scene of dissipation within.

"Never mind the tea, Raikes, but bring up a bottle of the Chambertin," said John jovially. "We're celebrating an engagement here."

The butler hastened to comply with this request, and John filled four glasses with the ruby liquor. Unexpectedly, it was Hettie who proposed the first toast.

"I'll give you Miss Chambers," she said. "It's only fitting, seeing that she's the bride-to-be. Besides, as far as I can tell, it's all her doing that this whole business has turned out as well as it has."

"You couldn't say truer, Hettie," said Lady Rexford heartily. "I'd say that it was a fortunate day for all of us when Miss Chambers took charge. Wouldn't you agree, Rexford?"

John looked into Claudia's eyes. "I couldn't agree more," he said.

Dear Reader:

I hope you enjoyed *Miss Chambers Takes Charge*. If you find a special romance and fascination in the Regency period, you might want to read my new series, *The Wishing Well*, which will be published by Zebra Books starting in July 2000.

The series will be a trilogy. Each book will be set in the Regency era, and each will feature a different hero and heroine. The action in all three books will center around a venerable well in the lovely southwest county of Devonshire, England. Whether the well really possesses mystical powers is a matter for argument, but each couple who encounters it finds the course of their lives—and loves—changed forever.

Passion, romance, and adventure have always seemed to me the very essence of the Regency. I hope to capture these qualities in *The Wishing Well*. Look for the first book in the trilogy, *Catherine's Wish*, in July 2000. An excerpt from *Catherine's Wish* follows this letter. I hope you enjoy it.

Sincerely yours,
Joy Reed

One

True to Aunt Rose's prediction, daylight was already beginning to fade by the time Catherine reached the great oak that marked the halfway point between Willowdale Cottage and Honeywell House. She continued doggedly on, however, leaving the well-traveled path across the Common to take a narrower footpath that went straggling off in a southwesterly direction. This path led Catherine, in succession, through a small spinney containing a cluster of workmen's huts; past the woods of the Abbey, the most important estate in the neighborhood; and past the disused quarry that had provided the stone to build the Abbey and several other local great houses. Here the path was bordered by an expanse of open heath, but it soon plunged into the woods once more. These were the woods of Honeywell House, and only a little more walking brought Catherine to the gravel drive that led to the house's main entrance.

Honeywell House was a handsome Elizabethan manor built of gray Devonshire slate and set amid extensive formal gardens. A much older house of the same name had once stood on the same site, and in fact the ruins of this ancient house were still to be seen in the woods beyond the gardens. The property had passed through several hands in its long history. It belonged currently to a certain Lord Westland, of whom almost nothing was known except that he possessed a huge fortune and an eccentric reputation. The residents of Langton Abbots generally agreed that it must have been this last characteristic rather than the first one that accounted for his leasing Honeywell House to the Earl of Lindsay the previous autumn.

Catherine mounted the front steps of Honeywell House and knocked briskly on the front door. A footman in livery with a powdered head admitted her to the house's entrance hall. It was typical of the Lindsays to cling to such niceties as hair powder for their servants, even when most of their neighbors were abandoning them. Catherine was shown to a small parlor off the entrance hall while the footman went off to inform Lady Laura of her arrival.

Lady Laura herself appeared a moment later, a beaming smile on her face. "Oh, Catherine, I am so glad you are here," she said, embracing Catherine, then taking her arm and leading her across the hall. "Why ever did James put you in this stuffy little parlor? You must come into the drawing room with the rest of us."

Catherine, who had already heard the sound of voices and laughter issuing from the room across the hall, tried unavailingly to resist as Lady Laura pulled her toward the drawing room. "But you have a party, Laura," she said. "I did not mean to intrude, upon my word. I only came to return your book and get the next volume if you were done with it."

"But I don't have a party. It's only Mary Edwards and Isabel Wrexford. And certainly you may have the book, but you must come in and sit with us for at least a few minutes before you start back. Sit down right here, Catherine. I'll order more tea and see about fetching the book for you." Pressing Catherine into an upholstered armchair, Lady Laura gave her a warmly reassuring smile, then glided off to see about book and refreshment.

Catherine was left sitting with the other two girls, both of whom had looked up as she came in. They were neither of them strangers to her. Mary Edwards was the daughter of the local doctor, a plump, dark-haired girl a few years younger than Catherine. Catherine knew no harm of her save that she was inordinately fond of gossip. Isabel Wrexford was a different kettle of fish, however. The Wrexfords had been among those families most outspokenly critical of Catherine after her return to Langton Abbots, and even now they maintained their policy of disapproval, never inviting Catherine to any of their parties and vouchsafing her no more than the coldest of greetings when they encountered her in public.

True to form, Isabel gave Catherine a frigid nod, then folded her hands in her lap and lapsed into disapproving silence. She was a pale girl with frizzy curls, a narrow, sharp-featured face, and an angular figure. This last she generally sought to disguise beneath a mass of lace, ruffles, and ruching, and her dress today was no exception. The skirt of her bronze-colored pelisse was trimmed with several flounces and a profusion of velvet bows, and an abundance of puffs, epaulets, and ruffles on the bodice made the top half of her figure as obtrusive as the bottom. Mary, too, was elaborately dressed, her hair a mass of plaits and carefully curled ringlets. Catherine surmised they had come together to call upon Lady Laura and they had dressed in their best out of deference to their hostess's rank.

The thought made Catherine smile, in spite of her irritation at Isabel's behavior. Her own toilette was a plain pelisse and matching round dress of green alpaca trimmed with black braid, while her chestnut hair was smoothly drawn back and pinned in a simple knot beneath her black felt toque. No greater contrast could have presented itself than her slim, upright figure when viewed against the frilled and furbelowed costumes of her two companions.

Mary, who shared none of her companion's disinclination to talk, greeted Catherine in a friendly manner. "So you have come to visit dear Lady Laura, too? Isabel and I just dropped by on our way back from the Mabberlys'. A charming visit we had there, did we not, Isabel?"

"Charming," agreed Isabel in a bored drawl. Turning her eyes to Catherine, she added with significance, "I wonder we did not see you there, Miss Summerfield. As your aunt's cottage lies so near Mabberly Manor, I would think you would always be visiting back and forth."

Since everybody knew that the Mabberlys, like the Wrexfords, refused to entertain Catherine in their home, this was hardly a tactful speech. Before Catherine could frame an adequate reply, she was saved by the reappearance of Lady Laura, who came bustling into the room with an apologetic smile, carrying the requested book in one hand.

"Here it is, Catherine. I'm sorry I was such a time finding it. One of the servants had put it in Mama's room by mistake. Ah, and here is the tea. Thank you, Mason." She smiled warmly upon the elderly maid, who had just entered the room bearing a teapot and a plate of scones on a tray.

The maid returned the smile as she deposited the tray on the table in front of Lady Laura. Catherine, accepting a cup of tea from her friend, reflected that there was a quality about Lady Laura that seemed to inspire nearly universal devotion. Mary also accepted a cup of tea, then resumed her attack on the subject that had apparently been under discussion when Catherine had arrived.

"I am sure you could tell us more if you wanted to, Laura dear. I have it on good authority that Lord Meredith has been seen not once but three times coming away from Honeywell House during the past week. And though I have the highest opinion of your papa, I cannot think it is Lord Lindsay who brings our wandering hero here so often!"

Lady Laura laughed, blushed, and shook her head. "You make too much of it, Mary. Lord Meredith has called here several times, but I am persuaded he only wished to consult with Papa about business."

"And I am persuaded it is something else entirely." Mary regarded Lady Laura with an arch smile. "Do you mean to say Lord Meredith has said no word to *you* during any of these visits?"

The flush on Lady Laura's cheeks grew deeper. "Lord

Meredith has been very kind," she said, a conscious smile hovering about her lips. "He has told us all such interesting stories about India."

"I am sure he has. I am sure he would like nothing better than to sit with you and tell you about his Indian adventures by the hour altogether. Upon my word, this looks serious, Laura. I believe the poor man has lost his heart to you."

Catherine observed that Lady Laura did not deny it. Instead, she only laughed again and said, "Well, you will have an opportunity to judge if you come to my party next Friday, Mary. I hope you will come, too, Isabel," she added, addressing Mary's companion, who had once more lapsed into silence. "And you, too, of course, Catherine. I quite depend on you and your aunt being there. Do you know Lord Meredith?"

"I met him a few times years ago," said Catherine cautiously. "But our acquaintance was of the slightest. I doubt I would know him to see him now. Is he really back at the Abbey after all these years?"

The question was addressed to Lady Laura, but it was Mary who answered it. She turned to Catherine with the zest of one delighted to find a new audience.

"Oh, yes, had you not heard, Catherine? Lord Meredith returned to the Abbey two weeks ago, and they say he means to stay and put the property in order. Isn't it too exciting? First Laura and her family coming here to Honeywell House, and now Lord Meredith at the Abbey. I declare, our local society is becoming quite exalted all at once!"

Isabel gave a thin-lipped smile. "For my part, I should not consider Lord Meredith any great asset to our local society," she said acidly. "It's scandalous the way he has allowed the Abbey to run down. My papa says he ought to have sold it years ago if he did not mean to live in it."

Mary protested this statement, and Catherine thought Lady Laura, too, looked less than pleased by it. "It was very bad of him to neglect his property, no doubt," Lady Laura said in her gentle voice. "But after hearing him talk, I am sure I cannot blame him for spending so many years abroad. India sounds a fascinating place. And you know he has also traveled in China and Japan and a great many other interesting countries."

"I am sure Lord Meredith had the best of reasons to spend so many years abroad, my dear Laura. You were not here when he lived in Langton Abbots before, but I assure you that his doings then were the talk of the neighborhood. It was quite scandalous how he went on. Why, by all accounts he was little more than a boy when he took up with the widow Cooper. And later on there was that business with that dreadful Radner woman—the one he fought the duel over—"

"All that was years ago," said Lady Laura, cutting short Isabel's exposition with a warmth unusual to her. "And I expect most of what was said about Lord Meredith then was as greatly exaggerated as it is now." With the hint of another blush, she continued, "You must know that I have talked with Lord Meredith several times since he has returned. I am persuaded that, whatever he may have done wrong in the past, he means to turn over a new leaf now and live as a nobleman of his station should."

Although her blush had grown deeper, she spoke these last words with a finality that seemed to forbid any further discussion of the subject. Isabel made no effort to take it up, but instead turned to Mary. "We have been so busy talking of Lord Meredith that every lesser subject has been neglected," she said. "I am sure I have heard nothing new for over a week about this business of that wretched girl down at the Crown. Is it true that the creature is going to live after all? Your papa is the doctor, Mary, and you know we all depend on you to keep us up to date."

"Oh, yes, it's quite certain now that she will live," Mary assured Isabel. "Her injuries were not so serious as Papa feared at first."

"But it's true that she was assaulted, isn't it? Not just beaten, but—*personally assaulted?*" Isabel spoke the question in an avid whisper.

Both Catherine and Lady Laura regarded her with disgust. Mary, however, replied quite readily, "Oh, yes, there can be no doubt that she was molested. Papa wouldn't give me any of the details, but I know he was quite upset about it. He said he couldn't imagine what kind of a monster would treat a woman in such a way."

"She was only a barmaid," said Isabel contemptuously. "And it's common knowledge that she was perfectly depraved where men were concerned. I'm sure no one ought to be surprised if a girl of that class gets herself beaten and assaulted. It would only be justice if they were all so treated, in my opinion."

Catherine thought this might be a barb directed in her direction. But it seemed to anger Lady Laura more than anyone, for she exclaimed, "Oh, you cannot mean that, Isabel! I'm sure no one could wish such a terrible fate on any of one's fellow creatures. Whatever this poor girl's failings may have been, she can have done nothing to deserve such a horrible experience."

"No, and it's so frightening to think that her attacker is still loose," said Mary with a shudder. "I declare that I am quite afraid to walk out alone nowadays, even just across the street. I wonder that *you* dare to go about alone as much as you do, Catherine."

This remark, spoken in a curious tone, reminded Catherine that her aunt was awaiting her return. She rose to her feet.

"I'm afraid my aunt shares your scruples, Mary. I must be getting back before she grows worried. It is a pleasure to see you again, and you, too, Miss Wrexford. Laura, I must take leave of you now. Thank you for the tea and the book."

Lady Laura also rose to her feet and accompanied Catherine to the door. "I wish you need not go so soon," she said, looking at Catherine wistfully. "It seems you only just got here. And what with one thing and another, we have had no chance to talk at all." She was too polite to speak against Mary and Isabel, though Catherine could see she had been irritated by the other girls' presence. "Could you not stay and dine with us?" she continued, looking at Catherine beseechingly. "I know Mama and Papa and Oswald would be very happy to have you. And there would be no difficulty sending you home in the carriage if your aunt dislikes you to walk after dark."

"No, thank you, Laura. You are very kind to invite me, but I am expected for dinner at the Cottage. I expect my aunt is already waiting for me."

Lady Laura graciously swallowed her disappointment and agreed that Catherine must not keep her aunt waiting. "But you will come to my party for Lord Meredith next week?" she urged, as Catherine turned to go. "I do wish you would, Catherine. It would mean a great deal to me to have you there. And I daresay Lord Meredith would like to renew his acquaintance with you."

So genuinely anxious did she seem to secure Catherine's presence at her party that Catherine could not find it in her heart to refuse her. "Perhaps, Laura. You know I must speak with my aunt before giving a definite acceptance. But if she is agreeable, I see no reason why we may not come to your party. Thank you very much for inviting us." With a warm smile and a last wave at her friend, Catherine set off again through the woods toward home.

The sky was getting darker now, and the path through the woods was fast being swallowed up by shadow. The clumps of trees on either hand loomed dark and menacing in the fading light, and every bush might have been the proverbial bear, or something even more sinister.

Catherine walked quickly, trying not to think of Mary and Isabel's conversation about the unfortunate barmaid and her assailant. It was, she reminded herself, only a step through the woods and another slightly longer step across the common. And there was no reason to suppose that the assault of the barmaid had anything to do with Langton Abbots in any case.

The Crown, near which the incident had taken place, lay on the outskirts of a neighboring village some miles away.

To divert her mind from the menaces with which her imagination insisted on peopling the landscape, Catherine reflected instead upon the things Lady Laura had said during her visit. Most particularly did she reflect on her conversation regarding Lord Meredith.

In common with most residents of Langton Abbots, Catherine was acquainted with Lord Meredith. During the time she had known him, prior to her departure to Miss Saddler's, he had not yet attained to his present title and dignities, but had been merely a dark-haired boy some years older than she who had the reputation of never declining a wager or a dare. Catherine could remember seeing him in the village now and then, and she fancied she had even spoken to him on occasion, but her memories on the subject were exceedingly dim. On the whole they were favorable memories, however. She preserved a recollection of a laughing dark face coupled with a lively charm that was very attractive.

Of course, even back then there had been whispers about his behavior. Isabel had not exaggerated in saying that his youthful affair with the widow Cooper had been a local scandal, and that had not been the only scandal that had tarnished his name during his residence at Langton Abbots. His crowning indiscretion had come at the age of twenty-one when he had fought a duel with the husband of the lady who had allegedly been his current mistress.

Catherine was away at school by the time this episode had taken place, but she could still remember the furor it had caused. Her aunt's letters had spoken of little else for weeks, and even the Cheltenham newspapers had carried a reserved but disapproving account of the incident. What made it more shocking still was that Lord Meredith, the guilty party, had emerged from the encounter unscathed while his opponent had been badly wounded—it was feared for a time, mortally wounded. This circumstance was held to cast a most discreditable light on the character of the young lord. It was no wonder that his father, in a fit of exasperation, had shipped Lord Meredith off to India to see what a prolonged sojourn in that country's torrid clime might do toward settling him.

By all accounts, he had prospered in India. Owing to the distances involved, reports of him had been necessarily few and far between during the intervening years, but the occasional news that had filtered into Langton Abbots had carried favorable accounts of his industry and acumen.

When his father had died unexpectedly, a few years after his migration to India, it was confidently expected that he would return home to the Abbey and settle down to a life of well-bred prosperity and ease like his ancestors before him. But Lord Meredith had confounded these expectations. Instead, he had chosen to travel farther afield—to China and Russia and even the mysterious island nation of Japan.

And now, having seen a good part of the world—and having enjoyed by all accounts more than his share of perilous adventures—Lord Meredith had decided to come home and settle at the Abbey. So Lady Laura had insisted, and Lady Laura's word was implicitly to be believed, as Catherine knew. Indeed, it seemed as if Lady Laura herself might have had a share in determining Lord Meredith's future plans. Reflecting on all she had heard of that gentleman's checkered past, Catherine thought that he and the gentle, virtuous Lady Laura made an unlikely pair, but there could be no doubt that Lady Laura was disposed to favor him. Her blushes when speaking of his intention of settling down told the story clearly enough.

"They say a reformed rake makes a good husband," Catherine told herself as she went across the common. "I hope that is true, for Laura's sake. I should hate to see her hurt."

It was completely dark by the time Catherine reached Willowdale Cottage. She was relieved to see the friendly glow of its unshuttered windows and the welcoming light thrown from the front door as her aunt came out on the porch to meet her.

"Oh, my dear, I was growing quite worried," said Aunt

Rose, the relief in her voice confirming the truth of her words. "Not but what I knew you must be perfectly all right at the Lindsays'," she added with rather less truth. "But still I cannot think it healthy to be out in the night air. There was a prejudice against night air when I was a girl, and even now, I cannot help but think there must be something in it."

"It has given me an appetite at any rate," said Catherine, laughing as she threw off her hat and gloves. "Will you forgive me if I sit down to dinner without changing, Auntie? I'm afraid I'm a trifle late already, and you know I wouldn't offend Cook's sensibilities for the world."

"Certainly I do not mind, my dear." Aunt Rose led the way into the dining parlor, where the table was laid for two. Having seated herself at the table and seen that Catherine was seated, too, she rang the bell, and the maids began bringing out the dishes. As Aunt Rose helped Catherine to roast duck, peas, and new potatoes, she inquired with interest after the inhabitants of Honeywell House.

"What had Lady Laura to say? I hope you found her and Lord and Lady Lindsay well—and her brother, too, of course. I remember your saying he had come to stay at Honeywell House recently."

"Yes," agreed Catherine, with a certain reserve. "But you know, Auntie, Sir Oswald is really only Lady Laura's half-brother. Lord Lindsay was a widower before marrying Laura's mother, and Oswald is his son by his first marriage."

She did not add that, in her opinion, Sir Oswald was a blot on the Lindsay family escutcheon. He shared none of Lady Laura's sweetness and virtue. On the contrary, having found out from someone or other about Catherine's past, he had treated her ever since with a leering familiarity that was very hard to stomach. Catherine trusted that by now he had learned she was not open to his advances, but she was still glad to be spared his company whenever possible.

"Well, I hope Sir Oswald is well along with the others," said Aunt Rose, pursuing her former line of thought. "Is Lady

Laura planning on attending the village assembly next month?"

"I don't know, for we didn't discuss it. It happens that she is giving a party of her own this next Friday. We are both invited, but I told her I would have to discuss it with you before I gave a definite acceptance."

Catherine had no real hope that Aunt Rose would refuse the invitation, for she knew her aunt's pleasure in parties of any kind. Nor was she wrong. Aunt Rose's face lit up at the magic word "party," and she at once began to question Catherine concerning the invitation.

"Next Friday, you say? I see no reason why we may not attend, Catherine. Is it to be a large party?"

"I suspect so. The Lindsays seem incapable of doing anything on a small scale. Their 'party' will probably be more like what you or I would call a ball."

"I always loved a ball," said Aunt Rose, looking childishly pleased. "But is this not rather short notice to be giving a large party, Catherine? If it is to be on Friday, and Lady Laura is only now giving out the invitations—"

"It is rather short notice, I suppose. But I expect that is Lady Laura's doing. You know that in that household she reigns supreme—I believe there is nothing Lord and Lady Lindsay or the Honeywell House servants would not do for her if she asked. It's a wonder she isn't spoiled beyond bearing, but miraculously she is not."

"She seems a very sweet girl," agreed Aunt Rose with enthusiasm. "I must say, I was surprised when the Lindsays decided to settle in an out-of-the-way place like Langton Abbots. But I am very glad they did. Lady Laura is such a nice, well-bred, pretty-behaved girl—just the kind of girl I like to see you associating with, Catherine. You know I cannot consider the village girls really appropriate companions for you."

Catherine laughed bitterly. "I suspect most of them would consider me an inappropriate companion for them, Auntie! Considering my scarlet past, I am lucky to be invited out at all." With a direct look, she added, "We need not pretend among ourselves, I hope. The plain fact is that I am damaged goods, Auntie. You know it, I know it, and so, I fear, does everybody else."

Aunt Rose looked embarrassed but mulish, as she always did when Catherine's past was mentioned. "Everyone can know nothing of the sort, Catherine dear," she said, blotting her lips energetically with her napkin. "They may suspect, but they cannot know that you did anything of which you need be ashamed."

"But I did," said Catherine with a twisted smile.

"Yes, but they have no proof of it," said Aunt Rose with energy. "And they should not assume without proof. That is the sign of a nasty mind, I always think—and that is one reason why I cannot like your being friends with the village girls. Some of them are very nice, I have no doubt, but the general tone of their minds is distressingly low."

Catherine, remembering Mary and Isabel's conversation, was inclined to agree with this statement. To change the subject, she ventured to repeat their remarks concerning Lord Meredith. Aunt Rose was interested at once.

"And so Lord Meredith is returned to the Abbey! I am sure I am very glad to hear it. I always thought he was such a nice boy. It was a great pity that events fell out as they did for him."

"To hear you talk, every boy you ever knew was a nice boy," said Catherine, smiling at her aunt. "And every girl was a nice girl. I suppose it is because people are constitutionally incapable of behaving other than nicely toward you."

Aunt Rose flushed with pleasure at this speech, but shook her head firmly. "Indeed, it is nothing of the kind. I always liked young Lord Meredith, and I always thought it most unjust that he should have been shipped off to India in that summary way. Many young men behave foolishly, after all. His papa ought to have made allowances—he was none too circumspect in his own youth, from all I have ever heard. And I suspect that if the truth about this duel business were to become known, that Radner woman would be proven to have incited the whole. I never liked her, you know. She always seemed to me a very coarse, unprincipled woman."

"So you see Lord Meredith as an injured innocent, do you, Auntie?" said Catherine, hiding a smile. Aunt Rose saw through her pretense, however, and shook her head at her niece once more, a reluctant smile on her own lips.

"Not an innocent, no, but it is my belief that his behavior was more foolish than wicked, Catherine. And I am sure that if he did do wrong, he has atoned for it years ago. Say what you will, India cannot be a *comfortable* place, and it must be very lowering to be separated from one's home and family for so many years. I, for one, am very glad to see Lord Meredith back at the Abbey where he belongs. I hope he will be very happy there."

Catherine concurred in this hope. Yet she could not help wondering privately if a life of travel and adventure might not be a happier one than was to be found in quiet Langton Abbots—especially for a person whose past was less than pristine.

ABOUT THE AUTHOR

Joy Reed lives with her family in Michigan. She is the author of nine Zebra Regency romances and is currently working on a historical romance trilogy set during the Regency period. The first book in the trilogy, *Catherine's Wish*, will be published in July 2000. Joy loves hearing from her readers and you may write to her c/o Zebra Books. Please include a self-addressed stamped envelope if you wish a response.

BOOK YOUR PLACE ON OUR WEBSITE AND MAKE THE READING CONNECTION!

We've created a customized website just for our very special readers, where you can get the inside scoop on everything that's going on with Zebra, Pinnacle and Kensington books.

When you come online, you'll have the exciting opportunity to:

- View covers of upcoming books
- Read sample chapters
- Learn about our future publishing schedule (listed by publication month *and author*)
- Find out when your favorite authors will be visiting a city near you
- Search for and order backlist books from our online catalog
- Check out author bios and background information
- Send e-mail to your favorite authors
- Meet the Kensington staff online
- Join us in weekly chats with authors, readers and other guests
- Get writing guidelines
- AND MUCH MORE!

Visit our website at
http://www.zebrabooks.com